MW01138790

Tiathan Eiula
And The War
of the Seven Fortresses

By C.J. Henning

Wisdom is found only in the inner reaches of those who seek it. In the world of Everstream, wisdom is found in the mind and Spirit of Jesuar. No one can find Him, but He is always there in front of all who seek the Truth. Power is found in the sword, the armor and the shield of Jesuar, but only used when no other options are available.

The wonder of life
Lives in the Great Oak.
Seeking is finding,
Finding brings joy,
Joy spreads love,
Love is Jesuar.
Jesuar is peace
In a land of turmoil.
Jesuar protects the innocent
From the evil around us.
Jesuar is strength
To defeat those who destroy
What was, what is,
What shall be
Everstream.

Inscribed on the trunk of the Great Oak.

Cast of Characters

Moshdalayrrimich (mosh-dial-air-ee-mick)
      Zelbiur Eiula (Zell-be-your E-oo-la)
      Tiathan Eiula (Tee-a-then E-oo-la)
      Ioroarka (eye-o-roar-ka)
      Miertur Eiula (Me-err-tour E-oo-la)
      Awlion Eiula (Aw-le-on E-oo-la)
      Outra Whorld
      Rhor (roar)
      Crymouth
      Trusk
      Jesuar (Yes-u-are)
      Shrodacrassniff (Shrod-a-crass-sniff)
      Carazaar (Car-a-czar)
      Thoos
      Krrool (cruel)
      Fraast
      Zarr
      Tenca
      Quardraille (Quar-drail)

Tranda

Hort

Sooma

Fraar

The Drearnok

Agraine Thrule

Thrun Thrule

Schill Thrule

Haavorn

TRAG ALPHABET

Hi-a	Ef'-if	hia-all
'ef-belief		
Ba-b	r-is	iet's-those
bati-but		
Si-c	T-the	et'-he
ba'veyo-believe		
Dy-d	A-as	tie-th
st'-st		
O-e	t-to	mo-were
	ties-this	
Ef-f	ef'-for	Ep'om-upon
	ba'oom-below	
N-g	W-in	om'-down
	mya'-will	
Et-h	ll'-you	llo-yet
	ba-efooRo-before	
Y-i	N-me	os-ous
	tim-tion	
X-j	ti'-it	ll'R-your
	ba'ady-behold	
V-k	OO-us	met-with
	ba'Rll-glory	

A=l   tn'-them   timst-township
            oi'R-our
N-m   st-sh   Ba'-able or ible
            metyn-within

M-n   M-wh   bam-been
            'll-ly
OO-o   es'-es or ies   P-P
Ep-p   N-ing   "Efoon-from
Kv=q   dy-ed   'ov-over

Ar-r   ba=by   esm-night
R-r   'ef-of   esdy=day
Es-s   ar-are   p'-eep
Ti-t   ad-and   mi'-way
Oi-u   ooR-or   siady-could
Vey-v   et'r-their   R'-er
M-w   ti-they   moot-not
X-x   M'-was   etti-that
ll-y   et's-his   o'-ie
ii-y   PoiRpa-purple   no'-green
'X-z   m'-ow   ardy-red
ms-ness   oi'-ou
oo-oi   baa-blue
Basiv-black   myti-white

Part Of The Original Manuscript

Mo ar mohiR omdy Tiyhitiehim
Oyoiahi eplpiesdy mohiRy'll oom
mhiti
et'mm' sihia'dy tiRoones vmooa' ti'
M' W etoomoor 'ef T dyllN
mhiR'aooR
ayN baetymdy etyn
MoRo ar mo himayoom oyoiahi sio'N
yati'yo baRohitie 'Efoon hivRhim
tieRoon estiyR'dy 'Efoon et's esydyo
t hiep'Roohiset etoR efhitiepR etoR
efo'ti
etoiRti 'Efoon T Roi'net estiooomes'
oom T nRoi'mdy epyoRsiN tieRo'net
T siooaes''ef etoR baoo'ties
T veyoRll etohiRti 'ef oveyoRst'
Rohin
mohiR T nRohiet oohiv 'ef XoesoihiR
A eto epRoonyesdy tiyhitiehim

esynetdy
met nRohiet Roayoef et's baRoom
st'ya' dyRyep'dy ba'oo'dy 'Efoon T
hiti'hisiv 'ef veyhiyvllRysiv
mhiR'yooRes
xoiesti hi efom etoi'Res ba'efooRo
sthiRep tieooRmes epRysivdy et's
sietym oveyom tieoi'net eto ethidy
sioonbadt et's nRohiti myti baohiRdy
nhimll tiynes' W T yhist' timoo
dyhilles

In the beginning before Jesuar
brought the Trags to the land of Everstream,
the forests were filled with animals and fruit
of every kind. The air was clean, the rain
pure and the soil produced a rainbow of
beauty in flowers, bushes and grass. Jesuar
brought forth the first Trags to help nurture
all the living things, but they disobeyed
Jesuar. The Trags decided to rule themselves
building tall spires to reach the heavens

hoping to find and defeat Jesuar.

The result of this disobedience was a corruption of life and language that brought into being the Arbushi, the Valvorri, the Valkyricks, the Modosites, the Rabel Ainians and those few Trags that were faithful to Jesuar. Mortarr, a rogue spirit that fought Jesuar and lost was now controlling most of Everstream. Small tribes ruled by bloodthirsty creatures like Nsaat with his Bantongues and Harkies were the most evil incarnations ever imagined.

The Seven Fortresses were built on the outer edge of Gimgiddo to control and enslave all those who came near to them. The fortress overlooked the Plains of Nord within the Valley of Gimgiddo. Rhor, the Gimgiddean ruler, was in full battle mode and terrorized all of Everstream. All the rulers now were vying for the control of Everstream and Mortarr led their yearning for power.

The Valkyricks were proud warriors,

yet terrible rulers, marched through Everstream forcing all they came upon to worship Mortarr or die. So, too, did the Arbushi who quietly killed or captured any stray traveler that came their way. They secretly looked for the day to bring down the Seven Fortresses and that day was coming closer.

Now the Great Rebellion was coming with the Trags led by Tiathan Eiula who hoped to break free of their bondage. Defeated in number, but not in spirit, the Trags escaped back through the Dark Forest while others took up the challenge against the Seven Fortresses.

This is the tale of that struggle.............

Chapter One
The Beginning....

"We are near the end." Tiathan Eiula paused wearily, on what he now called, Throg's Knoll. It was in honor of the dying warrior lying behind him.

"Where are we?" Awlion Eiula, seeing little breath from Akran Throg, stirred from his side to approach her father. Her feet hurt from the rough stones on the ground piercing through the soles of her boots.

"The very heart of Everstream near the Great Oak of Jesuar as He promised." Tiathan sighed with great relief. His brow still dripped blood from the attack of Valkyricks just a few hours before. Sharp thorns pricked his chin even though he had combed his great white beard many times in the last two days.

"I've never seen this Great Oak, father." Miertur, who shared his father's vision of Everstream, was not certain he wanted to enter this new land now that they were here.

"I've seen it only in my dreams." Tiathan calmed

his son, raised his hand allowing the
last of his fifty warriors and their families to rest. As First
Ioroarka, Tiathan wasn't only tired in body, but, also, in
spirit. The Trags had been wandering for many years in and
out of Everstream, living in other fortresses and other oak
trunks that were not theirs. "Yet Jesuar has told me that it is
as I have dreamed."

At last, Jesuar led them to an area of Everstream
that was their own, near the Great Oak where peace and a
permanent home were promised forever. He already knew
what he would call this place that was promised to them,
Quicksnatch. Quicksnatch because the Trags were so
suddenly pulled from Rabel Ain, where their cousins were
ready to slaughter them all because of the Trags belief in
Jesuar.

"Father, you act like there will be nothing to do, but
till the land and mind our own
Business." Ygueliav Eiula still hurt from the wounds of the
Bantongues that lashed their venomous fangs across his
legs. Even though the Bantongue warrior, an eight-legged
spider-like creature with the head of a Breen rat, didn't
break the skin, the poison still had its effect on his body.

Awlion and Akran saved Ygueliav from death with
quick arrows and spears, or else the last vision of life would
have been that of a grinning skull reaching for his neck. He
could not believe how fast these Bantongues, with such
bulbous bodies and overhanging snout, ran back
and forth in battle. They always seemed to be laughing at
you, even in death. Either theirs' or yours'.

Tiathan ignored his son's question since it was the

pain of a long journey that spoke more than his real thoughts. There were over five hundred who started this journey from Gimgiddo, where Rhor had cast them out. The land of Gimgiddo was fertile, rich with land and water. Rhor let them wander some distance before sending out his warriors to kill them all. Tiathan knew this was going to happen because Jesuar told him it would. Though he waited for the Gimigddeans to attack, the Trags were nearly destroyed in the ensuing battle. If it wasn't for a sudden storm, they probably would have lost everything.

Tiathan lost his mate, Arsonia, near the end of the battle. An arrow pierced her armor as she raised her spear in victory. It had been a sorrowful time, yet he was the 1st Ioroarka and Jesuar would not let him forget his purpose, his duty.

"If this is the heart of Everstream, we will never be at peace here." Awlion gently grasped her father's calloused hand, wrought with scars from so much fighting. Awlion was his youngest daughter, and the wisest of all his children. "I know you saw the Seven Fortresses that surround this place. Whoever lives around us may not want us to stay."

"It is only important that Jesuar wants us to stay." Tiathan kissed her hand explaining, rather, reminding his daughter of the obvious truth.

"At what price?" Awlion looked back at Arkran, who stared unseeing at the new land within Everstream. "We must bury him here overlooking our new home. May Jesuar be kind to him."

"Our new home will be called Quicksnatch."
Tiathan glanced back at his fallen friend. "For it's when life
is taken from us suddenly that we remember why we came
here."

"We live to die and be trodden upon." Ygueliav spat
on the ground, the scar across his face ran red with anger.
Kicking the dust with his wide-hooked toes, he
remembered their ugliness, and then quickly hid his
affliction. Ygueliav was the only Trag to be able to climb
trees and walls without rope or twine. When he was first
born, Tiathan thought his son was cursed, but soon realized
how quickly Ygueliav adapted to his crooked toes. Now all
Taithan's warriors envied Ygueliav for his affliction, when
they could see what he could do when lives depended on
tasks that appeared impossible.

"None will trod upon those who stand with Jesuar."
Tiathan tapped the point of his
sword on Ygueliav's barrel chest. "You've seen many
things, both wonders and lost dreams, but learned nothing."

"I've learned not to serve the Valkyricks in this or
any other place." Ygueliav pushed Tiathan's sword away.
"There's no fortress, no protection here from our enemies."

"You must do what you think best, my son."
Tiathan knew Ygueliav wouldn't last long in Quicksnatch.
Ygueliav was a warrior looking for glory and death, not a
farmer hoping for a quiet life. There would be no grief
whatever Ygueliav's decision for Jesuar would be his
strength and his guide.

"You won't stop me?" Ygueliav's surprised look
caused a rippled smile on Tiathan's lips.

"I cannot." Tiathan sheathed his sword and continued down the knoll as Awlion followed him. A large grove of gnarled oak greeted them with its low hanging branches some protection if riders should attack them. Tiathan already pictured sturdy homes that would protect them from the changing seasons as well.

"He has been comforted." Awlion approached Tiathan, pointing to the wrapped body of Arkran. A hole was dug with a small ceremony for a fallen warrior beneath a small young oak.

"Give him rest then." Tiathan ordered two Trag warriors near Awlion to help lower the body. Soon the last fifty warriors and their families circled the grave, now knowing the land was safe, and began to sing a warrior's funeral song in the ancient Trag language:

"Mom ahiesti mo noti
Oir olles MoRo dyn
Llo hia R voepti
W Xoost ad etyn
Moo Mhirties W tiohiRes
T estihill oiR efohiares
Mo llyveyoT dyo
T dyo Mo llyveyo
Moo RyNetti T dyo
OiR RyNetti T llyveyo"

As the procession left Arkran's grave, a shadow passed over the mound. Tiathan looked to see his youngest son, Zelbiur, run breathlessly toward him from the darkness of the Korwark Woods.

"We thought you were lost." Tiathan hugged his son, though it was hard since Zelbiur was taller by a full head.

"Father, I must go back." Zelbiur ignored the comforting hand of Awlion. "More important matters must forgo this reunion."

"What is it, my son?" Tiathan understood since Zelbiur was alone, when last he saw him, had at least twenty warriors behind him.

"Ten of our brothers have been captured by Nsaat, the one-eye." Zelbiur did not have to tell Tiathan the other ten warriors were dead. Tiathan, also, knew Nsaat was young and inexperienced in battle, but still the overwhelming numbers of army would be enough to defeat most of the enemies sent against him. "I need five warriors who will go back with me to free them. Nsaat will not expect me to return."

"Why not all of us?" Ygueliav stepped between them.

"This is a time for escape, not battle, my son." Tiathan was disappointed that Ygueliav did not understand the difference.

"We are not cowards!" Ygueliav insisted, turning to Zelbiur who turned away from him.

"Awlion?" Tiathan called his daughter over, not wanting to have to explain himself any further to Ygueliav.

"Yes, father?" Awlion hurried up to him, her golden hair untied, unkempt, bristling in the wind.

Pick five warriors who will go with your brother." Tiathan explained the situation to her, knowing she would not question the need or the purpose.

"Yes, father." Awlion ran to the front of the procession looking for volunteers.

"While we wait, Zelbiur, look before you at the land Jesuar has given us." Tiathan pointed toward a large grove of trees. "I have called it Quicksnatch for the way we have been uprooted so many times."

"It is a perfect name and I hope it is not our future ever again." Zelbiur liked what he saw, yet glanced off into the distance.

"What do you see?" Tiathan saw the strange look on his face.

"Something that is never right I'm sure." Miertur slapped his brother on the back.

"I see fortresses on three sides in the distance." Zelbiur always thought of the strategic purpose of every encampment they made. "They are far enough away which is to our advantage. We have marched through these woods, the Valkyricks have not, nor have any of the others who plague us. Our only threat in here is Nsaat and his Bantongues."

"What else do you see since your brother, Ygueliav, does not agree with you." Tiathan looked askance at Ygueliav.

"I see high oak trees to shower arrows and spears on any intruder." Zelbiur searched in all directions trying to notice as much as possible. "That lake near here is good for a quick escape by raft. I don't see anywhere we can be trapped if we are cautious. I have no time to say more. Our friends await."

"It is enough." Tiathan clapped his shoulders with pride.

"It's not enough!" Ygueliav walked angrily in circles. "We need moat and walls to protect ourselves. To show our enemies we will defy them!"

"And show them exactly our strength and position?" Even Miertur understood why this was a good place to live.

"You need to learn what it is to take advantage of your surroundings or you will perish, my brother." Zelbiur wiped some dried blood from his cheek; the scab causing him to itch was the part of his great left ear that was missing. Zelbiur was known for hearing a whisper from long distances. Many a time, Zelbiur heard advancing danger before the Trags did. The Trags survived numerous traps because of his warnings.

"Quickly, go, and bring our friends..... home!" Tiathan found it difficult to accept any place a permanent home, but Jesuar had promised this land to be theirs, so they believed it.

Zelbiur vanished into the encompassing darkness of Korwark Forest with five warriors as Tiathan turned to lead the Trags into their new land. He didn't know where the Great Oak was, but from a distance, anyone could see the huge spreading branches of a giant tree from any hillside. It could only be the home of Jesuar.

Tiathan stopped short for a moment, noticing there

was no singing of birds, specially the song of the Arrowail. No animals ventured toward or away from them as they approached. He relaxed when they turned into the glen leading to the Great Oak; a myriad of music filled the air. There was the chattering of Firetails which scattered a family of Tanneruns. Mammoth Butterflies shed rainbows on the ground as the sunlight filtered through their multicolored wings.

Miertur was in awe of the lush green fields surrounding the Great Oak with the blooming of every flower he had ever seen on his adventures to this new land. In the center of the glen was the Great Oak which appeared to reach the sky and was, at least, twenty warriors wide. The dense leaves on the overhanging branches hid from view whatever might be lying in wait above the trunk.

Tiathan approached the mighty oak trunk seeing fruit of every kind hanging ripe and ready to be eaten. All of the Trags gasped as one, seeing the bounty of food being offered that overwhelmed their senses.

"We must have a blessing for this moment." Tiathan turned to Awlion, knowing her ability to bring praise to Jesuar at a second's notice.

"Then we will ask Jesuar to give us one." Awlion turned to the other Trags, beginning to hum a tune before singing the words in the ancient Trag:

"oi'R shimdy R tieyes
oi'R tiyno ethies siono

MoRo ayefo R et's
Moo ayveyoes ef' esoono
llio oo ef' hia
Mo efoimdy T oohiv
efoimdy T oohiv
T xoost Mo sihia
Tihivo ooef oiaR Hoovo
oi'R xoiRmolles dyoomo
Moo nooRo Mo Roim "

"Greetings, Jesuar welcomes you." A very young
Trag dressed in white with a black cape
and a purple sash from shoulder to waist stood before them.
"I was not expecting you." Tiathan was perplexed.
The young Trag's blue eyes pierced into his soul and into
the souls of the others. His ears were slightly pointed, but
not so much that would be elfin. His nose was round, yet
did not fully carry the trait of a true Trag, at least, not any
of those who followed him. He looked unfit to carry a
sword and shield, but a sense of power seemed to flow
from him.
"I have not heard such music for a long time." The
young Trag bowed to them all. "I am Outra Whorld, your
servant, your Shroo."
"What is a Shroo?" Ygueliav did not like this at all.
He looked around trying to find out when the trap was
going to be sprung.
"A Shroo, Ygueliav." Ygueliav's eyes widened in
wonder since no introductions had been made, but Outra
continued, "A Shroo is one who speaks for Jesuar and

obeys what is said to him. Your father, Tiathan Eiula, was proclaimed First Ioroarka by Jesuar Himself because of his obedience to Him. Ioroarka means Warrior-king and you should obey him in all things."

"You were never in the visions I had of this place." Tiathan whispered in a low raspy voice.

"And why should you since I am only an instrument of Jesuar?" Outra gently grasped Tiathan's shoulder, leading him toward the Great Oak. "You and your kin will come inside, but your warriors must wait out here. They will be fed soon enough."

"I have no need to go in there." Ygueliav stalked away, slapping his sword against his shield in defiance.

"Ygueliav!" Tiathan started after his son, but Outra kept a firm hold of his shoulder.

"It was not expected that he would enter, let him go." Outra whispered to Tiathan.

"I will go." Awlion was anxious to see inside the Great Oak.

"Let's go!" Miertur grabbed his sister's hand as they raced each other to the great door before them.

Tiathan was still not sure that Outra with his glistening smile and strong grip could be trusted. He saw his warriors though relaxed, a wonderful peace seemed to encompass them all which made it seem all right to go inside. Sitting down they unbuckled their belts breathing in the fresh moist air of the fragrant flowers around them.

Tiathan hurried to Awlion's side as the high oak doors slowly opened to let them in. Inside, candles were lit giving a golden glow to everything that lay around them.

Tiathan stared at the long purple curtains draped from one end of the hall to the other. Gold lamp stands stood before a jeweled altar that seemed to call him closer. A dark stone rested upon an oak dish in the middle of the altar which appeared to glow as he came closer to it. He thought it was a trick of the candlelight or a soft glow from the very center of the stone beckoned him forward.

"I will tell you all you need to know in time." Outra Whorld took Tiathan's arm, leading him past another array of purple and gold cloth into an even larger room.

"This is glorious!" Awlion clapped her hands which stung somewhat as they were chafed from battle.

On various oak stands were draped three golden breastplates braided in part with silver chain. Two gold rings on each side of the room held two jeweled daggers in silver sheaths that glistened in the candlelight. Three swords were embedded into the floor in the middle of the room, each of the hilts had oak helmets attached. One spear fashioned in gold lay on the floor beneath the breastplates with two crossbows and two sheaths of arrows on either side.

"Even Jesuar must prepare for war." Outra looked at the surprised faces before him.

"It will be as Jesuar wishes." Miertur longed to touch such an array of weapons. At the other end of the room, he spied three shields, each with a different picture etched on its front. One was the first capture of the Trags over fifty years ago, the second of the great flood that only a few Trags survived, and the third was a picture of the

Great Oak.

"You obey without orders, Miertur." Outra was visibly pleased.

"It is because I understand things before they are said." Miertur recognized his gift long before he reached adulthood. He never fought the instinct to do the right thing, nor did he ever resist whatever Jesuar asked him to do.

"We have always been told that peace and life would not always follow us." Awlion relished the moment within the Great Oak, but realized it would not last. "With us death only follows more death. It is the way, our fate, for following Jesuar."

"Jesuar allows you the very choice between death and life." Outra's eyes blazed with the Spirit of Jesuar. "You're here for your father's sake, to decide what path you must take. Peace will really be your future only when the last of the evil of Everstream is vanquished."

"I don't know if we're prepared yet." Tiathan hoped the battles were over. Outra had just told them they were not and a cloud of sadness filled his heart. "I'm sorry if I offend you, but we lost many warriors just to get here. Now you're telling us we must go back and fight."

"No not all will go back, just you." Outra saw the look of dismay on Tiathan's face. "What I am showing you is only the start of your journey."

"I will go with you, father!" Miertur beat his chest.

"As will I!" Awlion raised her fist.

"It will not matter how many go with you, the

journey will be yours alone." Outra was touched by the devotion of Tiathan's kin. "For now eat and drink, refresh yourselves in body and spirit."

Tiathan then just noticed a table full of food and drink was prepared for them. How he had missed eating well was impossible to tell Outra. A white cloth with a purple sash covered the broad table showing off gold cups with a sweet red liquid next to loaves of dark seeded bread upon silver platters. Fruit and meat were piled high on golden trays ready to be eaten. This was a feast he had dreamt about so many times before and after battles. During the long journey, the rare moiments of peaceful nights, he almost tasted what he now saw before him. It was then he looked back, remembering his warriors outside.

"Now Tiathan, refresh yourself and your children." Outra saw his look of concern. "Those outside are being well attended to as we speak. Do not concern yourself for now."

"We must give thanks first." Awlion stopped short of the table.

"Yes." Outra nodded towards her sensing she was going to sing a song of praise.

Awlion blushed with his praise and confidence lavished upon her and then closed her eyes to hum a little before singing:

"Mo baaoes tieR efody
Ef' ayefo ad etohiatie
Ef' hia R ayefo
Metw Xoesoiar'es mohiatie
efody oi noiydyo oi
eshiveyo oi Baaoes oi
Hinom"

"After we eat you must be anointed." Outra spoke to Tiathan as they sat down.

"Anointed? As what?" Tiathan's ears seemed to curl as he wondered what else could happen to him.

"As First Ioroarka." Outra beckoned him to sit down. "You are Ioroarka in name only. Now Jesuar will give you the power that goes with the title."

"What power is that?" Awlion wasn't sure what magic could come with such a title.

"The power of leadership, the blessing of Jesuar and the allegiance of all Trags." Outra proudly smiled.

"Can we stay and watch?" Awlion was proud that her father would be so honored by Jesuar.

"We understand if we can't." Miertur added quickly so as not to offend Outra.

"You are expected to participate." Outra winked at them. "The three of you will enter the underground spring to don the armor of Jesuar."

"Since there are only three breastplates, you must have known Ygueliav would not be with us." Tiathan began to understand Outra a little more though his mysterious connection with Jesuar will probably never be explained.

"I knew and so did he." Outra tore the first loaf of bread in half before passing it around.

"But what of Zelbiur?" Awlion was sure her brother would not turn from Jesuar. "Does that mean he is not with us?"

"He's not here, but that is because he chooses not to be for the sake of others." Outra reached out to give Awlion some fruit. "He is honored here as you will be."

"Have you ever seen Jesuar?" Miertur whispered and yet his voice echoed throughout the hall.

"We all have." Outra answered without a hint of explanation behind his pale green eyes.

"You are a strange Trag." Miertur noticed a difference in Outra not only in his eyes, but his skin as well. Outra's skin seemed to be light brown in the candlelight where in the sunlight it appeared a yellowish tint. "I have noticed that your eyes were blue as waters outside the Great Oak, then a dark amber as we came inside while now they are green. What are you? Are you flesh and blood or spirit?"

"I thought they were blue." Tiathan laughed at the thought of Outra Whorld being anything than a representative of Jesuar.

Outra waited for them all to settle down again so he could finish the task ahead of him. He was bemused with the things that concerned them after the battles they fought together.

"Who do you think I am?" Outra passed a pitcher of red liquid that tasted like the Schew they remembered from Gimgiddo, only sweeter.

"Always a friend, I hope." Tiathan interrupted while walking over and patting Outra on the back. "And not a spirit."

"I cannot say, but Outra and I are friends always." Awlion did not think Outra would admit to anything he didn't want to.

"That we will be always, Awlion." Outra lifted his cup and saluted them all before he drank it.

They finished their meal in silence with Awlion staring at the many candles and strange writings on the wall. Shadows danced around them as a cool breeze flowed through the hall which stirred the flames back and forth as they ate. The spiced Notherhen melted in their mouths, various fruit moistened their palate and the hearth bread soaked up the gravy from the bottom of the plates. Awlion had never been in the Great Oak and now was in awe seeing the great hall and it seemed other rooms. She couldn't understand how all she saw could fit into the Great Oak she saw from the outside.

"Will you tell us about the writing on the walls?" Awlion couldn't contain her curiosity.

"It's part of the ritual." Outra was pleased Awlion noticed the sacred writings of the Great Oak.

Awlion let down her long golden brown hair feeling the coolness filter through each strand as if a great hand was gently stroking her head. She grew it long to hide the battle scars that covered her neck and back where only her companion Akran Throg saw them. She remembered in the Forest of Deen when Akran stood in front of her as a spear, thrown by a Valkyrick warrior, pierce d his chest. The memory brought tears and pain rushing to the forefront.

"It's all right." Outra seemed to read her thoughts. He rose up to the near wall and pointed to the inscriptions that lay there. "There are ten allegiances that you must make to Jesuar before the ritual is complete. The first is always prayer, the second is song, the third is obedience, the fourth is dedication, the fifth is charity, the sixth is baptism, the seventh is spiritual, the eighth is moral, the ninth is life and the tenth is prayer again. This is the ritual you must follow for it is the way of the Ioroarka and those that follow him."

"When do we start?" Tiathan was anxious to start.

"Now." Outra cast off his red and black robe revealing a second robe of pure white as the hair upon his head.

Since Trags usually relied on the moss of the field and leather of the Kalamada plant to make their clothes, Awlion thought Outra had to be rich to wear such fine cloth and live in such an elaborate oak. She was beginning to think that Outra was Jesuar Himself.

"Do not think that! I am not He who sits on the Throne of the Great Oak." Outra shook his finger at her. Awlion dropped her cup in surprise starting to rise from her seat.

"She is young. Forgive whatever thoughts you might have read." Tiathan protectively put his arm around her.

"You must put on these robes." Outra gave each of them a different colored robe; Tiathan a purple robe, Awlion a red robe and Miertur a blue one.

Quickly they each discarded their old oak armor and shredded undergarments before donning their robes. Each entered the water as Outra instructed them even though Trags were not accustomed to treading water. They trusted Outra even if they seemed to be rushed through their meal. Tiathan with his huge stumpy legs did not find the bottom of the spring very easily. Awlion and Miertur barely kept their heads above water. Miertur had the advantage of a longer nose to breathe above the surface if need be. Miertur never thought having such large nostrils was an advantage for anything except, perhaps, knowing when food was on the table.

"I'll read the ritual as it is written." Outra turned to the surrounding walls:

> "Jesuar has given you life,
> And life is neither sweet
> Nor everlasting till now.
> You are cleansed this day
> Until the time you turn away
> From Me or My servant,
> All things pass, I shall not.
> All things die, I shall not.
> All things fail, I shall not.
> Turn from Me and I shall follow,
> Lie to Me
> And I will show you the truth.
> Speak now your allegiance,
> And I will reward your faith.
> Raise your sword for Me

In honor and praise
And I will give you victory.
What say you?"

"We will now give You our allegiance as our forefathers have always done." Tiathan spoke for them all.

Awlion couldn't help herself as the music and words swam in her head bursting from her lips:

"Mo etohiR T mooRdyes 'ef Noost
etnet T esoomn 'ef mhitioR
etnet T nyefti t mhitioR
'ef tiRoitiet ad aooveyo mo nhitioR
moo sihiaes oo wtio baon
mhiti moomdyoRes mo efhisio
W oveyoRi'tietn mo areson
Ef' mhistoes metiti hi tiRhisio
T oveyya etti baoiRmes metw oo
T dyoibati etti ayveyoes hibaoiti oo"

Come out of the water and put on the armor of Jesuar!" Outra was pleased and smiled at each of them.

Outra directed Tiathan to the center suit of armor while Miertur and Awlion picked out their own armor. Awlion chose a bow with a quiver of silver-tipped arrows and two daggers that neatly fit under each arm. Miertur felt the smooth hard surface of his breastplate before reaching for a broadsword and battleaxe along with six star blades on his belt. He then picked up four daggers to hide in his boots and behind his back.

"Only the ancient Trags could have forged such weapons." Tiathan looked at his own broadsword engraved in silver and gold along with a shield of gold emblazoned with the letter 'J'.

"This is yours, also." Outra handed Tiathan a golden helmet with a crown of thorns upon it. "This Crown of Thorns sits on a complete circle with no beginning and no end; the thorns representing the difficulties of this life and the sacrifice Jesuar made for your soul. With this Crown you will serve Jesuar in war and in peace without comfort or peace for yourself. You will always make decisions to serve and protect those you lead. The golden sword represents justice not malice and it will serve you only in the right cause for Jesuar. Your shield is Jesuar's protection for you, but use it in strength not fear for fear will destroy you."

"I will wear this armor with honor." Tiathan noticed Outra withheld one terrible weapon from them. It was oddly shaped as the size of a large ball with metal spikes protruding from different angles. It was hinged to a long metal chain engraved with various figures of warriors past. He expected Outra would tell him about it soon enough.

"I see you're interested in Craxsmoore Guilding." Outra smiled while picking up the lethal weapon. "It is the wrath of Jesuar that you will need to destroy your enemies. It is the mighty hand of Jesuar in which whoever carries it shall be invincible in battle, but shall be weak if used just for the love of killing. Craxsmoore Guilding never leaves the Great Oak unless Everstream is threatened and then it is used as punishment toward those who stand against Jesuar. It can not and must not be used to conquer the innocent,"

"Why is it called Craxsmoore Guilding?" Awlion loved names and their origins.

"It is called that from the forger who made it, Arkson Guilding, and the township from whence it came, Craxsmoore." Outra smiled knowing that the explanation was simpler than what anyone might think.

"How disappointing." Awlion turned her back deciding that her weapons were more practical than such an unwieldy one as Craxsmoore Guilding. Certainly bows and arrows were much lighter and more lethal at a distance.

"We wish to build a township here." Tiathan changed the subject. "Will Jesuar bless this idea?"

"Why else would He have brought you here?" Outra embraced him to whisper in Tiathan's ear. "What will you call this township?"

"We will call it Quicksnatch because it symbolizes our escape from our enemies." Tiathan saw Awlion and Miertur nod agreement. "Who knows that we not be taken again in the future for I have had dreams that Mortarr is not finished with us."

"If it happens again, we will be ready." Awlion lifted up her bow.

"I will never be enslaved again." Miertur stood by Awlion's side.

"Not all of us will be staying." Awlion knew her brother, Ygueliv, was probably already getting ready to lead a few of the Trags back into the Dark Forest.

"Your brother will be all right for the present." Outra assured her though implied that her brother may be tested later. "If he does not stray far from Jesuar he will survive the coming storm."

"What storm is this? Have we not fought long enough?" Miertur wondered if the Trags will ever find peace.

"Peace will come soon enough." Outra seemed to read his thoughts. "For now build your township and enjoy the protection of the Great Oak."

"Come, let us go." Tiathan took off his armor. "If we are going to be under Jesuar's protection, we will let armor of war stay in the Great Oak."

Awlion was the only one who didn't want to give back her bow and arrows. Outra noticed her struggle and gently took her hand. Outra put the straps of the quiver of arrows over her head allowing her to take the weapons from the Great Oak.

"There are many uses for this bow so take it with you to stay sharp." Outra showed them all the door of the Great Oak and let them out. "I will be here if you need me."

****

Long months turned into fifteen years since Zelbiur entered the Dark Forest and never returned. Outra tried to reassure Tiathan and his kin that it was the will of Jesuar for them to wait in Quicksnatch. The pain of inaction took its toll as Awlion and Miertur demanded each day for their brothers Ygueliav and Zelbiur return. They had word that Ygueliav was alive and living in Rabel Ain, but Zelbiur was still lost. Tiathan begged for their patience, but eventually demanded it from them.

There was peace in Everstream until rumors started spreading that a new conqueror had taken control of the Seven Fortresses to the northwest of Quicksnatch. The conqueror's name was the terrible Moshdalayrrimich, which meant "he who conquers" in Valkrynese.

Stories from travelers who passed by the Seven Fortresses told stories that dimmed the bright afternoons of Quicksnatch with talk of war and battle. As long as there was peace in the land, it was only talk. Yet the news of a large company of warriors marching toward Quicksnatch forced Tiathan to decide whether to run or stand and fight. Many of the Trags in the township had not fought in years and it would time to retrain them.

"We just can't sit and wait for Moshdalayrrmich to trample all that we've built here." Awlion was already in battle dress with braided silver and oak breastplate. Her oak helmet was emblazoned with raven wings and as she approached Tiathan she carried her bow and arrows.

"Jesuar doesn't want war, but peace in Everstream." Tiathan heard the hollowness of his own words. Already Outra had told him that a few Trags were captured near the Dark Forest in the north and the hanged near the Cliffs of Angra.

The Seven Fortresses were sure to have dungeons

where many who ventured too close became its inhabitants. Unfortunately, the Trags were not considered valuable prizes so were often killed. Each of the fortresses were 160 stone high and 12,000 stone wide except the one at the end of the Valley of Gimgiddo. That one was 320 stone high and 36,000 stone wide with 20,000 warriors at one time or another. The smaller fortresses were on top of the mesas overlooking the valley with 150-1,000 warriors at a time. Six catapults were aimed directly toward the valley to shower any invading army with stone and flame. The main fortress was centered at the end of the valley with a black lake behind it call Theda Lake. The only escape was through a small pass that led past Mount Tarara, the sacred mountain of the Trags.

The Trags lived near the other side of Mount Tarara until driven out by the Valkyricks during their first time of bondage. If it were not for Jesuar the Trags would have been slaughtered on the Plains of Nord. Amalapek, leader of the Valkyricks at that time, lifted his sword in anger cursing the name of Jesuar and demanded to be struck down. When no answer came, except of the black wind, Mortarr, he felt it an honor to wipe out the Trags.

"I won't fight until I'm sure of our survival." Tiathan searched his mind trying to remember where he left the weapons Outra had placed in the Great Oak fifteen years ago. He was told then that he would go on a journey alone, but now he no longer believed it.

"I tell you now that you have no choice." Outra wandered in from the edge of Dark Forest as if on a friendly visit.

"I wish you would let me think for myself." Tiathan sighed heavily expecting Outra to clear his thoughts. "You made me First Ioroarka, but the decisions I make must always agree with your visions."

"It is the will of Jesuar as you well know." Outra understood Tiathan's dilemma. "Your spirit is strong, but not fully guided by what is right or wrong only by anger and pain."

"Sometimes I wonder and yet you are always right." Tiathan stroked his great gray beard with shards of white and black peppering it throughout. He turned to the Great Oak knowing he had to seek the guiding Spirit of Jesuar. The lives of so many Trags depended on his decision to fight or run.

Tiathan entered the Great Hall with Outra wishing that there was more time to prepare the Trags for war, but he knew they would never be ready. The years had softened them, cradled them like babies who still slept in their mother's arms. The past battles were now only stories to help fill the long days.

"Father?" Awlion followed him into the Great Oak interrupting his search for an answer, some miracle to keep the Trags from harm. "We must leave quickly."

"What has changed?" Tiathan looked from Awlion to Outra.

"Warriors have camped just outside of Quicksnatch." Awlion slid a second quiver of arrows over her shoulder. "We don't know who they are, but they wait by the lake."

"I am not worthy to wear Jesuar's armor, but I will take Craxsmoore Guilding with me." Tiathan saw the weapon in a dark corner of the Great Hall.

"They might be from the Seven Fortresses." Outra knew who they were.

"I've never seen them before." Miertur joined them inside. "Korallmykin, their Captain, knows you and demands your surrender." He smiled an all-knowing smile that Tiathan never surrenders, but plods relentlessly to battle.

"He's a stranger to me." Tiathan felt the cold relief of sweat down his neck. "Perhaps we can persuade him to leave us alone."

"But father?" Awlion objected to her father's

view of appeasement.

"I will go and face them alone." Tiathan patted Craxsmoore Guilding will wrapping it around his waist. "On second thought I will bring this shield just in case I cannot convince to leave in peace."

"Where shall I be, father?" Awlion knelt in obedience, but her fingers whitened as she tightly gripped her bow.

"Here in Quicksnatch." Tiathan knew his daughter would not like his answer.

"And what of me?" Miertur had no intention of being left behind.

"Follow me, but not with me." Tiathan stared hard into Miertur's eyes. "If I fall you must come back and bring everyone against them."

"There must be more." Awlion desperately wanted to go with her father.

"You'll lead whomever will follow us to Throg's Knoll until I or Miertur comes." Tiathan smiled to himself knowing she was her father's daughter. "Go no further."

"I will obey." She stood up with fire in her eyes. "I won't wait too long for you."

"I hope not." He kissed her on the cheek and walked past to the Altar of Jesuar, knelt and silently prayed. Standing up he turned one more time to Awlion.

"I wish I could give you a sign." Tiathan stared hard into her eyes.

"Watch the horizon for a flash of light and then watch for your father who soon be with you." Outra broke in to give her some comforting news. "Now go, all of you."

Awlion hurried out of the Great Oak with Miertur close behind her. They sprinted through Quicksnatch to find warriors willing to follow them. Tiathan stayed behind lying prostrate before the Altar of Jesuar. He repeated the words Jesuar Himself engraved on the wall above it. It was the prayer of the faithful in ancient Trag:

"lloiR mya mya siono
XoesoiheRes mya bao dyoomo
tieooRoinetoiti oveyoRestiRohin
a ti' r w T nrohiti oohiv
ef' nyveyo OO ad ethiveyonoRsill
adhidy OO T t tiRoitie
dyoayveyoR OO 'efoon ll'R omones'
ef' ll'R mya epoomoR ad veyoosio
sthia noiooyo OO ef' oveyor
oimtiya ll' ti' r moo nooRo
hinom"

"hinom." Awlion echoed from outside.

****

Flashfire Lake lay less than two miles from Quicksnatch. The winter storms extended the width of the lake some thirty feet in the last few months. Mirrored in the reflection of the water before him was the image of Korallmykin who stepped behind him hoping to cut off Tiathan's retreat. Tiathan was pleased to have the lake at his back.

"We've not been properly introduced, Captain." Tiathan watched as other warriors moved in a half circle around him. "Welcome to my home."

"Welcome? To your home? I am Korallmykin." He spat on the ground before Tiathan. As he unsheathed his sword his thorny elbows clicked against an oak breastplate. The other warriors who stood a foot taller than Tiathan lifted their shields and swords.

Tiathan wondered where this band of Krackian mercenaries had come from and who paid them to come to Quicksnatch. Krackians were known to fight for anyone for a price without conscience. They had greenish-blue hue to their skin with large eyes a protruding lower lip with two small tusks that appeared to curve toward their face. The fierceness in their faces was enough to frighten anyone who encountered them.

There were no warriors like this in the immediate confines of Everstream so they had to be called upon from the Havrll Mountains. Their bowed legs, much like a Korillian Grasshopper, were particularly suited for mountain fighting not here on sand and clay. There was a blue flame upon the Captain's brow which suggested a follower of Mortarr and a symbol of a mountain clan called the Brorskins. They rarely came this far east from the Forest of Deen.

"Today you die, Trag!" Korallmykin lifted his sword and shield to charge.

"Before you do so, tell me why." Tiathan tried to bide time as he unwrapped Craxsmoore Guilding from around his waist.

"For wealth, land and the honor to kill the great Tiathan Eiula! Why else?" Korallmykin was anxious to fight, but was amused how calm Tiathan stood before him with an obviously useless ball and chain.

"There's plenty here for everyone. Why here?" Tiathan let Craxsmoore Guilding dangle so they were all aware of it. Tiathan's shield made it obvious he was on the side of Jesuar which was not lost on these warriors.

"Because it is yours! Because you are Trags! When you die Jesuar is defeated as well!" Korallmykin sneered and bellowed.

"There's no reason for this." Tiathan tightened his grip on Craxsmoore Guilding preparing for the inevitable. In the name of Jesuar I will forgive your rudeness and let you live if you leave right now.

"Let us live?" Korallmykin and his warriors laughed at him. "I spit on Jesuar's name and will not let you die until you curse His name as well."

"Then I am sorry you have wasted your time and your lives coming here." Tiathan looked down at the long shadows of these mercenaries and knew it was soon time.

"Moshdalayrrimich was right when he put a bounty on your head." Korallmykin grabbed a spear from one of his warriors and threw it at Tiathan and missed. "You are an arrogant toad!"

Just as they started to charge, Tiathan knelt down placing his shield in front of his face as the first flash of light burst over the lake. It almost blinded him even with his eyes closed. It was Flashfire Lake's evening tribute to another day finished and now an aide to defeat the enemies of the Trags. Korallmykin would have known what was going to happen if he sent scouts ahead of him.

Korallmykin and his warriors did not shield their eyes nor did they understand the blindness that overcame them. Tiathan stood up watching them fight amongst themselves as Korallmykin continued his charge past Tiathan. He slipped into the water and sank quickly under the water since he never learned to swim. Without using Craxsmoore Guilding all the warriors were dead.

"Jesuar, your vengeance is great, but just." Tiathan ran quickly from Flashfire Lake to Throg's Knoll.

****

"We saw the great light of the lake." Awlion was the first to meet Tiathan. "No doubt their Captain saw it, too."

"He seemed overwhelmed." Tiathan winked knowing Awlion understood the outcome. "We must hurry before others overtake us. Moshdalayrrimich is behind the attack and he will not stop coming till we are all dead. How do we stand?"

"With those who have joined us, it would not take much to overwhelm our position." Awlion pointed to the twenty warriors that now surrounded Tiathan.

"What of those left behind?" Tiathan was concerned that Quicksnatch would be destroyed.

"Outra has taken them inside the Great Oak until

this is over." Awlion now could keep his mind on the battles ahead.

"Where is Miertur?" Tiathan searched the many faces for his son.

"He is already scouting ahead for safe trails to the west." Awlion was already concerned for her brother. "Where do we go from here?"

"Perhaps Rabel Ain if it is safe." Tiathan did not know what Jesuar had in store for them, but he was willing to venture forth to find out.

"I salute those of you who believe that Jesuar will be our protection and our guide." Tiathan nodded to this small company leading them into the Dark Forest.

The paths were just as overgrown as when they first came to Quicksnatch with the willowing of the Caridall and the screeching of the Pitmouse that did like the travelers coming through their homes. Shadows appeared as ghostly warriors who still roamed the thick brush and gnarled oaks with the evening moon above them. They marched for a few miles before finally seeing a familiar face smiling as if on a holiday instead of a dangerous journey.

"I have yet to understand why they call this the Dark Forest and why it is forbidden." Miertur embraced his father and sister. "The only thing forbidden in it is us."

"It is perhaps the legends of Nsaat and the Bantongues." Tiathan was glad to see him. "We've seen and fought against his Bantongues which you were scouting at the time and missed the fight."

"We plucked the Harkies from the skies with arrows, but many who were with us then are no longer here." Awlion proudly remembered the few Harkies she brought to ground.

"We know they are fearless warriors so I hope not to meet them now." Tiathan wanted to continue on, but they needed to rest.

"I never wanted to come back." Awlion raised her bow at the shadow that stretched across the trees in front of her. The arrow sprang from her bow finding its mark as a low loud wail pierced the air. The shadow quickly retreated back down the path ahead of them.

"What was that?" Miertur was surprised he was followed.

"A Bantongue and I loathe those creatures. I'll not be spied upon." Awlion strung another arrow as she surveyed the path ahead.

"Your deadly bow serves warning enough." Tiathan bade Awlion to lower her bow. "Jesuar is with us and if it is time to die, so be it. We are ready."

"It is not time, Tiathan." Another welcome voice

drifted towards them.

"I had hoped that my daughter did not see you as she did the Bantongue." Tiathan raised his hand in allegiance.

"Awlion does not like the shadows of any kind it seems." Outra Whorld slipped out behind a gnarled oak. He wore armor, but no sword. A red cloak masked the fact that the armor covered most of his body.

"I doubt I would have dented the armor you're wearing." Awlion thought Outra almost handsome and younger. He seemed less weak than the prophet of doom she was used to when living in Quicksnatch.

"Though now it is of no consequence." Outra bowed to her. "You would have missed."

"I always hit what I aim at." Awlion's smile melted away.

"You are no more than a few feet away." Outra tossed the red cloak over his shoulders; the letter "J" was scrolled upon his chest. "Shoot!"

"I never enjoyed your games, Shroo! Now is not the time to play with me." Awlion would not back down until Outra did. Only her father could make her check her anger when it was aroused, but she saw that Tiathan was not going to try this time.

"I am not playing, little princess." Outra stood

with arms crossed.

"Don't tempt me!" Awlion fitted arrow to bow.

"I do not tempt only teach what you should have known already." Outra stared into her fiery eyes.

Awlion raised the bow letting the arrow fly straight and to the mark of Outra's armor. Yet the arrow struck the ground in front of Outra. The Trags gasped in awe at what they saw. Tiathan walked over and calmly pulled the arrow from the ground and returned it to her quiver.

"Someday you'll learn that we're not like him." Tiathan smoother his daughter's hair and kissed her cheek.

"I'm sorry, Awlion, but it's a lesson better shown than spoken." Outra smiled. "I'm not here to battle your pride or to take it away. I'm here to show you the way and guide the Trags to their destiny. It is the will of Jesuar."

"I only hear it from you and not from Jesuar." Awlion was resigned to the fact that Outra could not be defeated, but she could. She had never embraced this Shroo who spoke of Jesuar as if they were related. She had only known war and the sadness of lost loved ones. A Great Oak and a little Trag in armor did not bring a great Spirit called Jesuar into her life. She knows someone is out there and there are times she doubts.

"You're still bitter that your brother, Zelbiur, has never returned." Outra sighed for it seemed an eternity since he told them they would see Zelbiur again.

"You are never to speak his name, Shroo!" Awlion drew her dagger as the tears welled up, yet she refused to let them drop.

"Perhaps we'll find out what happened to him." Outra tried to soothe her anger with comforting words.

"Outra, you already know what has become of him." Tiathan stopped the useless bickering with an angry look at both of them. "I expect to encounter Nsaat and his Bantongues near the House of Myrr. We need to speak of other things."

"We should have searched instead of listening to Outra." Miertur vented his despair before quickly turning away as Tiathan pointed a threatening finger at him.

"All things are known by Jesuar." Outra rested his hand on Miertur's shoulder. "Be faithful and understand."

"I am First Ioroarka!" Tiathan almost wept sounding like a Bull Toad in his grief.

"I must accept what Jesuar tells me through you." Awlion was still skeptical, but at least she had hope.

"But if my son is dead, I will know I stand alone and Jesuar has deserted me." Tiathan was tired and weary to convince himself if he had done the right thing for the last fifteen years.

"Do not be deceived with your ears or your heart." Outra warned them all. "See and believe what you know is true."

"So it shall be done." Tiathan felt his heart soar as Outra spoke.

"Look! The trees!" Miertur pointed to a Harkie that alit on a far branch smiling grotesquely at the small band below it.

"Do not slay me great warriors!" The Harkie hissed, its yellowed leathery face gleamed in the twilight. Its outstretched wings blotted out everything behind him.

"Come down here and speak with us!" Tiathan beckoned with his sword. "I will honor a truce if you will."

The creature's wings made little sound as it gently glided to the ground. It couldn't walk upright on its talons without using its wings for balance. The Harkies' eyes were flames of amber that brought shivers down the spines of those who remembered the battle that was fought in the same forest fifteen years before.

"I'm Trusk, the Scout." Trusk crossed his wings in front of himself and bowed to Tiathan while glaring at

Outra Whorld.

"What's your business, Trusk?" Tiathan scanned the brush behind Trusk for any Bantongues that might surprise them.

"I am not alone." Trusk saw Tiathan look away. "I would be foolish to enter your camp without escort. However, Nsaat bids you welcome this time."

"Why do you welcome us now?" Awlion did not trust him. "Many of your kind died at our hands fifteen years ago."

"As did many of yours." Trusk smiled recognizing the bow and arrows on Awlion's back. "I know you very well, little one."

"Call me that again and I will not honor our truce." Awlion was already itching to use her bow and arrows on him.

"We watched you at night from the air." Trusk turned to Tiathan. His ragged teeth curved inward to fine points causing a very fine drool of poison upon his lips. "We watched through your knotholes before your journey even began. We saw assassins trying to kill you at Flashfire Lake."

Trusk watched Awlion and some of the other Trags flinch slightly as their minds raced to think of the times they thought they saw shadows move outside their trunks. Trusk's eyes narrowed enjoying how uncomfortable he made them all feel.

"If we are welcome then where is our brother Zelbiur?" Miertur ventured to ask though he regretted the question immediately.

"I know not that name?" Trusk looked at Tiathan. "Another son, perhaps? No Trag has entered our domain since we last fought."

"Liar!" Miertur's sword flashed across Trusk's chest leaving a long slender wound that did not bleed.

The forest came alive with cries of anguish. Hundreds of Bantongues jumped from the underbrush and treetops with lances in their fore claws. The Trags saw them close up seeing their skeletal heads dripping with poison from their fangs. They had eight coarse legs and two fore claws to grasp weapons and warriors. Their huge black bodies made great targets, but were thick with fur and a leathery skin. A company of Harkies flew in a half-circle above them bearing stones and rocks to drop on their heads. The jagged jaws of the Bantongues dripped poison with the anticipation of battle.

"No, stay!" Trusk wiped the wound with some kind of liquid and was immediately healed. "I am well."

Miertur! Stay your sword!" Tiathan grabbed Miertur's sword and threw it to the ground. He then threw his own weapons to the ground, but kept

Craxsmoore Guilding hidden from vie with his cloak.

Peace was held by a slender thread. Tiathan knew too late what was happening and was unable to prevent it. Fortunately Trusk stepped back before the full force of the blade struck him. It seemed to amuse him as well of the lack of fear they all seemed to have. From the killing stare in Trusk's eyes, Tiathan knew that this was not a time to fight.

"Is this the great Tiathan Eiula we fought years ago?" Trusk taunted him. "The one who claimed he fought only to find his place in Everstream? Are you now the Shroo of the Great Oak? He turned to Outra Whorld who faced him without fear. "Are you eager to shed my blood so that you can claim victory in the name of Jesuar? I came in peace, but you took first blood. You'll never leave this forest alive if one more sword is raised against me."

"I swear by Jesuar that we will not raise another sword against you." Tiathan stood between Miertur and Trusk. He urged all the Trags to drop their weapons to ensure peace.

"Because your word has been known to be true, I accept your oath, Ioroarka." Trusk bowed again with the same honor due to his name. "Come, gather your weapons and follow us."

"To the House of Myrrh?" Outra watched closely as Trusk turned to answer him.

"No one enters or sees the House of Myrrh and lives." Trusk slowly turned to the western path before lifting himself up above them to show the way.

Within a mile the forest was quiet again as the Bantongues drifted back into the shadows or crawled up the trees. The only sound was the echoing footsteps of the Trags and the creaking of Trusk's leathery wings. As they walked the forest grew black from the overcast sky making it neither night nor day. Awlion and seven other Trags lit torches to guide the way ahead wherever that may be. Trample Spiders wove silken snares for anyone venturing too far from the path. The green and red bodied Trample Spiders spotted the trees above them waiting for anyone to fall into their trap.

Tiathan noticed that Outra Whorld had vanished into the underbrush no doubt to warn them in case of an ambush. Awlion thought Outra a coward, but was silenced by her brother who secretly hoped it wasn't true. The Trags walked into a clearing with a huge wooden throne at its center. It was obvious they had finally reached their destination as Trusk stood next to the throne.

"Rest here, Tiathan Eiula." Trusk backed slowly

behind the throne.

Soon hundreds of tiny eyes glistened off the torchlight. A low moaning whisper seemed to surround the Trags. Tiathan ordered swords and shields to be concealed unless necessary to defend themselves. A battle circle was formed as Awlion decided to aim her first arrow just behind Trusk for it was the biggest shadow she could make out and easiest to hit.

"Put down you weapons, Ioroarka!" A heavy thick voice thundered over the clearing. "I wish to talk, not fight!"

A monstrous figure emerged from the underbrush that even towered over Trusk who was three times the size of any Trag. One fiery red eye in the middle of his scaly head first appeared into the torchlight. The creature drew itself to the throne allowing his bulky green-scaled body to be fully viewed and feared. Behind him was an army of Bantongues and Harkies covering all sides of the clearing.

"I am Nsaat." He smiled seeing the fear on their faces. Trags considered themselves less than desirable in looks with some sporting large noses, others with scars from past wars, and tangled hair with long beards. Nsaat however, had fine honed razor sharp teeth and a tongue that split in half as he talked. When he walked the ground shook from his weight leaving dust behind in his wake. The Trags fought back their fear, but such a horrible sight made them tremble which pleased Nsaat.

As Trusk and three other Harkies built a pyre, Nsaat took on a more horrendous form. His green scales reflected the light of the fire as his hooves kicked the ashes away that burned too close to him. The three sharp talons on his claws clicked and snapped as he spoke.

"It is well." Tiathan saluted Nsaat with his sword before he laid it on the ground though he had respect for Nsaat.

"It is well." Nsaat's flattened snout pulled his lips back from his fangs. The single black horn upon his forehead moved slightly as his roving blood-red eye surveyed the Trag company. He waved Trusk away seeing the pyre was burning bright enough to see all his guests.

"You look troubled, Nsaat." Tiathan was not afraid knowing that even Nsaat had rules to follow when there was a meeting of peace.

"Will we not have the honor of receiving the great Shroo of Quicksnatch?" Nsaat looked hard into the darkness behind Tiathan.

"He probably thought it best not to irritate you

with stories of Jesuar." Tiathan could not help telling Nsaat the truth.

"It is best he never comes here again." Nsaat spat on the ground bringing sparks jumping in front of him. "I will not be as good a host as I was the last time."

"How tall this monster stands!" Miertur whispered to Awlion. "Four of us together on our shoulders would not stand so tall."

"If he has a heart his height will not save him from my arrows." Awlion kept arrow to bow just in case.

"May I be seated?" Nsaat's deep resonant voice vibrated the strings on Awlion's bow.

"It is your realm." Tiathan unwrapped Craxsmoore Guilding and set it on the ground beside him. He noticed Nsaat shift uneasily when he looked down at the weapon.

"Good!" Nsaat was pleased with Tiathan's homage.

"We're here to pass peacefully through the forbidden part of your forest." Tiathan was aware of the slight movement of the Bantongues on his left. "When first we met your warriors caught us fleeing our captors, the Gimgiddeans."

"Neither of us thought it helpful to talk first." Trusk interrupted bringing a cup of warm red liquid for him to drink. He offered the same to Tiathan, but he already knew it wasn't fit to drink so refused politely.

"To understand why we were there." Tiathan corrected Trusk.

"However we are talking now and soon come to some understanding." Nsaat forced a grisly smile.

"I understand first that three of your warriors are making their way behind me." Tiathan knew Nsaat couldn't be trusted as he pointed the warriors out without looking to his left. "If I pick up Craxsmoore Guilding we are finished talking."

"As much trust as you have with my warriors, they

were going to see who sits on the near branch to my right." Nsaat pointed to thick oak branch just above him.

"Very good, Nsaat." Outra Whorld clearly answered Nsaat. "I was only listening, but you have not lost your touch."

"But you have lost yours, Shroo. In an earlier time, I would not have noticed." Nsaat winced noticeably.

"Then nothing's changed." Outra climbed down entering the clearing with a swirl of his red cape hiding oak armor.

"One of your cheap tricks?" Nsaat was not

impressed clicking his talons nervously as Outra came closer.

"You gloat too much if you think I did not let you feel my presence." Outra was not smiling as he walked to Tiathan's side.

Something deadly was passing between them as Tiathan leaned ever so slightly towards Craxsmoore Guilding. Awlion noticed her father preparing himself for a fight so nudged Miertur who already steadied his hand upon his battleaxe.

"We have a long life to live before we finish this game, Shroo." Nsaat gripped the sides of his throne. "Yet, I can make it difficult for you to play."

Tiathan jumped over to grasp Craxsmoore Guilding firmly with both hands as Awlion aimed her arrow at the heart of Nsaat. Miertur jumped at the chance to put his sword to Trusk's throat.

"You've a brother, little one." Nsaat calmly stared at Awlion as his fiery red eye turned to a passive blue. His look pierced her soul and made her drowsy.

"Why does everyone call little this or little that?" Awlion felt her bow grow heavy, so heavy she dropped it to the ground.

"And you a son." Nsaat turned to Tiathan who

already dropped his gaze away from him.

Miertur stopped in his tracks seeing the effect that Nsaat on his family. He decided not to attack Trusk who already was waiting for Miertur to come for him. Everyone was at a standstill waiting for Nsaat to signal the fight to start.

"Do you remember this weapon?" Outra pointed to Craxsmoore Guilding.

"Yes, Shroo, but it is only as dangerous as the one who bears it." Nsaat slumped back onto his throne feeling weary of this game. There was a time he enjoyed playing with the Trags, but that time has passed.

"He has been trained with it and Awlion years of using the Bow of Cordell would make a decent fight." Outra broke the trance from which Awlion was suffering fearing she would soon be killed by the Bantongues not far from her. "Her brother bears the Sword of Akrin Thorn which has the blood of many of your warriors."

At the mention of Akrin Thorn's sword the Bantongues noticeably backed away from Miertur. Awlion reached down for her bow and again readied it for battle.

"I yield to you for now, Shroo." Nsaat grumbled. "I did not come to fight, but give you a warning."

"What warning is that?" Tiathan wanted to know.

"Your heads have a bounty on them from

Moshdalayrrimich." Nsaat didn't see any surprise on their faces.

"Old news." Awlion sighed as she placed her bow over her shoulder. She knew the moment had passed so resigned to fact that nothing would happen.

"We have asked to pass through your forest in peace." Outra stood at the hoof of Nsaat. "We, also want Zelbiur and any other Trag you have imprisoned in the House of Myrr."

"Why didn't you tell us where he was?" Awlion was restrained by Tiathan from approaching them.

"You may have them." Nsaat waved his talons indifferently. Zelbiur bores me with stories of Jesuar and the Great Oak of which I have no interest."

"Your judgment is just, Nsaat." Outra bowed before turning back to Tiathan.

"If you and your Trags are not out of my realm in three days, I won't be as merciful as I am this time." Nsaat snorted angrily as he pushed his throne aside and disappeared into the darkness. The Bantongues and Harkies followed leaving Tiathan and the Trags alone in the clearing.

"That wasn't too bad." Miertur winked at Tiathan as he sheathed his sword.

"We must leave quickly." Outra looked at

Miertur in amazement.

"Not without Zelbiur." Awlion insisted wanting to send an arrow after Nsaat.

"Nsaat will keep his word only to play a move in a bigger game." Outra tried to move them ahead.

"We should send our brother ahead as scout." Awlion teased. "Especially since he says he has no fear of monsters."

"I fear less because of your bow so stay close, sister." Miertur pushed Awlion away.

Tiathan ordered all torches extinguished till dawn hoping that Nsaat would think they had already left.
Awlion took three warriors to keep watch as other Trags dug trenches either for battle or sleep. Tiathan and Outra were at odds about leaving immediately and soon it was evident that Tiathan had won out. Outra and Miertur waited beside the fallen throne expecting Nsaat or his Bantongues to reappear at any moment. Hopefully, it would be to bring Zelbiur back to them.

"We don't know where the House of Myrrh could be." Miertur stopped Awlion as she walked by. "Or how to find it."

"And? So?" Awlion pulled her arm away thinking more a brother lost, then the one standing next to her.

"I see it in your eyes that you plan on finding Zelbiur on your own, but listen to our father and Outra. Wait." Miertur knew she would be lost going into the darkness alone.

"He will be released." Outra studied her face knowing how concerned she was for her brother.

"I am sure you will be led away from us if you go into the forest alone." Miertur still saw the determination on Awlion's face. The Dark Forest plays tricks on lone travelers."

"Then we must remember where they House of Myrrh could not be." Awlion tried to rationalize her need to go.

"Then we'll know where it is." Outra whispered aloud.

"No riddles. Outra." Tiathan did not want Outra to get into making riddles or they would all go insane trying to interpret them. "Awlion stay with the scouts and leave Zelbiur to me."

"Someone must do something." Awlion was anxious to do something, go somewhere. "Nsaat may kill him and send his body back to us."

"Then we must rely on Jesuar to keep him safe." Tiathan turned his back to the camp staring up into the night sky. He saw Trusk flying high overhead which told him Nsaat was aware they have yet to leave.

As the night brought out the many voices and sounds of the forest, many of the Trags relaxed enough to fall asleep. Tiathan kept watch seeing Awlion and Miertur fall asleep back to back near the throne of Nsaat.

Chapter Two

At dawn Zelbiur still was not returned by Nsaat. The Trags had already broken camp and were forming travel positions. Tiathan decided it was time to bring Zelbiur home no matter what the cost. They were only twenty strong, but Jesuar will lead and guide them.

"This day." Tiathan addressed the Trags. "We must begin our time of battle for one of our own. Already the Seven Fortresses press heavily on Everstream and the Gimgiddean, Rhor, will surely meet us from the west. First, we must rescue Zelbiur from the House of Myrrh. Many of us will meet Jesuar in this our sacred duty." He hoped they wouldn't have to fight, but Nsaat was untrustworthy. "I would do this even if one of you were held captive there."

"A mighty speech, Ioroarka, and I am sure an inspiring one." Trusk clicked his talons in mock appreciation. "Yet, unnecessary. Behold! Your son and his warriors!"

Zelbiur was the first to emerge from the underbrush with a blindfold over his eyes. It was obvious he was weak from his imprisonment of the last few years. Ten others followed with heads covered so that they could not lead Tiathan back to the House of Myrrh.

"My son!" Tiathan ripped off the blindfold and hugged Zelbiur. "Forgive me!"

"Nothing to forgive, my father." Zelbiur slipped to the ground and thanked Jesuar for his deliverance.

"We left you for dead, brother, and you show no anger?" Miertur hesitated to embrace him.

"If you had come, you would all have died at Nsaat's hands." Zelbiur smiled knowingly. "It was his plan to force you to leave Quicksnatch and rescue me. It was then he spoke of slaying you and enslaving the others in Quicksnatch. I prayed to Jesuar that you would not come."

"And Jesuar heard you." Outra stood behind him.

"This is sickening. Farewell." Trusk flew off to the west then turned south.

"And I heard you, too, Shroo." Zelbiur embraced Outra. "You came to me in dreams to comfort me and advised how to drive Nsaat to torment with the same stories of the Great Oak and Jesuar that drove us crazy when we were young. I thought he would kill me if I didn't stop."

"Yet, he didn't." Outra laughed at the thought of Nsaat screaming at Zelbiur to stop.

"No, he didn't." Zelbiur looked around for another familiar face. "Where is Ygueliav?"

"I'm sorry, but he has been gone these past fifteen years as well." Tiathan lifted his bristled brow and said no more.

"Our brother wanted adventure, so I'm sure he has found it." Awlion accepted whatever news might come in the future. "Rumor has it that he might be in Rabel Ain."

"How come you did not tell us that you knew Zelbiur was in the House of Myrrh?" Miertur was angry with Outra. "Why didn't you tell us that you were in contact with Zelbiur?"

"Would you have believed me and if you did would you not try to free him?" Outra already knew the answer.

"Of course we would have gone to find him." Awlion was not happy with Outra either.

"Then I was right not to tell you." Outra waved off any more conversation.

"I don't..." Miertur began to protest.

"Be quiet, my brother." Awlion grabbed his shoulder. "You have never won an argument with Outra ever."

"What do we do now?" Zelbiur looked to Tiathan and Outra.

"First, we will pray for your safe return and then sing thanks to Jesuar for your homecoming." Tiathan looked to Awlion who seemed to always have the right song for the moment.

"I know which one." Awlion cleared her throat and began the Forever Song which everyone knew by heart:

> "esN T efoveyor sioomN
> aroxooysio W efoveyor aooveyo
> dyhimsio t T etohiveyomall vey'oosio
> Rhiyeso ll'R ethimdyes t XoesoihiR
> ad esnyao hiti T efhisio 'ef ayefo
> mo ayveyo ef' etyn
> mo dyyo ef' etyn
> mo esN ef' etyn
> Metooeso mhino r XoesoihiR"

"Now to what we will do next." Tiathan felt rejuvenated from singing. "Tell me what you have heard that might help us get out of this trouble."

"I heard a great deal before Nsaat realized about my talent." Zelbiur pointed to his long extended ears. "They spoke of watching you in Quicksnatch and made plans often to attack. Each time Trusk saw warriors from the Seven Fortresses near the township. Nsaat fears them as much as we should."

"What plans do they have now that you back with us?" Awlion was anxious to move on to more important things.

"I heard little until they blindfolded us." Zelbiur gave a melancholy smile. "Nsaat had wax put into my ears to keep me listening to his plans."

"Why do you smile, my son?" Tiathan thought Zelbiur's imprisonment brought an emptiness where sanity should have been.

"After they bound me, someone pulled most of the wax from my ears." Zelbiur wondered if it had been Outra or a secret friend within the House of Myrrh.

"It was not me." Outra answered the unasked question.

"You must have had a friend in the House of Myrrh." Tiathan could not guess who would
have helped his son.

"What I heard was that we are to be attacked if we follow the path ahead of us." Zelbiur remembered that one of the Harkies made a strong point in mentioning the direction. "If we move south towards Rabel Ain we should come to no harm."

"Outra?" Tiathan looked to him for advice.

"It is a sound decision." Outra agreed, but was not totally ready to follow them to Rabel Ain and leave the Great Oak behind.

Tiathan and the Trags moved through twelve miles of sharp thorns and bristles until they found another clearing. This place was smaller than the last one, but the oak trees covered the azure sky while the branches kept them from view from above. Zelbiur listened for anyone nearby, but heard nothing.

"This is a good place to defend." Tiathan ordered trenches dug and a small wall built of stone in case of attack. The Trags were known for their fortifications in battle and the fierceness in their fighting when cornered. Open field fighting was a disaster whenever they fought in the open.

"What will we do now?" Awlion did not want to sit and wait.

"I will go ahead and see what lies beyond." Tiathan waved away the protests from Awlion and Miertur. "I am Ioroarka and it is what I decide I should do! Miertur, you will stay here with the company…"

"I will go with you." Awlion volunteered not

asking anyone else's opinion.

"No, I go alone." Tiathan said firmly. "When I come back, if it is safe, we will go west toward Rabel Ain."

"Jesuar go with you." Outra encouraged him to go.

"Farewell." Tiathan turned to begin slashing his way through the undergrowth.

"I will follow a second path then." Awlion waited for her father to disappear into the forest before she picked up her bow and arrows.

"You were told to stay." Miertur called after her, but made no effort to follow.

"He told you to stay." Awlion laughed at him. "He told me I could not go with him."

"He meant the same thing for you." Miertur did not find it funny.

"I can't hear you!" She vanished through a dark tunnel of trees.

****

Tiathan spent much of the day without a glint of sun or easiness of the path ahead. The dull green undergrowth continued to bar his way without ceasing.

Soon a flicker of light caught his eye. "Surely a campfire." He thought. "But whose?" It was too small for a company of warriors, but it bore a look.

On closer view, Tiathan spied a plucked Notherhen skewered on a small metal blade. No one sat near the fire so Tiathan unbuckled Craxsmoore Guilding and waited to see if anyone came back to the fire. The smell of the cooking meat made it difficult to sit and wait. Soon the temptation was too great and Tiathan moved forward toward the fire. Before he was able to reach out for a piece to eat a flash of light and heavy smoke nearly blinded him.

"Behold!" A cloaked figure appeared seemingly form thin air. "It is I, Carazaar! The Magician! Healer! Fortune Teller! Protector of Spirits!"

"And it is I, Tiathan Eiula, that nearly cut you in two!" Tiathan held his broadsword just beneath Carazaar's throat. One look and Tiathan knew Carazaar was full of mischief, not violence. The pudgy cheeks that billowed out from his frazzled beard only convinced Tiathan that Carazaar was not a threat by sword or lance. A quick glance at the magician's hands revealed their softness and lack of callous only betrayed the fat life he led.

"But, of course, I knew you wouldn't have killed me. For I can tell the future!" Carazaar stepped slowly back from the fire and Tiathan's sword.

"Oh? Really?" Tiathan drew his dagger with his other hand and threw it a hair's breadth from Carazaar's head.

"Of course, too, knowing the future one can always change the outcome." Carazaar began to sweat trying valiantly to keep to keep his dignity. "Come, fellow traveler, and tell me your needs."

"I look for many enemies, Carazaar." Tiathan retrieved his dagger and lay it across his knees as he sat back down near the fire. "Can you make my enemies disappear as you think you can?"

"Not on such short notice." Carazaar pulled a leg of Notherhen and offered it to Tiathan.

"I thought not." Tiathan smiled before giving thanks to Jesuar.

"As a Trag you'll need all the power at your command when you meet your enemies." He noticed the gesture of prayer while his mind raced to think how valuable Tiathan might be to him.

"I will?" Tiathan was amused at Carazaar's assumption that his magic tricks would be of any use to him.

"Perhaps I can teach you for a small fee the power of illusion?" Carazaar lifted his arm up high as he bit into a toasted morsel of Notherhen. "To make snakes, monsters, vast armies or even maidens appear before you very eyes! Look behind you!"

"I see nothing." Tiathan continued to eat, but did see the giant three-toed Anglarar racing towards him. Since he knew it was an illusion, he appeared unconcerned of the possible danger.

"Look again!" Carazaar was confused since he could see his own illusion as well. He watched Tiathan look back a second time, but there was no fear in his eyes.

"What do you see, magician?" Tiathan licked his fingers clean as he watched Carazaar stand up with a look of confusion.

"No!" Carazaar saw that the Anglarar was coming towards him, but it could not be possible unless it wasn't an illusion.

"Is there a problem?" Tiathan leaned back and watched Carazaar try to make sense of what he saw.

"Help me!" The magician tripped over his own feet as he tried to bolt away from the creature. Tiathan kept his back to the creature as Carazaar stumbled again trying to climb the nearest tree. He finally gave up to the fact he was going to die just as the image faded leaping towards his throat.

"Want some more Notherhen?" Tiathan

innocently offered him some meat at the end of his dagger.

"I see." Carazaar angrily dusted up his robe. "Obviously you have already mastered the art of illusion."

"I'm sorry. I don't understand." Tiathan feigned surprise. "It was you who said he was the master of illusion. I saw nothing to fear, but you did."

"Perhaps." Carazaar knew he was being taken advantage of by Tiathan. "Maybe I can surprise you with something you've never seen here in the pouch."

"I doubt you could, but you can try." Tiathan waited patiently as Carazaar dangled a leather pouch with various symbols along the bottom.

"Watch." Carazaar dumped its contents on an old oak stump.

"And what are they?" Tiathan watched him empty the pouch which seemed to reveal a mound of useless rubble.

"Among these stones are the mysterious forces of the Third Eye of Karatura that I show you now." Carazaar whispered low as if someone was close by listening. "It is said the victory of the spirits over Mortarr and Nsaat lay within these facets. These were the crystals of the conqueror Moshdalayrrimich!"

"Show me this wisdom!" Tiathan was interested, but it was more than the lifeless stones before that he wanted to hear about.

"First, you must empty your mind of all things good or evil." Carazaar became dazed as he moved side to side as he spoke. "Then I will place these crystals in a single row upon your chest. This pink crystal....very strong magic...will be placed on your forehead."

"Then what, magician?" Tiathan kept his ground reusing to tolerate anyone who professed magic or thought colorful stones had power over anyone."

"We will chant the song of the ancients." Carazaar was rocking back and forth now with his eyes rolled up into his head:

> "The living are lost
> In all their ways.
> No one will host
> Their soul, their days,
> But all searches end
> In grave's dark bend."

"It's a fool's chant." Tiathan was weary of Carazaar as he watched him almost dance in a fitful trance.

"Let me finish." Carazaar sighed heavily with his face shivering with some clouded vision only he could see. "These crystals have cured hundreds of their illnesses. It brought one Arbushi back to life."

"Enough! You mock me and you mock Jesuar!" Tiathan tossed a leg bone into the fire. "If I did not already know the truth, you would surely tempt me."

"Tempt you? No, I show you the way to happiness and wealth." Carazaar protested wondering if he lost his touch. "Look here! This will impress you. This is the Second Eye of Zebrac! Only one warrior holds the other."

"And who may that be?" Tiathan was hoping the magician would tell him something worthwhile. He had heard about the eyes of Zebrac, but thought they were just legends.

"Moshdalayrrimich!" Carazaar was proud to know the answer.

"You shall suffer the worst death imaginable!" Tiathan took the pink crystal from Carazaar, walked to a large stone near the fire and smashed it with the hilt of his dagger. What Carazaar didn't see was Tiathan changing the Second Eye of Zebrac with another crystal from pile of stones beneath him.

"You'll pay for that desecration!" The magician failed to Tiathan place the Second Eye of Zebrac in his pouch. "The wrath of Zebrac will descend upon us before the night is over!"

"Not before you tremble before the wrath of Jesuar for insulting Him with this trash!" Tiathan raised his arms as the sky grew dark with thunderous clouds and whipping winds. The remaining crystals on the ground were taken and crushed by an invisible hand. When it was over, Carazaar emptied his pockets of various stones and carved sticks with heads of strange creatures.

"How did you do that? I'm impressed! O glorious one!" Carazaar knelt before Tiathan. "I cast away all things before your power...."

"Stand up and do not kneel before me!" Tiathan was angry with sudden adulation. "I come in the name of Jesuar and not myself!"

"Whoever Jesuar is, I will kneel before Him after seeing such power that He has given you." Carazaar now lay prostrate on the ground.

"What about the magic crystals you vowed were the cornerstone of your magic and faith?" Tiathan had little pity for him.

Carazaar looked up at Tiathan showing dark circles under his eyes and a profound sadness of his soul revealed in his face. Whatever magic Carazaar had dissolved into a mass of quivering jelly as he cried before Tiathan.

"One cannot deceive without belief in something." Carazaar stood up shrugging away the question. "Seeing you with such power has taken away my belief in crystals and visions. Only the gullible I encounter believe in lifeless stones. These stones do not heal, do not bring wealth or bring long life. You talk of life then show me power. You have strength in your will. What you have shown me makes all that I have pale in comparison. I wish to learn more so I can be a great magician like yourself."

"I am not a magician." Tiathan pulled on his beard thinking hard about what to do with Carazaar. "I have no power other than what Jesuar allows me to have through prayer and obedience. Until you learn about Him and the Great Oak, you will never understand or enjoy the power you so desperately want. If you follow Jesuar you should not yearn for that power."

"Does this Jesuar have time for me?" Carazaar begged him. "I wish to learn more."

"You will learn nothing if you have no room to understand." Tiathan had little hope Carazaar knew what he asking of him. "Right now there is no peace in Everstream and I fear we have lost those we left behind.

Jesuar is not about power, but we need to leave this place quickly. I sense we are not alone."

"We?" Carazaar was delighted to hear Tiathan was going to take him along.

"If you are coming, I need to get back to my camp." Tiathan started to pack up his things.

"I want to learn more about Jesuar." Carazaar picked what little he had and joined Tiathan.

"To learn, you must leave all this behind." Tiathan pointed to his bag that held what was left of powder and crystals.

"It is all junk now anyway." The magician kicked two other bags into the fire. Flames shot high in the air as he clapped his hands. "Done! And done!"

"Somehow I do not think you know what you are getting into." Tiathan shook his head in wonder as Carazaar stroked his thick beard. His dull green eyes seemed to dance with anticipation while he followed Tiathan. "Yet, you're welcome to join us."

"How many of us are there?" Carazaar stopped dead in his tracks.

"My family and a few friends await my return." Tiathan was anxious to get back. "Do you have armor to wear, magician?"

"One moment." Carazaar relished the chance to

once more use his magic to impress Tiathan. He backed away from the smoldering fire letting a cloud of smoke and ash envelope him. Seconds later he reappeared wearing black and silver armor with a Gimigddean battleaxe. On the breastplate was the symbol of a Silverian Crow which convinced Tiathan it was an emblem of some lost tribe.

"Is that real or illusion?" Tiathan hoped it was real for Carazaar's sake.

"It was my father's armor which can withstand most of the weapons in Everstream." Carazaar was proudly thumping his chest.

"See that you use that battleaxe at my side and we will see if that is true." He stayed abreast of Carazaar to make sure it was safe.

"Ah, such a lack of trust in these times…" Carazaar waved him on into the deep underbrush.

It took hours to find his way back to the camp, but it worried Tiathan that it took little effort to find them. The campfire was burning brightly and there were no guards watching the path. A quick look told him that the Trags were not ready for battle, but more likely ready for a quick surrender.

"Where's Awlion?" Tiathan noticed immediately that his daughter was missing as he entered the clearing.

"She left when you did, father." Miertur wondered who the mysterious stranger was that followed him. "She went to scout the other paths out there. Who is this?"

"Carazaar at your service!" He bowed leaning on the handle of his battleaxe. "Magician, fortune teller, warrior…."

"Not now, Carazaar." Tiathan pushed him gently aside. "We must move to find her."

The Trags broke camp marching southwest to find Awlion. Tiathan worried that she might have already been captured. However, it wasn't too long before Awlion found them a few miles from the camp.

"Nsaat and his Bantongues are looking for us along the western paths of the forest." Awlion tried to catch her breath from the running towards the camp. "The only way now is south unless we return to Quicksnatch. It is my opinion that we will meet Rhor if we go south and Moshdalayrrimich is we go back to Quicksnatch."

"Then we will move south." Tiathan hoped there was reason for the choice, but one fight was as good as another.

"There are swamps with sucking mud and horrible creatures never seen before that protect a fortress called Modos." Carazaar spoke up seeing the look surprise from them all. "Believe it or not, no one will dare follow us. If we have to have a choice I would rather chance the swamps than certain death against those that follow us."

"We follow you, father." Zelbiur ignored Carazaar. Zelbiur was now fitted with an oak breastplate and shield that added to his confidence. He only found a lance to his liking as a weapon, but then he was not used to fighting at all since being imprisoned for fifteen years.

The small band of warriors soon passed the thorny underbrush of Nsaat's realm that led to a marshy swamp that stretched miles into the distance. There were no guards
watching over the oozing muck for no one sane would dare enter it willingly. Large drooping ferns covered most of the shore as did overhanging vines and ivy that framed the only path through the swamp. Strange sounds emanated through and under the water as long slimy creatures slithered past them. Tiathan could see the long tongues and diamond-shaped eyes watch as they slowly pushed their way through. Some of the horned heads seemed to be curious more than deadly as if it wasn't worth the bother to attack them.

"I don't like this at all." Awlion waded hip deep near Tiathan who already entered the black water.

"Neither do I, daughter." Tiathan sensed movement just ahead. "But Carazaar assures me this is the safest way."

"Are you sure he can be trusted?" Miertur pulled sucking insects from his arms.

"If you asked me that we first met, I would have said no." Tiathan looked back as Zelbiur and Carazaar were deep in discussion. "Now I think he lies only half the time."

Tho-o-o-o-os!

A brisk flying object sped by them. Tiathan and the others did not even see what it was, but braced for an attack. Something that fast would surely strike down half of them before they could raise their swords.

Tho-o-o-o-os!

It flew by again. It would have had to fly since the thick mud would slow anything down to a crawl. The smell of fear permeated the air which would only encourage whatever was flying past them in a blur.

"What creature is that?" Awlion drew her bow and placed an arrow hoping to quickly get a chance to shoot it.

"Everyone! Take off your capes and when I give the command cast them out in all directions!" Tiathan lifted his arms and waited for any sound. "Now!"

Tho-o-o!!!

A muffled thud, then a whimper was heard from under Awlion's cloak. The thing she clung desperately to, struggled fiercely as Awlion wondered if it had sharp teeth or lethal talons ready to rip through the cloth.

"I've caught it!" Awlion triumphantly raised her cape.

"Bring it out!" Tiathan was anxious to see it as well.

Awlion pulled out and cradled a furless thin creature with large eyes, wide mouth and pointed ears. Its hands had crooked fingers with feet larger than its whole body which kept it on top of the mud while running. It had no tail, but a large fur button at the base of its spine.

"It's not very cute." Awlion pouted wanting to give it to someone else to hold.

"Ugly you!" The creature stuck its blue tongue at her.

"It speaks!" Tiathan was happily surprised.

"It speaks!" The creature mocked him.

"We'll not harm you." Miertur moved to touch it.

"You bethcha." The creature jumped out of Awlion's loosened grip. What was left was the sound of Tho-o-o-os! as it sped off into the swamp.

"It was cute in an odd sort of way." Zelbiur

stared in the direction of the sound.

"Cute! Hah!" A voice was heard from a clump of reeds.

"Come back, little one!" Tiathan called out to him.

"Uh-uh, big one." The voice answered.

"At least tell us your name." Awlion looked hard into the shadows to see if it was close by.

Her answer was the same Tho-o-o-os! The sound disappeared far ahead of them until the marsh was again still and quiet.

"Okay then, we'll call you Thoos." Awlion laughed.

"Thoos?" the creature laughed back.

"Jesuar be with him." Tiathan whispered with a sigh.

"Peace!" Outra appeared from the reeds to their left.

"You seem to come and go as you please." Zelbiur was startled by his sudden presence.

"It is a gift." Outra smiled tapping Zelbiur on the shoulder.

"We must be very safe or in a lot of trouble for you to show up." Awlion avoided looking at him.

"It is in the will of Jesuar either way." Outra

raised an eyebrow.

"We are almost out of the swamp." Tiathan encouraged them all to continue on.

"So why are you here?" Miertur wanted to know.

"Can I not visit my friends without having a reason?" Outra skirting the question.

"You don't waste your time just visiting us." Awlion was more blunt than anyone else.

"True, but I have nothing to tell you that you don't already know." Outra moved forward with Tiathan.

"I don't like this." Awlion followed them a few feet behind.

The ground beneath them became more solid as they walked towards the sunlight at the end of the swamp. When the sky brightened, their spirits began to lift. However, the sound of trumpets greeted the Trags as they appeared from the edge of the great swamp. All but Tiathan and Outra stopped to listen in wonder.

"It is the sound of Moshdalayrrimich." Carazaar answered their unasked question.

"How do you know?" Awlion was wary of such things. No one could know who blew the trumpet unless they could see the encampment.

"Some days before I met Tiathan Eiula."

Carazaar couldn't wait to tell his story. "I had the honor of using my talents for Moshdalayrrimich and his warriors. They were good for my business and believed anything I told them. Almost everything I owned they bought. The First Eye of...." Carazaar saw Tiathan motion that he should not mention anything specific. "Well..anyway...They believe in the power of crystals and I was able to make my crystals glow in the firelight. They bowed down before this tremendous stone that shone like a mirror not far from their camp. We must be close to that place and they will not leave because they have made it into a shrine."

"Why did you not tell us this before?" Miertur was angry with the magician and wondered what his father was thinking bringing this outsider with them.

"You would not have believed me." Carazaar saw he was right by their expressions. "I told them that because of the great powers of the crystals I bore with me."

"But the crystals you had were worthless." Tiathan reminded Carazaar.

"True, but no one else knew that." Carazaar continued his story. "The great stone was at this place, but by using illusion I showed them that I could lift it up and place it before them. I told them they could do it, too, if they believed in the power of the stone."

"And Moshdalayrrimich believed you?" Tiathan was astounded with this bit of news.

"Yes, and I suspect they're still at the same place trying to lift the stone to take it with them." Carazaar listened to Tiathan's low laughter.

"Then you are a great magician!" Outra shook with mirth. It was a long time before anyone saw Outra laugh so hard. "I thought better of the so-called Conqueror. I do not accept magic or illusions and neither does Jesuar, but this is amusing."

"He is not as smart as Tiathan Eiula who saw through me right away." Carazaar shrugged at the limited compliment.

"It was Jesuar who allowed me to see the truth." Tiathan acknowledged the reason he saw through Carazaar. "But this is not our problem now. I'll go see for myself what mischief lies ahead of us."

"Alone again?" Zelbiur stood before his father straight and tall fully recovered from his ordeal. One thing about Trags is their ability to heal quickly. "I can hear what
they say without being seen. I should go with you, father."

"Yes, my son, but we should not walk together." Tiathan thought if one were captured the other would go for help.

"Agreed." Zelbiur understood without explanation.

"We don't have to worry about Nsaat and his Harkies." Tiathan turned to the other Trags. Still, take to the trees and by no means fight unless you are discovered. I leave Awlion in charge."

"But, father." Miertur did not like being left out.

"Miertur." Tiathan raised his hand to stop Miertur from protesting. "You will take three warriors to watch the path ahead of us. If you see or hear anything send up a flaming arrow to warn the rest."

"Would that not warn Moshdalayrrimich, too?" Miertur was not sure that was a great plan.

"It won't matter since they would know we are here already." Tiathan knew there would be little time if they were discovered.

"It is well." Outra was pleased with his plan.

****

Tiathan knew this wasn't the best of plans, but he needed to know who was encamped before him and their strength. Already, Nsaat was moving westward and this may be Moshdalayrrimich. It wouldn't surprise him if he met the army of Rhor as he scouted the area ahead of him.

Tiathan left Craxsmoore Guilding behind in the rotted inside of a large oak since he would have to crawl through tight spaces to keep from being seen. He was sure no one would stumble upon it within the short time he would be away. A small rise greeted him about a mile down the path, so he slowly crawled underneath some briars to reach the top. A ledge protruded in front hanging over the largest group of warriors beneath him. He counted only a few dozen which might have meant that Moshdalayrrimich might not be close by.

Creeping silently onto the ledge he looked down counting three companies of Valkyricks standing within the cave beneath the ledge. The others were standing around a large stone in the center of the glade. Upon the stone was none other than Moshdalayrrimich strutting back and forth on its smooth surface. He wore a red and black cape that accented his golden oak breastplate. His helmet had three multi-colored plumes that fluttered in the breeze. His frantic pace was that of a hungry predator looking for his first kill of the day.

"It is a wonderful view is it not?" A sword touched Tiathan's neck.

"As long as I can watch from here." Tiathan lifted his arms in surrender,

"Ah, I am sorry that won't be possible." The Valkyrick warrior shrugged his apology. He was taller than Tiathan and by the way his yellow eyes flared, he enjoyed teasing Tiathan. The nostrils of his flat nose snorted the derision he felt inside. Four other Valkyricks joined the first making it impossible for Tiathan to try to escape.

"I thought not." Tiathan relinquished his dagger to them.

"Moshdalayrrimich will be pleased/" The leader of the group smiled, prodding Tiathan down the hill.

"Shodacrassniff." Moshdalayrrimich waved the Captain of the guards toward him. "You bring a guest to honor me?"

"He begged me to bring him to you, my lord." Shrodacrassniff bowed before shoving Tiathan to the ground.

"You are a Trag." Moshdalayrrimich sneered at Tiathan not knowing who he was. "Worse, you're an old Trag which mean you are a leader of the Trags or some zealous fool. Either way, you smell of trouble."

"I am Tiathan Eiula, First Ioroarka of Quicksnatch!" He stood erect and defiant before the Conqueror.

"I'm not stupid! I knew who you were, Tiathan

Eiula!" Moshdalayrrimich spat out his name. "I, also, know your band of pathetic warriors are not far off. Do you think I would let you come this close and not know it?"

"Then maybe you also know why Jesuar sent me here?" Tiathan watched as the great Moshdalayrrimich eyes widened in anger.

"You don't mention that....thing in my presence!" Moshdalayrrimich toyed with the hilt of his sword. "Word has reached me that you have a wonderful weapon, a powerful weapon that can strike down ten warriors at a time."

"I have come in peace and you betray that peace." Tiathan felt the spirit of Jesuar well up inside him. He should not have been surprised that the Conqueror knew about Craxsmoore Guilding.

"You are not looking for peace, but war." Moshdalayrrimich stepped down from the great smooth stone. "There is no peace in Everstream or have you not heard of the trouble that surrounds us"

"We call upon all the inhabitants of Everstream to make peace in this time of possible war." Tiathan stared up at him noticing for the first time the wounds and scars on his face and hands. Looking around Tiathan saw that most of the Valkyricks had sores and ulcers on their bodies. They were ill from something he could not understand.

"There can no peace as long as Jesuar lives!" Moshdalayrrimich raged. "Even a spirit can be destroyed through the elimination of its followers. We, in the name of Mortarr, pledge our lives, our souls to this end."

"All that lives after such a war are the flowers on the graves of those who defy Jesuar." Tiathan spoke without fear. "What madness....What horror drives you to this monstrous end other than the allegiance to Mortarr who does not care about you."

"We not only stand with Mortarr, but stand with Karatura and Zebrac." Moshdalayrrimich reached into a leather pouch to grasp something tightly and was unwilling to show it to him. "It was foretold that some day we will have the power to defeat all our enemies and rule Everstream."

"Jesuar has told me about the Seven Fortresses and what you did to try to rule over them." Tiathan no longer
spoke for himself, but that of Jesuar. "Even now Rhor has taken over the Seven Fortresses while you stay here worshipping this rock. Your warriors suffer from a sickness no one has seen before. Greed and self-worship have defeated you without a single battle being fought."

"I hold in my hand the answers to life and death."

Moshdalayrrimich held out a brilliant pink crystal which Tiathan guessed to be the First Eye of Zebrac.

"Through this all health and life begins and ends." The Conqueror shook from within which crippled his thoughts. "This crystal will heal us all and will be the future bearer of our strength and security. We will win back the Seven Fortresses soon enough for we only wait for Zebrac to come to us."

"Kill him and be done with it!" Shrodacrassniff was already weary of this game. "All you do is talk, my lord."

"Be patient." Moshdalayrrimich raised his knotted hand which trembled under the pain he felt lifting it high over his head.

Tiathan watched as he turned to his warriors and raised high the First Eye of Zebrac for all to see. It was then that Tiathan reached into his pocket and brought out the Second Eye of Zebrac. The Valkyricks gasped as one seeing Tiathan threw his crystal at Moshdalayrrimich. The Conqueror was stunned as crystal hit crystal both smashing upon the smooth stone beneath his feet.

"Now where is its power?" Tiathan waited for the first blade to strike him, but none came.

"Zebrac will haunt you even unto death!" Moshdalayrrimich trembled trying to pick up the pieces.

"If you need another crystal, another Eye of

Zebrac, perhaps you can call on another magician to give it to you. How many eyes does Zebrac have?" Tiathan mocked their faith in rocks and stones.

"Die you worthless…" Shrodacrassniff raised his sword over Tiathan's head.

"Do not touch him!" Moshdalayrrimich waved his hand toward his Captain.

"Why, my lord?" His Captain never knew his leader to allow such insults to go unpunished before.

"It is of no consequence." Moshdalayrrimich calmed himself as he reached back into his pouch producing another crystal. It wasn't the eye of Zebrac, but it was bright pink with rainbow facets. He raised the crystal to the cheering Valkyricks. "Nothing can destroy its power! It is everlasting and never ending. No one can destroy it!"

Moshdalayrrimich listened to the growling cheers from his warriors who were slow to understand what was happening. Tiathan knew it was useless now to fight such false faith in rocks and stones. There were thousands of such things throughout Everstream, even ones that he used to skip on the surface of streams and rivers as a Tragling. Now they were looked upon as if they lived.

"You've learned nothing in all the years you've lived and ruled." Tiathan spread his arms in exasperation. "You deceive yourselves with this nightmare! Jesuar open their eyes."

"Jesuar? Now there is a fantasy!" Moshdalayrrimich pointed the pink crystal at him. "You can't touch Jesuar morning or night. You can't hold Him in your hand. There is nothing to touch or feel with Jesuar. But this!" He lovingly felt the smoothness of the crystal. "This has power and can be grasped by all who wish to touch it."

"It has a name then?" Tiathan watched his wrinkled brow quiver ever so slightly. He noticed Moshdalayrrimich's skin was jaundiced and translucent in the sunlight showing vaguely bone and marrow.

"I call it, Ishanbar, Life Bearer." He held the crystal high as his warriors moaned and bowed to the glistening light that emanated from it.

"And are you at war with all of Everstream?" Tiathan tired of this nonsense. "There are strangers in this land and you brought them here. If you crave the power the power of that crystal for life, why then try to destroy life?"

"I am the ruler of the Seven Fortresses...." Moshdalayrrimich leaned back against the cool stone that seemed to now be his throne. "Yet, I am a ruler of nothing."

"You have the power to destroy Everstream with your warriors and we yield to that power." Tiathan thought quickly of escape.

"But I don't rule you, Tiathan Eiula, do I?" Moshdalayrrimich became melancholy. "Do two walk together unless both agree to it? Does a Bantongue roar in the undergrowth when he has no enemy? Does Nsaat scream in victory when he defeated nothing? Does a Harkie fall into a trap when no snare has been set? When our trumpet sounds, do not the Trags tremble? When disaster befalls your township, is it not I who caused it? I proclaim to all my fortresses of Shadod and Tygep to destroy all those who oppose us and the spirits of Karatura, the taker of life and Zebrac, the giver of life."

"Jesuar says." Tiathan now was sure Quicksnatch was lost, but there was no time to mourn those left behind. "You may overrun Everstream, but your fortresses will fall behind you."

"Speak not His name!" Moshdalayrrimich rose up holding his ears and stomping his foot.

"Though you destroy most of us, the Trags will be saved and you will become dust." Tiathan spoke with the authority of Jesuar as those around him stood motionless listening. "Hear this, Moshdalayrrimich! On the day you declare victory over Everstream the altars of

Zebrac, Karatura and even Mortarr will fall. The horns that point to a crown will wilt from the heat of destruction. Jesuar will tear down all of the Seven Fortresses and each of your warriors will be dragged away by war hooks! The very last ones by fish hooks and cast into the black lake you
call Theda."

"How dare you speak to me this way!" Moshdalayrrimich calmed himself though the anger seethed beneath. "However, I am a benevolent ruler so I will let you speak one last time about Jesuar so that my warriors can laugh at you as you lie dying. My warriors will see, no matter what you say, I am greater than Jesuar and you will die by my word and my sword."

"It is blasphemy, my lord!" Shrodacrassniff pleaded. "Kill him now!"

"No, let him speak so you will know I am not afraid of Jesuar." Moshdalayrrimich seemed to look as confused as his Captain.

"Jesuar is He who formed the mountains, created the wind, cupped the waters and speaks his thoughts to me." Tiathan knew Jesuar himself had something to do with this moment. "It is Jesuar who turns dawn to darkness and treads the high places of Everstream. He is here in my heart and He is everywhere around us. Jesuar is His name!"

"Fallen are the Trags never to rise again! You've been deserted and no one to lift you up!" Moshdalayrrimich lifted his head above Tiathan. "I have seen your own clan split in so many ways with your son leaving you for the west. I have seen your warriors run from you as I invaded your lands." He raised his voice for all to hear. "But this I say the township or fortress that marches out a thousand strong will only have a hundred left and if a hundred strong will only have ten left when they come against me."

Tiathan waited for the cheers of the Valkyricks to subside. He secretly asked Jesuar for guidance and the skill to answer the mighty Conqueror, yet enough to bide him more time to escape from them.

"This is what Jesuar says." Tiathan could not understand why he was still alive. "Seek Me and live. Don't seek Rabel Ain. Don't go to Modos. Don't journey back to Mount Tarara for Rabel Ain will weary you, Modos will exile you and Mount Tarara will destroy you."

"And why do you even warnus?" Moshdalayrrimich
was amused with the threat. "We bring justice and harmony to Everstream.

"You turn justice into chaos and throw what is right back into the faces of those who stand against you." Tiathan knew they would not listen. "You despise those who tell the truth. You trample on the poor and force them to give you homage. You take bribes and deprive Everstream of their freedom. Therefore, though you live in stone fortresses you will not live in them again. Though you've stored warestumps of food and drink, you'll never again enjoy their taste."

"Then what do you recommend dear brother of death?" Moshdalayrrimich mocked him.

"Seek good, not evil so you may live." Tiathan listened to their laughter, but continued because he could not help himself. "Then Jesuar will be with you. Hate evil, love good. Maintain justice and Jesuar will have mercy on you."

"And if we refuse?" Shrodacrassniff looked to the skies waiting for a bolt of lightning to strike.

"There will be wailing in your fortresses and cries of anguish from your warriors." Tiathan felt a glow beginning to emanate behind him as he turned away from them. "There will weeping from your young as Jesuar passes through your midst. Woe to you who long for Jesuar on that day! That day will be darkness, not light. Are you better than all the others? You put off the evil and bring near a reign of terror! You lie on beds of gilded oak and lounge on mounds of feathered down. You're rich in

things, but poor in feelings! You don't grieve over the ruin of Everstream, but feast on the blood of your victims!"

"And who will mete out this justice?" Shrodacrassniff had enough this talk, but Tiathan could sense a yearning to hear more among the Valkyricks. The brazen words coming from Tiathan were not from a crazy old Trag, but seem to ring true.

"I only let you live this long, Tiathan Eiula, because you will pay for every insolent word you uttered to me." Moshdalayrrimich waved the Captain away. "It will slow and painful."

"Then you will hear all!" Tiathan voice shook the very stone, the very ground where Moshdalayrrimich stood. "Jesuar will smash the tops of your pillars so that the thresholds shake and cut off the heads of all who conquer and those who are left I will kill with Craxsmoore Guilding! Not one will escape though you dig down to the depths of Everstream, I, Jesuar, will reach down and take you! Though you climb the highest mountain, I, Jesuar, will bring you down! This Jesuar promises you!"

"Enough!" Shrodacrassniff looked to Moshdalayrrimich for a sign to kill him. "We have no more time for this!"

"It is true." Moshdalayrrimich stood above Tiathan with his sword by his side tapping his knee lightly. "We have no more time for this!"

As he raised his sword, Moshdalayrrimich glanced up at the brightness from atop the hill behind his warriors. His eyes, Tiathan noticed, were wide with surprise and awe. He lowered his sword and stared in disbelief

"Witchery! Demons!" Moshdalayrrimich screamed letting his sword fall from his hand.

Tiathan turned to look upon the hill seeing hundreds of golden warriors lined three and four deep. On a pure white horse was a warrior holding a great shield and lance ready to signal the attack. He could not see who was on the white horse because the ride wore a veiled helmet with three white plumes.

"Before your blade strikes me you will die by the arrows from those archers on the hill." Tiathan whispered to Moshdalayrrimich.

"It's not possible!" The conqueror cried out to his warriors who looked around in confusion and dismay.

"Let me go while you still live." Tiathan reached

out for his dagger from Shrodacrassniff. "We will not attack if do so."

"Let it be so." Moshdalayrrimich ordered Shrodacrassniff who obeyed, but did not know what to make of it all.

As Tiathan disappeared out of sight, Moshdalayrrimich looked back up the hillside, but the golden warriors were gone. The sun had set and only the beginning of night greeted their faces. What had happened was lost upon them all.

"What made you release him, my lord?" Shrodacrassniff tried not to sound too demanding though he was wroth with anger.

"Didn't you see the golden warriors on the hill?" Moshdalayrrimich was surprised his Captain would ask such a question.

"I saw nothing upon the hill except the sun through the trees, my lord." Shrodacrassniff thought he had lost his senses.

"There were too many for us to overcome." The Conqueror shook his head slightly confused. "Our main army is too far away to help us in time."

"Again, my lord, we saw nothing on that hill."

Shrodacrassniff insisted.

"Then why didn't you say anything?" He grabbed his Captain by the throat watching his narrow eyes bulge from the pressure.

"I felt as if I were in a dream and compelled to listen to him." Shrodacrassniff tried to think about why he said nothing. "I could not speak or move. Shall we follow him?"

"No, let him go." Moshdalayrrimich was confused as he sat down wondering what had just happened. "He won't go far."

"But he's still a threat." Shrodacrassniff anxiously tapped the hilt of his sword.

"He's a Trag." Moshdalayrrimich waved his Captain away.

"They are fierce fighters, my lord." Shrodacrassniff struggled mightily to keep from disobeying his orders.

"We will prevail." Moshdalayrrimich waved him off and stared off into the distance.

****

The trail Tiathan walked was an old riverbed stream with rocks and twigs strewn everywhere. Few sounds came from the surrounding forest except from a small brook that ran parallel with the riverbed. There was nowhere to hide since the vines and branches were so thickly entwined that it would take too long to cut a path with his sword.

A fork in the path made it difficult to decide where to go. He wondered if Zelbiur knew he was captured, and if so, if he knew about his release. Tiathan chose the rocky path that sloped down a long ridge into a small clearing. The other path led up a mountain that slowly disappeared into a dense fog. He knew this place for it was when Tiathan led the Trags against Rhor and his warriors. Horse tracks to the right led up the mountainside with clear tracks plainly seen. It was a sure decision that he would have to go the way down the mountain to be safe.

The sounds of battle echoed from the past after so many years of bondage under the Gimgiddeans welled up and pierced his soul. Tiathan could still see the hundreds of makeshift tents that covered the clearing before a great wave of water swept them away. He could Rhor and a band of warriors cursing him from a distance vowing revenge for all those who died. Even now he could hear the sound of hoof beats which seemed so close, so real.

"You have come to join us, Tiathan Eiula?" Rhor and ten of his warriors stood behind him.

"I expected to meet again, but not so soon." Tiathan started to draw his dagger, but was quickly overwhelmed.

"Chain him so that he doesn't trick us with his magic." Rhor relaxed when he saw Tiathan was chained from head to foot.

"It was never magic only the power of Jesuar!" Tiathan trembled under the weight of the chains.

"It was the same thing for me!" Rhor laughed. "If it wasn't done by the hand of Zebrac it wasn't real, only illusion."

Zelbiur tripped over some humped roots and sharp stones to try and reach his father in time, but it was too late. Rhor had Tiathan in chains and was dragging him through the muddy riverbed. Rage first enveloped Zelbiur before a plan formed in his mind. First, he would follow the Gimigddeans and listen to where they might bring his father. Then he could turn back and bring others to rescue him.

"Where do you take me?" Tiathan asked Rhor sensing Zelbiur might be close by.

"To the Mount of Zebrac where I will hand you over to your friend Moshdalayrrimich." Rhor savored a revenge he tasted for fifteen years. "Your Jesuar destroyed half my realm when we last met. I was disgraced before me warriors and I will have that revenge."

"I hope you heard that, son." Tiathan whispered to himself.

"What was that, old fool?" Rhor turned to strike Tiathan across the face until he thought
better of it.

"I meant no disrespect." Tiathan knew he would have to be patient to survive the march to the Mount of Zebrac.

"That's better." Rhor sat straight on his stallion looking and getting the admiration of his warriors.

Zelbiur watched as his father was dragged away. His yearning to do something was overcome with the caution he knew he had to have. Finally he decided to find Awlion and Miertur knowing that it would be better for his father if more knew where he was being taken.

As he crawled back away from the Gimgiddeans, Zelbiur felt his foot hit something that clanked. Looking over his shoulder he saw Craxsmoore Guilding partially hidden in an old trunk and a thicket of thorns. Elated, he grabbed for the chain to pull it out of the trunk only to prick his hands from the thorns.

"Only Jesuar knew I would be in this place and

help me find this." Zelbiur swung the mighty weapon over his head and liked the feel of it. However, he lost his grip as Craxsmoore Guilding smashed a large stone into small stones. Zelbiur hoped no one heard the noise it made.

He tried again, but this time he held it tighter. Sighing, he held it with both hands and swung it around his head. Again he lost his grip which only embedded Craxsmoore Guilding into a gnarled oak trunk. As much as he grunted and pulled he could not pry it from the oak.

"I was afraid to come sooner for fear I would distract you and your aim." Outra slowly approached Zelbiur from the shadows.

"That's not funny." Zelbiur was frustrated.

"Neither is what you must do now." Outra strode over gently pulling Craxsmoore Guilding out from the trunk. As he handed it to Zelbiur, he smiled.

"Why am I not going to like what you are about to tell me?" Zelbiur looked down at Craxsmoore Guilding and then at Outra.

"You have choices to make that will not be easy." Outra drew vague designs in the dirt.

"We must rescue my father." Zelbiur decided already what was important.

"He must go alone and you must return to the others." Outra stuck his finger in the middle of the circle he made.

"Will he be alive when we get back?" Zelbiur knew he would not like the answer.

"As Jesuar wills, it will happen." Outra wiped the ground clean as he stood up.

"I have heard that too often." Zelbiur winced tiring of being left outside the circle. "So my father may not be seen by us again?"

"You are needed elsewhere." Outra started back into the woods.

"Must I always guess what are you talking about?" Zelbiur spoke to the shadow that disappeared with slight whoosh. "Can you not speak plainly just this once?"

"Follow me! Is that plain enough?" Outra whispered knowing Zelbiur could hear him.

"Follow me, Follow me." Zelbiur mimicked and followed him.

****

"It has been too long." Miertur wanted to find Zelbiur and Tiathan. He was tired of waiting in silence. "And where is Outra Whorld? No one runs from us as fast as he does."

"We are to wait for father to return." Awlion tried to calm him down though she wanted to go find out herself where they were.

"No, I've decided!" Miertur pointed toward the Trags. "We leave to meet Moshdalayrrimich! And you can wait here if you like."

"You are disobeying father's orders!" Awlion turned to the Trags hoping they would listen to her. "Carazaar! What about you?"

"I cannot stay here alone." Carazaar shrugged. "Besides, my chances are better with your warriors than just you."

Carazaar pulled Awlion away from the rest and talked with her for some time. Miertur could not hear them which only made him more impatient. Having Awlion give ear to the magician angered him because he didn't want her under his spell.

"We go then to save our Ioroarka!" Miertur waved his sword toward the west as the Trags followed in single file.

"So be it!" Awlion sat down watching them all venture into the growing darkness. She listened a great while until she heard the sound of trumpets. She did not see Tiathan or Zelbiur and doubted the wisdom of waiting.

Awlion took what was left of the brown Hodge Bread and dried meat that lay over the fire on a spit. After putting out the fire and all traces of the encampment, Awlion took the path to the northwest hoping to find some part of her family. She had no idea what path would lead her to her father or the enemies of Everstream. Jesuar came to mind while trudging through briars and loose stones. A simple song came to mind that helped relieve the danger of the coming darkness:

"esN T esoomn 'ef XoesoihiR
onbaRhisio T mooRdyes 'ef esoomn
ef' hia r ef' nyveyom
hia r Romomody
W T mooRdyes
'Efoon T etohiveyomes
MoRo mo mya omtioR tieRoinet
esN T esoomn 'ef XoesoihiR
ef' mo ar T sihiooesom
mooti aytiao ooR efom
baoiti nhimll ad estiRoomn
moo mohiv omtioR
moo esooR'oom bao efoimdy
MoRo mo omtioR tieRoinet"

Far from the clearing she left Awlion heard voices ahead of her. They were not familiar voices, but low growls with angry thrashing through the undergrowth. Awlion knew the sound of Bantongues and found herself looking for a high place to hide. A full, leafy oak looked inviting enough as she quickly climbed up half way with bow and arrow ready.

"Get off my feet, Krrool!" One of the Bantongues pushed the other away with a sudden jarring of its thick scaly head..

"Don't walk so close to me then, Frasst!" Krrool tried to move ahead of him in their race to get through the forest.

The years took their toll on both of them with their legs creaking and popping as they walked. They were obviously not suited for scouting since anyone could hear them soon enough to hide. Perhaps it was the reason they made so much noise.

Krrool and Frasst seemed to be the only Bantongues nearby, but Awlion wanted to be sure before she let the first arrow fly. If they should cry out it would be only seconds before others surrounded her.

"I told you Nsaat would put us in front if you continued to beg for more important duties." Krrool was not pleased to be in the open and exposed to any enemy that would attack them.

"How could I know that when he said: 'I will put you at the head of all my armies!' he meant to throw us up here?" Frasst was unhappy, too, with his new duties and would be unhappier still if he saw the pointed arrow aimed at his heart.

Awlion slowly dropped her bow thinking that if she didn't get both, one of them would escape and alert the others. So she let them pass watching Frasst and Krrool bicker as they pushed their way east. The silence that followed only made her decision to wait more difficult. If she ventured down Awlion might walk right into Nsaat's warriors. If she stayed they may find her since Bantongues not only march in pairs, but scurry through the surrounding wood looking for snares and traps. All she could do was bow her head and pray:

"Jesuar, I await whatever direction
You will give me. I pray that
You will continue to use me
In whatever way you see fit.
Please watch over my father
And my brothers. I know
I go my own way, but you
Know my thoughts
And my mind for the best

For all concerned.
If I have offended you,
I ask for your forgiveness.
If I have disobeyed You
Correct me as You see fit.
                    Amen"

Chapter Three

Zelbiur reached the clearing alone where the camp used to be thinking Awlion and Miertur were waiting for him. The fire was still smoldering ash with no sign of life in the clearing. His first thought was that Moshdalayrrimich had captured them even though there were no marks or signs of battle. No, they must have gotten tired of waiting leaving to find himself and their father. The silence was overwhelming since Outra left some miles back.

"They are close by." Outra ducked beneath the sword Zelbiur sent over his head.

"You can't do that to me, Shroo!" Zelbiur smiled nonetheless knowing it was impossible to surprise the chosen one of Jesuar.

"You have ears..." Outra saw the sheepish grin that spread across Zelbiur's face.

"But not for you, my friend." Zelbiur grasped Outra's shoulders.

"I have trained a long time to make sure of it." Outra frowned.

"What is it?" Zelbiur listened hard for anything out of the ordinary, but heard nothing.

"I'm more concerned about your sister, Awlion, than your brother, Miertur." Outra studied the ground absently around them.

"Why is that? Is she in danger?" Zelbiur already was planning to find her.

"Awlion is alone." Outra changed his tone quickly to lessen the concern on Zelbiur's face. "Miertur, however, is being led by Carazaar who knows little and thinks less."

"Let us go and find Miertur before we search for Awlion." Zelbiur started to pick up his things anticipating a long journey.

"There is no hurry." Outra sat down upon a rock and watched Zelbiur struggle with as much as he could carry.

"We must rescue father, too." Zelbiur became torn as to what to do first.

"Tiathan must follow where Jesuar leads him."

Outra was concerned, but not concerned. "We'll do what we can with what we have. We cannot be separated and survive. The strength is in our unity, but that is the future."

"Then we will go and find Miertur?" Zelbiur twitched both ears as if he was trying to listen in all directions.

"If we wait a moment longer, we won't have to find him." Outra pointed to a band of oak trees to their left.

"I hear something now." Zelbiur turned his attention to the loud murmuring beyond the grove of trees.

"We've been marching all night!" Miertur was yelling at someone, but Zelbiur couldn't tell who it could have been.

"It's only a little farther." Carazaar insisted swinging his sword to cut the brush ahead of them.

"What's this?" Miertur was the first into the clearing realizing it was where they started their journey. "I should kill you, magician!"

"No Miertur." Outra stood between the two of them. "Carazaar did as Awlion asked and did it well, too."

"As Awlion asked?" Miertur turned to look at

Outra, then realized Zelbiur was standing behind him. "My brother it is good to see you, but where is father?"

"I'm afraid you have been deceived." Zelbiur could not contain the broad smile that spread across his face.

"Deceived?" Miertur stared at Outra with a look of outrage.

"No, not deceived...Yes, well you were deceived." Outra could not contain his mirth. "Awlion knew you would want to do something so she told Carazaar to be sure to keep you busy until my return."

"How could you?" Miertur was embarrassed now that he knew Outra did not trust him.

"It was for your own protection." Outra insisted realizing that Miertur took it too much to heart. "I protected you from yourself. If you led the Trags against Moshdalayrrimich and his warriors you would have surely died."

"I could not sit and wait...do nothing..." Miertur stammered wanting to hide beneath the nearest rock.

"I'm proud of you, my brother." Zelbiur embraced him.

"Why?" Miertur tried to pull away.

"Because it shows you are brave and worthy of being an Eiula." Zelbiur was serious to get all of this behind them.

"What do we do now?" Miertur was anxious to move on, too.

"Now we look for our sister whom you thought to leave behind." Zelbiur listened intently in all directions, but heard nothing that would give them a direction. "She's like us. Better to search or fight then to wait here for some disaster to overcome us."

"We must hurry, too." Outra waved them toward the path Awlion took.

"How do you know where she went?" Miertur wanted to know.

"Why do you bother to ask?" Zelbiur laughed.

"And our father?" Miertur looked hopefully at his brother.

"Captured by Rhor, yet I doubt they will kill him." Zelbiur hoped in his heart.

"Captured by Rhor, yet they might beat him up a little bit?" Miertur mocked him.

"Tiathan is too great a prize to be killed straight away." Outra echoed ahead of them already starting to drift into the shadows where he is best as their scout and guide. "They'll follow the ritual of Zebrac first before turning him over to Moshdalayrrimich as a peace offering. That way Rhor can do whatever he pleases for a while in Everstream."

"I thought Rhor hated Moshdalayrrimich?" Miertur was surprised.

"He does, but he cannot afford to fight Moshdalayrrimich." Outra sounded more distant. "Soon war will come when Rhor betrays him."

"What of the Arbushi? Where do they stand?" Miertur spoke louder thinking Outra was leaving them behind.

"Everyone will see the opportunity for power and success." Outra stood behind Miertur which startled him. "It is the way of Everstream for now even though there will be a time they will answer for the evil they possess. That is why we follow Jesuar so when judgment comes we will be on His side."

"Do we have a chance to save our father?" Zelbiur tried to get back to the point of their journey.

"If Jesuar wills so it will happen." Outra's voice drifted again in the breeze as he disappeared into the woods.

"I hate it when he does that." Miertur trudged through the thorns and mud as he started again marching the Trags west.

"Let us sing to Jesuar to take our minds off the journey ahead of us." Zelbiur thought of a tune before beginning to sing in the ancient Trag:

"oveyom W dyhiRvms
stodyes T ayneti
oveyom W tioRooR
sioones T xoll
Mom hia r epohisio
moo himnor myll bao
mo siov T vymndyoon
ad T maoorll
ad T etoomoor t sioono"

****

Awlion decided that the two Bantongues were far enough away to continue her journey. Following the path they came out would not do except to walk into the talons of Nsaat. Knowing that Nsaat's warriors always used a half moon march through the forest, she could not continue west to northwest. Awlion resigned herself to return south hoping she would find Miertur or Zelbiur.

"After her!" A voice from the sky shattered the silence.

Awlion shot an arrow into the heart of the Harkie that raised the alarm even though it was too late to retreat. Loud voices came with the crashing of twigs and branches which told her a company of Bantongues was racing toward her.

A war cry sounded to her right before quickly fading away. A second scream pierced the wood, but was much closer than the others. Six Bantongues appeared in front of her with two in the clearing and four in the trees. They grinned hideously even though they cautiously approached her.

"Krrool, get her bow!" Frasst stared down from the branch above her.

Awlion turned too late as Krrool slapped the bow and quiver to the ground. She was now unarmed as the Bantongues hungrily snarled with fangs dripping venom began to stalk her. They knew she was defenseless and were intent to play with their prey before killing her.

Awlion searched for a branch or stone to use as a weapon trying not to end her life without a fight. She prayed to Jesuar for a miracle even though it seemed hopeless. The Bantongues toyed with her by spitting venom around her. Even Krrool waddled down to join in the taunting.

Tho-o-o-os!

Before Awlion knew it her bow and arrows were in her hands. Soon after three Bantongues were dead and the others fled into the woods. Krrool and Frasst were the first to escape the volley of arrows.

"Thoos! Thank you and thank you, Jesuar!" Awlion ran from the clearing hearing the howl of the other Bantongues coming to the aid of their fallen comrades.

"Wrong way!" Thoos cried from behind a thorny briar watching Awlion turning south.

"Which way, Thoos? Show me!" Awlion heard the familiar giggle.

"This way!" Thoos sped past her toward a southern route.

It was hours before Awlion finally sat down to rest. She built a small fire before plucking berries from a nearby bush. When she turned around she found a meaty dinner of Notherhen already cooking on a spit.

"I hope you'll join me, Thoos." Awlion looked for the little creature who seemed shy though she knew he was also dangerous.

"Eat first." Thoos was somewhere behind her.

"Thank you, Thoos." Awlion bowed her head in prayer which brought giggles from the shadows.

A small stream trickled near her compliments of Thoos redirecting some water that passed by the camp. She cupped it to drink from time to time knowing that Thoos had something to do with this, too. What other bits of magic was this creature capable of and what would happen if Awlion angered him?

"Will you come out now?" Awlion finished her meal leaving a few thick pieces of meat for him to eat.

"Not now." Thoos stayed crouched in the shadows.

"Why?" Awlion was disappointed though she could his eyes glisten through the undergrowth.

"Ugly me." Thoos almost cried.

"No, don't think that or yourself." She held out her arms to accept him.

Tho-o-os!

"Oof!" Thoos crashed into her chest knocking Awlion over onto the ground. Thoos held her so tight that Awlion was unable to breathe.

"Wait a second!" Awlion tried to loosen his grip which startled Thoos.

"Tho-o-os!"

"No, come back, Thoos!" Awlion was becoming frustrated with this creature no matter how cute in his ugliness he happened to be.

"Not wanted." Thoos pouted in the darkness curled into a small ball.

"Yes, you are wanted, but you have to slow down." Awlion braced for another crushing blow only to find Thoos standing behind her. She turned to see tears streaming down his pale hollow cheeks. Awlion cradled Thoos in her arms for a long time and sang an ancient Trag lullaby while he closed his eyes to listen:

> "moRo dyhiRvms dymores
> hi ayneti mya stymo
> oioom hi mombaoRm bahibao
> a tiaRoinepoti tiaoes
> oiR xoost nyveyoes esynm
> oioom T mombaoRm bahibao"

"Good friend." Thoos mumbled thoroughly enjoying the moment.

"Good friend." Awlion gently stroked Thoos cheek.

"Stay friend." Thoos hugged her.

"Do you have a family, Thoos?" Awlion was ready to go to sleep and having Thoos on her lap would make it difficult.

"Family? Yes." Thoos was suddenly awake and alert.

"How many?" She was delighted to know he wasn't alone.

"Two. I get." Thoos was already jumping out of her arms.

Th-o-o-os!

Thip-p-p!

Thip-p-p thump!

Thoos had stopped short as two smaller creatures bumped into him. The third little creature did not stop in time and stumbled over the first one. The third one almost knocked over Thoos as well which made Awlion laugh out loud.

"Now we have Thip and Thump!" Awlion was pleased to name her new friends.

"Thump!" Thip laughed heartily as she pointed to Thump.

"Thip!" Thump laughed just as hard pushing Thip to the ground.

"One not learn stop." Thoos was embarrassed that he could not teach Thump to be like Thip when they traveled.

The young creatures seemed to be mostly eyes, ears, and a pair of huge feet. Their faces were more wrinkled and parts smoother than that of Thoos with no hair at all on their bodies. Thip and Thump playfully tripped each other as they played near the fire Awlion built up for the long cold night ahead.

"No mother?" Awlion looked into the distance expecting one more to appear.

"No…dead." Thoos snuggled back into Awlion's arms. Thip and Thump nestled on her shoulders as she lay down to sleep finding that they would keep her warm through the night. Thip and Thump played with her long brown hair making mustaches with the curls and scrunching their faces as they laughed and laughed. Awlion was surprised how light they now seemed which made her wonder what kind of creatures these were.

"How did she die?" Awlion wanted to know.

"Ogre." Thoos frowned as he closed one eye.

"Nsaat?" Awlion cupped her mouth feeling an overwhelming sorrow for him and his family.

"One eye ugly." Thoos hunched his shoulders.

"I'm sorry." She cradled his head while stroking the wrinkled spot over his eyes.

"Me, too." Thoos leaned against her closing his eyes. Awlion could not convince Thip and Thump to settle down so she decided to sing to them:

> "MyesepoRN momdyes
> baRohiteo T mhino
> XoesoihiR XoesoihiR
> y etohiR ll' eshill
> y hin ad esynet
> XoesoihiR XoesoihiR

moo tiyno oxyesties
.Efoon hioRo t tieoRo
XoesoihiR XoesoihiR
hia dy'Rositiyoomes
etohiR ll'R mhino
XoesoihiR XoesoihiR"

"Good night, Thoos." Awlion kissed his cheek feeling change from cool to warm.

"Night, friend." Thoos smiled.

Nothing else was said as the night passed uneventful. Crawler Crickets crackled and cricked nearby which only soothed their time of rest.

****

"What death would do justice to the great Tiathan Eiula?" Rhor had already ordered his warriors to tie him to two posts before the largest pink crystal had ever seen. Surely, it was not the same rock he saw earlier. Perhaps the firelight in the evening touched off the color or maybe the stone was different from what he saw before.

"This will not give you back your realm." Tiathan was unafraid uncertain whether Jesuar would help him or if Outra would make a sudden appearance.

Maybe Jesuar would allow him to be a martyr for Him.

"You see the great crystal of Zebrac before you?" Rhor's eyes flamed a bright red within the black circles of his eyes.

"It is only a large dead stone." Tiathan knew the crystal was thought to be the most powerful magical crystal in the whole of Everstream.

"This 'stone' is the lifeblood of my warriors." Rhor placed his dagger to Tiathan's throat. "It is the giver of life and the redeemer in death. We worship Zebrac and Mortarr as do the Arbushi only Moshdalayrrimich does not know this. When the sun rises it is perfect. When the sun sets it brings us peace and warmth. Your Jesuar cannot do that. Mortarr comes to us in flames and smoke before battle, but Zebrac gives us peace."

"I thought Mortarr was jealous of any other spirit?" Tiathan was curious about this change in Rhor's habits. He knew it was only the flame through a huge pyre that brought Mortarr to his followers and no mention of turning to a cold rock for comfort. Tiathan was confused because he knew Mortarr had no use for Zebrac and no one worshipped both at the same time. Rhor was desperate to grab hold of every power possible to save his empire.

"Mortarr can come to us in any way he wishes." Rhor grinned confidently. "Why not in the form of Zebrac as well?"

"It is true that Jesuar cannot appear from a rock or crystal." Tiathan watched Rhor swell in pride. "Yet, Jesuar does not need a stone to help you live in peace and harmony. You thrive in war and chaos not peace. Jesuar is, however, more perfect than this stone you stand upon. We do not wipe our feet upon Him as you do."

"We'll see, Tiathan Eiula." Rhor stuck his beak close enough to Tiathan for him to see the many battle scars upon it. Rhor looked older now with his feathered brow much grayer speckled with unhealed wounds on the sides of his neck. The leathery red sacks that hung on either side of his face enhanced the ruthless vulture that he was. His small beady eyes narrowed into slits as he spoke.

"Yes, Rhor, we will." Tiathan was just as defiant.

"Jesuar is finished. Zebrac has spoken to me in dreams and song." Rhor ignored Tiathan's comment. "Zebrac has told me that all of Everstream will be given to me when we burn down the Great Oak of Jesuar! Jesuar has no power against the soul of Zebrac or the Flame of Mortarr!"

"I have heard of this soul of Zebrac, but never heard that it could speak to anyone whether in dreams or in song." Tiathan watched Rhor's feathers bristle as he raised his talons toward the pink crystal.

"The hear it speak now in the very tongue of your ancestors!" Rhor picked up a cup of red liquid and threw it upon the pink crystal of Zebrac. Rhor became incoherent even frothing at the mouth. His warriors moaned in ecstasy and began to sway back and forth. Rhor then spoke in a slow dirge:

> "vey'sitiooRll W dyohitie
> hia ayveyo hinhiym
> W ad tieRoinet NooRtihiR
> ba'oody nymnaes' met dyoiesti
> dyoiesti hiRhies' Wtioo ba'oody
> NooRtihiR r T sioiep
> tiehiti etooadyes oiR ayveyes
> ef'oveyoR ad oveyor
> dyRymv t et's mhino
> esepyti oom T nRoimdy
> ef' ba'oody nymnaes met dyoiesti"

Rhor repeated the same song over and over again as the pink crystal glowed brighter and brighter. Tiathan wasn't sure if Rhor knew the effect was good or bad, yet the pink crystal glowed though the sun had set. Rhor began to tremble as he spoke until he finally fell to the ground frothing uncontrollably before seeming to sleep. Tiathan wasn't sure how much time passed, but it wasn't long enough.

"Did you hear Zebrac speak of this realm we call Everstream?" Rhor smiled as if he had the most beautiful dream.

"I heard nothing except the ravings of Rhor." Tiathan thought the direct approach would be what Jesuar would have him do.

"You didn't hear because you don't believe." Rhor turned to his warriors. "This is what happens if you lose faith in Zebrac, the Redeemer! You are deaf to his wisdom and to his peace! There are the privileged few who can hear Zebrac, but, my warriors, those of you who do not will soon be brought into the circle. Only when you realize Zebrac and Mortarr are one and the same will the power and the majesty of this life come to you!"

"Jesuar speaks to all those who follow Him clearly and without confusion even to those who hate Him." Tiathan felt the words well up and flow from his mouth. "Do you think when the wrath of Jesuar comes for you that this stone will protect you? Your stone is silent and cold for the things you care about. The voice you hear is only Rhor deceiving you. Those who hear the voice of Zebrac only hear it to stay close to you, Rhor. They feel only you favor them with wealth and glory. However the glory you offer them leads only to an eternal grave. I have seen Moshdalayrrimich stand upon a similar stone thinking it was the stone of Zebrac. What answer do you have for that?"

"Moshdalayrrimich is a fool!" Rhor spat upon the ground. "He knows nothing of the mysteries of Zebrac or his father, Mortarr. He was fooled by a mad magician who has made him believe he sits upon the throne of Zebrac."

"Not unlike you." Tiathan had to laugh.

"Gag him!" Rhor ordered the guard nearest to Tiathan to tie a heavy cloth over his mouth.

"You can stop Jesuar from speaking to you or defend yourselves..." Tiathan felt the cloth with leather bindings stifle his words.

"By morning we will start the ritual of Zebrac." Rhor grabbed Tiathan's vest drawing him closer to stare into his eyes as he spoke. "You don't know what that means, but it is better you do not. Sleep well, Tiathan Eiula, for it will be the last peaceful sleep you will ever have."

The night came as a rough blanket of darkness,

yet the Gimgiddeans did not sleep. Their low moans and chants kept Tiathan awake a long time. Fires were built around the crystal to keep the glow from ebbing. Tiathan prayed to Jesuar for help or if no help was coming, to die with honor. He finally fell asleep hearing a slow dirge from the warriors:

> "mo tiRombayo baoefooRo 'XobaRhisi
> Moo siRes' baomohitie et's tieRoomo
> mo etohiR ad oobaoll et's mooRdyes
> 'ef mhiR 'ef ba'oody 'ef esmooRdyes
> moo efohiR W bati'ao
> moo dyohitie W dyohitie
> ef' mo ar T sietooesom
> mo ar T efom
> Moo mya' ef' oveyor
> Roiao tieyes ahimdu"

****

"I know where we're going." Carazaar was the first to speak after a long silence.

"How do you know?" Zelbiur stopped the company of Trags so they might rest.

"I have been here before." Carazaar trembled

slightly. "I can see the Mount of Zebrac before us. It is there we will find Tiathan Eiula."

"What else is there that makes you tremble so?" Zelbiur saw the magician's hands shake and he took a deep breath.

"I discovered a great pink crystal in a box canyon some years before." Carazaar had to sit down upon the ground to relay his tale. "It was too large to take with me and too hard to break into smaller pieces. I left it there until I was captured first by Moshdalayrrimich and his warriors. At that time there was a huge rock that I convinced the Conqueror was the Altar of Zebrac. After a few days of illusions I convinced Moshdalayrrimich to let me go. Then I was captured by Rhor who I could not bring to the same place so I brought him to the box canyon. I used all my illusions to convince Rhor he had the Soul of Zebrac, but it wasn't until sunset and they built pyres around the stone that it glowed. I told them that I had brought the Soul of Zebrac to life and now they had to keep him alive with worship and offerings. At dawn the rock glowed so bright it blinded everyone so I made my escape. They thought Zebrac had consumed me as an offering and I doubt Rhor has left it since."

"Rhor believes this pink crystal is alive?" Zelbiur

was amazed.

"At first, no." Carazaar smiled meekly. "But then I spoke a strange language that made no sense to anyone and the crystal grew dim as I knew it would as the fires burned themselves out. I told Rhor that he was still an unbeliever and his warriors need to pay homage to Zebrac by
building the pyres higher and brighter. I told him Zebrac would not return unless he apologized and stoke the flames for his very soul."

"Don't tell me you had him tied to this crystal
through illusion?" Zelbiur was beside himself with laughter. "You are a master magician!"

"Not only did he apologize." Carazaar laughed with him. "He insisted I give him the power and the words over the crystal to have the power to call upon Zebrac himself."

"That is a worthy tale." Miertur was not so amused.

"I can be convincing when I try." Carazaar bowed his head in false modesty.

"Still, we must decide to save father." Miertur was still torn about leaving Awlion behind.

"It is easier to decide because we know where father is, but we might end up in a fight for our lives."

Zelbiur was ready for whatever might come at them. "We will save father or die trying.

"It is well." Outra broke his silence.

The Trags advanced their trek toward the Mount of Zebrac heading for the north side which was harder to climb, but fewer guards watching that route. Outra left them to watch for Moshdalayrrimich or Nsaat who might be somewhere behind them. The shadow of the wood lay a mile between them and the foot of the Mount of Zebrac which worsened the tension amongst the Trags. They had come close to the sound of what seem fighting a couple of times, but now it was real danger. Zelbiur felt the nervousness that seemed to overwhelm the company. Already he kept two Trags from killing each other over a piece of blackened bread. Their punishment was to fast and pray to Jesuar for forgiveness. The fasting would be easy since they were low on food, but the prayers came hard even for Zelbiur in these dark woods.

Zelbiur sent Miertur with two others ahead as scouts. An unspeakable dread overcame his ability to think clearly. Each step took greater effort as they tried to get to the base of the mountain. They all felt as if Jesuar had left them leaving them helpless. Zelbiur soon saw someone in the distance on a small rise. It looked as if Zebrac himself was chasing him. It was Miertur who waved toward the Trags, but he was alone as he raced toward them.

Listening with his eyes closed, Zelbiur could hear the snapping of twigs and branches before he heard the drawing of swords. Behind Miertur Gimgiddeans appeared with shields against their chests. Miertur took no notice which brought a cry up out of Zelbiur's throat.

"No! Miertur! Look out!" Zelbiur watched as the first sword pierced Miertur's side. "To battle!" He did not care how many of them there were. However, a second blade pierced the heart of his brother.

Zelbiur screamed with a fury that halted the Gimgiddeans in their tracks. There were only six warriors which the Trags overwhelmed in their anger. Zelbiur struck down the Captain who struck down Miertur. Then he fought the others with wild abandon and blood lust. The rage lasted long, but the battle was soon over with only Miertur and the two scouts dead. Zelbiur had the six Gimgiddeans lifted onto poles before burying Miertur beneath their glassy stare. He would come back and bring Miertur's body to the Great Oak.

"Don't worry, my brother." Zelbiur's anger clouded his thoughts. "You will be avenged! I swear by Jesuar!"

"This is not Jesuar's way!" Outra cleared his way

through the brush behind them. He had heard the fighting but was too late to get there.

"And what way is Jesuar's way?" Zelbiur felt betrayed and wanted to ignore Outra.

"I speak of the dead you have hanging before us." Outra pointed to the Gimgiddeans whose green skins were beginning to fade in the hot sun. "We fight to defend ourselves not butcher those who come against us."

"You did not see my brother, Shroo!" Zelbiur calmed himself. "Yet you are right. We are not butchers and I wanted to send a message for those who come against us that we are not cowards."

"Their vengeance on us would be greater if you leave them like this." Outra saw the hurt and anger in Zelbiur's eyes.

"Take them down!" Zelbiur ordered the Trags who hesitated to follow his orders.

"And bury them in unmarked graves so it will hard for anyone to find them." Outra kneeled beside the grave of Miertur. "I see and understand the wisdom of Jesuar. However…I'll miss you Miertur. I will miss you."

"We must go on." Zelbiur ordered the Trags to finish the burial of the Gimgiddeans and then get into formation. "We have others to find…and not bury."

"Walk with me, Zelbiur." Outra hurried Zelbiur a few paces ahead of the others. "We have little time to mourn Miertur, but I tell you this that he is with Jesuar at this very moment."

"I know even though I do not know why Jesuar did not protect him." Zelbiur fought back the tears.

"There is no time to discuss this right now." Outra changed the subject quickly. "I think I have found an ally to fight against Rhor and Moshdalayrrimich."

"We have no allies, just enemies." Zelbiur wiped his face from the tears that flowed freely. "Who would be foolish enough to stand against the Seven Fortresses except us?"

"Byabnol." Outra watched the rage ebb and flow in Zelbiur's eyes.

"The Dark Prince and his ghostly mist?" Zelbiur sneered. "What price do they ask of us?"

"Quardraille and his 'mist', Mortarr, refuse to give in to the threat of Moshdalayrrmich." Outra was pleased it wasn't welcome news to Zelbiur. "I'm sure they think of us as a nuisance more than an ally. We will be used as a distraction so Jesuar can use them for His own purpose."

"Then Jesuar causes confusion among us." Zelbiur pointed to the Trag warriors. "First, we take in a magician who also happens to defile the name of Jesuar with his crystal ravings of power. Then my brother is killed, my father captured and my sister…Wherever she might be! Now…" He was breathing heavily from the panic he felt inside himself.

"What else?" Outra knew there was more.

"Now, the most foul thing in Everstream might be our ally…and Jesuar will bless it?" Zelbiur was confused.

"You don't understand." Outra patiently waited for reason to reclaim Zelbiur's soul again. "Jesuar is allowing Quardraille to make his own decision to fight Moshdalayrrimich. We cannot do it ourselves and this will give us more time to find Tiathan without being interrupted by Moshdalayrrimich."

"I fear Mortarr, Shroo!" Zelbiur sighed knowing Outra was right.

"As you should." Outra wrapped his cloak around his shoulders. "There will be a time when Mortarr will bring as great as an enemy as Moshdalayrrimich against us. Zebrac has no power over anyone while Mortarr is more dangerous because he relies on fear and hate to survive. For now, his time exists at Jesuar's good grace for the purpose of the survival of Everstream."

"We must not continue on this path." Carazaar interrupted them.

"Why not, magician?" Zelbiur still did not trust Carazaar.

"It leads to the middle of their camp." Carazaar motioned Zelbiur to the top of a nearby knoll. "We must climb to the top over there or we will have no chance at all."

"And what's our plan when we get there?" Outra followed them even though Carazaar hesitated talking in front of him.

"I'm a master of illusion and magic." Carazaar nervously rubbed his hands together. "You will need to use their own belief against them."

"Save your illusions till we really need them, magician!" Outra rested his hand on Carazaar's shoulder. "I might know something better, Zelbiur. Do you have Craxsmoore Guilding hidden safely?"

"Yes, I do." Zelbiur glanced toward a heavy pack that one of the Trag warriors was carrying. "Maybe we can use you, Carazaar with a minimum of illusion to save our Ioroarka." Outra looked from the pack to Carazaar as a sly smile enveloped his pale face.

"As you say." Carazaar bowed slightly.

"I do not think I like this." Zelbiur looked up the mountain as ice and snow enveloped the top where they might have to travel.

"None of us will." Outra led them forward.

****

"It is time for the calling of Zebrac! His soul yearns for freedom!" Rhor placed his hands on the great crystal in front of Tiathan.

The Gimgiddeans cried out for joy with tears streaming down their ragged cheeks. It was strange for Tiathan to see such mighty warriors weeping and wailing in ecstasy. Gimgiddeans were known to be stone-face cold blooded killers. They were tall, strong in body and will, merciless and stoic. How a crystal could change this once proud company was frightening.

"Beware the curse of Zebrac!" Rhor was frothing at the mouth. "He soon will speak to us through me and only I can tell you what he says.

Tiathan noticed the change immediately. Rhor began to stop over to listen to the crystal. The Gimgiddeans began to chant again in the ancient Trag:

"mo ar oomo 'ef nhimii
oiR ayveyes mya' ayveyo hinhiym
MoRo dyohitie sthihia mooti ephies.
ef' mo ar T siRiiestihia nhixo"

All the warriors swayed back and forth as they repeated the phrase. It was then that Rhor walked to the forefront spreading his arms as he spoke. The veins of Rhor's arms seemed to press against his yellowed skin as if they were to burst forth with their lifeblood. Rhor lifted his talons upward as a small gurgling could be heard in his throat:

"Y ethiveyo sioono ef' ll'
ef' Y mya' moveyor dyyo
ll' eso' no 'efoon dyhim' t dyoiesv
tieoinet moveyor dyoiesv t dyhim'
Y mya' barn ll' ayefo
ef' ayefo r hia ll' barn
Y mya' barn ll' dyohitie
ef' dyohitie r hia ll' barn
etooady nii baRootieoRes W ll'R
ethimdyes
ad Y mya' nomdy ll'R moi'mdyes
Roiba ll'R olloes met 'XobaRosies ayneti
ad mohiytie mya' bao ll'R RomhiRdy

Y mya' moveyor ayo
llo tiRoitie r moveyor tiRoitie
Mhiti moomdyoRes sthia mo eso'
Mom ba'oody r stody ef' no."

A giant shudder shook the ground as the base of the crystal cracked near Tiathan's feet. A collective gasp enveloped the Gimgiddeans before they returned to their chanting. Even though the crystal cracked only fueled their fervor to speak to Zebrac.

"The sign of Zebrac!" Rhor wept uncontrollably. "The blood must be his!" He pointed at Tiathan who now looked to Jesuar for a miracle.

A puff of smoke exploded before the crystal shone brightly and then a cloaked figure stood with no arms in its sleeves and no face in the cowl. The Gimgiddeans waited in anticipation for the cloaked figure to speak not knowing who it was.

"I am Zebrac!" A great thunderous voice emanated from the cowl. "What are you doing, my brothers?"

"I...I..." Rhor's confused look comforted Tiathan because even he did not know what was going on.

"Did you not call for me?" Tiathan relaxed

slightly since the figure seemed less interested in him as in Rhor. "Won't you speak to Zebrac as you did to my soul within the crystal? I have been released to stand among you and embrace each of you."

"There's something wrong." Rhor stepped away from the figure.

The dark figure moved down toward Tiathan looming larger than before. Rhor missed seeing the blade that cut the bonds around Tiathan's wrists. Yet, he did catch a glimpse of Craxsmoore Guilding as it changed hands from cloak to Trag. Rhor had just enough time to avoid being crushed by the spiked ball as it swept over his head.

A score of warriors fell before Craxsmoore Guilding causing confusion and wreaking havoc that drove the Gimgiddeans down the canyon wall. Through the confusion Tiathan pulled the cloaked figure away from the crystal with him to safety.

"Carazaar! It's good to see you!" Tiathan addressed the faceless cloak.

"How did you know?" Carazaar was disappointed as he lost the illusion when Tiathan called his name. "I worked very hard to convince even you."

"It almost worked until I concentrated fully on you and not the illusion." Tiathan hurried Carazaar down the hillside.

Rhor and his followers could be heard following them until something started a rock slide with a shower of arrows that turned them away. Rhor cursed Tiathan and Jesuar for the destruction of the soul of Zebrac which was buried in the landslide. The great crystal was lying in great shards and no longer glistening in the morning light. Within the hour the Gimgiddeans started to pick up the pieces for themselves placing them in leather pouches. Another volley of arrows chased them into the Dark Woods as Zelbiur and the Trags emerged from their hiding places.

"How goes it, father?" Zelbiur hugged his father.

"I had hoped someone would come to rescue me." Tiathan was grateful to see them all again.

"What do we do now?" Zelbiur wanted to leave this place.

"We must go see your brother, Ygueliav." Tiathan patted the shoulder of his son.

"First, I must tell you that Miertur has been killed." Zelbiur looked down to the ground.

"When? How?" Tiathan was shocked.

"Before we came for you. He died in battle." Zelbiur sighed deeply.

"I will mourn later for we need help and may lose many friends before we are done." Tiathan looked among the Trags seeing some already missing. "What of Awlion?"

"Awlion is lost in the Dark Forest, but we still hope to find her." Zelbiur tried to be uplifting, but it was hard.

"I thought I felt a loss as my death seemed so near." Tiathan closed his eyes and prayed silently. "Yet I thought it was because…Tell me what else has happened since my capture."

As they traveled Outra joined them explaining what he knew before allowing Zelbiur to fill in everything else. After a while they all silently trudged through the forest on the way to Rabel Ain.

****

Awlion awoke to the sound of trumpets. Thoos had already left her to investigate leaving Thip and Thump behind. She rose up and used a branch to erase all traces of their encampment. When Thoos returned she wanted to be armed and ready.

Tho-o-o-os!

"What is it, Thoos?"

"Many warriors!" Thoos rolled his large blue eyes as he pointed to the path behind her.

"Moshdalayrrimich or Rhor?" Awlion didn't

think it mattered.

"Moshdalayrrimich." Thoos grunted before spitting on the ground.

"I feel the same way." Awlion spat on the ground, too. "Where shall we go friend?"

"Find more friends." Thoos pointed in the opposite direction.

"Where?" Awlion waited patiently.

"Rabel Ain." Thoos pulled at her pant leg to follow.

"Ygueliav is there! Are we close?" Awlion was excited to be able to reunite with her brother. It had been so long.

"Not far, two days." Thoos ran up the path and into the brush.

Awlion heard Thoos rush from right to left. She assumed he was looking for any warriors that might be hiding around them. She was able to relax a little searching the air for Harkies who might be scouting over her.

Tho-o-o-os!

Tho-o-o-os!

Tho-o-o-

The suddenness of Thoos stopping in midstride worried Awlion as she prepared her bow for battle. She refused to cry out for fear of warning whoever might be there. Awlion crept through the gnarled oaks until she spied a hanging net across the path she surely would have crossed. Thoos wasn't in the net probably because he ran so fast.

Two small eyes peered from a darkness beyond the net to keep Awlion from venturing further. She couldn't imagine where Thoos could have gone....except up into the trees. There wasn't a sound only the eerie stare from now two sets of eyes from the shadows. They did not seem to see her as if she was totally unimportant.

"Did you see that, Zarr?" It was clearly a Bantongues low growl.

"Yes, Tenca." The other whispered clearly surprised that the net missed its victim. "But there's nothing there! I told you this was a bad idea."

"I heard a rush of wind, yet saw nothing!" Zarr appeared first from the brush.

"That you hear anything anymore would surprise me." Tenca followed him into the small clearing.

Awlion could see the matted fur on their legs and the chipped talons on their sides which told her these were old Bantongues and outcasts. They were after food and nothing else. Still, they were dangerous with venom just as deadly as if they were still in their youth.

"Take care!" Awlion decided to cry out from behind her oak refuge. With bow and arrow ready she confronted the two Bantongues that towered above her.

"Oh! Oh! Oh!" The two cried out together as they tripped over each other to get away.

"Don't hurt us!" Zarr hid behind his brother.

"Him! Him! It's him you want!" Tenca pointed to Zarr who cowered behind a pile of rocks and then scampered behind him.

"Traitor! Traitor!" Zarr pushed Tenca in front of him.

"I am not! Take him!" Tenca pushed back and soon they were both at each other's throats. Awlion had to step in to separate them.

"Stop it this instant!" Awlion tapped them with her bow losing all fear of them. She decided it wasn't worth fighting them.

"We knew Nsaat would send someone to kill us!" Zarr groveled at the feet of Awlion which only embarrassed her since he was still towering above her.

"Kill him first Queen of the forest!" Tenca pushed Zarr aside while pleading with Awlion on bony knees.

"He's the eldest! Kill him first, O Queen!" Zarr

edged back toward the trees.

"I didn't come here to kill either of you!" Awlion wondered why she ever feared these Bantongues. "And I am not the Queen of this forest!"

"I knew it!" Zarr stood up proudly strutting back and forth. "You silly Notherhen, Tenca. I knew she was friendly."

"I knew it, too." Tenca quickly joined in.

"Did not!" Zarr frowned.

"Did too!" Tenca started to wrestle with Zarr again.

"How long has it been since you've both eaten?" Awlion kept up her guard just in case they were not as stupid as they seemed. Both of them looked thin considering her past confrontations with Bantongues.

"We're not sure." Tenca scratched his bald head parting the few hairs he had there.

"At least not today." Zarr rubbed his drooping snout.

"I have some food till I get to Rabel Ain." Awlion pulled out from her pouch some brown bread and blackberries to give to them.

"Thank you, mistress." Zarr and Tenca exclaimed as one while devouring most of it in one bite.

"It was not poisoned, was it?" Zarr squinted at

Awlion even though it was already too late if it were poisoned.

"Look!" Awlion pulled some brown bread and ate it in front of them though she was not very hungry.

"Wait here and I will return with something more substantial for you to eat." Awlion left them for a while coming back with two large Notherhens she had freshly shot with arrows. When she brought her offerings to the Bantongues they snatched her prey and devoured them quickly. Awlion forgot that Bantongues tended to eat things raw and was not a pretty sight.

"You are going to where?" Zarr felt stronger from his frenzied feeding.

"To Rabel Ain." Awlion was more assured of her safety,

"We know the way if you want company." Tenca grinned hideously which did not reassure her feelings about them.

"No one comes this way unless they are going to Rabel Ain." Zarr glanced down at her pouch as food magically pours forth from it.

"How far away is it?" Awlion tried to keep them talking instead of begging for more food.

"Not very far if you ride on my back." Tenca offered.

"Maybe one day, but why do you go there?" Zarr

was becoming more curious than Awlion wanted him to be.

"I am going to see my brother." Awlion decided to tell them the truth.

"I hope he will be safe by the time we get there." Zarr sipped water from a small stream nearby.

"Why is that?" Awlion didn't want to sound anxious, but her heart beat quickly thinking she might be too late to reach Ygueliav.

"Haven't you heard about the great battle which was fought not a few hours ago?" Tenca was preparing to tell the tale when Zarr interrupted him.

"Great battle? It was over in a short time." Zarr did not think it was worth the retelling.

"A black prince called Quardraille led a company of his black raven warriors against the camp of Moshdalayrrimich." Tenca enjoyed relaying the story as he remembered it.

"They were vultures who enjoyed killing and destruction." Zarr added. "Yet it was still a small fight."

"You sound like you think it was funny." Awlion remembered hearing trumpets which had to be the Arbushi riding to the fighting.

"Because you see Rhor had left the camp the day before with his warriors after meeting with

Moshdalayrrimich." Tenca became excited. "The funny thing was that Quardraille wanted to attack Rhor and instead met Moshdalayrrimich who nearly destroyed the Arbushi."

"How so?" Awlion was interested now in everything.

"Quardraille didn't use scouts so he wandered into the wrong encampment before he knew it was there." Zarr laughed heartily which was very creepy.

"What were you doing there?" Awlion would now know their allegiances or kill them trying to find out.

"Another funny thing was that when Quardraille retreated he ran into Nsaat and the rest of us." Tenca thought it more than amusing. "We did not join in the fight which Nsaat noticed and he cast us out."

"Nsaat had cast us out long before that since we were foraging for food for months." Zarr reminded Tenca. "We were not supposed to be anywhere near the fighting."

"We were curious." Tenca insisted.

"You were curious." Zarr nudged Tenca.

"Which way to Rabel Ain?" Awlion was tired of the banter.

"North." Zarr winced knowing he could never be

with Nsaat ever again.

"Nsaat told us if we interfere with him that others would come and kill us." Tenca became solemn again. "Sometimes he sends someone to torment us to make us go deeper into the Dark Woods."

"How long have you been here?" Awlion knew it must have been a long time.

"Three years now since we were left behind." Zarr sighed.

"We were unable to fight, scout or hunt so we were left behind." Tenca looked at the empty net before him, "We still can't."

"However, it does not stop us from seeing what's going on around us." Zarr had a dusty gleam in his eyes.

"We try to mind our own business." Tenca nudged Zarr to be careful about what else he might say.

"Not true!" Thoos finally spoke above all of them.

"A Thistmock!" Zarr spat on the ground. "Ugly bony things!"

"Ugly you!" Thoos shouted.

"We caught one by accident, but there was no meat to cook." Tenca ignored Thoos. "We had to let it go."

"Yes, but we hear Thistmock feet are a rare meal in Gimgiddo." Zarr suddenly felt a warm paste on his head.

"Ptoo!" Thoos spat on Tenca before he could move away.

"Thoos! Stop that!" Awlion shouted up at him.

"Cook you!" Thoos mocked them.

"Little pile of spuill!" Zarr grunted as he wiped himself off.

"He's my friend and I won't have you insult him!" Awlion drew her dagger which brought silence to the clearing.

"We're not violent, mistress." Tenca raised his broken talons. "We can hardly chew our food much less defend ourselves."

"We do have weapons, but they are old and not of much use." Zarr volunteered much to the chagrin of Tenca.

"So you just exist?" Awlion tried to understand how they could help her.

"There is nothing else we can do." Zarr shrugged.

"Perhaps there is." Awlion used her dagger to cut two sturdy branches. She sharpened them into two spears for the Bantongues hoping they would not use them against her.

"How does this help us?" Zarr asked.

"Now you are able warriors." Awlion looked at

the pathetic creatures who barely could lift their weapons.

"We have armor you know." Tenca meekly backed into the underbrush. Soon he reemerged wearing an old dented oak helmet and ill-fitting breastplate. The helmet was obviously too big for his head if that were possible.

"I have armor, too." Zarr scampered into the woods and put on his helmet as well.

"Ha, ha!" Thoos laughed above them.

"Thoos! Behave!" Awlion held back her laughter.

"We will not fight Nsaat or any of our own kind." Zarr warned her as he shifted his helmet so he could see better.

"We will run before we will do that." Tenca echoed his brother.

"Well, let's be off to Rabel Ain." Awlion reluctantly waved them forward

"Do I look all right, brother?" Tenca asked Zarr with his face half hidden by an oak flap.

"Fine. Fine." Zarr patted his brother's helmet. "We'll make great warriors even in Nsaat's eye.

"Like we were?" Tenca was hopeful even though he tripped over his spear.

"Almost, my brother, almost." Zarr helped Tenca up fixing his helmet which drooped to one side.

"Bad news, friend." Thoos jumped into Awlion's arms.

"I know friend." Awlion shook her head knowing these Bantongues would be of little use to her if they had to fight.

The path was clear and quiet as the band of warriors marched toward Rabel Ain. Awlion hoped the Bantongues might get discouraged and go back so she wouldn't have to have lie awake all night worrying about them. Unfortunately, Zarr and Tenca liked this new adventure and acted younger as night began to fall. The Bantongues refused to let Awlion do anything even making a fire to keep them warm.

"You might be better at hunting for food then we are, mistress, but we will cook and clean whatever you catch." Zarr was hopeful that Awlion would bring more Notherhen or a Grizzled Turkey.

"We will not have to worry about food since Thoos will soon be here with something for all of us." She leaned back and waited patiently.

Tho-o-o-os!

Before them was a freshly killed Notherhen that set the Bantongues in a frenzy of activity. Thoos left again as the Bantongues wandered into the forest to find sticks and stones to make a spit for the meat. Awlion was alone when she heard the first snap of a twig.

"Who is there?" Awlion readied her bow with the arrow pointed in the direction of the sound.

"I have not come here to harm you." A Voice whispered from the underbrush.

"Then come out and face me." Awlion refused to drip her bow.

"I am Agraine Thrule, daughter of Thrun Thrule of Rabel Ain. Who are you?" Agraine held her spiked mace tightly as she crossed over to the fire.

She was a Trag and a little taller than Awlion. She had gold bands around her forearms and wore a leather skin that covered most of her body. An oak shield was strapped to her back with a leather pouch and a skin for water. She had bright red hair that looked like fire on her pale skin. Her hard yellow eyes stared through Awlion like the warrior she was. On her ankles were painted two lightning bolts with the letter "J" on either side.

"I am Awlion Eiula, daughter of Tiathan Eiula of Quicksnatch!" She slipped her bow over her shoulder not wanting to fight her.

"We are both Trags, but I do not follow Jesuar."

Agraine kept her ground sensing danger nearby.

"I do follow him, but that does not lessen the fact we are sisters in a small family of warriors." Awlion started to smile.

"Death to Moshdalayrrimich and curse the name of Mortarr!" Agraine raised her fist in defiance.

"Death to Moshdalayrrimich and curse the name of Mortarr!" Awlion embraced her new friend.

"Where are you going?" Agraine relaxed a little.

"Right now I am more lost than understand where I am going." Awlion did not want to surprise her new friend concerning Thoos, Zarr and Tenca. "I'll take any advice where I can find my family and friends."

"If they know anything about these woods, they are already heading for Rabel Ain." Agraine rested her mace on the ground near her. "If not, we can give you food and shelter until you have decided what you will do next."

"I am at your mercy." Awlion bowed to her noticing a silver pendent with a circle next to a rising sun. "However, there is something else you should know."

Tho-o-o-os!

"A Thistmock?" Agraine was surprised as she rose to her feet.

"So?" Awlion wondered why Agraine was wary of her new friend.

"I hope you have not been feeding this thing or we will never be rid of it." Agraine started to lean over to pick up her mace.

Tho-o-o-os! Thip! Thip! Thump!

Agraine tumbled head over heels as all three of them hit her right at the knees and then vanished. Agraine quickly regained her feet and lifted her mace high over her head.

Tho-o-o-os! Thip! Thip! Thump!

Again Agraine was on the ground without a single swing to protect herself. Frustrated, she started to get up, but thought better of it.

"I think you've offended them, Agraine." Awlion tried not to laugh, but saw the anger in her eyes.

"You have befriended them?" Agraine trembled with anger.

"Yes and Thoos has saved my life more than once." Awlion offered her hand to help her up.

"Thoos?" Agraine grunted as she stood up waiting for them to come again. "You've given it a name?"

"Yes, Thoos is the older one. Thip and Thump are his young." Awlion could not understand the problem.

"You have no idea the trouble you've brought yourself and any of us who pass your way." Agraine was resigned to accept the situation.

"Thoos? Come out and meet our new friend." Awlion looked around in all directions.

"No, friend." Thoos cried out as Thip and Thump giggled nearby.

"Yes, friend." Agraine was resigned to be their friends as well. "But not willingly."

"Hug new friend, Thoos." Awlion knew Agraine saw the twinkle in her eyes.

"Oh, no." Agraine readied herself for the worst.

Tho-o-o-os! Thip! Thip! Thump!

Thoos had Agraine around the neck with a hideous grin on his face and a hold of her ankles. Agraine could not be mad looking into those pathetic blue eyes that seemed to swirl and dance around her in a dance.

"They are adorable now that I see them close up." Agraine broke down knowing she could not dislike these creatures. "Yet, it might be something about them that makes us like them."

"Whatever it is, I am happy to have them with me." Awlion picked up Thip and Thump who immediately started to hug her while playing with ends of her hair.

"You can let go now...Thoos." Agraine encouraged Thoos to let go, but he wouldn't until he kissed her cheek. "Ew-w-w! No kissing!"

Thoos laughed and ran away Thip and Thump following.

Tho-o-o-os! Thip! Thip! This time no thump.

"Any other surprises?" Agraine saw Awlion nervously looked behind her.

"As a matter of fact...." It was too late. Zarr and Tenca were already making their entrance.

"Bantongues!" Agraine reached for her mace and started toward the two of them.

"No, Agraine! It's only Zarr and Tenca...my friends." Awlion stood between Agraine and the Bantongues.

"You've named them, too?" Agraine was beside herself in wonder. "What magic is this?"

"No magic....it just happened." Awlion knew it was odd. "By the way, I didn't name the Bantongues. That is their names. Jesuar has put a strange group together for our journey."

"Who is this, mistress?" Zarr was fearful of the spiked mace.

"Is she here to kill us?" Tenca trembled though he still wore armor for protection.

"No, she is not here to kill you." Awlion patted his head gently. Tenca almost purred at her touch. "She is another friend."

"I must be crazy." Agraine sat down by the fire as Awlion related her story. Obviously, they weren't leaving too soon now. Zarr and Tenca could not keep silent so she let them finish the final part of the story.

"I am amazed." Agraine relaxed for the moment though having the Bantongues so close she kept on her toes. "If Rhor or Moshdalayrrimich should come out of the shadows and call you friend, I will dedicate my life to Jesuar for that miracle alone."

"No, no more surprises." Awlion leaned back watching the fire dance in front of her. Thoos soon brought two Notherhens to the spit which Zarr roasted slowly as the group took bits and pieces to eat as they cooked.

"Is this your first time in the Dark Forest?" Agraine asked between bites of meat.

"No, but it has been fifteen years since I entered this far." Awlion did not want to speak of her past.

"I have journeyed in and out of the Dark Forest many times." Agraine cupped a bit of water that Thoos had diverted through their camp.

"Tell us what you have seen so far." Zarr wanted to hear her story.

"Something strange and scary." Tenca already shivered at the thought of a good campfire story.

"Very well." Agraine sat up and wiped her hands in the sand around the fire. "I have been in the swamps of Modos and have come out alive."

"O-o-o-o-o!" Zarr and Tenca were both amazed already.

"We have heard of the dangers of those swamps, but never what was found in them." Tenca felt a tingle down his furry spine.

"Very few have lived to tell any tales." Zarr chimed up.

"We would never go there." Tenca leaned against his brother.

"I had been hunting for three days and caught nothing, saw nothing." Agraine started her story. "I did see a Grancin Deer which led me a merry chase further than I wanted to go, but I was hungry and did not want to go home empty-handed. I soon lost the deer and found myself waist deep in mud. I heard sounds that curled my hair and raised my skin which I had never heard before."

"O-o-o-o-o!" Zarr and Tenca were attentively rapt with her story.

"At first, I saw nothing that would connect the sound to any beast I had ever seen." Agraine stood as she talked. "Then there was a hissing sound around me until I saw the horned head of a serpent with fiery eyes and split tongue. It saw me before moving on as if I wasn't worth the trouble of fighting. I turned to get out of the mud when this huge horned head of some gigantic snake was looking into my eyes. I held my mace tight waiting to use it if it came too close. However, it just stared at me."

"What happened next?" Zarr was covering his eyes though there was nothing to see.

"It opened its mouth wide as if to devour me when I shoved the mace between its jaws." Agraine smirked seeing how enthralled they all were, even Awlion. "With my dagger I jumped upon its head and stabbed until it fell dead in the mud. It was then I noticed a thick fog surrounding me. I did not know what direction to go, but I remembered to retrieve the mace."

"What did you do?" Tenca tapped his bony legs against the ground.

"I wandered a long time in the fog, but could not

find land." Agraine stepped closer to the Bantongues gesturing with her hands. "There before me were monsters with ugly unnaturally formed heads rising above and around me. They slowly drifted into the air while looking down at me. Some were laughing noiselessly at me while others seemed to be screaming, but there was no sound. Still others looked at me with grim faces as if judging my worthiness to be near them. These ghosts, for they were ghosts since I saw right through them, did not close enough for me to strike them with my mace. They were there all night till the dawn when they and the fog disappeared with the sun. I found myself just a few feet from the embankment and escaped into the Dark Forest."

"That was a good story!" Zarr clapped his talons which unnerved Agraine who sat right next to them.

"Do you have another one?" Tenca was already scared enough that it would take hours before he would get a good night's sleep.

"No, that is enough for now." Agraine sat back down. "We have a dangerous journey still ahead of us. If I frighten you with stories, you will not be able to help us when the time comes. We will need you alert and unafraid to fight."

"You're right, Agraine." Awlion laid back her

head to rest upon a mossy stone. Thoos, Thip, and Thump quietly crept up around her and rested their heads on her shoulders and legs. Agraine smiled at the sight and relaxed.

Zarr and Tenca spent most of the night twitching and jumping at every night sound. They watched over Agraine and Awlion until sleep over came them as well. Thoos needed little sleep so watched the shadows ready to alert them all if any danger came their way.

.

Chapter Four

Thoos kept his distance for a few miles as the small band of warriors marched toward Rabel Ain. Zarr and Tenca complained about the length of the journey and what Nsaat would do to them if he found out Rabel Ain was their destination. Awlion and Agraine ignored the ramblings while learning each other's strengths and weaknesses.
Tho-o-o-os!

"Here, friend." Thoos was excited as he pointed toward a large clearing.

"Rabel Ain?" Awlion rushed to his side.

"Yes, we are here." Agraine walked into the clearing without fear.

"We best not go with you." Zarr stopped short of the clearing. Tenca stayed with his brother as Awlion continued on.

"I'll call you when we have told them you are with us."

Awlion agreed it was best for now.

"I'll tell them we're coming in." Agraine held up a small shell and blew a loud high pitched tune that echoed down the glen toward the battlements. A trumpet answered her call which prompted her to turn towards Awlion.

"I stay here, too." Thoos stepped back into the shadows.

"Okay, Thoos." Awlion realized how odd their group was and knew no one at Rabel Ain would understand their friendship.Awlion was soon able to see the makeshift fortress of stone and rock with oak battlements overlooking the clearing. Green and red flags flew at each corner which meant nothing to her. She heard an alarm which shortened their pace to a walk.

"Hold your fire! I know these warriors!" Ygueliav and two other Rabel Ainians jumped over the wall to greet them.

"Brother!" Awlion hugged Ygueliav.

"Sister!" Ygueliav kissed her cheek.

"Father, I have made a new friend." Agraine did not embrace him.

"I am Thrun Thrule and this is my companion for life, Schill Thrule." Thrun put his arm around his companion who was an older vision of Agraine. The difference was that Schill wore full oak armor and cradled a battleaxe in her arms. Schill had a shield with a pennant that had the name of Jesuar on it.

"I am Awlion Eiula." She stared at the shield.

"What is it you are looking at, child?" Schill lifted an

eyebrow with a some concern.

"I'm surprised." Awlion still stared at the banner.

"At what?" Schill was becoming annoyed.

"Your shield." Awlion pointed to the name of Jesuar. "I didn't know you were followers of Jesuar. We had been told you were of your own mind."

"It drives our enemies crazy." Schill laughed and thumped her shield without answering her question.

"Enough of that." Agraine thought this was a good time to tell them of their other friends. "We have others who followed us here."

"Friends? Bring them forward!" Thrun's smile evaporated as Zarr and Tenca came out of the forest in full armor.

"This is Zarr and Tenca, father." Agraine liked to see her father's weathered face trace new maps on his cheeks and forehead.

"Friends?" Thrun repeated as he backed away from these new visitors. He did not know whether to greet them or kill them.

"That's not all." Agraine pointed to Thoos who peeked out from behind Zarr.

"A Thistmock!?" Schill dropped her battleaxe and wrung her hands. She wanted to sound the alarm, but the calmness in her daughter's voice kept her from crying out.

"His name is Thoos." Awlion interrupted.

"Thoos? You gave it a name?" Thrun looked at Awlion in awe.

"Yes, father, and he has two young ones called Thip and Thump." She watched him blinked twice trying to make sense of it all.

"Oh, we will never be rid of it." Schill turned away towards the fortress gates.

A tall bow-legged warrior with a wrinkled snout and blue-hued scales on his arms cleared the walls and approached them. The warrior did not speak as he came closer. Awlion noticed a dark blue flame upon his forehead with his eyes a curious yellow and orange that blinked sideways making her a little nervous.

"Who is this?" Awlion grasped the hilt of her dagger.

"One of our friends." Ygueliav laughed as if his friend was stranger than her friends. "He and his warriors helped build this poor excuse for a fortress. We have little time before the battle begins. Is father near enough to help us?"

"I don't know where he is." Awlion kept an eye on the mountain warrior. She had heard of them, but never seen one close up.

"I am an Akrilla from the Havarill Mountains." He thumped his chest with hands that held sharpened nails on his fingers. He spoke in melancholy tones which oddly soothed Awlion as he spoke. "I am Haavorn, Captain of those you see behind me."

Awlion looked back on the walls of Rabel Ain and saw a number of Akrilla standing with spears, swords and jagged hammers in their hands. Awlion wondered how much they should trust these warriors, but they could say the same about her Bantongues.

"I must speak with my brother alone." Awlion pulled Ygueliav away from them.

"I understand." Haavorn bowed and returned to the fortress walls.

"He'll take some time to accept as an ally." Ygueliav waited for Haavorn to clear the walls.

"Father was separated from us when I left to look for him on my own." Awlion began to tell her story. "However Miertur, Zelbiur and Outra could be anyway by this time. I know they have broken camp and are searching for our father. The rest you know with my small following here to bring you up to date."

"I still would like to meet this Thoos." Ygueliav was amused seeing the possibilities of such a creature as a scout. The Bantongues still troubled him after so many bad encounters with Bantongues in the past. He nervously looked over at Haavorn who had no expression to read as they stood tall against the sky.

"What's the matter?" Awlion could see he was troubled. "Thoos is not dangerous to us."

"He will not come to me." Ygueliav noticed Thoos backing away.

"What about them?" Awlion nodded towards the Akrilla.

"Haavorn has fought Nsaat and the Harkies for thirty years so has no love or trust toward any of them." Ygueliav noticed that Zarr and Tenca recognized Haavorn and he hoped there would be no trouble.

"He'll have to understand." Awlion refused to compromise.

"We're two hundred and fifty Trags strong." Ygueliav was thinking out loud. "And there are fifty Akrilla warriors beside us which will give any army of Nsaat or Moshdalayrrimich pause to attack us."

"Are they so close?" Awlion wondered if they should already be inside the fortress.

"The Valkyricks are camped just ten miles from us, but we heard that the Gimgiddeans had left one or two days before." Ygueliav hoped Awlion might know something else. "Already we have had messengers demanding our surrender."

"What was your answer?" She noticed a smirk on his face as she asked the question.

"Arrows in the backsides." He laughed even though it was now a serious moment.

"Then I will stay with them." Awlion nodded toward

Zarr and Tenca who looked as nervous as Thrun and Schill. "I cannot abandon them since they are my allies. The Akrilla will not have them in the fortress and Thoos is afraid of you all. Besides, I can go find father and the our family to warn them of your troubles. Maybe I can cause some confusion as I go."

"Cause some confusion?" Ygueliav liked the idea. "Come inside and meet those who fought with us when we first came to Everstream."

"But not long." Awlion looked for Zarr and Tenca, but they had already wandered into the forest to hid within the trees. The cheers that greeted her softened her heart as Awlion entered the fortress. The Trags rose up as one raising their swords and shields in honor of the daughter of Tiathan Eiula. The Akrilla, too, bowed in allegiance which relaxed Awlion for the moment.

"You see?" Ygueliav slapped her shoulder. "We're one in battle then!"

"I hope." Awlion wondered how much her brother knew of the Akrillas. Her father had spoken of the warrior with a blue flame on his forehead that attacked him at Flashfire Lake. Every one of these Akrillas had the same mark even though some looked smaller than others.

"We will make sure you are well stocked for your trip when you are ready to go." Ygueliav stopped suddenly.

Agraine was the first to hear the trumpets in the distance. Ygueliav almost at the same time knew it was too late. There was movement on the right side of the woods as Zarr and Tenca stood out in the open looking up at the sky. Thrun and Schill raced over to the west wall as Awlion and Ygueliav scampered over to the north wall. Haavorn walked slowly with the Akrilla toward the south wall preparing his battleaxe while giving orders only his warriors could understand.

"I see Harkies!" Zarr screamed as he raced up to Awlion.

"Come inside and we will protect you." Awlion waved them to her.

"We cannot fight Nsaat and our own kind. Forgive us, mistress." Tenca agonized over what to do, but he and his brother would forever be criminals.

"I understand for Nsaat is surely with them." Awlion would not want them to do anything that would put them in danger.

"Nsaat is with them!" Zarr was dancing in place ready to run. "He cannot see us!"

"Do what you have to do, my friends." Awlion released them from her care.

"Again, forgive us, mistress." Zarr and Tenca left their weapons and armor behind as they ran into the Dark Forest. There was a flurry of activity in the fortress until a trumpet call stopped them in their tracks. The shouts of battle were heard across the clearing as horses, stallions and warriors on foot loped into view. The flutter of wings overhead seemed much too close for comfort, but Awlion looked up to see hundreds of

Harkies flying around Rabel Ain.

"I'm afraid you'll have to stay, sister." Ygueliav drew his sword and ordered the Trags to mount the walls with lances, battleaxes, bows and arrows.

"They have such beautiful armor." Agraine turned to her father.

"And such wonderful music." Schill patted Agraine's shoulder. "I would not think Nsaat would unite with Moshdalayrrimich, but there they are. These are strange times who live in and who knows what Jesuar has for us."

"They are still ugly creatures with so many characters in their faces and color of hair." Thrun watched the bow-legged creatures file into phalanxes of ten by ten as they readied g for their attack. Their long white hair seemed to make it impossible to see their emerald eyes with the yellow flame in the center. How they could fight with arms that reached the ground he could never know, but would soon find out.

Harkies flew overhead giving signals showing the weak points of Rabel Ain. Awlion sent arrows flying to keep them from getting too close, but there were too many to shoot down. For every one brought down, two more appeared to replace them. Torches were lit along the clearing as Moshdalayrrimich, wearing a silver and blood red robe, pranced on his black stallion into the clearing. He held a tall scepter with a golden globe upon the top which he used to point as he spoke. Snarling voices from the left in the forest alerted the Akrillas that

Bantongues were nearby.

"Awlion! Stay by me!" Ygueliav motioned to her to stand by his side.

"Ygueliav! We will protect the south wall if you can keep the Harkies from us!" Haavorn called over to him.

"Give me seven of your best archers and I will be able to protect him." Awlion was ready to go, but Ygueliav gently held her should while shaking his head.

"Stay with me, sister." Ygueliav insisted knowing how hard it would be to keep her from doing what pleased.

"Why?" she did not understand, but his look told her there was no changing his mind about it.

Agraine stood her ground tense and quiet as the first Valkyrick reached the makeshift wall. She silently drew her half-sword while preparing her spiked mace for the attack. The Valkyrick Captain grinned as he grabbed hold the top of the smooth stone. Agraine smiled back as she swung her mace at his head and then plunged her half-sword into his chest. Four others suffered the same fate before a spear glanced off her shoulder. The anger that blazed in Agraine's eyes should have warded off anyone else from approaching her. It took the defeat of ten more Valkyricks before the others avoided that particular part of the fortress. Alone she was more than they could fight so they ventured further down the wall.

"Bantongues!" Thrun had never seen Valkyricks and Bantongues fighting side by side. They all braced for an unimaginable fight that they could win.

Thrun and Schill were back to back as they fought off Bantongues that shot sticky webs of knotted cords at them. Behind the two were fifty Trags fighting Valkyricks as they breached the walls. Thrun kept an eye on Agraine in case she needed his help.

The battle was furious along the north wall as Trag and Valkyrick fell side by side. Ygueliav fought valiantly until a lance struck his shoulder forcing Awlion to see to his wound. He waved her away forcing himself upright to continue fighting.

"Have you no archers?" Awlion desperately shot volley after volley of arrows into leathery hides of the Harkies above her. Bodies piled up around her which some were still alive while others were mortally wounded.

"Light an arrow into those trees to the right." Ygueliav ignored her question.

It took three flaming arrows before the forest erupted into flames that spread quickly forcing Bantongues by the tens and hundreds from their hiding places. A shower of spears covered the sky as angry Bantongues, some still aflame, tossed their poisonous weapons at the fortress. Twenty Trags fell from the flurry as they were unable to escape at the time.

Haavorn with his Akrilla fighters decimated huge sections of Valkyricks with their double-edged battle axes. They never seemed to tire or looked for help. Neither did they hesitate when a comrade fell by their sides. The blue flame on their foreheads seemed to glow brightly with each blow of their blades.

Valkyrick warriors were advancing toward the south gate as Haavorn whispered into the curled ears of two Akrillas. Awlion was sure of treachery and readied her bow to pierce the heart of Haavorn first and then the others. She never felt comfortable fighting with them. Two Harkies drew her attention away as they reached out to grab her while flying by. Ygueliav beheaded one as Awlion shoved a dagger into the chest of the other.

"Something's wrong!" Awlion shook her brother while pointing to the south gate.

"It's all right." Ygueliav was unconcerned watching the two Akrillas move toward the south gate. The two Akrillas looked around before they unlocked the two great oak doors that held them closed. Awlion sent two arrows toward them, but only succeeded in embedding them in the doors. Haavorn saw the arrows fly, but did nothing except shake his head.

"Open the gate!" Haavorn ordered his warriors.

Awlion sent another arrow towards Haavorn who lifted his shield to block its path. She set another arrow to her bow, but a hand blocked her view. Angrily she turned to Ygueliav and wondered what he was thinking because it seemed clear Haavorn was betraying them.

"No!" Ygueliav struggled with Awlion to keep her from killing the Akrilla Captain.

"He is betraying us!" Awlion thought he was crazy to stop her.

"Let him be!" Ygueliav watched as hundreds of Bantongues entered the fortress screaming in loud high pitched screams.

"All is lost!" Awlion tried to reason with her brother.

"No. it is not!" Ygueliav hugged her.

"We cannot hold them now!" Awlion was frightened as more warriors came out of the fortress beneath the banner of Moshdalayrrimich. She did not see Nsaat, but she knew he had to be close.

The battle had only begun and the sheer number of warriors Nsaat and Moshdalayrrimich sent toward them would soon turn the tide against the Trags. It wasn't long before the Harkies started to drop rocks on top of them. The Harkies were too high for Awlion to shoot them down as both Trag and Akrilla fell before the onslaught. Some turned into the forest only to be pursued and killed by the Bantongues.

Awlion knew they were trouble though she saw Ygueliav was too busy fighting to be aware of the danger. Thrun and Schill already retreated to the south gate with twenty Trag warriors looking for an escape. Another victory yell followed them as Bantongues rubbed their spindly legs together causing a terrible vibrating sound while echoing throughout the forest.

"Let's go!" Awlion pulled Ygueliav away from his blood lust which she could see in his eyes. Agraine followed as Haavorn and his mountain warriors formed a barrier to give them a chance to get away.

"Haavorn! We've lost! Follow us!" Ygueliav called to him.

Haavorn waved his axe in acknowledgement, but continued fighting. His Akrilla warriors started to sing an old Trag battle chant which seemed to unnerve the Valkyricks:

"mo sihiRo moot ef' oiResoaveyes
mo ar hioRo 'ef ba'oody ba'oody ba'oody
ll'y ba'oody mya' bao stody
mo'epN Wtioo T nRoimdy
ef' mo sihiRo moot ef' oiResoaveyes
mo ar hioRo ef' ba'oody ba'oody ba'oody"

They beat their breastplates with their battleaxes denting the silver armor as they chanted louder. The Valkyricks hesitated just enough for Haavorn and his warriors to slaughter three rows of Valkyricks. A hundred and fifty Trags had fled the fortress leaving another fifty trapped in a circle by Bantongues and Valkyrick warriors. There was nothing any of them could do as more Bantongues climbed over the walls. Awlion and Ygueliav ran until they reached the edge of clearing stopping only after hearing a shout of triumph pierce the air. Awlion looked back to see Moshdalayrrimich raise his banner inside the walls of Rabel Ain. She also noticed that no one was following them, not even the Harkies, who were still circling the fortress instead of watching them.

"Moshdalayrrimich has his victory." Ygueliav tried to catch his breath. "He won't bother to chase us now. Thank Jesuar!"

"Praise Jesuar for that." Awlion echoed her brother's praise.

"He now believes we cannot defeat them." Thrun slowed to a walk as he put his arm around Schill. "But at what a cost."

"We need to find as many warriors who survived as we can." Awlion was already thinking of the next battle.

"Those who survived will meet us as we planned." Ygueliav was unconcerned which troubled Awlion. "We've no time to grieve for there are even more hardships for the living."

"In good time we will meet again." Haavorn appeared behind them with only twelve Akrilla warriors following. "My scouts are already looking for the wounded and strays to bring to us."

"We are safe which is all that counts now." Schill hugged Agraine and tended her wound.

"Good." Agraine slammed her mace into the ground as she sat down next to Schill.

"A great victory!" Haavorn was elated, almost dancing in place as he shifted the three toes on each foot from side to side.

"Victory? We lost!" Awlion thought Haavorn had lost his mind.

"No, Haavorn is right." Ygueliav wrapped his arm around Awlion's shoulders. "Soon Moshdalayrrimich will leave Rabel Ain and we will rebuild it properly.

"How many warriors did we lose?" Thrun became more sober when reflecting on the battle.

"Less than a hundred by my count." Schill thought out loud. "If all went well, fifty of our brothers and sisters will join us soon."

"What do you mean?" Awlion didn't understand what was going on.

"I had no time to tell you of our plans." Ygueliav patiently explained. "You were leaving us so it wasn't important at the time. The fifty you thought were trapped in the fortress purposely placed themselves there to help our escape."

"And we left them to die." Awlion slammed her bow on the ground in frustration.

"No, there were four areas of the fortress whereby they could escape at any time." Ygueliav brushed her cheek with the back of his hand trying to calm her down. "We dug tunnels beneath the walls which only we knew about. They could use those tunnels at any time to get away."

"How many should have escaped." Agraine looked to her mother just as she started toward the path through the Dark Woods.

"Most of them." Schill was the most skilled on guessing outcomes. "Counting the five hundred we sent ahead and those will meet us later. We should with all those meeting us to over a thousand strong."

"Now what are talking about?" Awlion still felt uninformed.

"We knew we didn't have a chance." Ygueliav laughed before pausing to remember those he left behind. "So we asked for volunteers to stay and fight knowing it might mean death to all of us. None of us could go with us because if Moshdalayrrimich saw even one of us gone, he would know we were up to something."

"That's why there were no archers." Awlion realized then why Ygueliav never answered her question till now.

"One thing I made sure of was that no archer could stay." Ygueliav sighed. "They all wanted to stay and fight. We will have greater need of them later. Besides, sister, you made up for all of them. Such shooting….I had forgotten how well you handled a bow."

"What's next?" Awlion decided she needed to know everything. "No more surprises!"

"We find father and the others and our reunion will be complete!" Ygueliav saw Thrun building a fire and guessed they were staying for the night.

"And our final destination?" Awlion was becoming impatient with her brother.

"The Seven Fortresses before the come to fight us again." Agraine dumped a few Notherhen on the ground. Thrun immediately started to pluck the feathers and prepare them for the spit. Notherhen were plentiful and had beautiful singing voices and the tastiest meat in the forest.

"There is a war coming and not like what you saw here," Ygueliav continued beginning to feel hungry. "Everstream is in trouble not because of the alliance of Rhor, Nsaat and Moshdalayrrimich, but because they bring Mortarr and Zebrac to fight with them as spiritual leaders. Jesuar forgive me, but we sacrificed our warriors for purposes of deception. We want them to think we are weak and cowardly."

"We don't think Rhor and Nsaat want to be second in command." Agraine rammed a branch through the Notherhen before putting it on the spit. "They will soon turn against Moshdalayrrimich whom Mortarr is displeased with and favor Rhor who will soon turn from Zebrac. When they start fighting amongst themselves we will be their thorn in the side."

"We must remember Quardraille." Haavorn reminded them.

"The Black Prince, Quardraille, is as we are, only a nuisance." Thrun waved the thought away.

"We will ask for volunteers to be captured in order to feed Rhor and Moshdalayrrimich information against each other. "Ygueliav is still forming a plan for all possibilities."

"If that doesn't work, we will lay traps with Valkyrick lances and Bantongue spears." Thrun snapped up a leg of cooked Notherhen.

"And if that doesn't work my warriors and I will join Moshdalayrrimich." Haavorn set his double chin on the handle of his battleaxe. "We will, of course, denounce you as traitors."

"That's not funny." Awlion snapped back.

"I have no sense of humor as everyone well knows." Haavorn looked at her curiously. If we join them when the battle of the Seven Fortresses begins, we will be in the inner circle fighting our way outward. I will kill Moshdalayrrimich myself or die trying."

"The attempt should confuse them enough for us to make an impression upon them with our archers." Ygueliav winked at Awlion who was still angry.

"I am still not convinced that I should trust you." Awlion stared hard at Haavorn who stared back with almost a serene look.

"Then here is my battleaxe." Haavorn handed it to her before lying on the ground with arms outstretched. "Do what you will to me."

"I didn't say I wanted to kill you." Awlion pushed the battle axe away from her.

"If you cannot trust me, all may be lost." Haavorn now stared through her. "It would take only one hesitation to turn the battle against us."

"My father was confronted by an Akrilla who tried to kill him." Awlion saw Haavorn nod in agreement.

"That was Korallmykin." Haavorn was silent for a moment. "He had no honor or family. He met a just end, but I am not him."

"We'll see." Awlion was still not sure.

The camp quieted down with scouts in the trees and down the path each with a trumpet or shoulder horn to alert them if trouble were near. Awlion thought Thoos would stay away with so many Trags around. As she drifted into a deep sleep while a tender hand touched her hair. Then she thought she heard "Friend."

****

"Smoke! I see smoke!" Zelbiur pointed to the sky ahead of them.

"This is not good." Tiathan worried that he may have lost another son.

"I will go ahead." Outra abruptly left them as he usually did in these situations.

"I hear something coming our way." Zelbiur wasn't sure at first before he screamed "Bantongues!"

"Trags!" Zarr and Tenca stumbled over themselves trying to reverse direction.

"Don't let them get away!" Zelbiur was already chasing them down.

"Oh my! Oh my!" Zarr and Tenca repeated over and over as they were cornered by the group of Trags.

"Don't hurt us! We know Awlion Eiula of Quicksnatch!" Tenca blurted out hoping it would stop the onslaught of swords and spears that they were certain to come.

"Awlion?" Tiathan stopped in his tracks.

"Me, too! Me, too! I know her, too!" Zarr saw Tiathan's reaction.

"No honor in killing these cowards." Zelbiur turned around in disgust.

"No honor! That's right! No honor at all in killing us!" Zarr shrieked hoping that his whining would make them offer mercy.

"We're cowards, no question." Tenca tried to hide behind Zarr.

"What about Awlion?" Tiathan talked rapidly as he closed his eyes to imagine what she still looked like. He tipped his sword under the hairy chin of Tenca.

"We saw her at Rabel Ain and she was well." Tenca had tears dripping down his fangs.

"Until the fighting started." Zarr saw the angry look Tenca gave him and regretted saying anything.

"Who was there?" Tiathan turned his attention to Zarr.

"Moshdalayrrimich and his warriors attacked Rabel Ain." Tenca answered for Zarr.

"Nsaat and our brothers were there, too." Zarr could not keep quiet.

"Nsaat and Moshdalayrrimich are allies?" Zelbiur was shocked by this news.

"Yes." Zarr bowed his head.

"And you did not fight with them?" Tiathan took his sword from Tenca's neck.

"We escaped with our lives because we would not fight against Awlion or Ygueliav...." Zarr tried to explain.

"Ygueliav is alive?" Tiathan was happily surprised.

"Yes, and..." Tenca wanted to continue.

"We must hurry!" Tiathan waved the Trags forward.

"What about them?" Zelbiur wondered if they should take Zarr and Tenca with them.

"Leave them!" Tiathan barely escaped having Zarr and

Tenca grovel at his feet.

"Thank you!" Zarr was already running down the path from them.

"Thank you!" Tenca was fast behind him. "I told you we should have stayed where we were.

"Then let's get back there while we still can." Zarr disappeared up a large oak.

As Tiathan turned the last corner entering the clearing as smoke and flames from Rabel Ain greeted them. The battle was already over and Moshdalayrrimich had moved on. Tiathan's heart sank as he was sure that he had lost both a son and daughter to the Valkyricks. Revenge never entered his mind only deep sorrow. The tears and anger would come later as he fell to his knees and prayed:

> "Jesuar, all things are possible
> Please do not forsake me
> In this time of need.
> Help me to find peace,
> Give me direction,
> Show me the right path for justice.
> If I have lost more of my family
> That I cherish, I love,
> Help me to keep my wits
> For in all things you are Jesuar."

"Father, we must go on." Zelbiur helped Tiathan up. "We will have time for prayer later and I will even join you."

"No, we need to enter and know for sure." Tiathan marched to the north gates of Rabel Ain. What he saw were bodies of Trags, Akrillas, Bantongues, Harkies and Valkyricks scattered everywhere. No one bothered to bury them.

"We must take the time to bury our dead." Outra walked up from behind and was overwhelmed by the loss of life.

"We will bury all of them." Tiathan looked for Awlion and Ygueliav among the dead.

Tiathan looked hard, but was relieved that his son and daughter were not there. The burials took them into the next day when Tiathan led them all with an ancient Trag hymn:

"mo estihimdy W moomdyhiR W himo
A hia tieNes ephies'
esoono tieNes xoisivoR tiehim ootieoRes
hia ayefo r eshisiRody
hia dyohities ar moot oxoihia
ef' XoesoihiR mhimties oies t ayveyo
ad omxooll T baRohitie W oies yoimnes

T mymdy W oies ethiyR
ad T xooll ef' yooveyo tioonotieoR
mo esynm T otioRmhia esoomn
ef' met XoesoihiR hia r otioRmhia"

"Is this what Jesuar wills?" Carazaar walked up to Outra not understanding the slaughter that was before him. The mounds of dirt now hid a terrible battle.

"It's what we all will suffer when we do not follow Jesuar." Outra snapped at him. "Do you think Jesuar expects us to kill ourselves like this?"

"This is not the time to question the will of Jesuar." Tiathan quietly tapped Carazaar's shoulder.

"Is there a good time?" Carazaar wondered out loud.

"I have seen these warriors before." Tiathan watched as two Akrillas were found lying dead outside the walls. "A few of them tried to kill me at Flashfire Lake."

"Then it was treachery." Carazaar seemed certain without really knowing. "They must have been betrayed from inside."

"How so?" Outra was curious how Carazaar could know anything by looking at these two bodies.

"These were the only two outside the walls leading away to the forest." Carazaar determined the number of warriors found inside Rabel Ain. "Trag and Akrilla lay next to each oher on the south wall. The attack was on the north wall, but none were found amongst the Valkyricks. The south gates were opened intentionally and not forced open with three Akrilla at the base. The positions bear out my belief."

"True enough if it were true." Outra smiled.

"We then must follow the path where these two were found and perhaps we will meet up with Ygueliav." Tiathan was now hopeful. "Gather your things and make ready as our journey continues."

Within the hour, Tiathan led the small band back into the Dark Forest to find Ygueliav and Awlion. He hoped he would not run into Moshdalayrrimich and his army until as Jesuar wills.

****

The blare of a short trumpet awakened the camp as Harkies flew overhead and Valkyrick warriors thrashed toward the camp. Haavorn and his warriors were the first to charge toward the sound as Ygueliav gathered the others in a circle awaiting the first sign of attack. Agraine pulled Awlion away with her and seven Trag archers leaving twenty feet between and Ygueliav.

"We can do more harm from this distance than with

fighting with them." Agraine confided in her.

"If anyone comes behind them we can strike first." Awlion agreed.

The first wave of Valkyricks came from the north as Ygueliav valiantly fought them back. Bantongues started jumping from the trees on top of some of the Trags. Awlion set arrow to bow as arrows already flew into the Bantongues direction. There were too many to kill as the circle of Trags started to collapse. Awlion realized that they were in danger as the loud thrashing became clear to their left. She started to run with the seven archers and Agraine fast behind her. Agraine began to hesitate, but knew it was the right thing to do. Awlion looked back to see Ygueliav fall from a spear in his side. As they left the small clearing, they heard the trumpet of victory sound. A deep sadness enveloped Awlion as she cut her way through the underbrush hoping no one was chasing them. It was hours before they dared to slow down to a trot. Awlion had no idea where she was and looked to Agraine for help.

"How lost are we?" Awlion whispered to Agraine.

"Not lost at all, but we are being followed." Agraine hurried them along. "We can rejoin your brother or the others for a while."

"Who is following us?" Awlion glanced back without seeing anything.

"Bantongues…a small company." Agraine anxiously

twirled her mace. "We cannot hide in the trees or in the forest. Our only chance is in the Caves of Gander. I hope we're the only visitors there."

"Won't the Bantongues follow us in?" Awlion worried that without seeing or hearing anything they would not make it to the caves.

"We have seven of the best archers in Everstream." Agraine hesitated before smiling. "With you, Awlion, that makes eight. The caves are small enough for us with the entrance that would force the Bantongues enter one at a time. They will be no match for us."

"Won't they wait for us outside?" Awlion saw the flaw in the plan. "There is no food or water inside these caves unless you know differently."

"They will wait for us." Agraine seemed confident. "I know another way out so we'll leave two archers at the entrance while the rest of us escape. When we are clear, I will go back and get them. By the time the Bantongues realize what has happened, we will be long gone."

"I'm glad you are with us." Awlion was relieved that Agraine was with them. "Thank Jesuar that we met and travel together."

"Thank whomever you will. I just like the challenge." Agraine patted Awlion's shoulder before moving on.

"What of your father and mother?" Awlion was

concerned for them even though Agraine acted indifferently as to their whereabouts.

"I saw them escape and will meet up with them later." Agraine's face paled slightly. "I saw the Akrillas fight through to the forest carrying Ygueliav with them."

"I thought I saw him fall." Awlion relived the moment in her mind, but still could not be certain.

"Nsaat knows who he is and will not kill him." Agraine said matter-of-factly. "I just hope enough of our brothers and sisters escaped."

They started to run nonstop till the Caves of Gander were in view. Agraine had thought the Bantongues might guess where they heading and try to block them off. As they approached the caves, riddle with openings, no one confronted them. Awlion led them into one of the lower caves which slowly slanted upward. It gave an easy view of the entrance and outside clearing. The opening was smaller than Agraine remembered so it helped to relax her a great deal. Agraine ordered in two rows of four including Awlion so they could give a continued volley of arrows at the invaders.

"Now what?" Awlion found it easy to let Agraine make all the battle plans. She let her mind wander to other things like where her father might be.

"Now we wait." Agraine sat down next to her. "You have changed in the little time we have been together, Awlion."

"How so?" Awlion was surprised to hear this from Agraine since they had known each other such a short time.

"When we first met we were equals." Agraine stared hard into her eyes. "Now you seem weaker and I need your strength as much as you need mine. Where has the daughter of Tiathan Eiula gone?"

"I am here." Awlion said without conviction.

"I may not always be near you to make decisions for you." Agraine looked down for a moment. "You must lead if I should fall."

"Jesuar has need for both of us, so I will leave it in His hands." Awlion blurted out tired of having to lead when she wanted to follow. Two of the Trag warriors turned to stare at them. Their conversation was of food and battle until the name of Jesuar got their attention.

"Tell me of Jesuar." Agraine was serious needing to pass the time with something other than staring at the rock walls.

"It will take time to tell you of Him." Awlion did not usually hesitate to speak of Jesuar or even sing about Him, but she was unsure of Agraine's intentions.

"We have plenty of time." Agraine leaned back with her hands resting behind her back.

"Jesuar is not the spirit of the trees, but He created the trees." Awlion began to think out loud. "He is the Spirit of the Trags even though He is not only for us, but anyone who believes in Him. We worship Him at the Great Oak which is found in the center of Everstream. He speaks to us, lives amongst us and shows us the way through His Shroo, Outra Whorld."

"Outra Whorld?" Agraine was not familiar with the name. "How do you know Jesuar exists?"

"Jesuar led us out of Byabnol and slavery." Awlion remembered the time of enslavement. "A great lake blocked our way as Rhor and his warriors chased us down the mountainside onto the plains. My father prayed to Jesuar for a miracle which came all at once. The lake split in two so that we could cross over to the other side. A huge pillar of fire held Rhor's warriors at bay while we made our escape. We hesitated until a voice from above called out telling us to cross the dry land."

"Perhaps it was your father that spoke." Agraine tried to understand the event.

"This voice shook the ground beneath us encouraging us to cross over." Awlion's eyes glazed over as she remembered how her skin chilled when she heard Jesuar's voice. "When we finally reached the other side, we looked back as the Arbushi followed after us. Then the waters collapsed on top of them as the pillar of fire disappeared."

"We must talk more of this, but we have company outside." Agraine picked up her mace tapping it against the wall in thought.

"They're coming!" Awlion saw movement across the clearing.

The first Bantongue crept into the tunnel trying to adjust to the darkness when the first arrow hit him in the chest. He howled with anger and pain as two of those behind pulled their friend from the tunnel. There was quiet for a while and then a shriek that echoed up the tunnel. Three Bantongues charged into the opening one behind the other hoping to overcome the Trags. A flurry of arrows hit their mark as three lay dead blocking the entrance.

"We have our chance." Agraine ordered their retreat leaving two archers behind. "I will come back for you."

"We will stay no matter what happens." One of the archers, who was older than all of them, waved her away. His bushy eyebrows and spindled beard made him look ferocious. The second archer was not much younger and just shook his head in agreement seemingly bored with all the fuss.

"Come, come, the rest of you before they see us leave." Agraine led the others away into the back tunnels.

The caves shifted downward from small to large openings with Glittermoss to light the way. Its green shiny glow allowed them to easily run down the paths behind Agraine. Stilt Spiders ran and hid from the advancing company seeming to worry that they may be trampled upon. A distant light greeted them from afar as Agraine headed toward it. Soon they were outside on top of a mesa overlooking a vast valley below.

"Stay here until I come back." Agraine returned to the caves to bring back the two archers.

In the caves, Agraine hurried back to her friends only to find the Bantongues had overwhelmed them despite the five dead that clogged the cave opening. She turned to leave only to barely avoid a cave-in caused by three Bantongues that were hanging by silken cords attached to the ceiling. Their combined weight seemed to weaken walls causing them to fall. She pulled out her short sword and twirled her mace knowing she would not get far if she didn't stay and fight.

Tho-o-o-os!

"This way, friend!" Thoos waved her to a narrow hole in the rock to their left. It was just wide enough to squeeze through and keep the Bantongues from following.

"I'm too big!" Agraine was afraid she wouldn't get through fast enough as she heard the Bantongues struggling to regain their feet.

Tho-o-o-os!

Within seconds, Agraine felt a thump against her feet knocking her forward into the crevice. Just as she pulled her feet up toward her, Thoos held on for dear life as the jaws of the first Bantongue snapped shut. Agraine could feel the hot breath from the hole where the Bantongue strained to get to them.

"Safe now." Thoos was wide-eyed from fear.

"Thanks to you, Thoos." Agraine smiled at him. "You are a true warrior!"

"Help friend is all." Thoos beamed with pride.

"More than that." Agraine was sure Thoos was blushing.

"Go, go, before they come round." Thoos pushed her ahead.

When they escaped in to the larger tunnels, Thoos ran off up toward the light. Agraine found Awlion and the Trags sharpening branches into spears. Some were making more arrows with honed stones to replenish the ones that were used. Thoos sped past Awlion as Agraine emerged from the darkness.

"Thoos? Where are you going?" Awlion was startled as Thoos ran by without even a hello or good-bye.

"We must hurry." Agraine tried to catch her breath."

"Are they following us?" Awlion knew they had lost the two Trags seeing Agraine alone and on the run. The look in her eyes showed the sadness from the loss.

"We must get the river before nightfall." Agraine pushed them all forward. "There's an island in the center of it that will keep us safe. I call it the fortress of Theble which is a safe haven where I made plans and can think clearly."

Within seconds, they were lost in the Dark Forest hoping no one was following. Awlion prayed as Agraine watched the skies for Harkies seeing only clouds and falling leaves. Soon the forest covered the skies where even the Harkies could not see them.

＊＊＊＊＊＊＊＊＊＊＊＊

"This way!" Outra called out to Tiathan and Zelbiur.

"Another battle?" Tiathan was more fearful for them all now seeing Bantongues and Harkies alike hanging dead from the trees.

"Father? Over here!" Zelbiur leaned over a fallen Trag.

"Ygueliav! My son! My son!" Tiathan embraced him even though the blood covered Ygueliav's face and chest.

"It is not as bad as it seems." Ygueliav smiled through the pain. "Most of the blood you see is theirs not mine."

"And what of your sister?" Tiathan was afraid to look for her. There was no other sign of life except the soft breeze that filtered past them.

"She escaped with Agraine." Ygueliav remembered seeing them run through the forest before he fell. "They suffered more than we did. I ordered as many to flee as I could before something hit my head. With all the blood, I am sure they thought I was dead."

"Thanks be to Jesuar!" Tiathan hugged his son again.

"I hear someone…Bantongues! Moving quickly our way!" Zelbiur waved warriors to various positions waiting for the attack.

"Be ready!" Tiathan crouched over his son willing to die to protect him.

"Do not hurt us!" A low growl came from a darkened arch of trees.

"Then come forth without your weapons!" Zelbiur readied his sword wondering trick would come upon them.

"We are friends of Awlion." Zarr slowly crept out into the light.

"It is those cowards we met on the road." Zelbiur recognized Tenca as he followed his brother into the clearing.

"We are not cowards! We are just very cautious as anyone to fight out own kind." Tenca still found it hard to be called a coward.

"Hold! Hold!" Tiathan raised his arms so that no one started a fight.

"We will show you our loyalty if you wish." Zarr kept his distance from them all.

"How can you do that?" Zelbiur did not trust them.

"Another of your Trags saved our lives by simply giving us food and words of kindness." Tenca offered though he knew they might believe him. "We told you of her on the road to Rabel Ain."

"Awlion Eiula?" Tiathan sheathed his sword and approached them.

"We came to Rabel Ain because she asked us to, but

when we got there we found Nsaat and other of our kind were there, too." Zarr looked down at the ground.

"We had to run because we could not fight our brothers and sisters." Tenca almost whispered hoping there were no scouts listening to him.

"Why are you outcasts?" Outra knew they were telling the truth.

"Because we do not like the taste of Trag and…" Zarr shut his mouth knowing he had offended them.

"We aren't like those who follow Nsaat." Tenca changed the subject while prodding Zarr with his spur. He did not know if he could help them forget what his brother said.

"We were cast out of the House of Myrr because we refused to kill for the sake of killing. We were willing to serve Awlion and until we find her again we will serve you." Zarr shuffled his legs nervously as he spoke.

"We saw you running away." Zelbiur looked to Tiathan for help.

"We were running away before changing our minds knowing there would not be another chance to redeem ourselves." Tenca tried hard to look into Tiathan's eyes.

"We have a hard time believing you, but Jesuar will know your hearts." Tiathan glanced over at Outra who seemed to nod in agreement.

"I believe them." Outra was not his outspoken self which bothered Tiathan.

"What do you think?" Tiathan whispered to Outra.

"I have never seen such a thing, but we are in strange times." Outra thought if the Bantongues could help, he was for it.

"We must find Awlion." Zelbiur thrashed his sword at the ground in frustration.

"Someone help me up." Ygueliav struggled to rise.

"I can carry him." Zarr offered.

"No, we take care of our own." Zelbiur grimaced as Zarr came close.

"Are we that disgusting to you?" Zarr was hurt. "Even Awlion, your sister, embraced us as friends."

"Is this what Jesuar means to you?" Tenca realized he hit a nerve by mentioning the name of Jesuar.

"How dare you mention Jesuar!" Zelbiur stepped toward them. "You followed Nsaat and have been the terror of Everstream. You have laughed at us and Jesuar…" He could not continue in his rage.

"If you are able to mention the name of Jesuar without hatred, I will embrace you." Outra walked over and hugged them both.

"And so will I." Tiathan just patted their heads.

"What can you tell us about Awlion?" Outra came back to the matter in hand.

Tenca scampered over the edges of the makeshift camp

since now the Trags felt they were staying there for the night. Bantongues were known to be able to judge the way others have traveled by sniffing the air and listening intently. The Bantongues were a formidable enemy because the Trags knew it was almost impossible to hide from them.

"She escaped that way to the west, but there are some of my brothers following them." Tenca drew on the ground with his claw. "I know Rhor is miles behind us, Moshdalayrrimich is just ahead of us and Nsaat has parted from them and is north of us."

"What of the Akrillas?" Tiathan was anxious to know if there were more of the bow-legged warriors who would try and kill him.

"They have followed Moshdalayrrimich, but they were seen at Rabel Ain with those who fought there." Tenca saw the news distressed them all.

"They are two miles ahead of us, at least." Zarr stared into the distance.

"Zarr has better hearing and can guess better at distances than I can." Tenca almost smiled. "He's very good at it."

"We'll leave everyone here except Zelbiur and you three who will go with me." Tiathan pointed to the largest of the Trag warriors.

"You will move faster with fewer to follow you." Outra agreed.

"Carazaar! Stay and bind my son's wounds." Tiathan ordered the magician. "You will be safe here now that the fighting is over."

"I can help with his healing." Outra knelt down and prayed over Ygueliav.

"I thought you might stay." Tiathan was comforted to know that Outra would stay and help Ygueliav. "When he is healed, join us."

"I will find you." Outra nodded toward him.

"Good. Now we must go." Tiathan made sure that the lead warrior still carried Craxsmoore Guilding and then started to run in the direction where Awlion had supposedly fled. Zarr and Tenca looked at each other wondering what they could do before quietly disappearing into the forest.

****

Awlion and Agraine ran ahead of the other Trags, but made sure they kept in sight of each other. It was getting dark before they were able to feel safe and rest. Awlion pointed to a craggy knoll that seemed to overlook the valley as a place of safety. It too the small troop until sunset to reach the safest spot and build a fire. As they sat down they viewed an encampment at the bottom of the hill with fires burning and warriors setting up hovels for the night.

"Arbushi! Crush the fire!" Agraine whispered harshly motioning the other Trags to stay low to the ground.

"How do you know?" Awlion wasn't sure from such a distance to see who they were.

"The insignia on the far right against the wall of rock." Agraine pointed to the red pennant with a large "M" surrounded by flames. "Only the Arbushi carry such a banner and do not fear anyone who sees their camp."

"How can we get by them?" Awlion saw guards posted every twenty feet. She could feel the heat of the large flaming pyre near the middle of the camp. One by one the Arbushi warriors threw personal possessions into the flames.

"There are only seven of us o we must wait for the right time." Agraine watched as the fire rose above their heads. How the flames got so high it could only be their special magic. Slowly a vision appeared within the flames which turned slowly to face them.

"What is that?" Awlion looked in horror at the monstrous ghostly head. It was five Trags high with flaming red eyes, pointed snout and ears that seemed to drip blood. Its mouth moved, but there was only silence. "And why can I not hear its voice?"

"It is Mortarr. I have seen him before." Agraine suddenly smiled to herself. "Only those who worship him can hear his voice."

The Arbushi gathered closely around the fire as a great cheer arose from their throats. To their right an Arbushi warrior in full feathered cape, silver helmet and holding two ivory scepters stepped beneath Mortarr. The other warriors started to hum as they swayed back and forth.

"Who is that?" Awlion was impressed though angry with the way the pompous warrior strutted around the fire.

"That is Quardraille." Agraine was herself fascinated with the ceremony that was taking place.

All eyes were on Quardraille and Mortarr as they spoke silently to each other. Still Awlion could not get close enough to hear what they said between them. The Arbushi stopped humming as Mortarr turned to them speaking in silence while they cheered and beat their shields with swords. Soon Mortarr stopped speaking and the Arbushi began to sin strangely enough in the ancient Trag:

> "naoomn onbaoRes
> MooRtihiR'es estiRomntie
> boiRmN efaost
> histoes ef' eshivo
> ayestiom mhiR'aooR
> etogiR OO moll'
> MooRtihiR' esepohives
> esepyRyties dymoa'
> W dyhiRv veyhia'es'

netooesti sihivoes
tieooRm efooRoesties
ad Basiv ahivoes"

    The beating sound of the shields grew louder as the Arbushi started to march around the pyre. Quardraille could barely e heard as he spoke to the image of Mortarr. Neither Awlion, Agraine nor the other Trags could hear what he was saying, but the effect on the other warriors brought out a great cheer. They began to sing again with great vigor:

"dyhimsie t T baohiti 'ef dyohitie
T onbaoRes esmo'ti W efanN esmooRdyes
tiehiti Ryep ad Romdy t Romom oiR estiRomntie
epyoRsio oiR etohirties
noati oiR esoiaes
esoo mo nhill eso' MooRtihiR'
mo nyveyo oiR ba'oo'dy
mo eshisiRyefysio oiR efaost
esoo mo nhill eso' MooRtihiR'
Mhiti r etooayoR tiehim T ba'oo'dy
etti efaoomes ad estiohines Ep'om T epllRo
Moo sihim metesstihimdy

T nymdy ad vey'esyoom 'ef MooRtihiR'
mo ar 'ef oomo nymdy oomo efaost
omoo esepyRyti W T esoia 'ef MooRtihiR'"

"Why are you smiling?" Awlion knew whatever Agraine was thinking had to be dangerous.

"Want to have some fun?" Agraine pulled out a small packet of a black shiny powder.

"What is that?" Awlion had never seen it before.

"Something that might divert their attention or it might lead them right to us." Agraine tied to one of Awlion's arrows. "Send it into the heart of the flames and then watch the expression on Mortarr's face."

Awlion did as Agraine asked sending the arrow just below Mortarr's ghostly image. An explosion ripped the vision into shreds before it quickly pulled itself back together again. Mortarr's face and eyes wobbled uncontrollably before a pained look enveloped him. Soon warriors came from all directions to find the one who defiled the image of Mortarr.

"Should we run?" Awlion was already giggling.

"They have no idea where it came from so we are safe enough." Agraine kept her laughter as quiet as she could.

"You are dangerous!" Awlion whispered harshly.

"You shot the arrow." Agraine whispered back.

"Now we have to stay up all night." Awlion stayed low to the ground.

Quardraille was shouting commands and pointing in all directions to his guards who ran back and forth without a clue who they were looking for. Four Arbushi warriors ran past the spot underneath where Awlion and Agraine lay. Their black feathers bristled as they searched far away from them as the sound of their bony knees clicking together as they faded into the night. Awlion was startled seeing their elongated faces with bright orange beaks that stretched forward to see into the darkness ahead of them.

"I love doing that." Agraine tried to keep her laughter quiet.

"You do this often? You'll get us all killed." Awlion refused to leave her safe hiding place.

"Come on! It's our best chance to escape." Agraine whispered harshly to them all.

The other five Trags did not hesitate to follow her as Awlion hesitated for a second. When she was sure no Arbushi warrior was close Awlion followed the rest of them. It was too dark to really find their way, but it was better to run now than to fight the Arbushi.

"It is safer with her than being alone." The last Trag

ahead encouraged Awlion on.

"I suppose so." Awlion reluctantly raced in the darkness.

Chapter Five

Quickly! Into the forest!" Zelbiur heard someone coming knowing they weren't there to greet them.

As soon as they hit the ground, a company of Arbushi on black stallions raced by the troop. They were looking one way and then the other for something. Fortunately they did not slow down to look very hard or they would have seen Tiathan and Zelbiur crouched behind a small boulder. The three archers that followed Tiathan were all brothers of the clan called Acoulla. They spoke little except with the accuracy of their arrows.

"What do you suppose is going on?" Zelbiur watched the Arbushi ride by with the stallions frothing at the mouths.

"We're in the center of some trouble since I do not think they were looking for us." Tiathan hesitated going any further.

"I guess war is inevitable with all these warriors wandering around looking for a fight." Zelbiur listened intently until the sound of hooves disappeared.

"Is it safe?" Tiathan waited a few more seconds before

asking.

"They are well past us." Zelbiur stood up and nodded to the Acoulla brothers who just grunted that they were ready to move on.

"I'm sure Awlion is near, but whether captured or dead, I cannot tell." Tiathan thought out loud.

"We need to stay off the main path if we are to be safe." Zelbiur pointed to a grove of trees beyond the next turn.

"It is in Jesuar's hands now." Tiathan agreed to let Zelbiur lead them. "A quick prayer before we go forward."

> "ef' ti' ll'R mya'
> ti' r nll mya'
> oo XoesoihiR nll aooRdy."

Just as they entered the grove, two pairs of sad yellow eyes peered from the shadows watching them leave. Zelbiur stopped for a second, but heard nothing from the bushes. Without a sound, the two pair of sad eyes dropped to the ground and followed them though the shadows.

****

When Awlion and Agraine came to the river with the island in the center, Awlion was disappointed since there was no castle or fortification. She only saw a pile of logs and rocks overlooking the water's edge. A raft was tied to a heavy post to which Agraine led them. It was then a terrible howling echoed from the shadows of the dark woods behind them. Bantongues surged from the treetops throwing netted webs in their direction. One of the Trag archers was caught and dragged away into the darkness. His two brothers sent arrows into the shadows hitting their mark. The eldest Trag struggled back to the river's edge joining all of them on the raft. Awlion and Agraine untied the raft as the Acoulla brothers continued their barrage upon the Bantongues. Soon they were all furiously poling toward the island.

"Don't let them get away!" one of the Bantongues hissed, but it was already too late.

"Hurry! Hurry!" Awlion pushed as hard as she could.

"It's all right, Awlion. They can't swim." Agraine hoped they could not throw their webs this far. "We should be safe soon."

Tho-o-o-osh!

Thoos left a fantail of water as he ran across the river and landed on the island before they did. The Bantongues stomped their feet in anger and frustration as Thoos taunted them from the dry embankment. One of the Bantongues slipped into the water in his rage and quickly drowned beneath the water.

"Thoos! Good to see you!" Awlion opened her arms to

the Thistmock as she jumped off the raft.

"Bad things!" Awlion could feel Thoos heart pounding as he nestled in her arms.

"Thoos!" Agraine was pleased to see him, too, but she noticed that the Acoulla brothers were not happy to see him.

"Who they?" Thoos looked curiously at the brothers.

"What's the matter, Mikar?" Agraine looked to the elder Trag, a warrior with numerous scars on his body from long years of fighting. His bow was the only one carved in oak with the symbols of his adventures and was looked up to by all the Trags as the most noble of them all.

"I am not sure, my lady." Mikar always had a curious look on his face.

"He is our friend and ally." Agraine made the decision final.

"As you say, my lady." Mikar bowed slightly and the matter was settled.

Agraine looked over the island with a disturbed look. There was something missing or something added that she could not account for at the moment. The great logs were locked together with rope and cord while the stones were placed atop of each other to make a wall.

"We have company." Agraine was angry that her fortress had been invaded seeing a single torch lighting one of the openings.

"Shall we go downriver then?" Awlion saw the light now and wanted to avoid another fight if it could be possible.

"No, it is my fortress and I will take it back." Agraine almost shouted as she readied her mace and short sword for whatever might attack them.

"It is my fortress and I will take it back!" A familiar voice mocked her from the darkness.

"Father?" Agraine saw Thrun strut to the water's edge with his arm around Schill.

"Ho! Agraine! About time you showed up!" Thrun waved to her. "I see you brought some guests with you."

"I didn't think anyone knew about this place, but now everyone seems to know." Agraine watched as the Bantongues danced up and down.

"We knew of this place for many years, but allowed you to think it was your secret place." Schill enjoyed seeing the confusion on her daughter's face.

"I suggested that one day this would be a safe haven for all of us. So here we are." Thrun hugged Agraine who struggled to keep decorum in front of the other Trags. "They cannot reach us or they would have killed us already."

"Well, we have roast Notherhen and Berryl eggs for dinner with wild carrots and onions you planted awhile ago." Schill rubbed her hands together. "Good to see you again,

Awlion and ….Mikar!”

"It is good to see you, too." Mikar bowed.

"You and the others will sit with us at our modest table. There will be no ceremony here." Schill waved to the other Trags, but they did not wave back.

"You forget our station, my lady." Mikar hesitated to follow her. "We are unworthy."

"Not any longer, Mikar, for we are all the same in these times." Thrun walked over and embraced Mikar who felt more awkward now than ever.

"This will remind you of your station!" Schill embraced each of them. "If you insist on stations, I will hug you every time you remind of it. These are times we must be brothers and sisters or we will fail in our fight to save Everstream."

"As you wish, my lady." Mikar did not want to embarrass himself any further.

"I am not your lady, I am his." Schill put her arm around Thrun who then kissed her cheek. "I am Schill to all of you from now on."

"And I am Thrun." He made it clear that Mikar was to agree.

"We are as equal as you and as much as a warrior." Schill was dead serious. "If we bleed and die together we will find there is no difference between us before Jesuar."

"Pardon me, my…." Mikar could not bring himself to

call her by name.

"O-o-o-o-o! A Thistmock!" Schill was beside herself with glee. "I have only heard of one, but it is obvious what you are!"

"O-o-o-o!" Thoos mocked her as he peeked around Awlion's legs.

"Come here, little one." Schill wiggled her finger.

"Go away, big one." Thoos wiggled his finger the other way.

"What a funny creature." Schill was not offended, yet pouted a little. "Perhaps later."

"Perhaps never." Thoos whispered so only Awlion could hear him.

"Behave Thoos." Awlion chided him.

"She crush me." Thoos protested.

"Maybe not." Awlion teased him.

"You hug first." Thoos stuck his blue tongue out at Schill.

"Our meal is getting cold." Thrun ushered them into a covered thatched room where all of them could sit around a slab of slate with trunk cores as seats.

Awlion looked back to see a horde of Bantongues scampering this way and that on the far shore. No doubt they were looking for some way to get on the island. By morning others would be sure to come. The smell of Notherhen deterred her thoughts enough to try and enjoy the meal. Then some sleep would be needed for the long days ahead.

****

"Behind us!" Zelbiur heard warriors rushing toward them.

"Who is it?" Tiathan could not hear anything.

"Bantongues! Many Bantongues! I, also, hear water ahead of us." Zelbiur tried to form a plan on the run.

"We cannot make a stand here." Tiathan looked ahead of them. It would be easier if they had more warriors to make a stand.

As they neared the river and the ground became soft as sand, the footing became more difficult. A few feet more and a small eddy swirled make the sand into mud making it harder to walk. There were overhanging vines and moss which seemed to slap their faces as they moved forward.

"This is a good place." Tiathan saw the confused look on Zelbiur's face. "This mud will slow them down and the fighting will be to our advantage. These vines are not strong enough to accept their weight so no Bantongue could surprise us from above."

"They are strong enough for us so why not climb up and

let them pass by?" Zelbiur would rather hide from them since he could hear they were outnumbered.

Zelbiur was the first to grab a vine and started climbing. The rest followed without question tying spears, battleaxes, bows and arrows to their backs. The rustling of brush and slurping of feet put them on alert with weapons ready. Tiathan prayed to Jesuar for victory if they had to fight, but he really wanted them to move quickly by.

"I hope they are still alive." The lead Bantongue spoke loudly, obviously not knowing Tiathan and the others were above them. "Awlion, daughter of the great Tiathan Eiula, would be a great prize for Nsaat."

"Vaarok! Hurry your pace!" The lead Bantongue pushed on.

"I am, Sensak." Vaarok mumbled something else which no one could understand.

Sensak stopped, looking up at the tall vines that hung down. He let the others pass as he scanned upwards thinking what a good place for a trap. He could not see the Trags from the ground for if he could he would see four archers aiming their arrows at his heart. The other Trags readied their weapons at separate targets waiting for Tiathan to signal for the attack. Tiathan was confident that the seven Bantongues below them would continue on without a fight.

"Sensak! Stop daydreaming!" Vaarok stepped up the

pace.

When the sound of the Bantongues faded, Zelbiur nodded to Tiathan that the danger was over. They all slide down the vines back into the mud. They waited to make sure they were alone before venturing along the same path.

"We have to find Awlion." Zelbiur anxiously pressed his father.

"Then we need to follow Vaarok and Sensak if we are to find Awlion." Tiathan purposely kept Zelbiur from rushing ahead. "They might know where to look which we do not."

"It would be too much to bear if she is lost." Zelbiur was beside himself with worry. "There is only death waiting for us if we follow the Bantongues. They will only lead us to Nsaat."

"That may be true, but Jesuar bids us go on." Tiathan patted his son's back.

****

"Wake! Wake!" Thoos shook Awlion from her sleep as the sun rose over the river.

"Trouble?" Awlion looked around seeing the others still asleep.

"Look! Look!" Thoos pointed to the sky.

"Harkies!" Awlion turned to sound the alarm when the first rock crashed through the roof knocking over the makeshift parapet with the force pushing her into the water. Something hit her hard, but did not knock her out.

"Not safe!" Thoos hurried to her side seeing a bruise develop on her head.

"Help me, Thoos!" Awlion begged him worried that she might drown.

Awlion could hear the others wake up as Trag archers shot volley after volley of arrows into the sky. Thoos pulled her to safety as she finally blacked out the pain. When she awoke, Awlion found herself in a burrowed hole in the ground with Thip and Thump by her side.

"Thoos?" Awlion unsteadily looked around for him.

"Yes, friend?" Thoos was immediately by her side.
"I need a place to heal my wounds." Awlion felt the blood ooze from her wound.

"Safe now." Thoos stroked her hair. "Near Swamp of Modos, my home."

"How far from Agraine?" Awlion was concerned she might not see her again.

"Safe from Bantongues." Thoos answer only told her they were far away for she did not hear running water.

Awlion fought her desire to sleep for fear she might never wake up. The tunnel was cool and comfortable as she lay on a bed of leaves. Thoos hummed a tune she never heard before and helped her to relax. Soon she forgot the terror that lay behind her and passed the day in a dreamless maze.

****

"I hear sounds of battle!" Zelbiur hurried toward the river.

"There! There!" Tiathan pointed to the Harkies dropping large rocks on the island fortress.

"We must help them." Zelbiur hurried his warriors up the side banks until they were in position to shoot their own arrows.

"Look above!" Tiathan saw a few Bantongues ready to pounce on them.

The Trags changed position sending a flurry of arrows into the trees. Bantongues dropped to the ground and charged the group that now slammed the point of their shields into the ground forming a wall against the onslaught. Battleaxes and arrows relentlessly brought down the Bantongues who soon wearied of the bloodshed and retreated back into the forest. Zelbiur found a large raft and ordered the Trags onto it to cross the river. As they poled to the island, the Harkies flew off to the east leaving the skies clear. A loud cheer of triumph greeted Tiathan and the others as they reached the island shore. Agraine was the first to come to them with open arms.

"I am Agraine." She introduced herself to them.

"I am Tiathan Eiula and this Zelbiur Eiula, my son." Tiathan saw her stop short at the mention of his name.

"You are Awlion's father." Agraine was suddenly saddened.

"Is she here?" Tiathan was at once excited.

"No, she was lost when the battle started." Agraine stared down at the ground. "I thought I saw Thoos pull her to shore, but then the battle became fierce and I lost track of her."

"Thoos?" Zelbiur asked.

"He is a Thistmock, a friend." Agraine saw that he did not understand. "Come, we will talk about this in the fortress."

Thrun and Schill came out to greet added warriors to their plight. Thrun was already laughing when he saw Tiathan who was not sure what to make of it.

"Cousin Tiathan! Do you not remember me?" Thrun embraced his cousin.

"Thrun? I thought you were dead or at least thinner." Tiathan was pleased to see him, too.

"I probably am dead since you last told me it was over my dead body that you would ever see me again." Thrun reminded him of something he long forgot.

"I remember now, but it was forgiven ages ago." Tiathan wanted no arguments now.

"Too bad you forgot to tell me yourself." Thrun slapped his shoulder. "I have a companion now. This is Schill who will also never forgive you for not telling me."

"If it is not truly forgotten I can make a bad meal as well as good one." Schill winked at him.

"It is forgotten and I beg your forgiveness for being myself." Tiathan smiled as he hugged Schill.

"We still have some Notherhen from last night if you are hungry." Schill offered the meat from a roaring fire.

"We will eat you out of trunk and fortress." Zelbiur chimed up as he passed them all toward the makeshift hall to start to devour anything still edible.

Now there were twenty warriors besides Thrun, Schill, Agraine, Tiathan and Zelbiur. The silence that followed from the forest was deafening as they ate and drank without a word passing between them.

"We keep missing Awlion." Tiathan finally took a deep breath before downing the rest of his scorched Notherhen drum stick. "It is as if Jesuar wants us apart."

"I doubt that, but we will eat before we look for her together." Thrun was happy to have his cousin by his side again after so many years.

"Tiathan Eiula!" A harsh voice echoed into the hall.

"Who is that?" Thrun was the first one to stand with sword in hand.

"Tiathan Eiula! Come forth!" The harsh voice repeated. Tiathan looked out to see a horde of Harkies standing with their claws holding a few of the Trags. One lone Harkie circled overhead waiting for Tiathan to answer him. Tiathan looked for the Trag that carried Craxsmoore Guilding, but he was nowhere in sight.

"Tiathan Eiula we must speak together!" The lead Harkie dropped down to the ground.

"If you come in truce, let my warriors go." Tiathan put down his broadsword. At this, the Harkie seemed to relax gesturing to his warriors to let the Trags go.

"I must speak with you alone." The Harkie's talons scraped across the stones as he approached Tiathan.

"Father?" Zelbiur wanted to protect his father.

"It is well." Tiathan waved him away.

"Very well not to draw your sword." The Harkie folded his leathery wings neatly behind him. He eyed Thrun and Schill who stood ready to defend Tiathan if need be.

"You know me, but I don't know you." Tiathan followed him to a far corner of the island.

"I am Srrahn, Captain of Nsaat's flying guard." As Srrahn bowed, his skin crinkled as the leathery folds rubbed against his wings.

"What news can you bring that would not mean our death?" Tiathan did not trust Srrahn at all.

"Like you, I choose honor through death in battle." Srrahn tried to persuade Tiathan of his sincerity. "Treachery has no honor much like Moshdalayrrimich whom we fight for at this time. This is a different matter that concerns your daughter, Awlion."

"Awlion? Have you captured her?" Tiathan caught himself reaching for a sword that he left behind.

"Very wise to have left your sword behind." Srrahn did not miss the movement. "I could lie and tell you we have her, but that is not honorable. Alas, no, she is near the Swamp of Modos. Some strange creature carried her off to his lair. We will find her soon enough. However, I will call of my scouts if you will surrender to us now. I will, also…." He looked toward Thrun and Schill. "….spare the lives of your friends for now."

"Never! As long as you don't have Awlion there is a chance she will escape your scouts." Tiathan stepped away from him.

"As you wish." Srrahn spread his wings and drifted a few feet away. "I am impressed, Tiathan Eiula, for you are the mighty warrior we have heard about. You are the great leader of the Trags and I would have been disappointed if you gave up so easily. I salute you even at the hour of your death. A worthy opponent."

Srrahn flew off to rejoin his company. Tiathan assumed

they would attack at once, but they all flew to the south. Thrun searched the riverbank for Bantongues or worse, Valkyricks, without seeing a single warrior. Whatever they were up to it would not happen directly.

"Strange that they would leave us alone like this." Thrun anxiously broke the silence.

"Where is Craxsmoore Guilding?" Tiathan looked for the Trag that held his weapon. Through the rocks the Trag came and offered the weapon to him.

"We are not alone." Zelbiur listened intently. "We have a large number of warriors coming our way. Some on horseback and others were scurrying through the trees."

"We must prepare for another battle." Agraine picked up shields and passed them out.

"Now we wait." Thrun sat down and drank a mug of brown Schew, a bitter syrupy liquid that, at first, revives the sense before drinking too much will cause one to pass out.

****

"Oh my!" Awlion thought she was hallucinating when she crept up the opening of the home of Thoos seeing strange creatures poke their heads above the dirty water. Some were out of the old books of Quicksnatch that portrayed long snouted eels with sharp teeth and three-pronged tongues that dripped poison into the waters around them.

"Stay from water. Will be safe." Thoos urged her back into his home.

"We need to get out of here, Thoos." Awlion still felt the bump on her head, but was aware of the danger they were in.

"Not safe." Thoos refused to budge.

"We cannot stay here." Awlion was just as stubborn. "Our friends… my family are looking for us."

"Then we go." Thoos was not happy yet wanted Awlion to be happy.

Thoos rushed her off to the left of the swamp where the great creatures hissed and bellowed, but did not follow them. In the muddy areas of the swamp were giant Brardor Slugs that her father told her he encountered when they escaped to Quicksnatch. Obviously, an arrow wouldn't stop them and their slowness made it difficult to capture anything.

Awlion was relieved to see the creatures were more intent on fighting each other than her. Soon Thoos had her on solid ground as she wept prayers to Jesuar for her good fortune. She prayed thanks and prayed for those lives lost trying to protect her.

"Where does this path lead?" Awlion saw only one road that lead from the swamp.

"To Byabnol." Thoos shivered at the thought of going

there. "And to Modos."

"Bad?" Awlion noticed her friend's apprehension. "Neither place is safe for us?"

"Quardraille." Thoos whispered. "Black Prince! Byabnol!"

"Take me around them both if you can, Thoos." Awlion wanted to get back to Ygueliav and Agraine as fast as possible.

"Dangerous, friend." Thoos was reluctant to continue.

"I know, friend." Awlion patted his head while urging him on. "If I'm captured you must find my father or Agraine to tell them where I am."

"I will." Thoos was saddened with the thought of losing her.

"Jesuar, protect us." Awlion shouldered her bow and quiver before drawing her dagger as they walked into the shadows of the Dark Forest.

It took a few days before they came within sight of the fortress of Byabnol. The stones were black as night with no sentries posted on the walls. Death stalked this place and Awlion wanted no part of it. All life had been sucked out of the trees and brush. So many burned out pyres seared the ground between them and the forest. Thoos shivered again at the sight.

"Must cross." Thoos pointed over to the stone path leading to a wooden bridge.

"I hope no one is watching." Awlion leapt up to a run as Thoos sped ahead of her to the other side of the bridge.

Immediately, an arrow flare soared into the evening sky as the drawbridge over the moat creaked open. Riders could be heard crossing over toward them as Awlion steadied her bow using a small log as protection. There was no chance for her survive this encounter, but she will take as many of the Arbushi as she could.

"Over here!" Thoos cried out to the galloping black stallions with fiery nostrils flaring. Then from behind the riders was heard "Over here!" Then from the right and the left were the same words confusing them all wondering which way to go. It sounded like a company of Trags had surrounded them.

The Arbushi stopped and stumbled upon one another as they searched in vain for the sources of these voices. It was then that Awlion's first arrow struck the lead rider. A second arrow found the heart of another which made more confusion.

"Ambush!" It was all Awlion heard before melting into the underbrush trying to find as much space as she could from Byabnol.

More riders came forth from the black mouth of Byabnol led by a great spectacle of a warrior with a red plume on his helmet framed by a flowing red and black cape. The Arbushi split up into threes and fours searching the outer brush and oak looking for anyone who did not belong there. A victorious cry from one warrior to another informed the warriors that there was only one enemy and they had found his trail.

"Thoos! It won't be long before they find me." Awlion saw him a few feet from herself. "You must go and find my father to tell him what has happened to me. If they don't kill me, watch where they imprison me. Don't try to help me by yourself!"

"Help, friend." Thoos wanted to stay.

Awlion advanced toward Thoos and pushed him aside. Three Arbushi nearly trampled Thoos as they rode to capture Awlion. The Thistmock was of no importance to the Arbushi and would rather ride over him as to look at him.

"Here! Here!" An Arbushi warrior leaned a double-pronged sword against her chest. "Surrender or you will surely die!" Thoos had already left without being seen which relieved Awlion a great deal. It was obvious that they would not kill her directly.

"Being outnumbered, I'll always surrender." Awlion dropped her weapons looking to make sure Thoos was really away.

"A female Trag! How insulting! The great warrior with the plume stood over her. "Do you know who I am, Trag?"

"You must be the great Quardraille." Awlion defiantly placed her hands on her hips.

"Ha! Brave are we?" Quardraille enjoyed her false bravado. He could smell the fear that was surrounding her however faint.

"She's mine, Quardraille." The warrior who found her spoke up.

"No, Elvoorn, this is the daughter of Tiathan Eiula." Quardraille listened to the others gasp in wonder.

"Then she must die!" A second warrior drew his sword.

"No, Achothorn! It is for Quardraille to decide." Elvoorn threw a noose around Awlion's neck and led her away into Byabnol.

Thoos watched from afar before quietly following them to the gates of Byabnol. He couldn't see where they were taking her as the drawbridge was being taken up. He did know that she was alive and guessed she would be taken to the center of the fortress where she would be imprisoned. Thoos headed east hoping to run into someone he knew before it was too late.

****

The silence was deafening just before the first rock crashed through the overhanging trees that protected the band of Trags. Tiathan looked up into the sky seeing none of the Harkies that were there before. Agraine gazed over to the shoreline finding three great catapults lined up with Valkyrick and

Bantongue warriors. Thrun's archers could not reach the shore with their arrows as the Valkyricks taunted them from afar.

"We must escape!" Thrun knew they would soon be crushed or captured.

"How? Where?" Tiathan was all for leaving the place as another stone crushed the table that eat from.

"Grab what weapons you can and follow me!" Agraine realized she knew more about the fortress than her father.

"They will see us if we leave." Thrun held her back.

"No, they won't." Agraine pushed over a great oak trunk seemingly bolted to the floor. An open hatch greeted them with a ladder leading beneath the ground.

"I should have known." Thrun grunted wondering how he missed it.

"It leads to a tunnel beneath the river and to the opposite shore." Agraine tried to hurry them on. "I dug most of this myself using brick and timber to shore it up, but it still leaks. We will be safe enough for I have used it many times to get here and back."Agraine led them all out just as the timber behind them fell from flying stones. Glancing back, Tiathan saw makeshift rafts with Valkyrick warriors approaching the island. With a sturdy tug of a rope, he pulled the oak trunk over the hole which would keep their escape safe for a while.

"The Bantongues are heading for the bridge down the river." Agraine pointed ti the black silhouettes scurrying in and out of the forest.

"We must stay together." Thrun insisted on keeping them close. "We need as much distance as possible to stay alive."

"I think we should split up in case of a trap so half of us can save the others if we are captured." Tiathan disagreed. "Some of us must escape to warn the others."

"We need scouts to be sure what lies ahead of us." Agraine added to the confusion she felt.

"We only need one to lead us." Schill interrupted them all. "And I think it should be our cousin, Tiathan Eiula."

"Why him?" Thrun was stunned that she would name Tiathan instead of him.

"Because he has fought more battles than any of us and won." Schill then began to smile. "Besides, if he leads us into a trap we will have him to blame and not you."

"I have been in that place before." Tiathan was not sure how to accept the challenge. "If someone must lead and take the blame, I will do so. I agree with Agraine that we need scouts and now what lies ahead."

"I will take three warriors with me." Agraine already picked three of the fleetest of foot to join her.
"I am not sure we should split up either, Thrun." Tiathan rethought his earlier decision. "I had hoped it would save some of us, but it might also destroy us all."

"I am sorry, cousin." Thrun apologized. "It was vanity

that wanted me to lead. You have the experience much more than I."

"I hope, cousin, you do not ever share that same fate. Experience of this kind only brings nightmares at night." Tiathan ordered the company of Trags forward to a clearing ordering them into a circle. "I know some of you do not believe in Jesuar, but I do. We will certainly fail without His help so if you follow me hear my prayer and hear His voice:"

"oo VN 'ef oveyoRestiRohin
XoesoihiR nll aooRdy ad nhiestioR
epRootiositi OO W tieyes oveyya etoi'R
y epRhill moot ef' vey'sitiooRll
bati 'ef oiR esoiRvey'veyhia
iet's Moo dyoo moot ba'veyo
nyveyo tnn' ba'ef
stoom tn' ll' ar oiR epRootiositiooR
ad aooRdy 'ef hia
ll' eshill y hin
ad y imesmoR XoesoihiR"

As they started to march west, the sound of thunder rumbled in the distance. The wind picked up around the company of Trag, but not on or through them. The trees swayed violently as dark clouds passed over them. Tiathan could see Harkies struggling against the wind before losing the battle and plummeting to the ground. Cries of pain and anguish could be heard around them as Bantongue and Valkyrick warriors fell back against the wind. Some who tried to stand their ground were shoved backward and impaled by tree and branch. From the sky came a great voice was heard:

> "esoo ll' vmoom y hin aooRdy
> 'ef oveyoRst'Rohin
> ad etoom y himesmoar T epRhilloRes
> 'Ef iet's Moon y aooveyo"

Thrun, Agraine, Schill and the Trags from Rabel Ain wept, kneeling down on the ground upon hearing Jesuar's voice. All of them trembled as they asked for Jesuar's forgiveness in their disbelief now faith renewed, now faith restored. The storm stopped and the wind subsided as the sun emerged overhead.

"Jesuar is pleased that you have heard His voice." Outra Whorld ventured out from the forest.

"Outra? What happened?" Tiathan knew seeing him by himself could not be good news. "Where are the others?"

"What news of my brother?" Zelbiur was still watching the skies, hoping not to see any Harkies flying overhead.

"Carazaar and the others have been captured." Outra

came to the point quickly.

"Who has them?" Tiathan knew it didn't matter, but he wanted to hear who it was.

"Moshdalayrrimich." Outra saw a tear in Tiathan's eyes. "But he wants you more than he wants to kill them."

"What shall we do?" Thrun approached them.

"When you face Moshdalayrrimich remember these words." Outra placed his hands on Tiathan's forehead:

"hia tieNes noiestie himesmoar t XoesoihiR
MotieoR ovey'a ooR noo'dy
moo'mo sihim dyoefohiet T himoomtiody
ef' ties etoi'R ll'R esoia r RokvoiyRody"

"His answer will be as has been foretold." Outra continued.

"nll himesmoar r ties
y hin moytieoR mooR noody
mootieN sihim dyoefohiti N
moot XoesoihiR ooR ll'"

"And you shall reply." Outra lifted his hand from Tiathan's forehead.

"tieom aoti XoessoihiR dyosiydyo
ad ll'R m'm epRydyo dyoiestiRooll ll'R"

"I know that there must be more meaning to this than the words you want me to repeat." Tiathan now knew that he would live long enough to meet Moshdalayrrimich face to face. "When Moshdalayrrimich and I meet again it will be the beginning of the end of the Seven Fortresses. I saw it as you held you held your hand to my forehead."

"It was not meant for you to know anything, but the future is itself and what you saw was what you wished for not what Jesuar has foretold." Outra cautioned Tiathan about interpreting visions.

"We are in a time of illusions with crystals that change visions of the anointed and the unenlightened." Outra spoke to them all now. "What you see may not be what it is and your enemy will look like your friend."

"We must have a sign or word to know each other." Zelbiur worried he might be deceived by the powers of Mortarr. "I've heard of strange visions coming from Mortarr that surround fortresses like Byabnol and even around the Seven Fortresses."

"I agree." Outra thought quickly. "For me ask 'When shall the dead arise?' and I will answer 'When all life dies.' No other answer, no matter how close, shall be accepted. You must strike the vision quickly before it reaches out to you or you wil certainly die."

"Jesuar be with us all." Tiathan bowed his head.

"And with you, Ioroarka." Outra embraced him. "Tell no one what I have told you, not even your family."

"I understand." Tiathan turned to Zelbiur and called him over.

"Jesuar calls me and I must return to the Great Oak." Outra raised his hand in blessing. "We'll meet again, but I don't know when. As Jesuar wills."

"Farewell." Tiathan gave the order for the Trags to move west. Zelbiur looked back for a moment only to see that Outra had already vanished into the forest.

"Where are we going, Father?" Zelbiur was concerned realizing the direction they were heading.

"We have no choice but to pass Byabnol." Tiathan saw the worried look on Zelbiur's face. "Awlion may have passed that way and then she might be their prisoner. We must find out."

****

Awlion had one small window overlooking the courtyards of Byabnol. There was a flurry of activity as catapults were being put in place, heavy logs buttressed oak panels that led from courtyard to courtyard and Arbushi warriors used short swords to cut sharp points on oak branches. These pikes were placed in open pits with bamboo and brush used to cover the top. One guard stood nearby to keep anyone from falling in by accident. In a far corner an Arbushi with great black plumes upon his helmet handed out small cylindrical objects to warriors with leather pouches.

"Have you noted our strengths and weaknesses yet?" Quardraille stood in the doorway of her cell.

"What good would that do if you plan to kill me?" Awlion was in awe of the Arbushi Captain despite her revulsion of the vulture warrior that stood before her.

Quardraille stood three Trags high with shiny feathers protruding from his silver and gold breastplate. A red and black cape covered his bony shoulders with a gold battle skirt enveloping his waist. She could see various weapons of war imprinted on each plate.

"You were captured not to be killed, but for bargaining." Quardraille almost smiled even though it would have cracked his orange neb with the effort.

"Bargaining?" Awlion knew what he meant even as she asked the question.

"The daughter of Tiathan Eiula should know what we bargain for." Quardraille's voice soured as he towered over her.

"He would not give himself up even for me." Awlion stared straight into his narrowly slit eyes seeing the red flames that sparkled within them. As she stared at Quardraille, the Captain relaxed and even laughed.

"Your family is to be honored." Quardraille paced back and forth with a look of admiration toward her. "You do not fear me. Even my warriors tremble before me, but you do not. I am truly honored, Awlion Eiula. Your father would be proud."

"If you insist on flattering me, do so while letting me go." Awlion did not know what to make of this new problem. Was Quardraille insane or just trying to confuse her?

"Ha! We are about to defend our fortress from Rhor and his pathetic army." Quardraille thoughtfully measured her reaction. "If you give me your word not to turn against us, I will allow you to fight by our side. If you do so, this is my word, I will release you. Of course, we would have to win the battle."

"Why is Rhor attacking you?" Awlion thought they were all allies.

"He has allied himself to the Gimgiddeans with at least two hundred Valkyricks who have followed him throughout Everstream." Quardraille was now serious. "There is no loyalty to one's own clan or to even Mortarr. Rhor is gaining strength and I fear he might even defeat us. I do not know how this involves Moshdalayrrimich, but we are pure and unified, allied to no one. We are under siege and will ask for Mortarr to defeat our enemies and protect us in our faith."

"Why would you release me?" Awlion realized that with Quardraille giving his word only meant how serious the situation was. Her father had to be warned, but only if she could escape Byabnol.

"Because you are right." Quardraille saw the surprised look on her face. "Tiathan Eiula would not surrender himself even for you. On your honor and mine, do we have a pact?"

"I am only one warrior so why do you need me?" Awlion still did not trust him.

"Moshdalayrrimich and Rhor will soon be our enemies." Quardraille looked out over the courtyard below. "They wish to conquer all of Everstream and I do not. I do have the warriors to even try."

"That is not entirely true." Awlion looked out with him. "If you defeat Rhor, would you not rethink taking Everstream by your sword?"

"Rhor is a fool where Moshdalayrrimich is not." Quardraille was becoming impatient with her. "I know of your ability with bow and arrow. Now I ask you again if you will fight for us?"

"Then I will give you my word as long as you keep yours." Awlion thought it better to be free and armed with Quardraille than be imprisoned in this tower. If Rhor should take the fortress she could still defend herself out in the open.

"My Captain, I have brought them to the courtyard as

you have ordered." Elvoorn bowed to him.

Quardraille led Awlion down the stairs to the front courtyard where a company of Arbushi awaited his command. Awlion saw they were standing in front of someone she could not see till they stepped aside. She was stunned to see Zarr and Tenca staring down at the ground before her.

"If it were not for these two, we would have not known your father is coming here to save you." Elvoorn was pleased to tell her.

"You ugly Wrathoads!" Awlion struggled to keep her anger down, but could not.

"They did you and me a favor." Quardraille tried to calm her down. "Now Rhor must worry about Trags that march from the east."

"You see, master, we have told you the truth." Tenca groveled before him.

"True enough!" Quardraille became impatient with them.

"Anything else we can do for you, master?" Zarr tried to get into Quardraille's good graces.

"Get away from me!" Quardraille waved them away. "Come Awlion, I have much to show you."

"What is it that you want from me?" She glared at Zarr and Tenca who looked at her strangely.

"Nothing now, except your help to defend the fortress."

Quardraille took her by the black-plumed warrior that was handing out round objects to other Arbushi. "Your father is of little importance until after the first battle."

"What are those?" Awlion did not want to talk about her father.

"These we call billets." Quardraille took one holding it up to Awlion so she could see it. "It is our own private joke. It is to send a loud and clear message that we will not tolerate invaders in our land."

"And these?" Awlion pointed to the curled black sticks lying on the ground.

"Those are hummers." Quardraille didn't bother to pick one up. "When you throw them they hum through the air before exploding."

"Tie one to my arrow." Awlion took her bow and arrow from a guard who carried them behind her.

"Do it." Quardraille nodded to the guard before encouraging Awlion up the stone steps to the parapet overlooking the clearing outside.

By the time Quardraille and Awlion reached the wall, Rhor had entered the clearing with his army carrying multi-colored flags and banners. Awlion could hear their drums and trumpets echoing around them with more pomp and ceremony than she had ever seen before.

"I love music before battle because it usually is up to me

to silence it." Quardraille's eyes sparkled as he gazed upon the forces against him.

"Elvoorn!" Quardraille called up one of his officers.

"Yes, my Captain!" Elvoorn stood beside him.

"Go, speak with them." Quardraille pointed to Rhor and his warriors.

"You do not seem worried." Awlion saw two or three thousand Gimgiddeans marching into position along the north wall.

Quardraille ignored her as Elvoorn rode out to speak with Rhor. For a few minutes Awlion could see Rhor waving his arms in anger. Before Elvoorn returned to the drawbridge, two arrows struck him in the back which pierced his armor.

"Elvoorn!" Quardraille jumped off the parapet and spreading our his wings, glided down to the ground with dagger in hand.

"They are advancing!" Awlion screamed, but no one listened to her.

"Mortarr!" Quardraille screamed in anguish.

"They are still finding their positions." Achothorn corrected Awlion.

Awlion sprinted down the stone stairs to stand near Quardraille. All the Trag tales she had heard of the Arbushi was only partly true since she still lived for the day. The Arbushi were not soulless beings, but seem to care about each other.

"Mortarr! If only I had the gift of life you possess I would use it now!" Quardraille wept for Elvoorn as the Arbushi around him watch him die.

All work stopped as some of the Arbushi started to sing in mourning:

"mo mya' no'ti hinhiym
baolloomdy dyohitie bahiti'aoefo'ady
Mom T ahiesti mhiR r efoi'netti
Mom T ahiesti dyRooep 'ef ba'o'dy
esoohives ymtioo T nRoi'mdy"

"I would give up everything to bring back our brother." Quardraille started to build a funeral pyre even though the battle was eminent. "Mortarr! Free me! You can have all of me, my soul, my body, my mind for the Gift of Life!"

"Only Jesuar has the Gift of Life!" Awlion was surprised to hear Quardraille beg for something that he could possibly have to possess.

"Mortarr has as much power to give the Gift of Life as ….Jesuar." Quardraille found it hard to mention Jesuar's name. He answered without thinking or caring.

The pyre in the middle of the courtyard sparked itself into flames as other warriors added brush and branch to build it higher. As the flames reached the height of the outside walls,

Elvoorn was placed in the center and consumed into ash. The Gimgiddeans hesitated as they saw Mortarr's face appear above the walls and seemed to speak to Quardraille. The Captain of the Arbushi was transfixed until he stepped into the flames himself. While Arbushi warriors screamed in rage and awe, Awlion stared into the flames beginning to see two images standing up and walking forward. It was Quardraille and Elvoorn!

"Jesuar! What is to become of us?" Awlion knew that Quardraille had given over his life and soul. What kind of creature would he be now that he has been blessed by Mortarr?

"Bow to Mortarr the Invincible!" Quardraille's eyes were aflame with anger and hate.

"Jesuar! Save me!" Awlion saw the change in him. No longer was he going to be a reasonable ruler and probably would not now keep his word to her.

"Speak not that name in my presence again!" Quardraille pointed at her with his dagger. "Take to the walls and be not afraid! If you fall, I will raise you up again. Our army will not suffer loss this day or any other day."

"What of our bargain?" Awlion had to know if everything had changed now.

"Despite the change…my new power…" Quardraille struggled with the words. "I must keep…my word."

"Thank you, Captain." Awlion thought it best to be humble and bowed to him.

"Do not be thankful for we will meet again and I will eventually kill you myself." Quardraille fought hard to keep his old self, but was losing fast.

The first volley of arrows found their mark as six Arbushi fell to the ground. Quardraille quickly pulled out the arrows and healed them instantly as he thanked Mortarr for the power. Rhor sent his warriors toward the walls and were greeted with billets exploding around them.

"Elvoorn, give me three of those hummers." Awlion saw the look of anger in his face. "Please?"

"Give them to her?" Quardraille ordered him.

"Watch this." Awlion tied the hummers to three arrows which shifted the weight in her hands. She took aim and released each one into the midst of the Gimgiddeans.

Rhor watched as his warriors fell from the barrage, yet there didn't seem to be a single Arbushi falling.

He rode closer to see how it could be possible for this to happen. He could not get close enough. His warriors were trying to scale the walls only to be forced back,

"What magic is this?" Rhor was afraid knowing that his army could perish without even breaching the walls.

"He seems to raise the dead and they fight all the harder because of it!" An escaping Gimgiddean told Rhor. "We cannot pierce their armor..."

"Are you mad?" Rhor pushed him away. Whatever it

was, he knew he would have to retreat. "We have the strength of Zebrac with us! Attack! Attack!"

The Gimgiddeans stopped short seeing the image of Mortarr rising over the fortress. When the vision started to move toward them, the Gimgiddeans retreated back to Rhor. Rhor had lost many warriors while the Arbushi were at full strength. It was not a hard decision for Rhor to retreat with most of his army already hiding in the forest.

"Shall we follow them, Captain?" Elvoorn was ready to go.

"We have the advantage!" Acothorn was already mounting his stallion.

"No, this is not the time." Quardraille looked to Mortarr's image and bowed down to it as the image spoke silently to him. He stood up and addressed the Arbushi. "We have long enough to prepare for our day that is to come. Be patient for now."

"Jesuar, what is to happen to me now?" Awlion knelt in prayer.

"What did I say about mentioning its name?" Quardraille almost spit fire at her. The heat of his breath soured upon her face as she felt the calming Spirit of Jesuar came upon her as she spoke:

"ll' eshisiRyefysio t dyonoomes

Mysiet ar moot XoesoihiR
noomestiR'es moot vmoom'
noo,estiR'es etti ar ynhines'
noomestiR'es ll'R efhitieR'es
dy'dy moot efohiR
ll' ethiveyo dyoesRtiody XoesoihiR
ll' ethiveyo efooRnooti XoesoihiR
Moo nhiveyo ll' bayRtie"

Quardraille struggled not to answer, but found it impossible to stay quiet:

"hi efyRo ethies bao'm vymdyaody
ball NooRtihiR'es mRhitie
oomo etti baoiRmes ba'oom
t dyoveyoi'R oveyoRst'Rohin
ad esoti efyRo t T noi'mtihiames
nll hiR'oomes mya' bao hinhiymst'
efhinymo mya' Rohiep ll'R lloi'mn"

Quardraille appeared to be relieved to finish until Awlion responded to his words, words inspired by Jesuar:

"ba'veyo ties etti XoesoihiR r T oomo

ad moo ootieoR mya' ooveyoRtihivo etyn
et' mya' epoiti dyohitie
NooRtihiR' ooR himll ootieoR
etti sthiRepom T efahistN esmoordy
Mysihi nRhiesepes T ethin'oR ef' xoidynonomti"

It was not over as Quardraille's eyes flamed with anger trying not to answer. He knew it was against Mortarr's will to continue speaking, but was compelled to do so:

"nll mymo mya' bao
T veyomoon 'ef esoRepomties
ad nll mhitioR
T epoo'esoom 'ef sioobaRhies"

Awlion felt the Spirit of Jesuar fill her mouth and mind as she stared straight through Quardraille without fear:

"tieom ties mya' XoesoihiRes mya'
ad eto eshilles ties
Y mya' tihivo veyomnomsio
oom nll omones'

Y mya' nhivo nll hiR'oomes
dyRoimv met ba'oo'dy
nll esmoordy mya' dyoveyoiR efaost
ad etohidyes mya' Rooa'hisiRooes' T dyoesoRti"

Quardraille took a deep breath, almost collapsing with the effort to stand. The Arbushi were entranced with the exchange though they understood little of it. Quardraille looked at Awlion as a strong opponent instead of a lowly Trag.

"You are gifted beyond what I would ever expect." Quardraille wanted to kill her. "For now there is nothing I can do. I gave my word to free you."

"The hand of Jesuar holds you back from killing me. I see this in your eyes." Awlion waited to see if Quardraille was going to change his mind.

"Mortarr is my strength…" Quardraille continued to struggle before straightening up suddenly. "Do not think you have persuaded me against my mission. I have already chosen my fate and if we meet again I will choose yours which will be death."

"I know." Awlion knew what he had lost.

"Make ready to ride!" Quardraille picked out twenty warriors before jumping on his black stallion. "You will join us for now." He glared at Awlion.

"You promised to let me go." Awlion protested as he

thought to use her bow and arrow one more time.

"And so I shall." Quardraille insisted.

"I'd rather be in the tower." Awlion struggled against the powerful guards who tried to put her on one of the small stallions.

"Then the tower you shall go." Quardraille waved her way.

As Awlion was led away toward the tower, she heard Quardraille ask about Rhor's position. She heard Zarr and Tenca answer him, but could not make out the words. The Arbushi guards pushed her down through a narrow hall leading to the stairway of the tower. They climbed the stone stairs high above the fortress walls into the same room and the same window. Then the guards left locking the door behind them.

"Jesuar." Awlion prayed as she stared out over the Dark Forest watching Quardraille ride out. "Please let Thoos find my father. Then give him guidance to lead them back here. I don't want to die alone."

She cried until sleep overcame her sorrow. The day grew dark as the sun pierced her tiny window with its last rays. No longer were the walls far from her, but closer now closing in on her. Finding a corner to lean against she wondered what would happen to her now.

****

"I have news!" Carazaar crashed out of the dense reeds to the right of Tiathan Eiula who almost cut off his head with his sword.

"If you value your life never do that again!" Tiathan would not have regretted to lose Carazaar as he seemed more a nuisance than a friend.

"But I have news!" Carazaar approached him again.

"Where is Ygueliav?" Tiathan grabbed him by the throat watching his eyes bubble from their sockets.

"Peace! Peace!" Carazaar gasped as he rubbed his throat.

"Don't try and use your illusions on me, magician, or I'll cut you in half." Tiathan loosened his grip to let Carazaar speak.

"I escaped to find you." Carazaar was surprised Tiathan was so angry. "I know where they have taken them."

"Who did you escape from?" Zelbiur could not believe even Carazaar could have escaped from any warriors.

"Valkyricks surprised us and took us all prisoner." Carazaar related the story as if he were still captured. "I stood with the others before Moshdalayrrimich and used the illusion of thirty Trags training their arrows on their great leader. He ordered his guards to protect them and during the confusion I slipped away."

"Surely they noticed that you were gone and what of Ygueliav?" Thrun found the whole thing amusing.

"No, for I conjured up an illusion of myself talking with Ygueliav which even he thought was real." Carazaar turned to Tiathan. "Even he didn't realize I was not there for over half an hour."

"Why did you not help Ygueliav to escape, too!" Zelbiur was angry with him.

"I could only conjure myself with the weakened power I have." Carazaar could se the disappointment in Zelbiur's eyes.

"Where are they?" Tiathan was impatient with him.

"Their camp is only a few miles from here and well guarded." Carazaar pointed east of where they stood.

"How did you find us?" Agraine already did not trust their new companion and found him a little frightening.

"I thank Jesuar for His guidance and pray for His forgiveness for using an evil art to escape." Carazaar bowed his head, but his voice sounded hollow.

"He tells the truth about where Ygueliav has been taken." Outra sensed that Carazaar was not sincere about anything else.

"What else do you know?" Tiathan saw that Carazaar was holding something back.

"I know where the camp is, but Rhor is not with them." Carazaar knelt to the ground and started to draw in the sand.

"This is the camp and this where they are keeping Ygueliav and the others. They are guarded even though it looks like a trap for anyone who might come to save them."

"What else?" Zelbiur prodded him on.

"Rhor and Nsaat were arguing with Moshdalayrrimich." Carazaar hesitated before continuing. "It is an uneasy allegiance. If they do not mend their differences, there will be a war like nothing Everstream has ever seen."

"We are already at war with all of them." Thrun kicked the dirt in front of Carazaar.

"As he has said, it will be a war unlike any we have seen in Everstream." Outra warned them all.

"There is a weapon that both Rhor and Moshdalayrrmich fear more than your Craxsmoore Guilding." Carazaar surprised them with his knowledge of Tiathan's weapon of choice. "Outra Whorld has told me of its history of other weapons in Everstream should I happen to come upon them."

"Before we step on your tongue, magician, tell us everything!" Zelbiur walked towards him.

"Friends do not mistreat each other this way." Carazaar glared into Zelbiur's eyes and tried to show he was unafraid.

"We've been betrayed too many times by supposed friends." Zelbiur refused to let it go.

"I will never betray you and this I tell you as a follower of Jesuar." Carazaar felt the hollowness of his words, but saw their eyes widen in amazement. "Yes, Outra has convinced me of my path in life. He also informed me that I am to give up my illusions and crystals to allow Jesuar to control my life and destiny. I have tried to do so, however, I forgot many things at the Valkyrick camp. Now…can we talk as allies and friends or do you want to just kill me now?"

"Jesuar has not struck you dead so I will apologize." Zelbiur stepped away from him. "But you can't blame me for my mistrust of you."

"Up to this point there was no reason for you to trust me." Carazaar felt a new power inside him. "Yet Jesuar will judge us both if you ignore what I tell you."

"It is well." Tiathan begged him to continue.

"There's a weapon called the Karalak which is a three-pronged sword from the family of Rhor." Carazaar drew again on the ground. "If the sword should fall into the wrong hands Rhor said he would be helpless to defend himself against it. Moshdalayrrimich laughed at him until Rhor told the story of the weapon that could defeat a whole army in the wrong hands."

"No such weapon exists!" Agraine turned away and sat against an old gnarled oak.

"He believes it to have the power to render the bearer invisible." Carazaar ignored her for the moment. "Now if he had both Craxsmoore Guilding and the Karalak no warrior could withstand him, not even Moshdalayrrimich."

"How does he know so much about Craxsmoore

Guilding?" Thrun was interested now.

"Craxsmoore Guilding has not been out of the Great Oak for a very long time." Tiathan was disturbed about this new information.

"One of your company must told him before meeting a horrible death." Carazaar was ashamed to tell them the whole truth. "He asked for Jesuar's forgiveness and yours. Tiathan Eiula, for his weakness."

"I wish I could ask for his forgiveness for not coming in time to save them." Tiathan sadly looked up to an empty sky.

"Now both Rhor and Moshdalayrrimich know of it." Zelbiur scoured the surrounding forest for the sound of warriors, but heard none.

"And Nsaat." Thrun added.

"We have other troubles now." Carazaar was not finished.

"What is that?" Tiathan was not ready for more bad news.

"Warathan of the Valvorri has declared his allegiance to Rhor and Moshdalayrrimich." Carazaar smoother the sand to draw again.

"I cannot believe that for they are mortal enemies." Thrun shook his head in disbelief. "I think he only bides his time to see what is going to happen."

"Where are they going?" Tiathan needed to know where they could sit out the coming conflict safely. "We are wholly outnumbered and need to find a safe haven."

"Moshdalayrrimich is already and we cannot retreat."
Carazaar started drawing circles in the sand. "Rhor will be
here by tomorrow, Nsaat has already left for here just south
of us and Warathan will be marching from the west."
"Going where?" Zelbiur did not know what it all meant.

"Is Rhor going to Byabnol?" Tiathan answered knowing
they were standing in the middle of the coming battle.

"To fight Quardraille." Carazaar agreed. "While Rhor
fights Quardraille, Moshdalayrrimich is looking for us and
Nsaat is using his Harkies to watch for Warathan."

"Such a lack of trust." Outra folded his arms.

"What do we do now, father?" Zelbiur was at a loss.

"Pray that Jesuar will tell us what to do." Tiathan turned
to Outra. "Is there anything you want or need to tell us?"

"It is in your hands, Tiathan Eiula…" Outra started to
say.

"…but you must leave us now?" Tiathan finished his sentence.

"Jesuar will be with you all." Outra left as he came
through the middle of the Dark Forest.

"We will rest until morning and then march to Byabnol
to find Awlion." Tiathan wearily sat down next to Zelbiur.

"And what if she is not there?" Thrun was concerned
they would meet any one of the three armies wandering through
the forest.

"Then we move on and find her somewhere else…"

Tiathan absently answered his question.

Tho-o-o-os!

"Thoos! Come here!" Agraine was excited to see him again.

"Friend! There!" Thoos was out of breath as he pointed toward Byabnol.

"The Arbushi have her?" Agraine guessed why Thoos was pointing to the west.

"Yes, but well." Thoos relaxed a little as he cuddled in her arms. "Where father?"

"I am Tiathan Eiula, her father." Tiathan was aware enough not to shout at the creature. His fascination with the Thistmock was evident to all of them. Then he smiled.

"She call for you." Thoos smiled back.

"Will Quardraille kill her?" Zelbiur blurted out.

"No, want you." Thoos pointed at Tiathan.

"Then we have time to plan and rest." Tiathan turned to the others. "First, again I say rest and prepare for a time we will not be able to rest. Thrun, Schill and Agraine will join Zelbiur and myself over a hot meal to decide what we must do."

"Must go now!" Thoos was angry. "Help Awlion!"

"No, my little friend." Tiathan smiled again at him. "I am happy you are Awlion's friend, but we need to know how to save her or we will all end up dead or in the same prison. Don't you agree?"

"Yes." Thoos was confused since Tiathan so easily treated him as an equal. He was not used to being treated this way.

"Make a fire before dark and use dry wood. We need to cook fast so we can put out the fires as quickly as possible." Tiathan ordered. "If our fires are seen, we will most certainly not see the morning. Many are looking for us so be careful."

"We need to hunt first before the fires." Zelbiur picked three archers and sent them into the forest. It took only two hours for two of them to return with Notherhen and Thrushtails for everyone to eat. A third had Ankaturkey and small game to the delight of the Trags.

This time Thoos stayed within the camp with Agraine feeling secure for the first time in a long time. As the night grew dark, their fires were eventually doused with sand and clay before a watch was set in all four corners of the camp. Soon the quiet restless sleep took over all of them with each one wondering what the next day will bring.

Chapter Six

"Mistress, wake up." Zarr nudged Awlion who jumped back as she opened her eyes.

"How dare you come here to me!" Awlion cried out wishing she had some kind of weapon to kill him. It was then she felt something behind her.

"Be quiet! The guards will hear you!" Tenca whispered in back of her.

"I'll quiet you forever!" Awlion gained her feet ready to start a fight.

"We will help you escape." Zarr tried to calm her down.

"You lie!" Awlion was still angry. But she lowered her voice anyway.

"You must listen to us or we will all die." Tenca crept to the door and looked outside the small window.

"Why should I believe you?" Awlion still wasn't sure what to make of all this. "Why did Quardraille greet you as friends? Why did you let him believe you were there to turn my father in?"

"He looks at us as followers of Nsaat, but we do not follow him now." Tenca tried to explain. "Why would he think we were friends of Trags when no one else would believe it?"

"Believe us because of this!" Zarr held out the key to the door.

"And this!" Tenca gave her a dagger.

"Your bow and arrows are already outside the gates waiting for you." Zarr tried to smile, but it only unnerved her.

"We did what we thought was right in order to save your life and ours." Tenca sighed knowing Awlion would probably never understand.

"How did you find me?" Awlion relaxed a little, but kept aware where each stood. Bantongues lacked the loyalty of friendship being creatures of Nsaat and Mortarr.

"We followed you and the little creature." Zarr shrugged his shoulders as if it was of little consequence to track her. "Your father must know you are here by now."

"It was not hard since you talk very loud when you should be silent." Tenca added without thinking he was being insulting.

"When we entered Byabnol, Quardraille wanted us killed, but we told him we helped capture your brother, Ygueliav." Zarr saw Awlion start to get angry again.

"He was captured, but not by us." Tenca anxiously explained while stepping back towards the back of the room.

"As Bantongues , Quardraille believes us because we are known to hate Trags." Tenca realized he had said it wrong. "He knows that it takes very little to change loyalties even to Nsaat. We are stupid creatures to him and knows we do not have the sense to lie."

"He thinks 'Why would Bantongues lie to me?'" Zarr almost laughed. "We have been practicing a lot since we met you."

"We know your father is heading here and we must get you out." Tenca liked to see Awlion happy and thought he could help.

"Here?" Awlion wasn't sure that was a good thing.

"Yes, here, of course!" Zarr thought it was obvious.

"He is looking for you." Tenca needed her to understand.

"Enough of this!" Awlion sheathed the dagger and took the key from Zarr. "How do we get out of this place?"

"Not down the tower stairs." Zarr was dancing with protest.

"But as a Bantongue…" Tenca had a thought.

"Down the walls!" Zarr finished the thought.

"Yet how we do it is embarrassing when it is done in front of strangers." Zarr hesitated to be the first to set up an escape.

"Dying here is even more embarrassing since you are

known as fearless warriors." Awlion leaned over and patted his head realizing now they were only trying to help. She was sure they were too dull to think of so elaborate a trap. Quardraille would just kill her if he had the mind.

"Our ancestors used an ugly way of spinning webs to trap for food and as a means of escape." Zarr explained as he looked to Tenca for help. "However, it has its uses when trapped in high trees or overhanging cliffs."

"I don't know what you mean." Awlion wasn't sure what they planned to do.

"Very well." Zarr looked at Tenca. "Show her."

"Me?" Tenca was horrified. "You're the one who thought of it. You should show her what we do when put into a corner."

"Oh, all right. Don't laugh." Zarr bent over and sprayed a long silk string across the room. The end stuck fast on the stone wall.

"And how is that trick supposed to help us?" Awlion suppressed a laugh while trying to think if this could help them.

"It's as strong as a rope and can help us escape sometime after dark to climb down the outside walls of Byabnol." Tenca saw that Awlion was not offended.

"But I don't want to touch it." Awlion already rubbed her hands against her clothes thinking about how it might feel.

"It's either that or fight our way out." Zarr insisted

knowing that fighting would be suicide.

"We'll carry you then even into the Dark Forest." Tenca offered a solution.

"All right then, I agree." Awlion was not totally satisfied, but staying imprisoned was not an option if her father may be close.

"We'll be back before midnight when the guard changes and the Arbushi begin to celebrate their victory." Zarr waved to her with his talons as they left her cell.

Awlion watched the Arbushi reinforce their walls and grounds in anticipation of another attack. She doubted Rhor would return, but the Arbushi would not be easily intimidated. She counted the number of warriors as they came and went through the courtyards. Easily three or four thousand were now moving about while young Arbushi were being trained to fight with swords and battleaxes. Others were taught to ride stallions and make weapons. The Arbushi were preparing for a larger war and not to defend their fortress. She had to get away to warn her father.

****

"Riders coming fast." Zelbiur nudged Tiathan before waking up the others.

"How many?" Tiathan jumped up to his feet.

"Twenty…maybe thirty with wagons behind them."

Zelbiur could not separate the two sounds.

"We cannot outrun them so we must fight." Tiathan pointed to a grove that surrounded the path. "Take half of our archers to the trees there. The rest of us will stand over in the ditch until they pass by to take the wagons from behind while you fire upon the stallions."

"Could we not let them pass?" Zelbiur was not so sure that this plan would work.

"I know we do not have the best of warriors, but they will have to do." Tiathan worried about their chances. "Send enough arrows to make them think there are more than there are."

"As soon as they reach us we will do our best." Zelbiur prayed that Jesuar would help guide their arrows.

"What's up?" Agraine brought Thrun and Schill with her.

"Follow Zelbiur into the trees for we are being going to have to defend ourselves." Tiathan ordered them away.

"May I suggest one more weapon against stallions?" Carazaar quietly wanted to help.

"And what would that be, magician?" Zelbiur couldn't help but show his disdain with Carazaar.

"Set a rope in front and behind them so that when they advance we can unhorse them and when they retreat we can knock them off again." Carazaar saw a smile envelope Tiathan's face. "If nothing else we can enjoy a good laugh before we die."

"Yes, we must have a good laugh before we die." Tiathan liked the idea and ordered it to be done.

"Then Schill. Agraine and I will stay on the ground behind those rocks so when they fall we will use our battleaxes to finish them off." Thrun liked the idea and thought about the advantage that it would give them.

"Agreed." Tiathan waved them away.

Just as they were able to settle into position, the sound of hooves echoed down the path. Around the bend came twenty Arbushi riders followed by two wagons covered with cloth. As they passed Tiathan, he could see the wagons had food and weapons protruding from the back. Within seconds, the first six Arbushi were down on the ground with arrows in their chest. The company picked up speed just as they hit the rope lifted just a foot off the ground. Six more Arbushi fell to the ground finding Trags dropping from the trees to attack them with battleaxes.

"Now!" Tiathan ordered his warriors toward the wagons that stopped on the path.

The Arbushi riders turned to protect the wagons when the second rope was secured and another four riders fell to the ground. Trags fell on them with Schill and Thrun with battleaxe and sword until all of them were dead or dying. Tiathan noticed one escaped with an arrow in his side traveling towards

Byabnol. There would be little time to leave the area.

"We cannot catch him." Tiathan kept Zelbiur from chasing after the lone rider.

"He will tell the others." Zelbiur protested.

"No doubt he will." Tiathan turned his attention to the food and weapons.

"We are well supplied now." Carazaar beat them as he tore sheets of cloth to help carry away the supplies.

"What are these?" Tiathan held a cylindrical object in his hand before tossing it in the air and catching it again.

"Don't do that!" Carazaar snatched it away from him.

"Why not?" Tiathan thought it wise to let Carazaar explain before he thumped him on the head for interfering in his game.

"It explodes." Carazaar saw the foggy look in Tiathan's eyes. "Like this!" He threw it far into the forest so the explosion would not harm them.

"Oh." Tiathan nervously backed away from the wagons.

"They are safe until they are thrown upon the ground." Carazaar reassured him. "I only know of these things from Moshdalayrrimich who was given one by his captains. It was found on an Arbushi warrior that was captured earlier that day. He was quickly put to death. Moshdalayrrimich gave one of those to his shield bearer who accidently dropped it outside his tent which killed him and four others instantly."

"They will come in handy." Zelbiur rubbed his ear from

the unexpected explosion that was so loud within in his hearing. "Since you know so much about them, you can drive the wagon. I will take the other."

"We must hurry." Tiathan thought about the Arbushi wanting to take revenge.

"We must find someplace secure and safe to hide." Zelbiur still felt weak from their fight.

"These wagons will only slow us down." Tiathan had second thoughts about taking the wagons.

"Jesuar? Show us a safe haven." Jesuar prayed quickly.

"There!" Tiathan looked over at the trees seeing a mountain peeking over them. "Mount Hamiar! I remember from some of the old maps that it is the only mountain within miles."

"Come! All of you! This way!" Outra ran up to them from the path ahead. "There are Bantongues waiting for you just beyond the trees."

"Take what food and weapons you can." Tiathan decided to leave the wagons behind.

Zelbiur picked out twenty leather bags and filled them with billets and hummers while Tiathan packed the food, water and skins of Schew for the Trags to carry. Thrun set fire to the wagons left behind so the Arbushi would have little to use.

"That will keep them from using anything against us." Zelbiur said out loud.

"You better run ahead before the fire sets off what is left

of the billets." Outra encouraged them down the path.

As they moved away from the forest and off the path, they could hear the Bantongues howling anger just before the wagons exploded. A second explosion broke the silence as the Arbushi rode into view. Tiathan could see the Arbushi sixty strong following their trail. On the east side were Bantongues over one hundred strong massing at the bottom of the field ahead of them. The Trags reached a rock ledge twenty feet from the top where it was wide enough to hold all of them.

"They've stopped." Zelbiur saw the Arbushi setting up camp.

"The Bantongues, too." Tiathan scouted the east side.

"We must build a wall." Zelbiur was already thinking of a defensive position. He scoured the rocky area seeing stone and fallen timber on all sides scattered about. "We can use the stone for a wall with openings just large enough for us and then place the timber on top so we can extend the mountain over us. We'll use whatever we have to tie the timber together and use dirt to push over the top."

"Do we have enough time?" Tiathan knew it would take all night and part of the next day to finish.

"Whatever we do will be more than what we have now." Carazaar was already carrying the first stone.

"It couldn't get any worse." Zelbiur started towards a pile of rocks himself.

"Over here!" Outra called them over to see in the distance a great army, four abreast, marching toward them. The army seemed to stretch for miles.

"It must be Moshdalayrrimich!" Tiathan knew the Seven Fortresses was the only place capable to have such an army.

"And Rhor." Zelbiur added noting the different languages he could hear even from that great a distance. He wondered at the decision to make a stand in this high place.

"And Nsaat." Outra pointed to the Harkies flying over the same warriors.

"If we are not ready by morning, we will not be able to defend ourselves." Zelbiur ordered every Trag to different positions hoping to make up time by using a chain to bring rock and timber to the right place. For once he would have liked the night to be almost endless so they could protect themselves.

****

"It is time, mistress." Zarr gently woke Awlion from a restless sleep.

"Then we'd better hurry before I have second thoughts." Awlion sighed as she prepared for a long drop to the ground. There were no guards in the hall leading to an open turret.

As they started down the walls, Awlion shivered as a sudden thought occurred to her. What if the Bantongues were freeing her under Quardraille's orders hoping to follow them to find her father? Still, it was better to be free than in the tower. She would have to change any plans they might have when they finally were safe in the forest.

No alarm was made as they reached the fortress walls and ran into the dark corner of the forest. There the journey became slow and arduous until they reached a niche to climb up on. Awlion looked back to see shadows of guards with torches roaming the courtyard they had just left. No way could they climb the walls without being seen. With the rising of the moon they would be clearly seen from any part of the courtyard even at this distance.

"We have to chance it." Zarr was the first to speak about the obvious danger.

"I fear they'll see us."Tenca was more cautious.

"Then we will have to fight." Awlion gripped her dagger tightly. "If we make it over the top I hope you are right about my bow."

"It is there, mistress." Zarr was annoyed that she didn't believe him.

"This is not the place I want to climb, but over there." She pointed to the west wall of the mountain. "Past that guard."

"Guard?" Tenca saw nothing.

"I see him." Zarr whispered.

"How do we get past him?" Tenca wasn't sure they could get past him.

"I think over there." Zarr saw an opening where they could pass by him without being noticed.

"I have a better plan." Awlion smiled at Zarr. "Zarr, show me again how your ancestors caught their food. Not yet though until we can get closer."

"I..." Zarr at first did not understand until a gleam of light crept into his thoughts. Thinking hard at what she wanted him to do, he nodded in agreement.

It was easy to pass through the shadows to a dark opening that led near the Arbushi scout. The scout already seemed agitated making it difficult for Zarr to spray his trap.

"You've got to get closer, Zarr." Awlion pushed him closer.

"And what is he sees me?" Zarr pleaded.

"You're the honored guest of Quardraille out for a nightly stroll as all Bantongues are want to do." Awlion whispered back.

"That's right, I forgot." Zarr was reassured before turning back to her. "What if I miss?"

"We won't be here if you try again." Awlion waved him forward.

"I'll not miss then." Zarr confidently walked up to the

guard, turned around and sprayed him totally with a silken web. Within seconds he was wrapped up and hanging from a tall tree.

"Well done." Awlion was upon him instantly. "Will you let me ride on you so we can make the best time?"

"Thank you, yes, mistress." Zarr raised his head in pride.

"Enough of this nonsense!" Tenca was impatient to leave.

The ground moved so fast Awlion could not see where she was going. Zarr and Tenca spun a small web to keep her safely on Zarr's back. They keep away from climbing trees in case Zarr might knock Awlion off his back.

****

By morning their work was complete as some still slept while others sharpened swords and spears. Still others tried to add to their compliment of arrows. There was no movement below in the Arbushi camp. Tiathan saw Harkies flying overhead as Bantongues paced back and forth around the ledge beneath them. His eyes felt heavy with sleep before he drifted off again.

In his dreams, Tiathan saw a great fortress filled with gold, silver and pearls. The tables were filled with food and kegs of Schew. Along the walls were weapons of all kinds glittering in the sunlight. In his dream Flashfire Lake surrounded the mighty stone walls spewing smoke, fire and ash blistering both stone and mortar. Soon the fortress sank beneath the surface of the waters, but just before it disappeared an army of black warriors with red capes flying from their shoulders rode out upon the plains hacking everyone in its wake with axe and sword.

A golden warrior stood alone in the path as they rode down upon him with anger and fury. He wore a crown of golden thorns with a gold breastplate, sword and shield. With a cry of "Jesuar" he laid sword and shield upon them. The black warriors screamed in pain and fell around him. It was then Tiathan woke up to cries of panic.

"They're coming!" Zelbiur readied his warriors.

"Let them get close enough so we cannot miss!" Tiathan looked down the ridge.

From the skies came a horde of Harkies carrying rocks and stones to drop on top of them. Bantongues were heard scurrying and scraping as they climbed the rocks beneath them. Agraine calmed Thoos as he started ti run back and forth inside the walls.

"Thoos! Leave us!" Agraine wanted one of them to survive.

"No leave friend!" Thoos' eyes bugged out with fear.

"No, go find Awlion and tell her where we are." Agraine changed her tone making it a command.

"Yes, I go find Awlion." Thoos liked the idea and shot out through the small window down the slope. No one realized anything except a faint breeze pass them as Thoos escaped.

"At least he will be safe." Agraine told her father.

"He would only be in the way otherwise." Thrun agreed.

The thunder of the stones rolling down the mountainside above them shook the timber. The first Bantongue stuck its fangs inside the near window toward Zelbiur, but could not reach him. A moment later the creature was gone. More stones rolled over the top of the timber only to strengthen the roof against the onslaught. The Trags lost only three warriors from the stones that collapsed part of the side wall. Now as the Harkies dropped more stones they rolled from the roof onto the Bantongues killing over thirty of them.

"Jesuar be praised!" Tiathan leaned back in wonder.

"If they keep this up we can leave in peace within hours." Carazaar laughed at the sight.

"It will not be over that easy." Zelbiur listened intently out one of the windows.

When the excitement died down, Tiathan helped build a fire in a niche of the mountain with a small crack sending the flow of smoke through the top. It provided a good spot for cooking where they could dine without interruption. Water was provided by a small streamlet that spurted from another crack in the wall. Tiathan knew it had to be the work of Jesuar since no water could be found so high up on the ridge.

"I have never seen such a thing!" Thrun laughed long and hard. "We did not use a single arrow!"

"It was the work of Jesuar!" Tiathan reminded him.

"Truly, yes, it was." Thrun was still amazed and grateful.

"Maybe Jesuar will fight each day for us." Agraine was trying to be amusing knowing their fate would be settled soon enough.

"We can hope and dream." Zelbiur listened intently through the small openings in the wall.

"Hear anything, my son?" Tiathan waited a long time before asking.

"They are very angry with the Harkies." Zelbiur left the window. "The Harkies could care less. One said 'Trag or Valkyrick all the same to us. Besides, you have Moshdalayrrimich. Why do you care?"

"Moshdalayrrimich? I don't understand that." Tiathan mused before letting it go. Nothing seemed to make sense to what was going on in Everstream.

"We will not be so lucky tomorrow." Carazaar felt a chill run down his spine.

"If we are to be victorious or defeated let it be with Jesuar on our lips." Tiathan stood up. "Let them hear we are not afraid of them. Let us sing the song of Meridrok:

"nhill mo oveyoR eso'
T estihiRes W T mynetti esvll
nhill mo oveyor mhivo
t efo'a T nooRmN dyom
nhill mo moot epoRyst
ba'efooRo mo etohiR XoesoihiRes mhino
nhill mo efoRoveyoR
Bao hiet epohisio met ohisiet ootieoR
nhill mo hiamhilles esN
W xoollefoia sioabaRhitim
nhill me epRhill hi epRhilloR
'ef tiehimvesnyvn ad tiehimves
nhill mo naooRhiefll
nhill mo eshimsitiefll
nhill mo eshinhiefll
T mhino 'ef XoesoihiR"

  There were no more attacks that day or night. Everyone left as Moshdalayrrimich advanced more toward Byabnol than near the mountain. Quardraille seemed to be more on his mind than the Trags and set up four encampments on all sides of the mountain as well as Byabnol. A pink glow emanated from the western camp telling Tiathan it was where the Valkyrick leader had his own special tent. The glow was what was left of the crystal of Zebrac. As things began to settle for the night, music came up from the western camp and drifted up toward the Trags:

> "ba'ady T olles 'ef 'XobaRhisi
> siRllestihia aooRdy 'ef hia
> baRynetmoes' stymo oom OO
> nooady OO ymtioo estioomo
> sthiRepom OO met ll'R epoomoR
> esepohiv t OO ll'R na'Rll
> stymo baolloomdy T esoim
> naoom baolloomdy T noo'm
> ll'R sthidyoom r oi'R ayneti
> naesstomn efoRoveyoR methim OO"

"We cannot wait for them to come to us." Zelbiur wanted to leave the mountain.

"You are right." Tiathan agreed. "They would not expect such a small company to venture down the mountain except to escape."

"What have you planned?" Zelbiur saw the sparkle in Tiathan's eyes.

"You and Thrun will take half our company back to Rabel Ain." Tiathan looked over at Thrun and Schill. "That means that you, my cousins, will go with him."

"I will stand and fight with you!" Thrun was not happy.

"We will fight together, but not this time." Tiathan embraced his cousin before whispering. "I want you to protect my son since he is the only one I have left if I cannot save Ygueliav or find Awlion."

"Then it is a good reason to go." Thrun calmed down and agreed.

"I intend to stay!" Agraine slammed her spiked mace on the ground.

"And so you shall as well as Carazaar." Tiathan already decided he wanted them with his adventure to come. "The rest of us will go down and visit Moshdalayrrimich. If Ygueliav is still with him we will rescue him. There should be thirty or more warriors around him which we will need if we are forced to return to this place."

"I wish to go with Zelbiur." Carazaar did not like this plan.

"I think not." Tiathan refused to accept his offer. "I may yet need your illusions."

"And what of my vow to Jesuar?" Carazaar complained.

"It is as empty as your faith in Him." Tiathan surprised even himself with such an honest comment. He could see that Carazaar was surprised and relived.

"How do you know this?" Carazaar meekly bowed his head.

"I know Jesuar and He knows me." Tiathan explained looking right through him. "If you were changed I would know it. The Spirit of Jesuar would be upon you, but it isn't."

"It must be true because I do not feel His presence." Carazaar wept which Tiathan could was real feelings. "I tried to convince myself it was different…I cannot explain why…"

"No matter now." Tiathan dismissed him with a wave of the hand. "Jesuar still has use for you anyway."

"When shall we leave?" Zelbiur knew he could not argue with his father once he made a decision.

"Now." Tiathan was still forming his own plan. "The largest opening between the four camps is east of us. They know we are heading in the direction of Byabnol so there will be more scouts north and south. It should be easy to retreat to Rabel Ain."

"We'll see." Thrun wasn't so sure.

"I'm sure Outra will meet you at some point if you need help." Tiathan was already worried about what he was going to do.

"What if you need help?" Thrun was still concerned.

"It would be too late for you to help us by the time you learn of it." Tiathan encouraged them all to leave. "Jesuar has other plans for all of us and you will be needed again."

"Let us go then." Zelbiur looked out one of the openings

and so nothing that would hinder their journey. One by one they left the makeshift fortress.

Tiathan let them venture down the mountainside before taking the rest of the Trags toward Moshdalayrrimich's camp. The green glow easily guided them to the western camp. No guards were posted except in a couple of trees where a few carefully placed arrows rid them of that annoyance. The drums and singing drowned out their cries before they hit the ground.

"There they are!" Carazaar saw a fenced in section of the camp with forty Trags chained to posts. Eight guards stood around the fence, but it was obvious that they did not expect them to escape.

"Do you see Ygueliav?" Tiathan was looking hard without finding his son.

"Yes." Agraine spotted Ygueliav near the center of the Trags. "There!"

"Agraine, take archers on the left and wait for me to get close to the tent of Moshdalayrrimich." Tiathan saw a thick grove of trees overlooking the camp. "Carazaar, take five warriors and ready yourselves to free everyone within the fence. I will visit their leader and perhaps even bring back a trophy."

"Shall we stand and fight?" Agraine knew if they did there was no chance of escape.

"No, send two volleys of arrows and then go back to our stronghold on the mountain." Tiathan hoped it would work so all of them would end up in their safe haven.

"Good, we can try our new toys." Agraine pulled out a few hummers.

"Do not wait for me either of you." Tiathan looked at Carazaar and Agraine.

"I didn't think we would." Agraine smiled at him. "Just don't get there before us."

Within minutes, Tiathan was able to crawl next to the great tent listening to the laughter of the Valkyricks. Another voice intrigued him as one he had heard before, but who it could be eluded him. He cut a slit in the side and peeked in seeing four Akrilla seated at the right hand of Moshdalayrrimich. Lifting a cup of Schew in salute was Haavorn which made Tiathan want to unwrap Craxsmoore Guilding and fight no matter what the cost. What gave him pause was a bright red sword leaning on Moshdalayrrimich's left side. It was then the arrows tore through the top of the tent causing panic and disarray as explosion threw dirt and warriors in all directions.

"We are under attack!" One of the Valkyrick warriors shouted from outside.

"To your posts!" Moshdalayrrimich jumped from his throne leaving the red sword behind.

Haavorn glanced down at the weapon as he surveyed the panic around him. With a quick gesture the weapon disappeared beneath his cloak. Haavorn hurried toward the other side of the tent, cut open part of it and escaped into the night. Tiathan followed close by as Haavorn pushed aside Valkyrick warriors that stood in his way. Haavorn entered quickly into a far tent without being seen. Tiathan followed trying to reach the backside of the tent without being seen. He sat close to the cloth wondering if he should look inside or wait until Haavorn left the tent.

A light was extinguished after a soft rustling of dirt and cloth. Tiathan waited a few minutes listening to the Valkyricks vent their anger and frustration of losing the Trag prisoners. He was glad to hear that no one was caught which left the rest to him. Slowly and quietly he cut an opening in the cloth and entering in. The point of a sword greeted him just behind the right ear.

"Welcome my friend." Haavorn urged him to sit on the ground.

"We are not friends." Tiathan could not reach his short sword or have time enough to use Craxsmoore Guilding in such a confined space.

"Yes, we are." Haavorn put his sword away. "I told you what my plans would be if we were separated. I have done my part and you must do yours."

"I saw you steal the red sword." Tiathan did not trust him still.

"Ah yes, the Karalak." Haavorn uncovered it from beneath his bed of straw. "It is yours, of course."

"How easily you give up such a powerful weapon." Tiathan was wondering when the trap would be sprung.

"Easy for me for I do not want or need it." Haavorn saw the surprise in Tiathan's eyes.

"This would help you rule Everstream." Tiathan could not contain himself.

"Why would I want to do that?" Haavorn gave him a look of scorn. "I have enough trouble feeding my own warriors much less the whole of Everstream. Besides, I do not like most of those I would have to rule. I am a traveler, a mercenary, fighting when I want and going where I feel like going. I do not need anything else."

"But your loyalty is to Moshdalayrrimich." Tiathan remembered the toast Haavorn made to the Valkyrick leader.

"My loyalty was to your son first and no other after that." Haavorn was insulted. "Now go before we are found out and be sure we never meet again."

"I thank you for my son." Tiathan now knew why Ygueliav was still alive.

"No thanks is needed. Now go!" Haavorn turned his back on him thinking how the Trags talk too much at the worst of times.

Tiathan left with the Karalak, but now had more weapons than he could possibly handle. The trek was slow and tedious because he had to skirt around the camp in order to get back up the mountain.

****

"Do you know where we are?" Awlion asked Zarr and Tenca. "Two days and we seem lost as ever in this forest."

"We are far from Byabnol which is the most important problem we face." Zarr crushed small trees and brush underfoot to make a path through the forest.

"Quardraille must know we have betrayed him." Tenca sounded nervous.

"Still, we must find my father or be lost out here forever." Awlion insisted as thorns tore at her arms and legs.

"What else can we do?" Zarr shrugged as only a Bantongue could shrug.

"Ah, there is a path ahead and perhaps it will tell us where we are." Zarr hurried to the clearing before the others.

"We must rest for a while to make sure we are not running circles." Awlion sat down upon a rock to the right of the path.

"I'll scout ahead." Zarr already started toward the trees

that shaded the path and scurried up the nearest oak.

"And I'll stay with you." Tenca lay next to Awlion who leaned against his rough skin. "I'm too tired to go on anyway."

The clouds above Awlion leisurely drifted over her as if nothing of any importance was happening beneath them. The sky had neither the smoke or orange hue of destruction that pervaded the sky not so long ago. It was so quiet and Awlion fell asleep feeling the gentle breeze across her face.

"Stallions!" Tenca jumped up pulling Awlion by the collar up into the highest oak overlooking the clearing.

They slumped behind two huge branches where no one could see them except a Harkie overhead. There were no Harkies and if there were they would only see a Bantongue watching a band of Arbushi riding into view. The Arbushi were not looking for Awlion, but maybe a place to camp.

"We're nearer to the fighting than I want to be." Awlion still felt a chill when she looked into the face of the Bantongue. Yet, Tenca's weary eyes lessened the fear she used to have of them.

"We'll know for sure when Zarr returns." Tenca reassured her, but it was a long time before Zarr came back.

"I've never seen such madness." Zarr broke into the silence trying to catch his breath. Awlion never heard him coming even though Tenca did.

"What's happening out there?" Awlion offered what

little water she had with her.

"Warthan of the Valvorri has come to Everstream." Zarr drank furiously with what little water there was to drink. "He's advancing from the west."

"Is he going to join Moshdalayrrmich?" Awlion needed to know though it would not make much difference in the numbers against them. "If he does we can only fight small battles to lessen the numbers."

"We saw Arbushi riding toward the south." Tenca offered not knowing if Zarr had seen them, too.

"They passed under me even though they saw me in the trees." Zarr was indifferent to the danger. "Moshdalayrrimich is nowhere to be seen."

"That may be good news." Awlion relaxed a little.

"The only ones who have not committed themselves are the Modosites." Zarr was thinking out loud. "We know little of Modos anyway."

"The Modosites?" Awlion heard of them, but never had seen one.

"They live beyond the Swamps of Dreer and are protected by the most vicious creatures in all of Everstream." Zarr explained with a slight tremble in his voice.

"I've heard they breathe fire and have more than one head to devour their prey." Tenca added with a slight shiver as well. "They know no reason and kill for the love of killing.

The Modosites have some power over them with their fortress called Modos in the very center of the swamps."

"And if that is true why should they care what happens to the rest of us or Everstream?" Awlion hoped their journey would keep them from Modos so she wouldn't have to meet any strange creatures at all.

"Because it is their nature to rule everything." Tenca only expressed the opinion that he had heard from Nsaat.

"We are not near Modos so we have nothing to fear." Awlion was deep in thought.

"Maybe not for you, but I cannot get Modos out of my mind now." Zarr trembled at the thought,

"Did you see any of my fellow Trags anywhere?" Awlion pressed Zarr for an answer.

"No, nothing except a few pieces of arrows on the path." Zarr thought it was important. "There could have been a fight, but I could not tell."

"You're hiding something." Awlion was becoming angry.

"I did not want to worry you, mistress." Zarr sighed heavily. "I did find scouts from Rhor's camp that spoke of your father."

"Tell me everything!" Awlion stood in front of him with her hands on her hips.

"Your father is some miles ahead at Mount Hamior." Zarr hesitated before deciding to tell her everything. "Tiathan and Zelbiur have split forces with Zelbiur retreating back to Rabel Ain and Tiathan staying in some cave on the mountainside. The number of Trag warriors is so small that Rhor has left the camp of Moshdalayrrimich to meet with or against Warathan."

"They do not stand a chance against the Valkyricks." Tenca was dismayed for Awlion.

"I have seen Jesuar use three Trags to defeat a whole army." Awlion was pleased to hear that her brother and father were still alive. "But what of Ygueliav and Miertur? Have you heard anything of them?"

"Not of Ygueliav, but we heard that Miertur was killed not long ago." Zarr looked miserable telling her of a vague rumor.

"That cannot be true!" Awlion was shocked to hear that she might have lost her brother.

"It is only rumor, mistress." Zarr wanted to change the subject.

"If there are few Trags on the mountain maybe Moshdalayrrimich will march around them." Tenca was hopeful for Awlion's sake.

"They cannot be reached now." Zarr was thinking of

what else they could do.

"I want you to lead me to my father." Awlion patted Zarr on the head.

"No, mistress." Zarr sounded very sure of himself which surprised Awlion.

"Why not?" Awlion heard the strangeness in his voice.

"We can help your father best if we stay unknown to all those around us." Zarr looked to Tenca for help in explaining.

"We have the freedom to set traps and cause diversions which can drive them crazy." Tenca hideously smiled. "We can come and go into any camp we choose…"

"Except Nsaat's camp…." Zarr reminded him. "…or Quardraille's."

"Every mile or two we can set up our cords to trip up the Arbushi stallions or anyone passing through. We do not have to be around when it happens." Tenca was getting excited to be of help. "True, it would only annoy them more, but what great fun!"

"We can dig pits with wooden stakes to slow down the Valkyricks." Zarr looked for branches to get started on the stakes.

"I see the wisdom in all this since no one would know who they were fighting." Awlion understood the joke. "I know how to make bows that will shoot arrows without someone pulling the bow. Anyone who comes by will think they are being attacked, but no one will be there."

"We'll be safely away before it happens." Zarr was laughing.

"We cannot be sure your father might stumble upon one of the traps." Tenca cautioned Awlion.

"Jesuar is with him." Awlion was certain their plans of traps and weapons could be set without any Trag stumbling across them.

"With this, let Jesuar be with us, too." Zarr knew they needed all the help they could get.

****

Tho-o-o-os!

"I know that sound." Tiathan was not having any luck getting back to the mountain. "Come here, little one."

"Uh-uh, big one." Thoos replied with a giggle.

"Why are you here?" Tiathan searched the fading light without success.

"Your daughter." Thoos slowly crept out of a creeping fog that was beginning to sweep the forest.

"Awlion still lives! Have you found her?" Tiathan allowed Thoos to be cradled in his arms.

"Don't know." Thoos watched him get comfortable and felt a certain peace by holding him. "Am sorry."

"Is she still in Byabnol?" Tiathan wanted to know.

"No, escaped." Thoos smiled as Tiathan's face brightened with hope.

"How far away is she?" Tiathan tried to be patient with him.

"Too far." Thoos wondered if Tiathan would rub his head and nuzzled under his arm. "No go to mountain?"

"Too many guards." Tiathan was not so sure he should try.

"Fog help." Thoos closed his eyes.

"Maybe." Tiathan thought the fog might help.

"What I do?" Thoos waited for an answer.

"Find Awlion and then come back to see me." Tiathan sat down and allowed Thoos to go.

Thoos rushed back into Tiathan's arms for a final hug before he left. Tiathan knew he was not alone in his thoughts as Jesuar gave him a vision of the way the Trags should be led. Family was not as important as Everstream and Everstream not as important as Jesuar. He knelt in prayer after he was sure Thoos was well away:

> "XoesoihiR etooadyes oi'R ayefo
> metym T baoi'mdyes 'ef aooveyo
> moo ootieoR efhisio mo eso'v

moo ootieoR ethimdy mo tihivo
oi'R bahiti'ao r baolloomdy
T esoi'mdy 'ef ovey'a
oi'R bahiti'ao r
ad hiamalles mya' bao
W T esepyRyti
'ef oi'R esoi'aes
ad T Ro'nes 'ef oi'R nymdyes"

Tiathan got up and hurried into the thick fog toward the sound of trumpets and drums only to be stopped by the waters of a river with no way across. He could see from where he stood that the rock fortress on the mountain was under attack. He doubted he could reach it in time.

"Ioroarka!" A voice startled him from behind.

"Carazaar! What are you doing here? Why are you not up there?" Tiathan was both angry and happy to see the magician.

"I stumbled while running up the mountain." Carazaar cautiously walked up to him. "When I regained my feet, there were too many Bantongues in front of me. They didn't see me so I was able to escape. I have been wandering around for hours."

"How did you get here and find me?" Tiathan became

suspicious.

"The little creature that seems to appear and disappear at will." Carazaar spoke of Thoos. "He said you might be lonely so brought me here."

"Yes, I was with Thoos a while ago." Tiathan looked forlornly at the river.

"I made such noise wandering in the forest it was easy for Thoos to find me." Carazaar was uneasy with the fact they were standing out in the open. "I was glad that he found me and not the others. He said you were close by."

"We need to pass the outer camp and cross this river to join them on the mountain." Tiathan was anxious to help those already fighting.

"How about a raft?" Carazaar suggested.

"The wood around us is too rotten." Tiathan already thought of that.

"We can wait for the waters to recede." Carazaar tried to think of a spell that would make it happen.

"Then by this you will know that Jesuar is with us." Tiathan unwrapped Craxsmoore Guilding while handing the Karalak to Carazaar who felt the power of the sword surge within him. Tiathan knelt and repeated the prayer of life"

"y nyveyo hia t XoesoihiR

ef' XoesoihiR r hia y vmom
mo ayveyo t nyveyo ayefo
ad met etti ayefo
XoesoihiR r ymesydyo OO hia
y sihia' oom etyn
t ephiRti T mhitioRes
tio' efRo' OO efRoon dyoestiRoisitim"

Tiathan began to twirl Craxsmoore Guilding around his head as a low rumble shook the ground and the sky glowed an eerie blue. The waters before them crashed against themselves beginning to swirl around in a giant eddy. A loud gasp was heard from beneath the waters as the steady swirling parted the river leaving a small path to the other side.

"We must hurry." Tiathan led them across the dry bed to the other side.

"I have never seen such power!" Carazaar couldn't suppress his amazement. "Why doesn't Jesuar let you destroy your enemies with such power?"

"It is not for Jesuar to decide how our future unfolds for it would mean we would not have free choice."

Tiathan wrapped Craxsmoore Guilding around his waist thankful he did not have to use it. He vowed to himself he would not test Jesuar again. "How easy it would be for Him to squash us all and start over again."

"Jesuar allows so many to die." Carazaar did not understand. "We may not exist at all if He does not come to our aid."

"It is a matter of choice, Carazaar." Tiathan knew he had little time to spare even though Carazaar's concerns needed to be answered. "Jesuar can force us to do what He wills, but has decided to let those in Everstream choose for themselves. Outra has spent many years telling us this and we have come to accept it."

"But if you obey Jesuar…" Carazaar wouldn't let it go as they hurried to the other side of the river. "Why are the Trags the most to suffer for it?"

"That I cannot answer." Tiathan laughed suddenly realizing it really didn't matter if there was an answer or not. "Yet, I will tell you we are on the right side of this."

"We must hope that Warthan has come to fight Rhor or Moshdalayrrimich." Carazaar was now more serious as they reached the far embankment. "If he does we have a chance to get everyone out from the mountain."

"Let us get there first and see what Jesuar has for us to do." Tiathan tapped pulled Carazaar up and away from the clearing. "We must keep moving."

Carazaar knew the way around to Mount Hamior so Tiathan allowed him to walk ahead. If there were any traps, Carazaar would be the first to find them knowing what to look for. He led Tiathan to a high hill overlooking the valley below. There were now seven encampments within range of Mount Hamior; four of Moshdalayrrimich, one of Rhor's, one of Warthan's and one safely in the distance which must have been Quardraille's camp.

"We must get closer to Rhor's camp if we are to learn of anything." Tiathan saw the red flag of the Gimgiddeans flying over the closest encampment. "He always had the loosest tongue in Everstream and he looks like he has made peace with Warthan."

"They will have scouts and guards." Carazaar was not sure this was a good plan.

"They will be watching for warriors three times our size." Tiathan smiled.

"Where is that red sword you carried over from the river?" Carazaar noticed that both Craxsmoore Guilding and the Karalak were hidden from him.

"Both are hidden and safe from everyone." Tiathan was pleased that Carazaar was talking so much he didn't realize that he had dropped the Karalak into a rotting trunk and Craxsmoore Guilding he let slip behind a cracked stone as they walked. You need to watch more closely if you want to survive in the future."

"Outra told me that if I do not fail you or Jesuar, I would receive the greatest gift and power of all." Carazaar was thinking of the Karalak.

"It is not what you think, but more than you can imagine." Tiathan felt sorry for the magician that believed illusion and a sword were the greatest gifts he could receive.

"What if I fail?" Carazaar worried back and forth.

"We will bury you near the Great Oak in honor of your attempt." Tiathan played with his mind.

"Somehow you do not give me the confidence I need right now." Carazaar stopped short staring at him.

"It is all we have to look forward to…if we fail." Tiathan urged him on.

There were no guards behind the camp which made it easy for them to find cover amongst the oaks. All eyes were watching the camp of Warthan and a great pillar of fire in the middle of the tents. It would have been easier to rescue Ygueliav from Rhor then it was from Moshdalayrrimich, but Rhor probably knew that when he gave his son to the ruthless leader of the Valkyricks. The sun was setting which would make it easier for him to sneak through the camp without being seen. As the darkness grew, so did the pillar of fire. It was then that Tiathan realized that Rhor had broken away from Zebrac and now worshiped Mortarr. The ugly monstrous face of Mortarr formed from the ash and smoke. Soon a murmuring grew into a mournful dirge as the Gimgiddeans began to sing to the image:

"oi'R dyohidy etooveyoR W dyRohimes
mo eso'v et R mhimdyoRN esoiaes
T efyRo r oi'R sioonefooRti
ad oi'R noiydyo t NooRtihiR'
mo efohiR mootieN W T mynetti
ef' mo ar mynetti siooveyoRN dyhill
baomhiRo basiv RydyoR
ef' eto sioonoes t estioya ll'R esoia
moo esepyRyti mya eshiveyo ll'
moo sihiveyo dyo'ep omoinet
t dyroom' oi'ti ll'R siRyes'
ef' mo ar T moepethiaoin
ephiRti etohiveyom ephiRti ohiRtie
efanes' oom oi'R efo'ti
nRhibeyes' aoefti W oi'R dyoist'"

"They are gaining strength through Mortarr." Carazaar was frightened and excited at the same time. "Mortarr challenges Zebrac now, but will soon challenge Jesuar Himself."

They are not through." Tiathan hoped to learn from their song so continued to listen:

"moo noRsill W ayefo
moo Rost' W dyohitie
mo mya tihivo etooady 'ef ll'R etohiRti
ad nhivo ll' vmo'a t NooRtihiR'
moo xoihiRtioRes nyveyom
moo esoiR'omdyoR stom'
mo ar T moepethiaoin
ephiRti etohiveyom ephiRti ohiRtie
efanes' oom oi'R efo'ti
nRhiveyes' aoefti W oi'R dyoist'"

"It has been written of such a thing, but do not fear Mortarr for he is finite." Tiathan turned to Carazaar. "Jesuar shall always be."

"Don't leave me alone, Tiathan." Carazaar tried to stop Tiathan from going forward. Tiathan pulled away from him and then turned around.

"Watch for me." Tiathan whispered. "If there is trouble, cry the call of the Notherhen."

"What if they are hungry and come to kill this Notherhen?" Carazaar complained that someone might take a shot in his direction.

"Then growl like a Grontar." Tiathan shook his head in dismay. "They won't venture close to that and if you're good enough I might avoid you, too."

Tiathan was up against the braided tent of Rhor hoping to hear their battle plans. He unsheathed his dagger to poke a hole into the side to see what was going on. Rhor and his warrior counsels let out a cheer which muffled the slitting of the tent cloth. He made it large to crawl through and hid behind a Gimgiddean battle shield leaning against a ceiling pole. No one could see him unless they picked up the shield.

"Here comes our messenger from Warthan." Rhor greeted one of his scouts who was out of breath and obviously tired. "Take your time, Kapar. We'll wait for your report. Mora! Bring us a drink of water! Better yet a mug of Schew!"

A young female Gimgiddean in full armor offered Kapar a cup, but he refused it. She then drank it herself before spitting most of it at his feet. She walked back to the throne which Tiathan can tell was slightly smaller than Rhor's on his left. Tiathan guessed Rhor had a companion which was like him with a past and prideful.

"Warthan begs your forgiveness, but he has only heard from his scouts that Moshdalayrrimich has left the Seven Fortresses and destroyed Rabel Ain." Kapar stood straight as he gave his report. "I don't believe he would waste his time fighting Rabel Ainians and now would fight a small band of Trags on the mountain."

"Warthan lies well, but no matter." Rhor laughed playing

with the black curls on Mora's head.

"He wants to know your intentions whether you will join this great army of Valkyricks or stand with him in fighting against them." Kapar waited as if an answer was forthcoming.

"And what did you tell him?" Rhor leaned over against the rail of his throne.

"That we did not know what the Conqueror's intentions were ourselves." Kapar stared into the glistening eyes of Rhor. "However, it should not concern him. I told him he should return to his fortress and leave the valley so there would be no misunderstanding of his presence."

"What was his reply?" Mora hissed at him. Her green skin seemed to visibly crawl as she stared through Kapar. Mora had the bloodline of the Akrillas, Modosites, and Gimgiddeans which made her a rare creature. Her skin was pale green with a face elongated from chin to crown that stretched her flaming yellow eyes into oval spheres that shook fear into those who saw her. However, that fear she instilled made Rhor love her all the more. Her hands were mere claws that were suited for battle, but little else. Her feet were round with three talons for toes that scraped and scratched the stone step beneath her throne. It was meant to intimidate and it worked very well for Kapar was sweating.

"He laughed, my Queen." Kapar appeared confused, not knowing what to make of Mora's obvious hatred for him.

"It could only mean one thing and that is Warthan is her

to fight Moshdalayrrimich and anyone to who follows him." Rhor slammed his dagger into the oak throne.

"We will have to change our plans for tonight, my King." Mora was disappointed.

"Mortarr must send us an answer." Rhor lifted a piece of pink crystal and stared at it absently. "If only there was some truth in this crystal. I can see Mortarr, but I cannot see Zebrac."

"I never could see Zebrac." Mora lifted a second piece joining it with Rhor's own. A flash of light dazzled Tiathan and then slowly faded away.

"It will be done." Rhor threw the crystals to the ground as Mora smiled with satisfaction.

"We must make sure our special guest does not escape again." Mora licked her leathery lips.

"If only Tiathan Eiula were in my grasp instead of his son this would be a very special day." Rhor clapped his claws together.

Tiathan's ears pricked up as he heard his son was a prisoner of Rhor. Did not Carazaar rescue him from Moshdalayrrimich? What was Ygueliav doing here? Tiathan looked for a quick way out even though he hoped to see that Ygueliav was all right. A guard now stood where he cut out an opening making it difficult to get through.

"We must leave our guest secure for another day." Rhor stomped back to his throne. "I will enjoy seeing the Valkyricks waste their warriors attacking that anthill of Trags on the mountain."

"Jabdar!" Mora called to a guard outside the tent. A one-armed warrior drew back the curtains and entered without fanfare.

"Yes, my Queen!" Jabdar bowed before her.

"If in the heat of battle the camp is overrun." Mora smiled at him with her fangs dripping venom. "Make sure the Trag is beheaded and his head taken to the cave of Mortarr."

"Your wish is mine, O Queen." Jabdar bowed and left.

As Rhor ordered his warrior counsels from the tent as Tiathan grabbed the opportunity to slip through the hole in the tent. Before retreating to the clump of trees where Carazaar was waiting, he watched where Jabdar went. A small tent with black and white flags lay just within the circle of fires to his right. There Jabdar tied the flaps back and entered.

"You know what's going on?" Carazaar was delighted to see Tiathan knowing now that he would not have to sound like a Notherhen.

"Did you know they recaptured Ygueliav?" Tiathan gave a wary eye toward Carazaar.

"No, he left with the others." Carazaar was just as surprised as Tiathan.

"He is in that tent over there." Tiathan no sooner got the words out when an alarm was sounded throughout the camp. Rhor was screaming ay his guards as they flitted from one end of the camp to the other.

Soon the forest was filled with warriors picking up swords, shields, battleaxes and lances as they went. Tiathan knew they could not do anything until things calmed down. A second alarm sounded as riders broke into the camp circling with scouts crying out that Warthan was attacking a Gimgiddean company only a mile from their position.

"Mount up!" Thor seemed to breathe fire as Mora almost danced with delight at the coming battle while picking up daggers and a sword.

"We will go now for Ygueliav." Tiathan pulled a reluctant Carazaar up toward the tent.

As Rhor and his warriors left to face Warthan, Tiathan and Carazaar ran toward the black and white flags. None of the Gimgiddeans noticed the two as they rolled themselves behind the tent.

"Let's do this quickly." Carazaar was sweating again.

As they entered the tent, Jabdar immediately drew his sword and confronted Tiathan. Tiathan had only a dagger with him so ran back outside the tent forcing Jabdar to follow him.

"I know of you, Tiathan Eiula." Jabdar was pleased to pit his strength against the great Ioroarka.

"But I know little of you." Tiathan looked up at him.

"You'll have little time to remember." Jabdar struck the first blow that glanced off Tiathan's shoulder knocking him to the ground.

Carazaar jumped to his feet and entered the tent to save Ygueliav who was tied to a post in the back of the tent. After he was freed, Ygueliav and Carazaar escaped into the forest. Ygueliav realized that Tiathan was fighting Jabdar and wanted to go back. Carazaar pulled him away pressing Ygueliav away from the camp.

"I lost this arm by your son's sword and only fitting that I get my revenge." Jabdar pointed to his vacant sleeve. "Now you'll lose your life by mine.

"That is for Jesuar to decide." Tiathan threw his dagger against the breastplate of Jabdar. The blade stuck fast, but did not penetrate through.

"A good try, Trag, but so unworthy an opponent." Jabdar pulled out the dagger and threw it back at him. Jabdar's sword grazed Tiathan's head as he tried to pick up the dagger. A second stroke pierced Tiathan's shoulder forcing him to drop to one knee.

"Jesuar, help me." Tiathan whispered.

"You're finished!" Jabdar sheathed his sword and then picked up the wounded Trag flinging him into the underbrush. "I don't kill wounded unworthy creatures. I let them die slowly of their wounds."

Jabdar spat in Tiathan's direction before reentering the tent finding it empty. After realizing Ygueliav had escaped, Jabdar roared in anger before mounting a stallion to search for his lost prisoner. The camp had only a few guards left as the fires burned brightly into the night sky.

****

"Hurry you two!" Awlion encouraged the two Bantongues toward her fallen father. It had been such a relief that she had seen her father enter the camp. After traveling for so long she was glad to reach him in time.

"We're not young toadies any more, mistress." Zarr huffed his way towards her.

"Cover us." Awlion told them when they reached Tiathan whose wounds were serious enough that he had to be carried.

"Awlion?" Tiathan thought he was delirious from his wounds.

"Tenca? I'm putting my father on your back so we can bring him to the others faster." Awlion lifted Tiathan with Zarr's help the broken body of her father onto the back of Tenca.

"Yes, mistress." Tenca obeyed even though he saw the resistance in Tiathan's eyes. "First, assure your father that we will not eat him."

"Don't be foolish, my father has no fear of you." Awlion

was not so sure seeing the fear in her father's eyes as she tied him down.

"Daughter, you are too trusting with my body." Tiathan whispered in her ear before they started for Mount Hamior.

"Here! Here!" Carazaar was the first to see them. Ygueliav showed the scars of battle on his face, but was healthy nonetheless.

****

"Seeing you makes our decisions easier." Ygueliav hugged his sister.

"It will be good to see Zelbiur, but I heard rumors of Miertur…"Awlion saw the downcast look of Carazaar and Ygueliav.

"Zelbiur is well and the rumors of Miertur are true…." Carazaar's voice trailed off.

"He is dead then?" Awlion felt the breath leave her and not come back again.

"Yes, and Zelbiur has left for the Great Oak with Outra." Ygueliav had already heard everything from Carazaar. "They will be picking up the remnants of the Trags from Quicksnatch and Rabel Ain for we fear that war is inevitable against the Seven Fortresses."

"Your father and I stayed to rescue Ygueliav and others

captured by Moshdalayrrimich." Carazaar made it sound heroic, but there was still fear in his voice.

"My cousin, Thrun, is in the fortress on the mountain." Tiathan felt his strength returning.

"And Agraine?" Awlion was happy to hear they were all alive.

"Yes, we must return to them." Tiathan suddenly thought about the weapons he left behind. "Ygueliav, come here quickly.

"Yes, father." Ygueliav bent over to listen as Tiathan told him where he hid Craxsmoore Guilding and the Karalak. Within minutes, he was off and running back toward the far end of the camp. Most of the Gimgiddeans were already away from the camp, so it was simply finding the hiding spot and take the weapons away with him. As he looked he found only the Karalak, but not Craxsmoore Guilding. When he returned his face told Tiathan everything he wanted to know.

"Where is it?" Tiathan held out his hands.

"I do not know." Ygueliav placed the Karalak next to his father.

"Jabdar must have found it somehow." Tiathan was heartbroken, yet the Karalak seemed to give him strength. "I think I can walk with you now."

"But your wounds…?" Carazaar was amazed to see that Tiathan's wounds had somehow healed.

"It must be the Karalak, but at what price?" Ygueliav

noticed a certain fierceness in his father's face that was not there before.

"It may also be the hand of Jesuar." Tiathan even doubted his own words as the need to fight surged through his veins.

"We've much to talk about, father." Awlion changed the conversation.

"We must get Craxsmoore Guilding back." Tiathan ignored her. As he raised the Karalak, his grip nudged a lever that splayed out two other blades turning it into a trident. Awlion gently tried to take the sword from him, but he held it ever more tightly.

"What's happening?" Awlion was afraid as she turned to Carazaar.

"Leave it be for now." Carazaar appeared to be calm even as the Karalak dazzled him from where he stood, "I have heard of the strange healing powers of that weapon, but also that it changes its bearer many ways."

The glow subsided from the Karalak as Tiathan was able to stand upright. He swung the blade this way and that while raising it high in the air so everyone noticed its brightness. It was then that they all noticed that Tiathan's beard had changed to pure white.

"The Karalak is now the weapon of Jesuar!" Tiathan felt

both strength and anger well up inside him. "We'll get Craxsmoore Guilding back and show those who oppose us that Jesuar of the Great Oak is the real ruler of Everstream."

****

"Why do we come this way?" Thrun asked Tranda Marr, the best scout of the Trags besides Tiathan himself. Outra had already left to go ahead to meet them at the Great Oak if they got that far.

"We must bypass the House of Myrr to get back to Quicksnatch." Tranda drew three paths on the ground. She had the sharpest eyes as Zelbiur had the sharpest ears. The difference was that Tranda had deep blue piercing eyes and many feared to go near her. Tranda had been alone most of her life so devoted herself being a scout for the Trags. Her travels through the Dark Forest provided worthwhile with the present danger they were in.

"Nsaat is not there so it might be safer to go directly to Quicksnatch." Zelbiur kept a wary eye on the path ahead.

"I would not chance it since the House of Myrr is always protected." Tranda insisted. "The path to the left would lead us to the House of Myrr, the idle path to the Void of Deen, and the one on the right leads to Byabnol. The only safe way is through the Void of Deen."

"I have never been through the Void of Deen and it may

be just as dangerous as any other path." Zelbiur did not like the choices at all.

"I am willing to go wherever she says." Schill did not see the difference in any of the paths since they all seemed dangerous to her as well.

"In the Void of Deen I cannot hear anything more than what you can hear." Zelbiur heard stories that his father told him about his adventure through the Void. "It could only be a few feet or not at all."

"If we fear it then those who follow us will fear it, too." Tranda searched Zelbiur's face knowing that he was aware that they were being followed.

"Hopefully more than us." Zelbiur sighed.

"Do you know more than us?" Thrun was sure he was missing something in their conversation.

"Will you follow me, Prerman?" Tranda turned to her brother who had no skills except that of the bow and arrow.

"As the hand of Jesuar is upon you, I will follow." Prerman did not hesitate to support her. "To death's door and beyond, my sister."

"As always." Tranda brushed away the jet black hair from his eyes and kissed his forehead. One attribute Prerman had was his burnt olive skin that made it impossible to find him in dark places like a cave. When he steadied himself in one spot and slowed down his breathing, even Zelbiur could not find him.

"The Void of Deen has no path beyond this point, but I can get us through soon enough." Tranda used her sword to hack away at the thick undergrowth.

Although Zelbiur could see her swinging the sword, he could hardly hear it strike as they entered a very quiet world. The Trags followed Tranda for most of the day before one of the warriors began to shake and cry out as if in pain. Zelbiur and Thrun didn't know what direction was east or west only followed Tranda who seemed to know where they were going. The sun seemed to rise and set from the same place. The moon rose overhead before turning around to set at the same place it arose.

Zelbiur was taken aback with the quiet in the Void and he realized he could hear a lot more than those around him. There was a faint sound of flying Irthas, Notherhens and howling Kranacs which sounded like cries for help. If there were warriors close by he wouldn't hear them in time. Everything moved in slow motion once they were in the Void and it was unnerving.

"It's too quiet, Prerman." Zelbiur shouted though Prerman could only read his lips.

"That's why it is called the Void." Prerman laughed without a sound or echo. "It will eventually cause insanity if you get lost in here."

"Peace!" Zelbiur heard Tranda's faint voice though she was not three feet from him.

Zelbiur dispatched the Trags in a semicircle battle line. Thrun and Schill stood on the outside line as Zelbiur made his stand in the center. The silence was maddening to them all.

"What is it?" Zelbiur finally asked her.

"We've reached the end of the Void." Tranda pointed down into a glen with a log barrier that lay glistening in the morning fog.

"What troubles you?" Zelbiur tried to readjust his hearing.

"I'm not sure." Tranda strained to see what might be behind the logs.

"Bantongues, maybe fifty strong." Zelbiur regained his hearing which almost deafened him. There were harsh whispers and familiar cries of sorrow coming from behind the logs. "And Trags."

"Are you sure?" Tranda knew better to ask that of Zelbiur, but could not understand how the Trags had come so close to the Void.

"I hear Arden Warkman complaining as he did when he was forced to earn a day's wages in Quicksnatch." Zelbiur smiled. "I hear Madvark Tillger consoling his companion, Tharta, who is crying very loud."

"There are three Bantongues guarding the outside

camp." Tranda motioned to Zelbiur.

"Oakran! Paldour! Zalmac! Take care of the guards!" Zelbiur ordered the only warriors carried lances. He looked to the other Trags. "You four will go with Tranda and the rest of you with me. Thrun, move to the right and Schill to the left."

The three Bantongues were easily dispatched without a sound since they almost asleep at their watch. Zelbiur moved closer to the camp listening to various conversations that were being held throughout the glen, but heard nothing that could help them. Bantongues were such an ignorant lot who could not think for themselves. It was then he stopped in his tracks when he heard the name "Apadalpa" which meant 'He who escapes'.

"Escape!" Zelbiur worried over the word as he turned to the others. "We must hurry."

He waved the Trags forward as five of his warriors race into the woods which sounded the alarm with fifteen Bantongues racing behind them. There was nothing he could do to join the fight that was to ensue since he had a chance with only about twenty Bantongues left to fight. Thrun had his archers ready their arrows as Zelbiur peeked over the log fence seeing the captive Trags digging through the dirt wall that held them. Zelbiur gave the signal that arrows and spears into the chests of ten Bantongues who already were approaching his position. The captive Trags were surprised before turning to use their shovels and pickaxes as weapons against the Bantongues.

It was a short fight as the remaining Bantongues fled into the forest.

Frightened, the Bantongues ran into the five Trags coming back from their fight in the forest. An older Bantongue raised his talons as the others came to his side trying to form a fighting phalanx to protect themselves. The freed Trags took positions near the Void of Deen waiting for Zelbiur to order the attack.

"Come, my brothers, quickly before others come to their aid." Zelbiur ordered the Trags to dig in before the attack. Trag archers gave their daggers to those without weapons and held their ground by breaking the ends of their shovels to act as lances.

More Bantongues came out of the forest and advanced singing their battle chant:

"dyohitie t iet's moo dyoefll OO
dyohitie tiya' dyohitie ethies sioono"

The Trags held their ground without fear for Jesuar put their fate before them and vengeance was now foremost on their minds. The first wave of Bantongues were struck down with a hail of arrows and the violent thrust of splintered lances. The second wave broke through the center of the Trags killing four and barely missing Zelbiur with their dripping venomous fangs.

"For Jesuar!" Zelbiur cried slashing his sword left and right without ceasing.

"Zelbiur!" Tranda cried as two Bantongues overwhelmed her with their talons almost at her throat.

"Here!" Zelbiur jumped on the closest one to him almost beheading the creature with his sword.

"And here!" Thrun pierced the heart of the other.

"And here!" Schill shoved a spear into the throat of the same creature.

"Tranda!" Zelbiur picked her up though she didn't seem to breathe. Suddenly she moved slightly and opened her eyes seeing him looking worried about her.

The Trags fought valiantly though many died in the effort. The Bantongues soon retreated back toward the forest until they heard another Bantongue war cry. Fifteen more Bantongues appeared giving the others renewed strength and will to fight on. The war chant was sounded again as they regrouped into one large phalanx to finish the Trags once and for all.

"Be ready! Close ranks!" Thrun ordered the Trags as Zelbiur hurriedly covered Tranda with a shield and cloak. Her wounds made her weak and he did not want to lose her.

"Archers! Behind me!" Zelbiur retook command and set twenty archers left putting them in four separate rows one behind the other.

The Bantongues began their charge shaking the earth as they ran. The first row of Trags let fly arrows one row after another so that a steady flurry of them would blot out the sky. Many hit their mark as the black furry bodies flew like wheat from a scythe. By the time any of the Bantongues reached the Trags on the small knoll there were only ten left. The battle still raged for another hour before it was over. Every Bantongue was buried before the Trags rested from battle. Trags lay buried beside Bantongue with the honor due them.

"How many of us are still alive?" Thrun was too weary to count.

"Seventeen archers, twenty lancers and the four of us." Schill counted quickly.

"How is Tranda?" Zelbiur asked Schill who was attending her with cloth and splint.

"She will be well for now." Schill stroked Tranda's hair as she would her own daughter.

"We'll rest here for the night and then march to…" Zelbiur pricked up his ears almost hearing something in the distance. "This may not be the only camp of Trags around here. We'll search for others in the morning."

"Then to the Seven Fortresses!" Thrun raised his fist in defiance.

"It is inevitable that we go there, but with two thousand

Trag warriors instead of forty-one." Zelbiur lay down to sleep. He spent the night now and again looking to see if there was any change to Tranda before finally drifting off into a deep sleep.

CHAPTER SEVEN

"If we wait for the outcome of the battle between Rhor and Warthan." Tiathan drew circles in the dust. "We'll know their strengths and weaknesses. Perhaps Warthan will allow us to pass through the mountains beyond. He has given us safe passage before even though we are on the brink of war."

"He will kill us." Carazaar was blunt and to the point.

"How so?" Tiathan was a little annoyed as he gripped the Karalak tightly. The weapon never left his side since he was given it.

"I've seen his meaning of sanctuary with the Valkyricks and Gimgiddeans." Carazaar explained feeling a salty taste in his mouth. "He has killed many in their sleep."

"If he suffers heavy losses he will think twice about attacking us." Awlion thought out loud, wondering how she could get the Karalak from his hands. A slow change was evolving in her father's manner and decisions that was not like him at all. "Maybe we can go around all of them to the mountain. We are too few to make any mistakes in this."

"We best go alone without them knowing we are here." Ygueliav was tired, yet wanted to go on.

"We know Warthan." Zarr spoke for Tenca who nodded agreement. "He makes alliances like the Akrillas. When the battle starts, he will betray us."

"You all have spoken well, but I will tell you what we are going to do." Tiathan was impatient with them all. "I must have Craxsmoore Guilding back and I want all of you to have ideas how we can do this."

"Send me." Awlion wanted to get away and think about what to do as her father was changing before her eyes.

"And us." Zarr and Tenca stood with her.

"We can't spare any of you." Tiathan stared at her hard. "You would take Craxsmoore Guilding from me?"

"I will go anyway, father." Awlion wiped a tear from her eye. "The Karalak is changing you and you must give it up."

"It is mine!" Tiathan struggled with the effort to throw it away, but couldn't. "You will not have my blessing if you leave of even the blessing of Jesuar."

"Then pray to Jesuar for your sanity." Awlion started away with Zarr and Tenca close behind.

"My daughter's life in your hands, Zarr…Tenca!" Tiathan raised the Karalak as a warning. "Bring her back safely!"

"We hear and obey, great Ioroarka." Zarr and Tenca bowed together.

Awlion and her two protectors soon vanished into the wilderness beyond the clearing where Rhor set up camp. What she planned to do Tiathan didn't know   and surprisingly didn't care. He struggle with the thoughts as he looked down at the Karalak.

"We are not going to Mount Hamior, but to the mountains of the Drearnok." Tiathan changed their plans abruptly.

"But those mountains are fifteen miles away from here." Ygueliav was stunned at his father's decision to go somewhere else so abruptly. "What so my cousin, Agraine, and all those trapped up there?"

"We must allow Jesuar's will to work." Tiathan knew his pain even though he could not let emotion override his belief of the will of Jesuar.

"Father?" Ygueliav realized how far his father had changed.

"Yes, my son?" Tiathan looked away from him.

"Why do we go to the mountains of the Drearnok?" He had no reason why they would go near such a place.

"We once, before you were born, lived there." Tiathan's eyes glazed over in thought. "It was the home of Jesuar before the Great Oak. There were no fortresses or different warriors fighting amongst themselves in those days. We dwelt at the base of the mountains where there were thousands of us at peace in Everstream."

"Until the day of the Drearnok." Ygueliav remembered well the story.

"The Drearnok came quickly and silently." Tiathan shook his head sadly not realizing he had dropped the Karalak to the ground. Ygueliav quickly picked it up and hid it under a gnarled oak. "From the depths of Everstream and the Black Lake devouring every Trag that crossed its path. Some of us even worshiped the monster."

"What did it look like?" Carazaar became very interested.

"It was a slithering, leathery creature with three heads with each one having its own voice." Tiathan tried to visualize it. "If it wasn't for them arguing with each other concerning the creature, we would have lost fewer of our warriors trying to fight it. The scales were like sturdy oak shields with no weak spot that could be used against it. The Drearnok could spit venom and fire fifty yards and kill anyone who was unlucky enough to be standing in front of it."

"Much of the danger of the Drearnok was not in its venom, but the hatred it brought to all the Trags." Ygueliav closed his eyes and recounted part of the story. "It demanded that all of us bow down and worship at his feet. Many of us refused and were forced from the mountains."

"What of Jesuar?" Carazaar could not understand.

"Jesuar warned us that the Drearnok promised was coming." Tiathan's voice saddened as he spoke. "Some of us laughed, others were afraid, but we did nothing to prepare for that dark day."

"The first head of the Drearnok promised that we would live forever if we worshiped it." Ygueliav, too, came under the spell of the tale. "The second head promised us wealth and the third head promised us that we would see Jesuar."

"Jesuar spoke from the mountains." Tiathan stared absently for a few seconds before continuing. "But we could not hear Him because the Drearnok spoke close into our ears. We believed it could show us Jesuar until the creature told us it was Jesuar."

"And we believed." Ygueliav stared blankly at the ground. Though he never experienced it, he knew turning from Jesuar must have been terrible. He was not sure how anyone could turn from Him, but bondage was so foreign to Ygueliav because of the freedom he has shared with his father all his life. How desperate for life they must have felt.

"What did Jesuar do?" Carazaar looked first to Tiathan then to Ygueliav.

"Jesuar allowed the Drearnok to make a pact with Rhor, our enemy." Tiathan was getting angry now. "And put us into bondage. We were traded for the mountains of our forefathers as Jesuar and Notfer Whorld, Outra's father, left us there to the Great Oak of Quicksnatch. Jesuar would not speak with us except through Notfer because we disobeyed Him."

"Is the Drearnok still in those mountains?" Carazaar wasn't sure he wanted to meet it, but wouldn't mind seeing the creature. "Can it still deceive us?"

"We don't know." Tiathan knew now that they must return to Mount Hamior and then realized he no longer held the Karalak. "Thank you, my son,"

"We still must take it with us, father." Ygueliav now saw the father he knew and loved. "It might even be useful if we have to fight the Drearnok."

"We have more important work ahead of us." Tiathan felt a renewed strength and purpose. "Our friends and family await us on Mount Hamior if I am right."

"You have changed your mind about the Drearnok." Ygueliav wondered how quickly the effect the Karalak away upon his father.

"No, only to let our friends know where we are going." Tiathan believed going to the mountain was the best path no matter the danger.

****

"I don't know why they haven't attacked us." Agraine looked out the small opening down the mountainside.

"They know they can defeat us so why rush if there is nothing else to do?" Mikar hoped they would never attack. "Isn't that right, Stilkyl?"

"I don't care either way." Stilkyl lifted an eyebrow toward her companion as she sharpened spears and lances for the coming battle.

"There is no way the others can reach us." Agraine looked around at the eighty-two strong warriors trying to defeat thousands from the ground and the air.

"Then it will be an even battle." Mikar tried to keep a straight face. "If the others were here they wouldn't stand a chance."

"Too true, Mikar." Stilkyl stifled a laugh.

"I would like to see my father and mother again." Agraine stared into the noon day sky dotted with Harkies looking at the forest below.

"The Harkies have spotted something." Mikar followed Agraine's stare.

"Whatever it is, they aren't too concerned." Agraine did not see them raise an alarm, just drifting with the wind watching whatever it was on the ground.

****

"They see us." Carazaar looked up at the Harkies overhead.

"They are unsure of what they see because of us." Zarr was the first out from the forest. Tenca and Awlion followed tired from scouting and hiding from various warriors that crossed their paths.

"Then let us make it easier for them to understand." Tiathan led them off the path and out of sight.

"We must rest for a while." Awlion looked as tired as she felt.

"What news of Craxsmoore Guilding?" He turned to Awlion.

"Jabdar has it." Awlion was relieved to find her father was no longer under the power of the Karalak.

"What now?" Ygueliav waited to see what miracle his father could pull off now.

"We will use Zarr and Tenca as our way to the mountain." Tiathan saw the look of relief as he had changed his mind about the Mount Hamior. He started to cut Vandal Vines for rope.

"What will we use these for?" Carazaar questioned the logic of cutting the vines.

"We will tie ourselves to the bottom of Zarr and Tenca so they can take us up the mountain unseen." Tiathan told them of his plan.

"With all that hair we will not be seen from the air or, if we are lucky, from either side on the ground." Ygueliav liked the idea.

"I am ticklish." Zarr protested.

"We'll try not to move around too much then." Tiathan would not hear of his complaint. He then turned to the few Trags that followed him. "Everyone else will meet us on the far side of the mountain. If we do not come by nightfall, we will never be there."

As they trekked their way toward the mountain, the Harkies followed for a full mile before they turned back. The underbelly of the Bantongues were hot and smelly, but their lives depended on getting through to the others. The climb up the mount was rough since they were stopped by Valkyrick and Gimgiddean guards who were really not interested in Zarr or Tenca so let them pass.

"Hold there if you value your life!" Agraine had five archers train their arrows on them.

"Agraine? Good to see you again!" Zarr almost smiled.

"Zarr? Tenca? Where are the others?" Agraine's heart leapt.

"Tied beneath us and I must say I thought it was good of

me not to laugh when passing so many guards." Zarr shook Tiathan and Ygueliav loose.

"I tried not to scratch. Carazaar was very itchy." Tenca shook him loose as well. "I hardly noticed Awlion."

"Awlion, sister!" Agraine almost climbed out of the opening. "Come in quickly before you are seen."

"You understand that we cannot join you?" Tenca turned to Zarr. "We must allow this to look good."

"Yes, Agraine?" Zarr looked towards her.

"Yes, Zarr." Agraine knew what he was going to ask.

"Are your archers good enough to not kill us?" Zarr winced at the thought of being shot with an arrow.

"I think here." Tenca pointed to a spot on his left side. "This would be the place to….you know."

"We can't shoot you." Agraine protested, but knew it had to be done for both their sakes.

"Do it quickly because they are watching." Zarr closed his eyes waiting for the pain to begin.

A moment later they both had an arrow sticking out from their sides. The wounds would heal quickly and the scars left behind would be a badge of honor. Zarr and Tenca scurried back down the mountain hearing the laughter of the guards as they passed. No one saw that they left something behind and only pride was their temporary wounds.

"As glad as I am to see you." Agraine steadied her elation in seeing them again. "You should not have come back here."

"We had to since I could not desert you." Tiathan embraced her.

"If they find out you are here, they will certainly attack us." Mikar could not keep still.

"Would you rather we leave?" Carazaar was surprised that they were not welcome. "However, our transportation has gone down the mountainside."

"There is no way now." Stilkyl looked out the small portal seeing a party of six Bantongues and twenty Valkyricks approaching their position.

"We will leave after dark." Ygueliav backed away from the light pouring in from the portals. "They are searching the forest for us and if they do not find our trail, they will know we are here."

"We do not interest them." Agraine was relieved and insulted, but at least they were alive."

"What we need are the scales of the Drearnok." Tiathan was angry that he would have to confront the creature again as those who followed him.

"Scales of the Drearnok?" Carazaar was not happy with this new thought. "It would turn us to ashes before we could get close enough if what you say is true."

"The scales can be fashioned into shields and breastplates which could withstand the strongest and sharpest sword." Ygueliav saw the wisdom and folly of the adventure.

"The Drearnok knows me and will not kill us until it exacts a price." Tiathan knew he could not kill it, but thinking of the Karalak he saw a chance to defeat it.

"You have seen this thing?" Carazaar was amazed and impressed with him. "And lived to tell of what you encountered?"

"Only a few of us will go." Tiathan looked over who was there. "Awlion, Ygueliav and you, Carazaar will have to come with me. We will need six warriors to join us with large sacks, spears, bows and arrows. This way no member of my family can stir the anger of our friends out there. We will meet up with the others we sent ahead.

"Our visitors have stopped at the bottom of the ledge." Stilkyl watched as the warriors spread out beneath them.

"Well, what do we do now?" Carazaar paced back and forth.

"We have time for me to tell you a story." Tiathan sat him down. As his thoughts and mind drifted back to a more terrible time, he remembered the things he wanted to forget. "In the early days during our bondage, Rhor proclaimed that any day celebrating Jesuar was banned under penalty of death. It was by our own stubbornness that we immediately proclaimed a holiday for Jesuar. It started as defiance and then it turned into a blood bath when Rhor came with an image of Zebrac carved in a crystal. He told us to bow down to this image and we refused. It resulted in the death of four hundred by the sword and the breath of the Drearnok. The Drearnok allowed Rhor to rule because it couldn't watch all of us at the same time. The only reason he stopped the killing was that there were fewer Trags to do their work and more of his warriors had to make up the shortage. For our future safety we never had a public display of loyalty to Jesuar, but in our tents we prayed in our hearts and worshiped Him."

"It looks like that time has come again." Carazaar glanced out the portal watching a Valkyrick Captain order his warriors to offensive positions.

"However, we made swords and daggers in secret, but we should have let Jesuar's will be done." Tiathan continued his tale. "I was spoken to directly by Jesuar to face Rhor and demand our freedom. I hesitated and things became worse. Finally, I stood before Rhor and made the demand to be freed and he refused. His warriors laughed at me until the voice of Jesuar came from my mouth. I told them that plagues of the worst kind would descend upon him and his warriors. For two months sickness and death visited our captors, but we remained healthy. Rhor saw this and finally let us free."

"That is when you came to Quicksnatch?" Carazaar interrupted though he wanted to hear the whole story.

"No." Tiathan was patient with him since the retelling of the story relaxed him. "Rhor let us go and then had second thoughts sending his warriors against us. We knew only Jesuar could save us now for the Drearnok would certainly find us. In the great valley of Gimgiddo we stood with the Seven Fortresses in front of us and Rhor's warriors behind. They advanced with drum and trumpet as we trembled before them. I had no fear then, but even I saw our own destruction. As the Gimgiddeans marched around us we fell to our knees in prayer. We heard their war chants, screams, hoof beats and war horses pounding in our ears." Tiathan stopped for effect.

"Then what?" Carazaar was captivated with every word.

"It was then Jesuar spoke to us from above." Tiathan continued:

"I am Ichtar!
I am Icthus
I am the Fisher of all!
Woe to Zebrac!
Woe to Mortarr!
Who raises their swords against Me?
Who raises their swords
Against those I have protected?"

"Lightning flashed from the sky." Tiathan raised his voice for effect. "Torrents of rain flooded the valley except where we stood in awe as their warriors cried out in anguish:

"Great Zebrac save us!
Magnificent Mortarr help us!"

"Then there was silence in the valley." His voice was
hushed as if still in awe of what had happened so many years
before. "When the rain stopped and the mist lifted before us, the
great army of Rhor was laid waste. Only a few warriors who
stayed on the hillside were spared. We escaped to Quicksnatch
fighting Bantongue, Valkyrick and Gimgiddean along the way.
Rhor had a few hundred warriors left behind in his fortress. He
allied himself with Moshdalayrrimich up to this day. Now he
has a greater army which we fear will try again to control
Everstream."

"I am amazed and thankful you told me this great history
of the Trags." Carazaar bowed to Tiathan.

"We have had the good fortune to see firsthand what
Jesuar can do." Tiathan became more thoughtful, stroking his
white beard as he spoke. "But over the years the memories
become vague, forgetful images of thing past. We chose what
was important and what was not for our own purposes. The
Great Oak was quiet a long time before Moshdalayrrimich
decided to take control of Everstream. When we realized our
disobedience to Jesuar, our families were taken from us and we
were cast into the Dark Forest. Now those of us who are

scattered throughout the land must reunite if we are going to gain back Jesuar's favor and blessing."

"The sun is setting." Agraine did not want them to go and it would be dark soon so they could escape. She knew most of them would have to stay and fight.

"Peace to you all." Tiathan looked over the small force he may never see again.

"Hur-rah!" They cheered as one in salute.

Agraine and four other archers shot flaming arrows into the guards at the bottom of the mountainside. A small fire forced the guards to leave their posts and tried to put it out. Tiathan, Ygueliav, Carazaar, Awlion and the others slipped unnoticed down the mountainside towards the mountains of the Drearnok. Agraine watched as long as she could until they disappeared from view. It was then that she saw the Bantongues climbing trees and surrounding the fortress they had built. Above the evening sky as the moon rose higher, Harkies flew in threes and fours scouring the countryside for anyone who did not belong. The hour had come to fight and she prayed that Jesuar would let them die with honor and give Tiathan more time to escape. She may never know if they would have success as she released the first arrow into the night sky.

****

The journey was longer than they expected. Each hour

forced them to think harder of the task ahead than of their friends behind. They marched through the Black Hills of Avenknel and into the Breen Forest where the Stilt Spiders ventured from caves and mines to raise their young for two short weeks before quickly returning to their nests.

The Valley of the Drearnok lay just beyond the Breen Forest as familiar as any other place in Everstream. The fog that filtered through the trees was really the breath of the Drearnok, heavy and filled with musk from the evil it spewed over so many years. Tiathan hesitated to be the first into the clearing just below the cave where the Drearnok lived. It was also the bleak dungeon where the Trags suffered for years before they escaped. Rhor found many Trags throughout the countryside and some still were bound into slavery.

"I will go first, father." Awlion stepped out into the morning sun.

"No, I must go first if we are to have a chance." Tiathan quickly overtook her already realizing that they had awakened the Drearnok.

A blast of heat melted the air they breathed as sand pelted their faces creasing their cheeks with pain and the cry of anguish from the shadows chilled their very bones. Into the sunlight came the Drearnok, a three headed slithering creature that rose twenty feet in the air. Small leathery wings fluttered on each side of its heads, its triangular eyes flamed a fiery red and yellow and the slippery lathering sound from its forked tongues rained venom to the ground.

"Tiathan Eiula!" The Drearnok's first head sneered towards him while the other heads looked over the rest of the group. Has-s-s it been s-s-so long s-s-since we las-s-s-st parted?"

"Not long enough." Tiathan watched the coils of its skin expand and contract.

"Oh, we are devas-s-stated that you have not vis-s-sited us-s-s s-s-sooner." The second head of the Drearnok moaned.

"Are there no more Trags to torment?" Awlion was followed by the others with Carazaar hiding behind them.

"No, no, all gone." The third head seemed pleased to see her. "All that mattered have left without a word of thanks-s-s." A deep, soft laugh shook the ground.

"It was-s-s not our fault." The first head of the Drearnok drifted down closer to Awlion.

"But let us-s-s talk of things-s-s." The second head stared straight at Carazaar.

"S-s-someone new?" The third head stuck out its flickering tongue at him. Come clos-s-ser our friend."

"I think not." Carazaar refused to budge.

"Do not fear us-s-s." The first head gently pulled back away from them.

"We have s-s-seen vis-s-sions-s-s that you could only dream about." The second head almost whispered.

"We have fortunes-s-s no other one could poss-s-sess-s-s." The third head added while studying Tiathan who never seemed nervous nor sweated in its presence.

"We poss-s-sess-s-s s-s-spirits-s-s at our command to avenge any wrong." The first head twisted its head around and over them all.

"To heal." The second head spoke louder.

"To conquer." The third head dripped venom.

"And to bring plagues-s-s." The first head finished with a flourish.

"You can join us-s-s, Carazaar." The second head saw the surprised look on the magician's face. "You are like us-s-s and not at all s-s-should be with them.

"Yes-s-s, we know who you all are." The third head drifted back down toward them.

"You, Carazaar, want all that we have and more." The first head lowered itself on the other side of Carazaar. "You don't want Jes-s-suar or even to be with thes-s-se ....Trags-s-s."

"How do you know what I want?" Carazaar sputtered.

"Fight them, Carazaar!" Awlion tried to encourage him, but the soft seduction of the Drearnok's words have already affected him.

"We know all, don't we, Tiathan Eiula?" The second

head sniffed impolitely at Tiathan.

"No, not all." Tiathan turned an whispered to Awlion and Ygueliav. "As I strike its sides, you and the others pick up the scales and leave the valley. Do not wait for me."

"We cannot leave you, father." Awlion protested.

"You must leave me for the sake of the others." Tiathan insisted. "Jesuar will be with you."

"We will come back for you." Ygueliav would not hear of anything else.

"No, stay away." Tiathan grabbed his shoulder. "If you return, I will not be found here."

"Then I will stay." Awlion clenched her teeth.

"I order you to go because Agraine will need you." Tiathan felt the hot breath of the Drearnok behind him.

"Carazaar unders-s-stands-s-s us-s-s." The first head of the Drearnok refused to be ignored.

"Follow us-s-s and we will give you the power you s-s-seek, Carazaar." The second head swayed back and forth to mesmerize him.

"If you follow Jesuar as you told us, then do not listen to them." Tiathan warned him.

"I...don't...know." Carazaar was already under their hypnotic gaze.

"Yes, you do! Obey Jesuar!" Tiathan shouted at him, but Carazaar was already walking past the |Drearnok and into the cave behind.

"So easy." The third head's thunderous laugh echoed throughout the valley.

"Go, our friend! Through the gates-s-s of the Drearnok." the first head was triumphant as Carazaar disappeared into the darkness.

"You have brought others-s-s for our pleas-s-sure." The second head turned to the other Trags.

"No more!" Awlion let loose an arrow that shattered against the Drearnok's scales.

"No less-s-s!" The Drearnok used its mottled tail to knock Awlion off her feet.

"Stay!" Tiathan drew out the Karalak pointing it at the creature. "In the name of Jesuar you will obey his own!"

"O-o-o! A nas-s-sty weapon you have!" The second head mocked Tiathan.

"Keep your distance or we will find out its true power!" Tiathan waved the blade in the air.

"We know its-s-s true power. Do you?" The third head almost smiled.

"Obey Jesuar!" Tiathan said again.

"Obey?" They all laughed.

"We have never obeyed Jes-s-suar." The third head spit flame.

"Why s-s-should we obey Him now?" The first head

tried to strike at Tiathan's feet.

"You know this weapon?" Tiathan just missed striking its head.

"Oh, yes-s-s, we had it forged in our mines." The second head seemed not to fear it.

"Do you think you could kill us-s-s with that?" The first head bobbed up and down menacingly above Tiathan.

"Good for us-s-s that you have it for the longer you hold it, the clos-s-ser you come to us-s-s." The third glared at him.

"I will not give it enough time to corrupt me." Tiathan handed the Karalak to Awlion.

"Devious-s-s!" The first head shook violently.\

"Mis-s-schievious-s-s!" The second head echoed.

"Malicious-s-s!" The third head bobbed up and down.

"S-s-surely, we can s-s-speak of better things-s-s." The first head of the Drearnok kept its distance.

"Yes, we want the Trags you have kept prisoner for the past fifteen years!" Awlion swung the Karalak moving it from one hand to the other feeling the evil power swell within her grasp.

"We could take you as-s-s pris-s-soners-s-s as-s-s well." The third head hissed horribly at her.

"S-s-stay with us-s-s and we will s-s-show you the riches-s-s of Evers-s-stream." The second head stared into Awlion's eyes.

"S-s-stay with us-s-s and you will be as-s-s Jes-s-suar Hims-s-self. You will be more powerful than ours-s-selvess-s-s-s-s." The third head bobbed and weaved above her.

"If I stay I will be cursed by Jesuar. My riches are my family and my weapon of choice is the bow and arrow." Awlion was defiant and stood her ground. "I may die by your hand, but all the riches I could ever want would be found in the arms of Jesuar."

"You have at least four hundred Trags in your caves." Tiathan wanted to get back to business. "Send them to us now!"

"How dare you!" The second head snapped at Tiathan who quickly took the Karalak from Awlion and split the creature's jaw.

"Hurt me! He has-s-s hurt me!" They said in unison even as the wound quickly healed. The Drearnok stomped its foot and swished it rattling tail in anger.

"I could cut off your head, but then we could not negotiate until it grew back again. "Tiathan smiled slightly.

"You have forgotten who we are, Tiathan Eiula!" The first head belched flame and smoke.

"You are the Drearnok, punisher of the living and the dead." Tiathan know the saying by heart from the bondage he had endured. "You are the weapon of Mortarr who cannot survive except in fire and smoke. You do what Mortarr cannot do. Even Jesuar sees need of you only as a reminder to all who love Him that evil lives in Everstream, too. You and Nsaat come from the same black pit and will return there when Jesuar puts an end of the reign of Mortarr."

"You remember well, Tiathan Eiula, even adding a little bit of nons-s-sens-s-se on your own." The third head narrowed its angry eyes.

"You cannot hypnotize those of us who follow Jesuar." Tiathan waved the Drearnok away. "Our prayers and the Spirit of Jesuar protect us."

"Protect you and yours-s-s maybe, but not the others." The first head looked over at the other Trags.

"Let us-s-s tell them of our power and s-s-strength." The second head licked what was left of its wounded mouth.

"No, in the name of Jesuar you will be of service to us!" Tiathan struck another blow at the neck of the Drearnok sending scales to the ground.

"He dares-s-s to attack us-s-s again!" The first head was irate blasting fire and smoke into the air.

"You cannot believe you have a chance agains-s-st us-s-s?" The third head was still stunned that Tiathan would try.

"Spread out! Use the scales as shields!" Tiathan ordered the Trags. He knew spears and arrows were useless, but they might confuse the Drearnok enough for him to strike the Karalak upon it.

"The Karalak cannot kill us-s-s!" The third head did not

sound as convincing as before. The Drearnok noticeably started to step back.

Arrows and spears rained against the Drearnok giving Tiathan opportunities to strike again and again. A hundred scales fell to the ground which the Trags gathered up in sacks while evading the smoke and flame from the creature. Awlion shot an arrow into its mouth causing it to howl in pain. More arrows struck the inside of their mouths though the dragon spit them out as fast as they could. The Drearnok ignored Tiathan in order to stop the barrage.

Ygueliav ordered the Trags to retreat while grabbing Awlion by the shoulders to force her back. Tiathan continued to force the creature towards its lair. The Drearnok hissed and moaned as the Karalak struck scale and leathery skin.

"Enough!" The first head screamed.

"Leave me!" Tiathan turned to the others.

"We cannot!" Awlion pleaded against leaving.

"Leave now!" Tiathan hid within a pile of rocks and scales.

"Enough!" The three heads unleashed a scalding stream of fire and smoke that enveloped the place where Tiathan hid himself.

"We must go!" Ygueliav led the Trags away.

"No!" Awlion tried to go back, but Ygueliav pulled her away.

"We will have you all!" The Drearnok looked at its wounds before limping back into its cave.

Ygueliav and Awlion mourned the loss of their father as they hurried away from the valley. The scorched earth and rock could not have had any other result than the death of Tiathan Eiula. When they were safe enough away they sang the Song of Burial:

"mo noi'Rm T dyohitie
'ef T mhiR'yooR TvN
moo baRoi'nhiet OO etoRo
mo noi'Rm T aooes'
'ef T efhitieoR moo aody
OO t efRo'dyoon
mo sioaobaRhitio et's ephies'N
oomall baosihioieso hio ayveyoes
met oi'R aooRdy XoesoihiR"

****

Zelbiur brought his company of Trags just a mile from the Great Oak as the sun was setting in the west and a soft breeze at their backs. A squeal of surprise echoed from the evening sky as a great shadow covered the drifting clouds overhead. Whatever creature it was, it hid in the darker shadows of the wood.

"What business do you have with us?" Zelbiur could hear the heavy breathing. "You have come a long way to be silent."

"Your ears have always betrayed me." A Crackling voice whispered from the wood.

"Come out, Onigel, and speak your mind." Zelbiur placed his hand on Thrun's shoulder as he started to raise his battleaxe.

"A Troop Bat!" Thrun spat out the words in disgust. "No good will come of this!"

"You wish to kill me then? Come, let us embrace in battle." Onigel waddled into the dim light. His leathery skin crinkled and stretched as he walked. Onigel's dark red eyes pierced the growing darkness making his wrinkled face more terrifying than it already was.

"Stop it, both of you!" Zelbiur stood between them. "Since you came alone, I must think this is important to both of us."

"As you say, it is important to us son of Tiathan Eiula." Onigel breathed heavily wanting to tear Thrun apart, yet he did not want to break the truce.

"What have you to tell us?" Schill spoke softly as she gently pulled Thrun away from him.

"We, too, fear Moshdalayrrimich and his warriors." Onigel found it hard to talk with them without a bitter taste in his mouth. It was shameful that he even was asking for help from any Trag.

"We need allies to fight them when the war comes as it soon will. Already, Rhor and Warthan have left Mount Hamior by separate routes. Quardraille is reinforcing his fortress and has changed with the power of Mortarr. It will not take long before the war will begin. We do not want to ally with any of them because we are satisfied to live in caves and do as we please."

"Why won't you join any of them?" Zelbiur was not sure what Onigel was asking of them.

"We do not know which one Mortarr favors even though Quardraille has some special gift from him." Onigel hesitated before continuing. "Is this Zebrac even someone we need to be concerned about? It is well known that your family speaks with Jesuar and not to us. Perhaps you can tell us which one will be victorious so we can go back to our caves in peace."

"None will win if they turn their back on Jesuar." Zelbiur saw Onigel drop his head in sorrow.

"I had hoped you would give me a straight answer, but it as I expected." Onigel turned angrily away. "It was not easy for me to come to you and you mock me with words of Jesuar. Why

I should waste my time…"

"I did not mock you, but told you the truth, great king of the Troop Bats." Zelbiur stood cautiously away from Onigel who turned and glared at them all. He minded the talons and claws that could easily rip them all apart.

"I cannot follow Jesuar as you know…" Onigel looked hard at Zelbiur.

"I know you are a great king and we have been enemies for a long time, but I will tell you this that Jesuar would welcome you even now if you come to Him." Zelbiur saw Onigel shudder from the thought.

"Will I have to worry about you in the coming battle?" Onigel waited for his answer.

"We would rather not fight either, but I tell you this…" Zelbiur thought before he spoke. "Do not look to the west for you answer for the sun will set upon you as easily as the sun rises. Death awaits us all."

"Thank you for that son of Tiathan Eiula. Your father has taught you well." Onigel slightly bowed before spreading his wings and took flight against the moon.

"If we had captured him, we could have forced him to make peace with us." Thrun was enraged that Zelbiur let him go. "He would not have done the same for you."

"He did make peace with us." Zelbiur calmed Thrun down. "He did not come alone for I heard hundreds of Troop Bats following him as he flew off."

"I did not hear anything." Schill looked up into the sky seeing nothing.

"I could." Zelbiur left it at that.

As they approached the valley where the Great Oak stood, hundreds of tents and hovels surrounded its trunk. One cheer greeted them as they were soon to be joined with more and more Trags who recognized who Zelbiur was. Thrun and Schill were pleased to see so many in good spirits.

"I think I recognize some of them." Schill hugged Thrun's arm.

"As do I." Tranda slipped up from behind them still rubbing the healing wounds on her body. She was still tired, but this was a welcome sight."

"It is a miracle indeed!" Prerman picked up a young Trag that strayed from his mother.

"Who leads you?" Zelbiur called out into the camp.

"Jesuar!" Many of them responded in kind.

"As He does us!" Schill raised her sword in triumph.

"I speak for them." An older Trag strode up to Zelbiur. The Trag's hair was white as snow and the wrinkles on his face showed the years of toil and bondage. One hand seemed crippled even though he could still grasp a sword and spear if need be. "I am Zekiah Zorn who have led them to the Great Oak and await His word where we must go."

"I am Zelbiur Eiula, son of Tiathan Eiula, First Ioroarka of Everstream." Zelbiur new Zekiah understood who he was. "Your answer has come."

"An impressive ancestry to be sure is yours. We are equals before Jesuar." Zekiah beat his chest with his fist as bits of cloth shed from decay. "I know of your father and you, big ears!"

"Big ears!" Thrun took offence for Zelbiur whose eyes grew large as he recognized who he was speaking with.

"Zee? Uncle Zee?" Zelbiur laughed hysterically as he embraced the old Trag. "So long I would never have recognized you! Too long!"

"You were very small when we last talked and I am insulted you do not remember me." Zekiah feigned anger and hurt.

"You are no relation to me." Thrun tried hard to remember him.

"No, Thrun, he has made an honorary uncle so long ago. Then he left us for adventure and danger." Zelbiur turned back to him. "You never sent word that you were all right and we thought you were dead, Zee."

"No, I have come full circle and Jesuar has brought me here." Zekiah tried to keep an air of dignity about him.

"We will all be dead if we stay here." Thrun grunted. "We have spoken with Onigel and he is not happy that we gave him the wrong answer about our loyalties. He will most certainly come for us."

"Jesuar protects us." Zekiah nodded though agreeing with him should convince the others to feel the same. "We do not fear what lies beyond our camp. If we do not venture far from its branches we will be safe through Jesuar's protection."

"Know this." Zelbiur wanted to rap his ears so Zekiah would listen. "It is no longer a safe haven for any of us. Come now with us with sword and shield or you will lose your protection. The hour has come and we are here to bring you away as Jesuar commands."

"If you speak for Jesuar be assured we will follow you." Zekiah did not budge from his comfortable spot within the seat of a gnarled oak.

Zelbiur knelt in front of the oak door of Great Oak and prayed:

> "XoesoihiR mo efohiR T oimvmoom'
> ar mo dyoestiymdy t efynetti
> ar mo t nhiRsiet W ll'R mhino
> dyoes' ties tiRhin esepohiv ef' ll'
> ooR ar mo dyosioyody hinhiym"

The wind blew gently against the billowing tents picking up speed until a strong gust lifted their makeshift homes away. No Trag now had a shelter or bed when it was over. The wind stopped as quickly as it started. The Trags understood the message they were sent and started packing what weapons, food and water they could find.

"We believe in signs." Zekiah stood before Zelbiur. "Specially when it is so obvious. Where should we take the Traglings?"

"We leave them in Lebeth for Jesuar has told me to go there first." Zelbiur looked over the small army that was now his to command.

"We have one thousand, eight hundred and fifteen warriors." Schill was already counting for him. She had always been good with numbers and can count within seconds any large group of warriors. "There are two hundred too young to fight or too ill to travel."

"When did Jesuar speak to you?" Zekiah looked strangely at Zelbiur.

"He whispered in my ear while you were chasing tents." Zelbiur smiled.

"Very funny." Zekiah was not amused.

"Almost ready." Tranda tested her arm with swinging her sword one way and then the other.

"You have healed well and quickly, Tranda." Zelbiur was pleased to see her on her feet again. "The spirit of Jesuar is upon you."

"Some of them have never fought before." Thrun was discouraged as he surveyed the many Trags that stood before them. "Many of them have no weapons other than knives for cutting fish, shovels to dig their own graves and pickaxes to clean their teeth as much as fighting against any foe."

"It will have to do for now, Thrun." Zelbiur worried that they were marching to disaster. "Listen to me sons and daughters of Jesuar!"

The murmuring stopped as all eyes turned to Zelbiur who patiently waited until all the Trags were close enough to hear him. He was not sure what he was going to say, but let the spirit of Jesuar take hold to give him the right words.

"All of you must kneel before the Great Oak. Think of Jesuar and I will lead you in prayer." Zelbiur turned his back on them and knelt down. He heard them all follow his lead as they knelt together before the Great Oak:

"mo esepohiv ll'R mya
W efooRoesti ad noi'mtihiym
ll' dyoo moot etydyo 'Efoon OO
ll' dyoo moot Roim himhill
Mom mo sihia' ll'R mhino

XoesoihiR aoo'v ef'OO
sio'v oi'R efhisio W T dyhiRvms
ef' mo ar hiamhilles aooesti
ad moveyoR efoi'mdy
oxsioeptu Mom ll' sihia' OO
moom mo epRhiyeso ll'
hies ll' tihioinetti OO
XoesoihiR W T nRohiti oohiv
ba'oes'dy r ll'R mhino
oveyoRst'Rohin r ll'Res
Mhiti ll' eshill sthia' bao dyoomo
etoRo hinoomn OO tieoRo "Efoon OO
bao met OO ties dyall
efooRnyveyo OO yef mo efhiya
ayefti OO oiep Mom mo efhia'
aohidy OO himhill 'Efoon ovey'a
dyoayveyoR OO 'Efoon NooRtihiR'
ef' ll'Res r oveyoRst'Rohin
mom ad efoRoveyoR"

Slowly the small Trag army ventured away from the
Great Oak. No one saw the oak door slowly open as they left. A
gentle sigh lifted into a passing breeze and eventually was lost
through the fluttering leaves of the surrounding oak.

****

Awlion led the small company of Trags back through the forest. Ygueliav was still grieving over his father which hindered his judgment. He was unusually quiet as were the other Trags who looked back from tiem to time to see if the Drearnok was chasing them.

"How many scales do we have?"Ygueliav broke the silence trying to change the subject. "Everyone, we are safe enough here so count what you have."

"I have twenty." Awlion counted the ones in her sack. "They are so light."

"It is why the Drearnok can fly overhead without difficulty." Ygueliav knew the stories now were true that he learned when he was a young Tragling.

The other Trags counted eighteen, twenty-six until they came to a total number of one hundred and twenty-eight. Ygueliav was visibly disappointed since there would be many more who needed its protection.

"Not as many as we need, but more than we expected." Ygueliav did not think the sacrifice of is father was worth such a paltry trade.

"He is gone." Awlion understood his thoughts. "We have to mourn later. With these scales we have shields for as many warriors. Our archers do not need them."

"I don't think we'll be able to sneak up the mountain to meet Agraine." Ygueliav hoped the Valkyricks and Gimgiddeans had given up their search.

"Then we'll find another way to them." Awlion was determined to reach her friends.

"Let us keep moving and be there in time." Ygueliav stood up and urged them forward.

****

The Drearnok had retreated to its cave while licking its wounds that now would not heal for hours. Outside, underneath the rubble, a hand moved and a foot jerked. No one heard the low moan of Tiathan Eiula who was alive, hurt and a little scorched. The scales of the Drearnok that covered him saved his life from the searing heat and flame. Cries of anguish echoed from the cave as those inside paid the price of the Drearnok's pain.

"This will not do, Jesuar." Tiathan felt a surge of strength and renewal flow from the Karalak that he still held. He brushed burning ash from the tip of his beard as he struggled to stand.

For most of the day he picked up scales and traveled few a miles to make sure the Drearnok did not follow him. Tiathan used what rock and branch he could find as tools to hammer the scales into shield and armor. He had to build a carriage to drag the pieces of armor behind him since it was the only he could carry them back. His anger drove him instead of the spirit of Jesuar and it did not bother him. What scale did not bend with the rock, he used the Karalak to force it into shape. He was able to form a conical helmet with curled flaps and a corner that strayed to the left of his nose. A shutter was set to shield his eyes if the Drearnok belched flames upon him.

Tiathan knelt of the ground and struggled to pray the Prayer of Ladien, his father's father, who first defied Mortarr. Ladien passed through the flames of Mortarr and survived to free the Trags from their first time of bondage. He knew the prayer by heart, but the power of the Karalak fought against the memory:

"y st'himdy etoRo W ll'R epRoesomsio
XoesoihiR ll'R st'Romntie
r hia y ethiveyo t hiesv ef'
y sihim moot dyoo ties mytieoi'ti ll'
baRhisio no ef' T efanes'
baRohitieo ef' no tieRoi'net T esnoovo
dyoayveyoR oi'R omonll 'Efoon ties epasio
etooady oiep nll Rynetti ethimdy

hies him ymst'Roinomti 'ef ll'R mooRdy
efRo' OO 'Efoon ties baoomdyhino
ad tihivo iet's moo ar ll'R oom'
t dyoo met hies ll' mya'
ef' mo ar ll'R esoRveyhimties
Moo Mom mo etohiR ll' eshill y hin
Mo himesmoar XoesoihiR"

All pain had left him as his spirit filled with purpose and direction. The strength of the Karalak subsided as the spirit of Jesuar took control. Tiathan ventured back to the caves expecting to end the feud. The howl of the Drearnok could be heard feeling its pain and anger when it found Tiathan was still alive. The spirit of Jesuar and the armor of the Drearnok already warned the creature of Tiathan's presence.

"Tiathan Eiula! You are a s-s-stench upon my nos-s-strils!" The Drearnok screamed in torment from its cave, but Tiathan could easily hear it.

"Not for long." Tiathan strode defiantly forward. "Not much longer will you smell my presence!"

"Then die!" The Drearnok's three heads shot a sheath of flames at him. Tiathan knelt to the ground dropping his visor and felt the heat flow past him.

"No, it is you that Jesuar calls." Tiathan ran into the cave swinging the Karalak left and right.

"To the death then!" The first head of the Drearnok snapped at Tiathan only to break its teeth on his shield.

For the next hour they fought as scales and soon blood fell against the dusty floor of the cave. Roars and screams of hate came from the Drearnok as it tried to crush Tiathan, but it realized that hi armor was made of its own scales. Still it fought and bit only to find the battle would soon be lost. The Drearnok was exhausted and frustrated that it could not defeat Tiathan. It finally backed away from the Karalak and Tiathan who wielded it.

"Enough, Tiathan Eiula, I yield this time to Jes-s-suar." The second head cried out.

"Then let the Trags go!" Tiathan demanded.

"Let it be s-s-so." The third head drooped down to the ground while hissing in anger.

Out from the depths of the cave came two thousand Trags which some of them were old warriors Tiathan knew. Others came with their young Traglings who looked weary and sick. They are looked warily at the Drearnok who made no move to stop them.

"Come with me! Jesuar has freed you!" Tiathan hurried them out before lowering his voice. "Pass it on to pick up as many scales as you can. We will need the armor later."

As the last one passed by him, Tiathan sensed one last prisoner hiding in the shadows. He strained to see who it was, but whomever it was retreated further into the bowels of the cave. Tiathan walked towards him even as he back away.

"Come. You cannot stay here." Tiathan waved him forward.

"I cannot for I am ashamed." The voice of Carazaar seemed to weep with each word.

"We are all weak." Tiathan reached out for him, but Carazaar would not take his hand. "I, too, was held captive here. Jesuar forgave my weakness as He will forgive you if you ask for it."

"I cannot forgive myself." Carazaar wept even more turning away toward the Drearnok.

"Come with me and we will pray to Jesuar together." Tiathan heard the Drearnok coming toward them. "Hurry!"

"Leave him Tiathan Eiula. He is los-s-st to you." The first head of the Drearnok almost sounded benevolent. "Carazaar is-s-s s-s-sacrificing hims-s-self for the others-s-s. I will deal with him."

"No! None shall be left behind!" Tiathan advanced toward Carazaar.

"Yes-s-s one will." The second head pierced the darkness of the caves. "Do you think we do not hear the voice of

Jes-s-suar? We fear Him and we hate Him, but His-s-s word is-s-s final even for us-s-s."

"Carazaar as-s-sked Jes-s-suar to be a sacrifice for the others-s-s." The third head spoke though it annoyed him to acknowledge Jesuar at all.

"Jes-s-suar s-s-spoke to us-s-s, but we mocked Him until you walked back into our cave." The first head looked despondently to the ground.

"Jes-s-suar s-s-said we would be des-s-stroyed by your hand if we refus-s-sed to listen." The second head found it difficult to talk about it.

"We s-s-still did not believe until we s-s-saw our blood from wounds-s-s that did not heal." The third head still looked to its side unwilling to look at Tiathan. There was a deep gash beneath its scales that pained it greatly.

Jes-s-suar protects-s-s you for now." The second head tried hard not to spit venom in his direction. "But if you do not leave us-s-s for neither the Karalak or your armor will not s-s-save you."

"I cannot believe Jesuar spoke to you." Tiathan wavered under this new information. "Jesuar? Tell me what I should do?" The earth floor shook as rocks fell from the walls. Behind the fallen rock was a smooth surface where an invisible hand wrote:

"y ethiveyo esepoovom"

With tears in his eyes, Tiathan turned and left Carazaar behind. A second quake cracked the top of the hill causing a landslide that sealed off the mouth of the cave. Tiathan had just enough time to escape the small boulders that fell his way.

"Where do you take us?" The oldest Trag faced Tiathan. His face was so withered with age and years in the dark, no one would have known him except Tiathan.

"Asken Phar? Do you not remember me?" Tiathan removed his helmet.

"Tiathan Eiula!" Asken cried for joy and then slapped the side of Tiathan's head. "What kept you so long away from us?"

"The fear of the Drearnok instead of the strength of Jesuar was my thought." Tiathan answered honestly.

"I thought we would never be free." Asken took a deep breath of fresh air.

"Well, for a while anyway." Tiathan winced causing Asken to worry what was happening throughout Everstream.

"Where do we go and whom do we fight?" Asken still knew the look of war.

"We will first give praise to Jesuar." Tiathan knelt as did all the others:

"XoesoihiR oi'R efRo'dyoon
R 'ef ll'R dyn

y hin oomall him ymst'Roinomti
'ef ll'R xoidynonomti
mo moom nyveyo ll' oiR ayveyes'
ad nyveyo ll' oi'R oobady'omsio
t dyoo hies ll' mya'
moot hies mo mya'
mo epRhill ef' ll'R ba'oes'N
ad met etti ba'oes'N
mo etooady ll'R mhino eshisiRody
T mhino 'ef XoesoihiR"

From the rocks came a voice:

"ba'oes'dy ar ll'
Moo r ayvo ll'
hi mhitim eshiveydy ball XoesoihiR
et r ll'R styoady ad etoaepoR
ad ll'R naooRyos esmoordy
ll'R omones' mya' sioomoR ba'efooRo ll'
ad ll' mya' etRhinepao dyoom'
et'R etynet epasies'"

"Outra Whorld! How did you find us?" Tiathan

recognized the voice and realized the question was of little importance.

"I came at Jesuar's request." Outra climbed down to face him. "I will take those you have rescued and bring them to Agraine. You will be sent alone into the forest of Deen to gain strength in spirit and body. The Karalak even now corrupts you."

"Then take it from me." Tiathan offered it to Outra who refused to touch it. The sad look in Outra's eyes worried him, but not enough to release the weapon.

"It is up to you to overcome the evil within it." Outra stepped closer to him. "Jesuar cannot lead if you serve two masters."

"Then I will throw it away." Tiathan offered.

"If you can then do it." Outra waited patiently.

"No problem." Tiathan spun around lifting the Karalak over his head. He was unable to let it go.

"You had it too long." Outra knew it was Jesuar's sake that Tiathan used it in the first place. "Go now and Jesuar be with you."

"Will we meet again?" Tiathan was afraid of what he might become.

"It is in your hands and Jesuar's not mine." Outra lifted his hands to speak to the other Trags. "We march to the mountain where Agraine wants for your help. The scales you carry will be your shield and armor as well as your sword. Guard them well for others will have need of them as well."

Without another word he Trags left Tiathan behind. The sun was setting which made the loneliness even more overwhelming. What road he should take? How would overcome the power of the Karalak, he did not know.

CHAPTER EIGHT

Zelbiur tried hard to keep the small army of Trags from deserting back to the surrounding townships. Few believed they would ever return if they followed Zelbiur into battle so a couple here and few there filtered to the back of the column before disappearing into the forest. They had not gone more than three miles when darkness slowed them even further. The fluttering of wings only made them jump at their own squeals of surprise.

"We have company." Tranda walked close to Zelbiur. Just ahead of them stood Onigel with a host of Troop Bats behind him and assuredly there were hundreds more in the forest around them. Zelbiur saw the deep red eyes that seem to flare up from the shadows. Talons clicked on every side serving the very purpose of unnerving all the Trags.

"We cannot let you pass Zelbiur Eiula." Onigel stepped

closer balancing his body with his huge leathery wings.

"Do you fight us then?" Zelbiur slowly placed his hand on the hilt of his sword.

"Not if you turn back." Onigel narrowed his beady eyes warning Zelbiur by his look that a sword is raised the Trags would be destroyed.

"Jesuar calls us forward." Zelbiur hesitated enough to let Onigel relax.

"Then it will be on your head when all those around you die." Onigel almost was capable of a smile.

"No, Zelbiur, let us turn back." Thrun saw they had no other decisions to make.

"Are you afraid. Thrun?" Zelbiur was surprised.

"We have no advantage and no skilled warriors to fight them." Thrun glanced from side to side.

Zelbiur looked in all directions seeing shadows upon shadows in the dark forest. Even he understood the uselessness of fighting such a mass of warriors. They could not fight on Onigel's terms and retreat was not an option.

"My uncle has more sense than I." Zelbiur heard the soft mocking laughter and the word "coward" whispered among the Troop Bats. He ignored the insult as he ordered the Trags back toward the Great Oak.

"Until sunrise?" Tranda anxiously fought the urge to send at least one lance into the heart of Onigel.

"Until sunrise." Zelbiur gritted his teeth hearing the victorious chatter behind him as they left.

****

"Someone is following us." One of the Trags from the back ran up to Ygueliav.

"Who is it, Bankoor?" Ygueliav prided himself knowing all his warriors. It was a trait he was sure he received from his ancestors. It was a special gift that mirrored Schill's gift of numbers.

"Whoever they are, they are not afraid to approach us." Bankoor refused to go back and find out.

A black cloud enveloped the narrow passage from the valley behind them. As they walked through they saw the bones of warriors and unwary travelers which made them cautious. Ygueliav ordered swords drawn and arrows set to bows as a distant thunder shook the ground beneath them.

"Battle circle!" Awlion ordered as three shadowy figures loomed just inside the black cloud.

"Who dares prepare for battle against us?" A dark grumbling voice pierced the valley.

"Who comes sneaking behind us that we should trust you?" Ygueliav tensed realizing the voice was familiar from a long time ago.

"You are one of Eiula's brats!" A second voice laughed. "For only one of his family would be unafraid of us."

"They know you!" Bankoor was now even more

frightened as were the others. "They are giants…! As big as the Drearnok!"

"And no less dangerous." Ygueliav warned as he strode out to meet them.

Out of the smoky mist came the three giants whom Ygueliav knew to be the Brothers Fantom. They were part of the offspring of the Drearnok though offspring was a poor choice of words. The three brothers were brought to life from a pact between the Drearnok and Mortarr. What magical illusion or hateful source brought them into being no one knew. One good thing Ygueliav knew was that they were not as smart as Mortarr or the Drearnok.

"For the benefit of your friends I am Dreegan." The first brother looked down upon them. "And these are my brothers Sorrell and Piethan."

The three brothers were very different in their looks. Dreegan had one furrowed brow that connected one eye to the other, a bulbous nose with a large wart on the left side and scars on the right side of his face. Sorrell was a fat, bungling creature that looked like a giant Trag with pointed ears and vacant listless eyes. Piethan was the thinker with narrow eyes colored in blue and red specks, a thin neck and a large mouth with fang-like teeth. All three were bow-legged with arms dangling almost to the ground. Ygueliav believed Mortarr and the Drearnok had a sense of humor putting these three together.

"We come in the name of Jesuar!" Bankoor blurted out without thinking as his nervousness got the best of him.

"There is no Jesuar." Dreegan scoffed. A loud snort blew from his bulbous nose shaking the large wart violently.

The Brothers Fantom refused to believe they were akin to anyone else in Everstream. To prove their differences they had no qualms killing and devouring anyone who came into their valley. Each brother was condemned for the evil they did by Jesuar. Outra warned them of these brothers who now stood before them.

"But there is Mortarr for we have seen him!" Sorrell sat down to study the small group. He was obviously disappointed that they were so small with little meat on their bones.

"I have not seen him." Piethan shook his wrinkled face. "So you are both wrong. Neither exists. In fact, I could prove we don't exist either if you give me some time to explain…"

"Oh, no." Dreegan sighed heavily with a look of frustration and pity cradled his face with pain. "We will be here for days listening to you until we actually wish we didn't exist."

"I saw Mortarr once in a bonfire." Sorrell continued without listening to the others.

"You have no faith in me at all, Dreegan." Piethan complained while thoughtfully staring into the sky. "I could do this all afternoon…."

"Do what?" Dreegan had no idea what his brother was referring to as he looked up at the empty sky seeing a few clouds and nothing else.

"Mortarr looked fearsome in the fire with his huge head, jagged teeth and tear=flamed eyes." Sorrell's own eyes widened in wonder. "I thought I would faint from fear."

"Oh, shut up, Sorrell!" Dreegan nudged his brother.

"I told you he doesn't exist except in illusions and dreams!" Piethan wanted no more of this conversation.

"Maybe we can press on while you three can continue your discussion." Ygueliav started to walk away until a small boulder rumbled past him.

"You wouldn't leave us now?" Dreegan picked up another heavy stone. "It would not be polite."

"You must stay for dinner." Sorrell almost drooled with anticipation.

"Broiling your guests is not polite either." Awlion noticed the fire behind the three brothers which the smoke covered before the brothers appeared. On it were the charred remains of something Awlion did not want to guess.

"We did not intend to invite you." Dreegan was annoyed with Sorrel for now they had to treat them as guests instead of a meal.

"We stumbled upon your lair by accident." Ygueliav

motioned the Trags to lower their weapons. "We did not come to fight you either."

"If we thought that was your intent, you would all be on this spit already." Dreegan could not hide the hunger in his voice. "Trags are rather too lean for us. Now Valkyricks..." He pointed to the raging fire. "They have a lot of muscle and fat."

"Then what do you have in mind?" Awlion insisted though hearing the other Trags started to shuffle their feet nervously behind her.

"We have not spoken to anyone in many years." Piethan looked to his brothers. "Only ourselves and you see how well that has kept us sane."

"So now you are invited guests." Sorrell was excited to have company.

"Lead on then, but we will have to decline dinner." Ygueliav knew they would be safe for a time. The brothers were honest though terrible hosts. Since they were invited death was not eminent.

As they ventured into the lair surrounded by boulders and gnarled oak. Bankoor saw hewn rocks with chests of gold, silver and jewels. These were treasures no Trag thought they would ever see let alone possess.

"There is wealth beyond reason here!" Bankoor whispered without thinking.

"Yes, wealth." Dreegan heard him though it was in a

whisper. "It is wealth to those who can use it. We do not need any of it ourselves."

"Then why keep it?" Bankoor wondered what good it was for them.

"Because it means so much to those like you who ventured close enough for us to capture." Piethan licked his thick calloused lips.

"We have little need of it ourselves." Ygueliav gave Bankoor a warning glance, but he ignored it.

"So you say!" Bankoor slapped his knee in disbelief.

"It is a burden that will only slow us down and dull our wits." Ygueliav sat closer to the warm fire.

"How so?" Dreegan was intrigued as he snapped bone and sinew from the spit. His brothers followed suit and then threw the remains in a niche behind them.

"We are on a mission for Jesuar which takes us far from here." Ygueliav was grateful that the horror of the fallen warrior was taken from their sight. "And to reach our destination we must go through swamp and mountain. To have such a heavy load would sink us in the swamps and cause us to fall off the dangerous ledges of the mountains."

"You said it would dull your senses." Piethan reminded him.

"We would worry about losing the treasure and make decisions that would not keep us safe." Ygueliav relaxed that he could keep the brothers talking and forget about their stomachs.

"Besides, the treasure is yours and not ours for we are not thieves." Awlion had her hand not far from her bow.

"So you can keep your wealth." Ygueliav reassured them while staring hard at the other Trags who might think of stealing something.

"How different!" Dreegan clapped his chubby hands together.

"Then what are in your bags that you carry on your backs?" Sorrell noticed that the Trags did not place them on the ground when they sat by the fire.

"A trick perhaps to claim our gold!" Piethan wanted to see what they hid from them.

"You!" Dreegan would get back to the bags, but he saw the yearning in Bankoor's eyes.

"Me?" Bankoor shook with fear.

"Yes, take what you will." Dreegan waved him away towards the treasure.

"You have our permission." Piethan smiled at his brother's thoughts knowing already what he had in mind for Bankoor.

Bankoor looked at Ygueliav and then Awlion before running towards the chests of gold and silver. The Brothers Fantom laughed heartily as Bankoor raced toward the first chest. He almost dove into the middle of the coins while the other

Trags watched in confusion.

"You see!" Dreegan's voice thundered throughout the valley. "You lied to us!"

"No, we haven't." Awlion almost in one blurred moment sot an arrow into Bankoor's left leg sending him to the ground just before he took the first coin.

Bankoor fell hard writhing in pain looking back in surprise at Awlion. No one went to help him except Sorrell who picked up Bankoor and tossed him back into the circle of Trags. Ygueliav wondered if the brothers would take up arms against them.

"We will deal with you later." Ygueliav ignored Bankoor's cries while he faced the other Trags. "Take him and bind his wound while we decide his punishment."

"It is still a trick." Piethan was not convinced.

"No trick." Ygueliav noticed a Courgner prowling around the blood pool Bankoor left behind. Looking at Dreegan he lifted his hands defensively. He nodded to Awlion who understood exactly what her brother wanted. A single arrow brought the Courgner down where it stood.

"Now we are hungry and with your permission will put our meal on the spit." Awlion walked over with two Trags to place the Courgner onto the fire. He tender meat would be more welcome than anything the brothers could offer.

"We apologize for our bad manners." Sorrell was intrigued with Awlion, yet wary of her bow.

"You say you came in the name of Jesuar?" Dreegan knelt close to Ygueliav. "Did you come here to kill us for you had many chances since you came to us?"

"We did not know anything about you and Jesuar did not tell us whether to kill you or not." Ygueliav answered before lowering his voice. "If Jesuar wanted you dead, it would be so."

"Then let us talk for a while." Dreegan leaned back near the fire.

"What proof do you have that Jesuar exists?" Dreegan drew circles in the sand in front of him. "Prove it to us that we may know the truth."

"Faith is the proof I have and what I bring." Ygueliav pulled a browned piece of meat from the spit.

"That is no proof at all." Piethan snorted using his webbed fist to pound the ground.

Ygueliav bowed his head and prayed over the food he was about to eat:

"ba'oes' ties efoo'dy
ef' mo eosRveyo
t esoRveyo hinhiym"

"The greater existence is shown through faith that something exists." Ygueliav ignored Piethan's response. "Instead of proving something that exists. To handle something, to touch someone like Jesuar disproves His existence. To see and know what He has done for Everstream only proves He exists."

"Logical, only if proving nothing exists." Piethan tried to reason out this new thought. "For if you cannot touch anything except to prove it doesn't exist, then why concern yourselves of its existence in the first place?"

"I am proving that Jesuar does exist, but you can do it in a natural way." Ygueliav saw the confused look on their faces.

"How can you do that?" Sorrell lifted his head high though deep in thought and muddled in comprehension.

"Does this Jesuar speak to you?" Dreegan was now very interested.

"Yes, but not like we speak with each other…" Awlion struggled to keep out of the conversation. "It is like the wind or a gentle breeze. A thought not of your own. Sometimes it is a thunderous storm or an invisible hand writing on the wall."

"I would like to hear this Jesuar and judge for myself." Piethan was skeptical, but confused.

"I have heard the voice of Mortarr, seen his face and felt the warmth of his fire." Dreegan found it hard to believe anyone else but Mortarr existed.

"Someday you shall see and hear Jesuar." Ygueliav knew they were lost and when they heard Jesuar it would be their judgment day.

"Only the good and those that have been called by Jesuar can hear Him." Awlion looked over at the dead warrior now the food of the Courgner and Klak Crow.

"Nothing can be good or evil except in the eye of him who stands to watch over all of us." Dreegan explained as he followed Awlion's stare toward the Valkyrick's bones.

"There are so many gray areas that good and evil are often blurred." Piethan checked the fire before adding wood.

"That is only an excuse for the weak." Ygueliav spat out a piece of fat that lodged in his teeth, "Whenever you choose to do the wrong thing it is because you do not fear the consequences. It takes strength to stand up for the right cause no matter how many disagree with you."

"But if you stand for the wrong thing when everyone around you tells you it is wrong, what is the difference in knowing what is right?" Piethan only confused the matter for his brothers.

"If you know it is wrong then there is no justice standing up against it." Ygueliav was losing the logic of the conversation.

"But what if you think it is right?" Sorrell added to the conversation. "Worse yet, what if you were taught the wrong thing was right?"

"Then you condemn yourselves for not knowing it was wrong." Ygueliav stood firm. "We all know what is right and wrong from in here." He beat his chest. "We choose to believe one or the other out of convenience."

"Not so." Dreegan shook his massive head as his hunger had abated as their conversation progressed. "For if we are taught young enough that the wrong things are right and the right things are wrong. We can never know the difference."

"Yes, you would as you watch and learn from others." Awlion was tiring of a conversation even she was losing understanding of where they were going. "If others are hurt by what you do, then it is wrong. If what you do benefits only you, then it is right." She wondered where she was getting these thoughts until she felt the spirit of Jesuar comforting her soul.

"True enough!" Piethan was almost satisfied.

"If we are taught to be evil...." Dreegan could not let it go and his eyes darkened as he spoke seeing most of the other Trags had fallen asleep. "Then why concern ourselves if we can only change by seeing the results of our actions or those around us? If I burn you beyond recognition even now, it would benefit me and my brothers as tasty meals. How do I learn it is wrong to make dinner out of you as you make dinner out of this Courgner? Should we starve for whatever good may come out of not eating our enemies? I am hungry though and would like to get on with our own meal."

"Oh." Awlion raised her bow and arrow not knowing what Dreegan was really talking about. Her brother had them so confused they were starting to make sense.

"Fear not for we will not have you for dinner or breakfast." Piethan eased her mind with a gesture.

"At least not this time." Dreegan stood up and walked back to the far niche scattering the Klak Crows for one more morsel.

"I am thankful for that!" Awlion's heart beat fast looking to her brother for a nod to escape or fight.

"We would not have let you eat the Courgner if we were going to kill you." Sorrell explained as he leaned on his elbow. "We do not like a variety of tastes with our meals. The Courgner is too sweet for our palates."

"That is a good thing, is it not?" Dreegan's flaming eyes betrayed the mischief going through his mind. The brothers were known for strange conversations and changing moods. When they got bored anything could happen.

"For now…Yes." Ygueliav was now thinking of escape instead of battle. The Brothers Fantom would certainly not let them go now since they had someone to talk with for hours on end. It was obvious that they only killed first and never talked with their food, only themselves.

"You carry bags that seem very precious to you." Dreegan saw that each Trag clutched rather uncomfortable looking satchels as they slept.

"They're of no value to you." Awlion kept a close on

them.

"We are even more interested." Piethan reached over past Awlion.

"To take what is not yours is a bad thing." Awlion raised the point of her arrow between Piethan's eyes.

"Let him see, Awlion." Ygueliav knew when they slept the bags would be taken from them anyway.

"It is not theirs." Awlion refused to lower her bow.

"And not rightfully ours either." Ygueliav offered his bag of the Drearnok's scales to Dreegan.

"That is wise." Dreegan was already standing behind Ygueliav with fists raised to squash him.

"The scales of the Drearnok?" Piethan laughed himself silly as Dreegan emptied the bag.

"Some treasure!" Sorrell snorted.

"Take the trash and welcome to it." Dreegan tossed the bag back to him.

"How did you come by the scales?" Piethan was only slightly interested.

"We picked them up as we traveled throughout the valley." Ygueliav lied hoping the subject would not be brought up again.

"We were lucky that the Drearnok did not hear or see us." Awlion took his cue to broaden the lie realizing the truth was not necessary.

"The Drearnok does not easily miss travelers in his realm." Dreegan did not accept their story, but did not care either.

"He has a fondness for Trags." Sorrell sat up losing his smile.

"He is very possessive of his scales." Piethan was aware what his brothers were thinking. "Yet, you have many bags of his scales with you. There is something you are not telling us."

"And who cares?" Sorrell burst out in laughter. "They have worthless scales so they can brag the Drearnok. So what?"

"What do you think of Zebrac?" Awlion changed the subject.

"Zebrac?" Piethan scoffed. "Thick head of stone! Lifeless crystal followed by fools who look for light instead of the illusion of Mortarr."

"I rather like Zebrac." Sorrell almost whimpered.

"Dolt! Do not let Mortarr hear you say that!" Dreegan slapped Sorrell on the back of the head. "You forget where you came from?"

"Who is greater then?" Ygueliav nudged Awlion as he gestured toward the Trags. "Mortarr or Zebrac?"

"I still like Zebrac because his stone is smooth and cool not like the flames of Mortarr." Awlion thought fast realizing the only possibility for escape might soon come to them.

"Yes, yes, I agree." Piethan felt a surge of energy. "Though I must insist that neither exists, except for the convenience of the weak, who must believe in something."

"Quiet! Both of you and let me think!" Dreegan paced back and forth.

"Think of what?" Ygueliav prodded. "Was it not you that so strongly believed in Mortarr? Do you doubt now as your brothers do?"

"I do not doubt! I have seen him!" Dreegan turned his back as Sorrell and Piethan stood beside him.

The Trags picked up their bags as Awlion whispered in each of their ears. The Brothers Fantom were too involved with their discussion to notice their guests were leaving. Ygueliav wondered what Awlion was telling them.

"I saw Zebrac's mantle which was a great pink stone that glowed from sunrise to sunset!" Awlion ventured to the other side of the fire. "I say Zebrac is greater!"

"I, too, Zebrac!" Bankoor called out though bound head to foot and carried by two warriors.

"And I!" The other warriors echoed just before venturing around the first turn from the lair.

"See, Dreegan!" Sorrell stood in triumph. "I told you, you were wrong. Mortarr is not greater than Zebrac."

"I don't believe either one is greater." Piethan saw the

flush of anger color Dreegan's face.

"I have seen Mortarr." Dreegan grabbed both Sorrell and Piethan and shook them furiously causing rocks and stones to shake loose around them.

"And I have seen Sorrell!" Sorrell grabbed Dreegan's ears and pulled hard.

"And I have seen neither!" Piethan was able to break free of Dreegan's grip.

"Go!" Ygueliav waved the Trags away that still waited for him.

"I will wait for you." Awlion backed away to the safety of some low hanging branches before aiming her bow and arrow at Dreegan.

"Mortarr!" Dreegan raged.

"Zebrac!" Sorrell stumbled towards the fire pulling Dreegan with him.

"Who cares!" Piethan tried to break them apart.

"I do!" Ygueliav yelled as his answer seemed to spur them on.

Now no one was concerned as Ygueliav and Awlion fled from the lair. The ground shook as the three brothers fought which eased the minds of the Trags who thought they might be pursued. It was hours before they finally dropped to the ground, exhausted, but safe.

****

"We must find a way around the Troop Bats." Schill was anxious to get back to Agraine.

"I can hear them close by." Zelbiur still suffered from their insults.

"It is nearly sunrise." Thrun patiently sat near the fire. "We will be able to escape soon.

"Onigel will follow us no matter where we go." Tranda feared the Troop Bats more than any other enemy. "How will we fight them?"

"Set the forest on fire." Zelbiur knew the Troop Bats hated fire.

"What?" Schill was surprised.

"If they follow us, we will set the forest on fire." Zelbiur thought it was the only answer.

"And where will we be when the forest is aflame?" Thrun lifted a furry brow.

"Where I tell you to be." Zelbiur smiled to himself.

"I have a better idea." Tranda gently held Zelbiur's arm.

"What is that?" Zelbiur wondered what grand plan would come from her.

"We will move south until the Troop Bats are assured we are not going to meet Agraine." Tranda thought her plan a good one.

"What if they continue to watch us?" Thrun saw how easily that plan could fail.

"Then our goal would be to find as many warriors a possible and eventually meet outside the Valley of Gimgiddo." Zelbiur was thinking of the possibilities.

"It is in Jesuar's hands." Thrun was not thrilled with the plan.

"The only other thing is to stand and fight." Zelbiur did not like that idea even as he spoke.

"Not with these…" Tranda's voice trailed off.

"Most of them would be dead after the first hour of battle." Schill agreed. "We have the numbers, but not the warriors."

"Then we either stay here or head south." Zelbiur waited for an answer.

"We move south." Thrun did not want to stay.

"I think we could save some time if we leave half our warriors here to train so Onigel won't know what we have done for a few days." Zelbiur heard a whisper in his ears giving him the idea. Perhaps Jesuar knows best and is telling him so.

"That might work." Thrun liked the plan. "Someone they

know must stay behind."

"I agree." Zelbiur stared at Thrun whose heart sank before he heard what Zelbiur had to say. "We must raise tents and hovels to make it look like everyone is here."

"Schill and I will stay on so Onigel will recognize us." Thrun volunteered before Zelbiur had to say it. "You, Awlion and Tranda lead the rest to the south. May Jesuar be with you to help Agraine in time."

"No, my uncle, it is you who must get to Agraine in time." Zelbiur saw the look of surprise on Thrun's face. "Do you not know that when Onigel finds out we have tricked him, he will lead most of warriors against us? When he does that, you must march to the mountain, too. One of us needs to get there in time."

It took most of the night to pitch tents and finish lean-tos, but by morning it was an impressive landscape of a mighty camp. Slowly, three and four Trags at a time wandered off into the woods. Some came back with firewood while others waited for Zelbiur to meet them. It took most of the morning as six hundred Trag warriors managed to move three miles south without any of Onigel's scouts seeing them. Zelbiur had cut a slit in the back of his tent where he crawled off into the underbrush without being seen. Tranda and Awlion called out loudly that they were going to hunt for food and brazenly left the camp toward the north. The scouts ignored them since there were only two who wandered off.

****

For two days the Troop Bats scouts lazily watched as Schill and Thrun trained the remaining Trags in sword and bow. The Trags practiced battle circles and four line archery at imaginary enemies. The camp looked as full as it always had. The scouts thought the Trags all looked alike so did not miss Zelbiur or Awlion who were now far to the south. It wasn't until the wind seemed to shudder that the scouts rose up wary of the disturbance coming their way. Onigel and a host of Troop Bats shook the trees as they flew in from the north.

"We have company, dear." Schill looked to Thrun.

"Call everyone out." Thrun waved to a guard standing close by.

Soon a trumpet sounded alerting all in the camp to come forward with weapons ready. Onigel immediately saw that the number of warriors were not the same as when he left. Landing a few feet from Thrun, he decided to be cautious as he looked in the brush on either side for a trap.

"I wish to speak with Zelbiur." Onigel wondered where the leader of the Trags could be hiding.

"He sleeps." Thrun stood his ground. "Speak with me."

"What I have to say is for him alone." Onigel narrowed his eyes guessing something was amiss.

"As you can see, Onigel." Thrun walked up to him unafraid. "We have done as you asked. Why are you here?"

"My scouts have not seen Zelbiur in two days." Onigel already knew there was something wrong. "Is he that tired that he cannot speak to me for a moment?"

"He did have a rather difficult adventure." Schill quickly quieted as Onigel glared at her.

"I am not a fool!" Onigel screamed at them. "Take me to his tent and I promise not to wake him."

"We do not trust you." Thrun protested as he hoped to gain more time.

"Nor I you." Onigel started to walk through the camp. "Where is he?"

"Find him yourself." Schill drew her dagger and waited.

"You think too much of yourselves." Onigel sneered at her as he stared at the small dagger in her hand.

"No, I think too little of you." Schill waited for him to approach her, but he did not.

"I do not have to search for him." Onigel looked deep into Thrun's eyes. "He has already left camp with half of this camp."

"Hunting for fresh game for all those you see here." Thrun smiled.

"With one gesture you will be the first to die." Onigel smiled back without making the move for tnhe Troop Bats to attack.

"With one gesture you will be the first to die." Thrun raised his arm as fifty archers aimed their arrows at the great bat.

"You have done well with two days of practice." Onigel looked askance at them. "Yet, it would be a waste of fifty arrows. I have better things to do. Where did they go?" He surprised Schill with his question seeing her glance to the south.

"I have no idea." Schill realized what she had done.

"Thank you. A question that surprises will always get the answer in a gesture." Onigel bowed to her before flying off.

Most of the Troop Bats flew off to the south leaving only a hundred or so warriors behind to watch Thrun and Schill. Thrun stared at the Troop Bats flying toward the south until Onigel vanished through the clouds.

"Get ready to march!" Thrun shouted to the Trags.

"I am Elogin who now commands these warriors." A large Troop Bat landed near Thrun. "You will continue as you have until Onigel returns."

"I think not." Thrun picked up a lance and threw it at his feet. "We march before sunset!"

"I forbid it!" Elogin was amazed that Thrun would start a fight.

"Good for you." Schill walked by him blowing a trumpet three times as the Trags rallied around her.

****

The air seemed to shudder as hundreds of Troop Bats came from the north. Zelbiur heard them before anyone else thought anything was wrong. He looked to Tranda and on an impulse kissed her as if for the last time.

"Took you long enough." Blushing, Tranda readied her bow knowing that something was wrong. She stuck several arrows into the ground in front of her. She could send a whole quiver of arrows into the air faster than any other Trag in their company.

"Full battle circle!" Zelbiur hoped the two days of training was enough to give them a chance.

"Pray to Jesuar for our deliverance, Zelbiur, or we will be lost for sure." Tranda set the warriors four rows deep.

"Stand ready as I pray." Zelbiur knelt still not seeing the Troop Bats, but heard Onigel give orders to his warriors:

"tieoRo r moo oomo ayvo ll'
XoesoihiR dyoayveyoR OO

oieso oi'R mohivms
ad nhivo ti' oi'R estiRomntie
ayefti oi'R hiR'oomes
t dyoefohiti iet's
moo estihimdy hinhiamst' ll'
stoom tn' ll'R estiRomntie
tieRoi'net oi'R mohivms"

"Arm yourselves!" Tranda saw the first wave of Troop Bats passing the tree line.

"Send as many arrows into the air and don't bother to aim." Zelbiur knew that sheer volume would bring down many of them as they flew into the barrage.

Onigel led the first wave until he was about a hundred yards of the battle circle. Onigel was brave, not stupid. He waved his warriors on knowing that many would die. The purpose was to get the Trags down to fighting with sword and lance which would give the Troop Bats the advantage.

"Loose arrows!" Zelbiur saw his first arrow hit its mark felling a Troop Bat at his feet,

Hundreds of arrows took flight finding easy targets in the midst of the dark cloud hurtling towards them. The vastness of the Troop Bats would deplete their arrows quickly. Four Trags were carried off into the forest by larger warriors while twenty others fell to their talons and venom. Zelbiur looked down at the ground seeing blood seeping beneath his feet from fallen warriors. Suddenly the sky was clear and the battle was over. The Trags cheered over the hundred or so bodies of Troop Bats lying dead or dying.

"No time! No time! Tranda? Send runners to see what arrows can be used again!" Zelbiur sent ten warriors to pick up those arrows that were not broken or cracked.

"They will wait for nightfall." Tranda started to panic though not fearful of fighting, but did not like Troop Bats. She remembered when her mother was carried of by one of Onigel's warriors never to be seen again.

"Start fires every ten feet so when they come again we can set fire to the forest if we need save ourselves." Zelbiur ordered the Trags as he picked up sticks and brush to build a pyre.

"Won't we be in the center of the fire?" Zekiah kept his silence for a long time and now wondered if this was a good idea.

"We are far enough from the edge of the forest." Zelbiur thought the answer was sufficient.

"There is a lot of dry grass between us and the forest." Zekiah stopped short seeing the icy stare from Zelbiur.

"We will see the light shine in their eyes and have easy targets even in the dark." Tranda took Zekiah by the shoulders willing him to be quiet.

For the next few hours Zelbiur and Tranda sent arrows into the overhanging branches hitting the scouts that ventured too close. Zelbiur heard the chattering of the Troop Bats around them. They made enough noise to keep him from hearing Onigel and his battle plans. Frustrated, he thought of sending a flaming arrow into the dense forest. Then the chattering stopped.

"Battle circle!" Zelbiur looked into the night sky as the fires illuminated a hundred feet in all directions. "When they come, the first row will shoot arrows straight ahead.while everyone else into the night sky when the stars are blotted out."

"We could not gather enough arrows that were still in one piece." Tranda warned them. "After we use what is left, it will be sword and dagger only."

"Have the rest of them use the broken arrows as daggers." Zelbiur could not worry about it now.

"Then Jesuar help us. We will suffer greatly at their hands." Tranda trembled as she searched the night sky for them.

"Light your arrows!" Zelbiur called out even as the air buzzed with activity. "Let's see what's going on."

Fifty flaming arrows struck tree and brush surrounding the Trags with fire. Some of the trees had Troop Bats that were set aflame. The skies lit up as the first wave of Troop Bats started toward them. The small glen might also be consumed, but at least they would see them coming.

"Ready arrows!" Zelbiur raised his bow as he saw the first angry face streaking towards him.

"Jesuar! We come to You!" Tranda lifted her bow as the night sky grew darker and the moon disappeared from view.

****

Tiathan awoke with a start feeling something crawling beneath his shirt. He stuck his hand inside pulling out first one than another furry little creature. Tiathan shook his head in wonder how they got inside his clothes, but they did not appear to be a threat.

"Qwa." Tiathan sighed in resignation.

"Qwa-a-a?" The Qwa answered staring at him with sad green eyes and then jumped out of his hands to snuggle close to his hairy chin. Two more rolled up to Tiathan and sighed as they cuddle up next to him. They were small balls of fur that crept up to many a traveler they trusted during long cold nights. They always sensed those who were safe and who were not to be trusted.

The Qwa were known for leading lost travelers to safety. In times of trouble they would bounce up and down to warn of danger before disappearing into the underbrush. They were not fighters now would they have much of a chance against any warrior that meant to kill them.

The thing that disturbed Tiathan the most was their eyes. The eyes of the Qwa held all their expressions of joy, affection, anger and sadness. The other thing was no matter how you held them, their eyes followed you as if they floated upon the fur. Tiathan felt as if he held melting wax when he picked them up. The Qwa could eat even though they appeared not to have a mouth. Did they run down the path ahead of him or did they roll? He could not tell. He saw no feet when they moved along the ground, but he was glad to have them around.

Tiathan fell back into a deep sleep after checking the horizon for anything that might be following him and remembered that the Qwa would warn him if there were. As he slept he dreamt again of the Seven Fortresses. This time he was overlooking the valley seeing great slithering creatures marching toward the main fortress walls. In the dream, he tried to get closer until a pounding upon his chest awakened him.

"What is it?" Tiathan saw the Qwa jumping up and down on his chest. When he was awake they scattered into the forest. Tiathan slipped into an old oak trunk and watched the path behind him.

"He must be here." A Bantongue thrashed around behind the gnarled oak behind Tiathan.

Tiathan slowly pulled out the Karalak waiting for the Bantongue to find him. He wished Outra had taken the Karalak away from him though he would be defenseless now. The need to use the Karalak almost overpowered his need to be safe.

"Tiathan must have already left here." The second Bantongue answered.

"Outra told us we would find him near here." Tiathan recognized both of them.

"Zarr? Tenca? What are you doing here?" Tiathan pulled himself out of the trunk. He was happy to see them as he climbed into the open.

"Tiathan Eiula! We have come to bring you a message from Outra Whorld. Then we must return to Agraine." Tenca rushed up to him.

"We would hug you, but we wish not to crush you." Zarr kept his distance.

"What news do you have?" Tiathan was happy, too, that neither of them tried to hug him.

"Agraine and the others are safe for now." Zarr began as Tenca huffed at the interruption.

"Moshdalayrrimich is still camped close to the base of the mountain and is in no hurry to attack." Tenca inched Zarr off to the side.

"Rhor has left him to meet with Warthan even though we do not know if it is to join him or not." Zarr nudged Tenca back.

"An alliance?" Tiathan didn't think it was possible.

"Nsaat stays with Moshdalayrrimich even though he

speaks he might leave him." Tenca shook his head as if he was as confused as the situation seemed to be.

"We heard news from a messenger that Onigel of the Troop Bats have kept Zelbiur and Awlion trapped near the Great Oak." Zarr saw the sad look on Tiathan's face.

"Zelbiur is well." Tenca hastily added. "Moshdalayrrimich sent word that he wanted the Trags alive as long as they stayed near the Great Oak."

"They are alive until Moshdalayrrimich returned there to enslave them all." Tiathan thought out loud wondering if he should return to them.

"Word has it that Zelbiur is arming and training the Trags he found at the Great Oak." Zarr almost whispered as if someone else was listening.

"How many?" Tiathan was hopeful.

"Over two thousand strong." Tenca proudly told him.

"Probably not as many, but enough to put up a good fight." Tiathan wondered why Outra sent him away alone. Even Zarr and Tenca were told to leave after they gave him their news.

"That is all we know." Zarr shrugged allowing his leathery skin crackle as he move side to side.

"Do you know what I must do?" Tiathan hoped they might know something.

"Only that what you do must be done alone." Tenca

could not help him.

"Then you must leave me so I may find out my destiny." Tiathan offered his hands in friendship. "Goodbye my friends. I hope to see you soon."

"We are your friends and are in the comfort of Jesuar." Tenca saw a look of joy in Tiathan's eyes and then a look of confusion.

"Could not a Bantongue pledge himself to Jesuar? Must he be a Trag only?" Tenca was indignant.

"I am happy you follow Jesuar and some day we will talk about how this has come about." Tiathan knew few who were not Trags have accepted Jesuar.

"This pleases you then?" Zarr was barely listening as he looked back into the sky where he saw Harkies searching the forest above them.

"Yes, it pleases me greatly, my brothers." Tiathan embraced them as best as he could.

"Then we must leave so those scouts will see us and give you more time to get away." Zarr was the first to turn to leave.

"One day…" Tenca nodded agreement.

Tiathan watched them disappear quickly into the forest with a sadness in his soul. He sat down between the rocks to hide from the Harkies wondering which way to start his journey. He closed his eyes to pray to Jesuar:

"T xoi'Rmoll r aoomn
ad y ethiveyo moo dy'Rosiyim
XoesoihiR esomdy no
MoRoveyoR ll' mo'dy no
Esepohiv t no
etoomoveyoR ll' myst
y noo aohidy no"

"Qwa-a-a." Three Qwa rolled up to his feet staring up at him.

"I guess you are an answer to prayer." Tiathan laughed at Jesuar's sense of humor. "Lead on! Take me wherever Jesuar leads!"

The Qwa rolled ahead of him to the north and Tiathan followed hoping it was truly Jesuar's answer to his prayer. Going to the north led to more dangers than other part of Everstream. What adventure would confront him? What creatures would want to defeat him?

****

"Keep everyone in line!" Thrun pushed and shove the rag tag army into position.

"You cannot leave!" Elogin thought his presence would

keep the Trags there, but Schill was the first to walk by him.

"We are not leaving only taking a walk up a mountain." Schill glared at him.

"We will attack!" Elogin did not know what else to say.

"Then we will destroy you.' Thrun calmly waved the Trags ahead.

"I will inform Onigel of your escape." Elogin was beside himself what to do about this. He was told the Trags left behind would not be a problem and that they knew little of fighting.

"And what will Onigel do to you when you tell him?" Schill was bemused at the empty threat.

"If you let us leave now we can continue our journey without interruption." Thrun almost walked over him.

Elogin flew off barking orders to the small army of Troop Bats hiding in the forest. Some three hundred warriors rose up into the sky as a show of force. Thrun watched and waited until Elogin approached him again.

As he alit on the ground, Thrun drew his sword to defend himself.

"We will attack if continue this way." Elogin was now angry.

"And we will defend ourselves." Schill turned to the Trags who were standing and waiting. "Battle circle! Ready bows and arrows!"

"You have caused this, not I!" Elogin anxiously returned to the sky.

"Show no fear for Jesuar is with us!" Schill lifted her sword.

Elogin frantically swooped up and down with his warriors displaying signs of strength, but Thrun patiently waited till they were closer. Elogin decided the only thing he could do was fight. He worried what Onigel would say when he found out that there was a battle. For now it didn't matter, Onigel decided to fight.

"Loose arrows!" Thrun gave the command seeing the horde of Troop Bats diving toward them.

Tens of Troop Bats fell dead to the ground as the first volley of arrows hit their mark. Twelve Trags crumpled where they stood as the first wave of warriors flew through their lines and tearing apart those who were in their way. As more Troop Bats fell to the ground, the others became suicidal in their rage. Thrun only worried now if they had enough arrows to finish the fight.

"Don't stop!" Thrun urged them on as more than half of the Troop Bats fell from the sky.

"This is butchery!" Schill could not understand why the Troop Bats kept coming knowing they could not withstand such a barrage of arrows.

"Maybe we can stop it." Thrun looked as eleven more

Trags suffered the death blows of the Troop Bats.

There were less than a hundred Troop Bats when Thrun picked up an oak horn and blew loudly into the air. The Tag stopped fighting and even Elogin was surprised to hear the horn and hesitated. No one was sure what the horn meant so waited for Thrun to speak.

"Speak to me, Elogin!" Thrun lowered the horn.

"I have nothing to say!" Elogin wiped blood from his wings.

"You are defeated and we wish you to live and not die at our hands." Thrun heard a harsh murmuring behind him, but ignored it.

"Your warriors disagree." Elogin heard them, too.

"They do not understand." Thrun knew Elogin would not give up. If he let him go, Elogin would return with Onigel to fight again.

"Neither do I" Elogin needed this time to regroup his warriors.

"If you attack us again, none of you will survive." Thrun warned him.

"If we do not attack, Onigel will see to it that none of us survive." Elogin answered with a hint of sadness. "We know and understand why we do this."

"Then do what you must do." Thrun allowed a tear to fall knowing either was that Elogin would die no matter what he did.

Elogin led a final attack as Thrun ordered his archers to use bow and arrow to finish the battle. Within minutes it was soon over. Schill cried at the senseless killing and the fallen thirty-three Trags that lay around her.

"Bury them all both Trag and Troop Bat." Thrun ordered the Trags who complained, but did as they were told.

"We must leave this place as quickly as possible." Schill reminded him.

"We will travel north and then west to meet Zelbiur and to keep Onigel guessing where we went." Thrun thought he might zig-zag all over Everstream to keep them safe.

"Jesuar will be with us." Schill now believed they would not find Zelbiur in time.

It took most of the afternoon to bury all the dead. Thrun stood on a knoll overlooking the mass graves of a terrible battle and bowed his head in a short prayer:

> "XoesoihiR hisi'oepti iet's
> Moo efoi'netti ties dyhill
> noiydyo OO W oi'R xooRmoll
> t MoRo oomall ll' vmoom"

CHAPTER NINE

Tiathan approached what he knew were the Dark Caves of Rethan Amier because the mountainside was almost one huge gaping mouth with a high ledge. On the ledge were two smaller caves that made the mountain look like it was soundlessly screaming in pain. The blackness of a moonless night greeted him from the inside. Before he entered the Qwa rigidly stood still. Tiathan knew they would not follow him in.

"Thank you my friends, I can go on from here." Tiathan leaned over and patted their furry heads.

"Qwa-a-a." They sadly answered and rolled away.

As he stepped inside, a couple of Banter Bats flew by him watching from a safe height to see if he was dangerous. Deciding he wasn't a real threat, they flew on back inside the cave. The walls dripped mineral water down its sides leaving small pools of crystallized pearls here and there. The pearls would have been valuable if Tiathan had time to pry them loose from the cave floor.

He heard a rustling behind some crevices and reached for his dagger. He did not want to show the Karalak until he had do. A second noise behind him almost knocked him over.

"Aw-w-wk!" A yellow-bellied Screamer almost danced on his feet. "What are you DOING HERE? We don't allow anyone to come into our home WITHOUT AN INVITATION!. Aw-w-wk!"

"I'm only passing thr---" Tiathan started to explain.

"Aw-w-wk!" A second Screamer pierced his ears with its loud voice. These creatures could never talk softly and they were well named for they relentlessly pursue their prey incessantly until madness sets in. "We don't want explanations, just results! KEEP WALKING!"

"DON'T STOP!" The other Screamer bumped him to the ground with his belly as he raised his voice as the sound pierced Tiathan's ears. "We have no time to waste TALKING TO YOU!"

"We have barely enough time to speak WITH EACH OTHER!" The other one smiled at his friend.

"I did not…" Tiathan was bumped to the found again.

"You should not INTERRUPT US." Both Screamers bent over him with their furry yellow feathers sticking outward. Tiathan absently noticed their webbed feet had only two toes that curled upward. "We did not INTERRUPT YOU!"

"But you have…" Tiathan was losing his temper.

"Are you speaking to us?" The smaller of the two Screamers asked. "If you wish to ask us something, then just SAY IT! Don't be SHY!"

"We are happy to tell you anything as long as it is NOTHING about SOMETHING which means ANYTHING that can be said about SOMETHING." The larger Screamer beamed with philosophy.

"That is to say, we wish to tell you what we DON'T KNOW before we tell you about we DO KNOW, which is little I'm afraid." The smaller Screamer lowered his voice to a yell trying to make things clearer.

"Aw-w-wk!" The larger Screamer nearly deafened Tiathan who had no idea what they were talking about except whatever it was became incessantly noisy.

"Why don't…" Tiathan tried to escape the two Screamers, but they followed him down the cave tunnel.

"If we can be of any ASSISTANCE, please ask him." The two Screamers pointed at each other. Then they both abruptly stopped talking.

"Finally, peace." Tiathan wondered why they stopped, but was glad they did.

"We know better than to follow you DOWN THERE!." The larger Screamer shook its head.

"Beware the Starmass Stranglevines." The smaller Screamer warned him as he struggled not to shout.

"What are Starmass Stranglevines?" Tiathan warily looked around him.

"They will FIND YOU! If you do not find THEM FIRST!" The smaller Screamer turned and waddled back away from Tiathan.

"Aw-w-wk!" The larger one agreed following the smaller Screamer back to the main entrance for the next traveler to enter.

The tunnel wound its way deeper into the mountain. All Tiathan saw were simple vines cascading up and down the walls. He decided not to get too close in case the Screamers crept up behind him. A loose rock knocked him off balance forcing against the glistening walls. Quickly, the first Stranglevine wrapped itself around his waist and then a second around his neck. His right arm was free to pull out the Karalak which he used to cut himself free. Tiathan hurried further ahead seeing a soft glow in the distance. He hoped that whatever was there would be more of a welcome sight.

A strange slurping sound echoed down the tunnel toward him. Tiathan found his feet sticking to some eerie substance on the ground. One more turn and he would enter the lighted cavern ahead of him. He was not expecting the sight that greeted him which made him pale noticeably.

"Tharkanian War Slugs." He said under his breath. These behemoths were attached to the ceiling, walls and slowly moving on the ground before him. Some of them still had unhealed wounds from past battles.

"Who-o-o?" The voice of heated bellows greeted him from behind.

"I thought you were long gone." Tiathan stared up at the mammoth beast as its tendrils moved left and right to appraise him. He tried hard not to show fear even though as slow as they were now, their reputation of moving quickly over their enemies was well known.

"Hid-den...not...lost." The great War Slug oozed as it struggled to speak. "I am Foozakhan."

"I am Tiathan Eiula." He saw scars and sores upon its side and back. Though the scars were old, the pain still must have been great. Tharkanian War Slugs were known for their quick healing powers since they had no vital organs to injure. A sword would rip open one part and within seconds would heal itself leaving a scar for a long time. "You are in pain. Can I help?"

"Help?" Foozakhan's deep resonating voice crippled the air around them. A soft rumble shook the ground that Tiathan thought was Foozakhan laughing at him.

"Yes. Help." Tiathan thought he might be in danger if Foozakhan became angry.

"What...can...you...do?" Foozakhan breathed heavily trying to form each word so Tiathan could understand.

"If you sit beneath the limestone droppings." Tiathan pointed to the pale liquid that spotted the cave ceiling. "It would seal your wounds and give you armor to protect you from your enemies."

"It..would...slow...us...down." Foozakhan stifled a rumbling laugh as considered the thought. "Too heavy...We...would...be...more...vulnerable."

"When the limestone hardens, it would equal the strength of any stone." Tiathan could not think of them being slowed down by a couple hundred pounds of rock.

"We...need...the poison juice of the Antiar Star." Foozakhan was able to speak clearly now that he had some practice from such a long time of silence. "It is a flower that rejuvenates us, heals us, but is deadly to you."

"Where is it and I will get it?" Tiathan offered without hesitation.

"At the top of this mountain where the Banter Bats protect them from us." He bellowed sadly. "We have tried to climb up to them, but we are weak and slow as the Banter Bats destroy the flowers before we get to them."

"What does the flower look like?" Tiathan didn't think anything short of an avalanche could stop these behemoths.

"A black pitcher filled with water." Foozakhan sounded weary.

"Then I can empty the juice into a cask or water pouch to

bring it back down to you." Tiathan's mind ignored the danger and looked for something to carry up the mountain with him.

"I must warn you that if you drink of it or splash a drop upon you, you will die." Foozakhan warned him again.

"Then I will be careful." Tiathan looked finding two empty casks which upon looking closer were rotten on the inside.

Tiathan hesitated going back the way he came because of the Screamers that waited in the darkness. Stumbling to the entrance of the cave he could hear the Screamers deriding some poor Banter Bat that landed too close to them. Quietly he slipped past them and to the outside where he looked for something to make into a container. The only thing he could find was a large section of an oak stump which was only one foot wide and two feet high. He was able to use a rock to stop up one end while he cored out the center. To make it easier to carry Tiathan use a leather strap to tie each corner and wrap around his shoulders.

Climbing up the mountainside was difficult as the stump smacked the side of his head every other stride. Halfway up, he wondered how he would get down without spilling the poison on himself. Just before nightfall he found the field of Antiar Stars which were actually black flowers with a purple leaf in the shape of pitchers. Setting down the trunk, he tipped each flower down the opening he had made until it was almost full.

"Now what?" He said out loud. His hands began to shake thinking of the task ahead.

"Bring it to me." Tiathan was startled to find three War Slugs slithering behind him. "You have done well, Tiathan Eiula."

"This was a test?" Tiathan was angry, but did not show it.

"Yes, it is our only way to trust you." Foozakhan did not hesitate in his speaking though it was still slow and deep sounding.

"Then maybe you can help me." Tiathan hoped to get something out of his trouble.

"First, give us the water." Foozakhan slithered up to him extending his mouth towards the log.

"Water? You said this was poison." Tiathan now felt betrayed.

"It is not poison, but it is a healing salve for our wounds." Foozakhan sucked the log dry as he gave off a deep resonating laugh that shook the ground. "It may not be safe for you to drink though."

"Has anyone tried?" Tiathan was tempted to try it.

"No, not one other." Foozakhan was not sure what Tiathan had in mind. "Why has Jesuar brought you to us?"

"You know of Jesuar?" Tiathan was surprised.

"We seek His favor and listen to His voice as you do."

Foozakhan began to his story to him. "During the Tharkanian Wars we carried warriors over mountains and fortress walls. Thousands died under our march and we thought ourselves invincible. We do not age as you do until now. Our disobedience has been our own curse so our wounds heal slowly and our pace becomes slower. We hide in the caverns below from Quardraille and the Arbushi who now possess the power to destroy us. We have become frightened since Jesuar seldom talks to us now. Mortarr is gaining strength while Zebrac is soon to be lost forever."

"My father spoke of you once and even that was very little." Tiathan struggled hard to remember what he lost.

"We are the warriors of Jesuar and Mortarr is the fury of the coming wars." Foozakhan continued with a weariness in his voice. "Before Moshdalayrrimich, before Rhor, was Tharkan who ruled Everstream. We did his bidding until Utter Whorld came as a prisoner who told us of Jesuar and our hearts lifted with hope. We were tired of war and killing the innocent."

"He never mentioned any of this to me." Tiathan wanted to hear more.

"Tharkan was the first to build the pyre of Mortarr." Foozakhan bowed his head a little. "We helped him. He had taken many prisoners for slaves, but those who could not work or were too old…too young… were cast into the fire. The evil was so great that day that a face appeared within the flames.

When the face spoke all who heard him turned to listen. He said his name was Mortarr, Bringer of Death, Healer of Wounds, who said Everstream would be ours forever if we remembered the flame. Mortarr promised us a long life, prosperity and success in war. We believed him until Utter Whorld told us differently. If Utter Whorld had come sooner, we would not have listened to Mortarr."

"It is not unusual to bring a deaf ear to any of the Shroo." Tiathan smiled to himself. "Now it is Outra Whorld who speaks for Jesuar."

"We did not get what Mortarr promised." Foozakhan continued acknowledging to Tiathan that he heard what he said with a tilt of his head. "But only we, not Tharkan nor his warriors were discontented. When we followed Jesuar, Mortarr voice was silent. We saw his lips move, but no word, no sound came to us. Mortarr's voice and face contorted in anger as he looked at us till we realized it was time to escape. Tharkan never knew we could speak or even think so we acted the dumb creatures of burden that he believed us to be. When Mortarr told him we had given our allegiance to Jesuar, he laughed. He did not know what was in our hearts. That night we left we brought your father and Utter Whorld with us. Soon after we joined in the fight against Tharkan until he was defeated near the center of the Dark Woods."

"I am grateful for the help you gave my father." Tiathan bowed and gestured his loyalty to Foozakhan.

"Jesuar told us of your coming here and to test you as we have." Foozakhan lowered his voice. "You have been corrupted by the Karalak and if it had overcome your soul you would not have come to this place. What we say to you is if you have need of us, send for us and we will come."

"What now?" Even though the thought of walking away was strong, Tiathan did not know where to go next.

"Jesuar has spoken to us and has told us to send you toward the east where you will be renewed in your spirit or perish in the corruption of the Karalak." Foozakhan waited to hear Tiathan's response.

"Then I live or die by heading east?" He knew time was crucial to help the Trags. "There is little time for me to worry what will happen to me."

"Do not question the voice of Jesuar!" Foozakhan was impatient with him now. "Do you not see that already you struggle with the word of Jesuar? Have you ever thought to defy Jesuar as you defy him now?"

"I will go." The thought of going away from his friends raged within him. What terror has the Karalak placed itself inside him? Did Jesuar question his loyalty?

"Go then, Tiathan Eiula! We will meet again." Foozakhan turned with the others and started back down the mountain.

"As Jesuar wills." Tiathan struggled to say the words. He

tried again to throw away the Karalak even though the weapon would be useful in any battle ahead of him.

"That is a good start." Foozakhan disappeared over the ledge.

It was a difficult climb down the mountainside in the dark. Tiathan was on the way where he was to find life or death as Jesuar willed. He could not think of the right prayer to pray and it bothered him that it was so hard to remember the words of the weary traveler whose words brought safety and guidance who prayed it:

> "Mhiti ayoes hietohidy
> y dyoo moot vmoom
> T Roohidy r ayoomn
> ad tiyno r stooRti
> nhill nll xoi'Rmoll
> bao eshiefo ad tiRoio"

****

"I see movement below." Agraine alerted the others. It had been a long time since anyone paid attention to them. A few spears hit the side of the walls only to let them know someone was watching. "Anker! Watch the north side! Stilkyl! The south!"

"They will not be here in time!" Anker hesitated before shooting an arrow into a shadow that moved near his portal.

"Keep that fire high so we can use it for our arrows!" Agraine knew he was right as she tried to think of some way for all of them to escape.

From the sky came boulders and rocks crashing on top of their meager fortress. This time they did not roll down the hill. Agraine looked into the faces of each Trag warrior as if for the last time. A long talon shot through the portal knocking her to the ground.

"Agraine!" Anker used his sword to cut the talon in two. When he looked down Agraine did not move and did not seem to breathe.

"What can we do?" Stilkyl pulled Anker back to the fight.

"She may be lost…Leave her!" Anker's anger took over his reason. "Fight to the death and the glory…." The word seemed empty to him. ",,,of Jesuar!"

****

Tiathan journeyed half a day before coming upon another maze of caves. It looked like it was a good shelter from the dark clouds that were drifting his way. If the Bantongues or a hundred other creatures that were looking for him and did not find the same shelter, he would safe. As he entered one of the dark openings he could swear he heard subdued laughter. Looking closer, he saw hundreds of glistening orbs almost gem-like staring at him. Perhaps it was flint rock mirroring the last bit of sunlight from the walls. As he walked further, he raised the Karalak and waited for whatever might come his way.

"Stranger among us." A brittle voice spoke above him. Then laughter pierced the silence around him.

"Who speaks to me?" Tiathan tightened his grip on the Karalak.

"Edgy, this one." The voice snickered.

"In the name of Jesuar stand before me or be the coward you are!" He crouched in a battle stance.

"Coward! Me?" Something flew past Tiathan's head.

"Now who's edgy?" Tiathan started to spin in a circle knowing whatever it was could fly at him from any direction.

Soon hundreds of eyes were staring at him instead of reflections from the stone walls. He knew now he was in the lair of Troop Bats and could not possibly get out alive if they did not allow him to. Even the Karalak did not deter the Troop Bats from taunting him.

"Who will speak with me?" Tiathan hid the Karalak as a sign of peace.

"I will if you promise not to kill me." The brittle voice spoke again.

"Very well." Tiathan waited patiently.

"I am scout." A very small, undersized Troop Bat with fiery red eyes and a crooked nose crept out of the darkness.

"I came looking for shelter and this how you welcome visitors?" He thought it best to take the offensive.

"Visitor? No one invited you here." Scout's nose twitched with confusion.

"Then I ask for your hospitality." Tiathan waited for the laughter to die down. He knew he had a chance for if they what was happening on the mountain, he would be dead already.

"Brazen he is, Scout!" A deep, darker voice came from above. Tiathan watched as a great Troop Bat waddled toward him. The Troop Bat's face was frozen in anger and contempt with no mercy etched in his eyes that stared vacantly toward Tiathan.

"Yes, brazen." Scout stepped aside to let him pass as his leathery skin scraped the floor as he passed.

"I like that and so you shall have our hospitality because it pleases me." The great Troop Bat struggled with its weight.

"As you wish, o king." Tiathan bowed keeping a wary eye on those around him.

"I have not seen you before." He beamed with pride at the mention of being addressed as a king.

"Nor I you." Tiathan kept his distance. "Who do I stand before?"

"Bazarath!" He puffed with pride at his own name.

"Bazarath? I have heard of you!" Tiathan recalled his name mentioned after the destruction of the Township of Pure Water. So many dead without a battle or a warning.

"Perhaps as the most feared of warriors and a visionary of Everstream's future." Bazarath listened to the applause and cheers as they echoed off the walls.

"Feared, yes. Visionary, no." Tiathan watched Bazarath's eyes narrow with anger.

"Who are you to mock me?" Bazarath used his wings to double his size to intimidate Tiathan. "What is your name?"

"I am Tiathan Eiula, First Ioroarka of the Great Oak of Jesuar!" Tiathan calmly stared into the eyes of Bazarath.

A frenzied sound of gnashing of teeth and wings greeted his answer. Bazarath paced back and forth with this new information and not knowing how to save face in front of his warriors. It was unusual for him to hesitate in his decisions.

"I take it you have heard of me?" Tiathan enjoyed his discomfort.

"Why are you here?" Bazarath heard of Tiathan without saying so. His manner changed to one of deference from one great warrior to another. "Are you here to avenge Pure Water?"

"I did not come for you." Tiathan thought fast. "I did not

know you were here. Outra Whorld sent me this way."

"I know him, too." Bazarath winced hearing Outra's name.

"You bring death to us." Scout looked to Bazarath for a sign to kill Tiathan, but it never came.

"You know the story of Tripis?" Tiathan stared deep into the eyes of Bazarath who flinched slightly. "It was he who Jesuar sent against you."

"It is of no importance now." Bazarath waddled away from him. "You give us meaningless names. If you have come to insult us, then our hospitality only goes so far."

"Tripis will find you soon enough and I have no intention of fighting you here." Tiathan moved so his back was to the near wall of the entrance.

"You keep mentioning his name as if we should know him." Scout did not like the way the conversation was going.

"I do not come to insult you, but warn you that Jesuar rules Everstream." Tiathan never raised his voice which probably kept Bazarath from trying to kill him. "What I tell you is the truth."

"There is no truth." Bazarath turned to the darkness that yearned to embrace him. "I have no more time for this. You have one night here and then you must leave unless you wish to leave now?

"As you say…or command?" Tiathan watched the flurry

of wings follow Bazarath into the deep recesses of the caves.

"I do not know what you are talking about and I think it is not safe." Scout waited for the rest of the Troop Bats to leave.

"Then answer me some questions." Tiathan took a liking to Scout. "First, what is this place?"

"These are the caves of Morgg." Scout whispered though they seemed to be alone. "He is not here now, but you don't want to be here when he comes back."

"Who is Morgg?" Tiathan patiently leaned against the smooth cool cave wall knowing that he was safe for the moment. As the daylight dimmed, the inside of the cave grew brighter. A shiny moss glistened off the ceiling making a fire for light unnecessary.

"Morgg is the last the tribe of Ono." Scout kept his voice low. "An evil creature that fights us all the time. Many of us have died by his sword and his bare hands. His skin is dark green to match the trees and brush in the Dark Woods. No one can see him until it is too late except in here. He has only one good eye for which Bazarath takes credit. I was there and saw what really happened."

"What really happened?" Tiathan was interested in case he was confronted by this Morgg.

"Morgg was blinded in one eye when Bazarath tried to escape from Morgg's grip on his legs." Scout remembered it as if it were yesterday. "When Bazarath flapped his wings he accidently poked Morgg in the eye blinding him. Morgg was forced to let him go and so the story."

"Why not make peace with him?" Tiathan smiled as if it were that easy.

"If that is possible, wait and you make peace as he steps on your head." Scout giggled. "Now tell me of Jesuar."

"Jesuar is ruler of all things both high and low." Tiathan began to explain hoping he could keep it simple for Scout. "We learned of Jesuar through our first Shroo, Richstone, who came to live with us. Richstone told us of the Great Oak of Jesuar while we were in bondage. He told us that when we were free of bondage that he would not be seen again."

"What happened to him?" Scout was confused.

"It is a mystery we still talk about to this day." Tiathan mused for a moment Great Oak no one was allowed to enter unless they followed the path of Jesuar."

"What path was that?" Scout was enthralled with the story.

"The path of truth and faith." Tiathan saw that Scout was still too young to know what he was really talking about. "It may be hard to understand."

"Help me understand. What is truth?" Scout was sincere with his fiery red eyes now a soft orange.

"You must turn away from those who do not believe in Jesuar." Tiathan saw Scout's eyes tear up. "There can no future for you if you follow Mortarr. Mortarr is death and does not care about you. Bazarath does not care about you for you are only a worthless scout."

"I cannot leave my Troop." Scout cried out in anguish. "I have not yet been accepted. I would be cast out and die without them!"

"You will die if you stay with them. Follow Jesuar and live." Tiathan sat down next to Scout. Jesuar is heard through the wind, the trees, but mostly in your heart. Have you seen Mortarr?"

"Yes and we fear him." Scout shivered. "We fly close to those camps who send flames into the air with the vision of Mortarr in the center. He is real. I know this to be true."

"Mortarr is mostly a mist in smoke." Tiathan tried a different tact. "You could fly through him if you dared. Jesuar is greater than Mortarr. Why do you think Mortarr and Zebrac curse his name? If Jesuar were not a threat to them, they would not bother to mention His name except in a curse."

"How do I know He exists if I have never seen or heard Him?" Scout looked around as if Jesuar or Mortarr might hear him.

"When was the last time Bazarath allowed anyone to enter his cave and live?" Tiathan stared hard at Scout.

"Never." Scout's eyes widened.

"It is through the grace and fear of Jesuar that I still live." Tiathan closed his eyes as the weariness of a long day was now overcoming him. "It is by His intervention that I still live and will continue my journey tomorrow."

"Where are you going?" Scout wondered out loud.

"Wherever Jesuar leads me." Tiathan did not want to go long into what was happening behind him. He started to drift off into sleep though it was dangerous to think Scout could be trusted.

"Would you fight Morgg?" Scout disturbed Tiathan's sleep.

"If I must." Tiathan laughed as he scratched his nose in thought and absently touched the Karalak for reassurance. Obviously, Troop Bats had a short attention span so he just answered whatever questions Scout asked him. "Jesuar defends me and gives me strength."

"Would you kill him?" The fiery red eyes were back as Scout searched the caves for anyone who might be listening to them.

"If it is possible not to kill him, I will not." Tiathan saw that Scout did no want to understand.

"Is that what Jesuar tells you to do?" Scout clicked his small talons anxiously.

"No, but he knows our heart and if we kill for the love of killing he tells us this is wrong." Tiathan saw the change in Scout so decided to look for a place to sleep. "Life is sacred. I would rather live in peace and not have this mission. Jesuar tells me that my future has no peace."

"Can I go with you?" Scout stepped closer to whisper into Tiathan's ear.

"I must travel by day and you travel by night." Tiathan reasoned with him knowing Scout could not be trusted on such a journey.

"I can sleep in your sack during the day and guard you at night while you sleep." Scout's voice brightened, but his eyes were still a deep red.

"I will think on that." Tiathan drifted off again. He knew Scout would not break the uneasy truce between Bazarath and himself. He also believed Scout would not be near him when he awoke.

While he slept Tiathan dreamt of a great fortress under attack by warriors from all over Everstream. The vision was dim since the fighting was so fierce clouds of smoke and billowing flames blotted out the sky. Sweat poured off Tiathan's brow as horses and warriors attacked him from all sides. Then the vision vanished bringing him the deepness of sleep and the comforting obliteration of time.

****

"More stones coming!" Mikar watched Stilkyl hold he ears as the rocks crashed upon the roof of their small fortress.

"Stay where you are!" Stilkyl looked over the fallen body of Agraine.

"We cannot escape!" Anthor Cragg, the oldest warrior there, tried to keep spirits high though all was lost. "Listen to me!" He shouted above the din and everyone listened as they fought to the Lament of the Fallen Warrior:

"tioRo r moo dyoefohiet
W ayefo met XoesoihiR
tioRo r moo efohiR
tieoi'net dyohitie r mohiR
a mo estiehimdy oi'R nRoi'mdy
ef' XoesoihiRes' eshivo
oomyll oi'R ayveyes'
eto sihim tihivo
tieoi'net mo esao'ep otioRmhia
mo mhivo W naooRll
ef' eto mya' tioa' OO
et's moveyoRomdyN estiooRa"

"Look out!" Mikar tried to save Amhor before the boulder crashed through the roof on top of him. Bantongues and Harkies broke through the opening dragging away Trags who still fought though in the jaws of death. Six Valkyrick warriors climbed down into the middle of them with swords and daggers high. Many warriors fell from the onslaught as Mikar tried to run to Stilkyl's side.

"Mikar! Behind you!" Stilkyl screamed in vain as it was too late.

"Stilkyl?" Mikar was in shock as the blade of the Valkyrick warrior pierced his heart. The Valkyrick approached her with a grimace of pleasure that she would be next.

"No, not yet." Stilkyl released an arrow from her bow which struck the Valkyrick in the throat. Other arrows followed as she brought down Harkie and Bantongue alike until trumpets sounded as the north wall crumbled to the ground. Bantongue, Harkie and Valkyrick warriors ignored the remaining Trags to scurry back down the mountainside. Stunned, Stilkyl wearily collapsed next Agraine wondering what had happened.

****

"What's this?" Tiathan jumped at the booming voice standing over him.

"You must be Morgg." Tiathan tumbled away from the heavy foot that crashed near his head. He readied himself for a fight as he took out the Karalak to protect himself.

"You not belong here!" Morgg kicked the Karalak out of

his hand.

"I hope my being here doesn't distress you." Tiathan pulled out his dagger and lunged at Morgg. He managed to stab his great toe as he rolled past Morgg.

"You dare attack me?" Morgg was in a rage as he threw stones at Tiathan.

"I was warned by Bazarath and Scout that you would not welcome me with open arms." Tiathan ducked easily from each stone. "They were right."

"They lie!" Morgg thundered as he drew a sword that he carried on his back. "I gentle. You not hear me kill you. Come embrace me!"

"I think not." Tiathan could tell that Morgg acted without thinking so decided on a different plan. "Come get me, Mort."

"Morgg! I am Morgg!" He ran headlong toward Tiathan who rolled and stabbed him on the other foot bringing Morgg down against the near wall. His head crashed against a ledge that jutted out which knocked Morgg unconscious.

Quickly, Tiathan pulled down some of the thick vines growing along the wall and tied Morgg up. He then gathered wood to start a fire to cook a small Notherhen that happened to wander too close to the cave. It was two long hours later before Morgg began to stir.

"I am Tiathan Eiula." He took a bite of roasted

Notherhen.

"Why do this?" Morgg licked his lips at the meat roasting in front of him.

"Better than having you crush my head." Tiathan thought a moment before offering some meat to him as a peaceful token.

"Let me go and I repay you." Morgg struggled with his bonds.

"Repay me with a rock or a sword?" Tiathan saw the scars on Morgg's face and arms. His one eye looked sore and infected.

"They lie to you! Many lies!" Morgg screamed down the empty caverns. "Where Scout?"

"Probably heard you and found some place to hide." Tiathan didn't think Scout would stay close by.

"He promise protect you?" Morgg laughed until he started to cough uncontrollably.

"It doesn't matter." Tiathan understood Troop Bats more than he wanted to know.

"He go, bring friends." Morgg became serious. "Scout bring others. They kill me."

"You are safe for now and so am I." Tiathan offered him a bite to eat, but at the end of his dagger.

"Never safe." Morgg looked curiously at Tiathan's dagger seeing the gold hilt encrusted with jewels. He struggled again trying to get free before sighing heavily as he gave up. "What reason you here? Look for me?"

"Jesuar sent me here." Tiathan took another bite seeing Morgg stiffen his back when he mentioned Jesuar.

"I no quarrel with Jesuar." Morgg searched the cave walls for Troop Bats.

"He knows." Tiathan sensed Morgg was more relaxed now that he had eaten. "But you turn your back on Him by stealing and beating the Trags in Everstream. This is not right."

"How you know this? Trags do this to me!" Morgg turned his head to show his scars. "Trags no want me. Try to kill me. Say I am different. Ugly."

"I did not know this until Jesuar showed me in my sleep." Tiathan almost felt sorry for Morgg. "Those who hurt you no longer come this way. The ones you and the Troop Bats attack are innocent travelers."

"None innocent." Morgg shot out his wide, parched lips. "I do what I please."

"Not anymore."

"Then I kill you!"

"I think not."

"Let me loose!" Morgg gritted his teeth. "See who favored!"

"A great battle comes and I sense Jesuar will need you." Tiathan struggled to hear Jesuar's voice, but could not. He looked for the Karalak without success. He was relieved not to be able to find it.

"Never!" Morgg fell backwards with his head turned away from Tiathan, "He no need me."

"Then you will be left behind." Tiathan felt pity for him.

"Leave me alone!"

"I cannot."

"Release me and I reward you." Morgg turned looking desperately into Tiathan's eyes.

"What better reward can I have than that of Jesuar?"

"Then trade." Morgg looked at Tiathan's dagger.

"What for?" Tiathan threw another log on the fire.

"Your dagger." Morgg sat up. "It is valuable. I give you freedom. Go, never come back."

"That's not a good trade when you are the one bound and I am free already." Tiathan kept a wary eye on him.

"It Jesuar's will?" Morgg had a hint of a smile on his face.

"Do not tempt me, Morgg."

"If they come we both die."

"I doubt that will happen."

"Soon."

"I have till morning. You don't." Tiathan knew what Morgg said would be true if the Troop Bats come back. He leaned back thinking of a good song to sing which relax them both:

"MyesepoRN mymdyes
baRohitieo T mhino
XoesoihiR XoesoihiR
y etohiR ll' eshill
y hin ad esynet
XoesoihiR XoesoihiR
moo tiyno oxyesties
'Efoom etoRo t tieoRo
XoesoihiR XoesoihiR
hia dy'Rositioomes
etohiR ll'R mhino
XoesoihiR XoesoihiR"

"What song that?" Morgg glared at him.
"Jesuar is trying to speak to me and tells me that you will someday follow Him." Tiathan felt more at peace now. "I fear the hatred within your soul and find it hard to believe what I have been told."
"Curse you and Jesuar!" Morgg kicked the ashes from the fire sending sparks against Tiathan's chest. "I never follow Him! I here because of Jesuar and Trags!"

"How so?" Tiathan saw the tears well up in his eyes.

"When I young, I play with Trags." Morgg spoke in a daze seeing the past as if he were reliving it. "They not see me as different. One day I grow big. They laugh at me. I hurt who laugh at me…accident..son of Graystone Arkara. He curse me in name of Jesuar. No one talk to me again. Trags throw rocks, beat me with sticks. Drive me out of Township. Jesuar name on lips as they beat me."

"It was Jesuar who cursed you." Tiathan calmly told him. "If He had cursed you, you would have heard Him yourself."

"You lie!" Morgg broke one of the vines holding him, but he was still secure.

"Jesuar has sent me to tell you that you are no longer confined to these caves." Tiathan gently touched Morgg's forehead and said:

> "tieoi'net ephiym r ll'R ayefo
> ad esoief'oRN moveyoR omdyes
> W ties esnhill noestioiRo
> bao etohiady ad RonobaoR
> XoesoihiR r ad mya'
> hiamhilles bao ll'R estiRomntie
> ll'R noi'dyo ad ll'R sioonefooRti
> hinom"

The swelling and infection around his eye healed quickly which surprised Morgg. Tiathan wondered if the power of the Karalak had something to do with the healing. He then chided himself for even thinking that Jesuar had no hand in it. AS Morgg regained his eyesight, Tiathan ventured to tell him more.

"Jesuar has a purpose for you if you let Him come to you." Tiathan watched as Morgg shook uncontrollably.

"No, no, no!" Morgg started to weep. "All years lost? You say go back?"

"It's over now." Tiathan started to weep with him.

"No, it not! Morgg's rage helped him break free of his bonds. Once free Morgg started toward Tiathan. "You mock me!"

"This will only lead to your death, Morgg." Tiathan readied his dagger though his heart was not in it.

"I care not." Morgg tried to grab Tiathan by the head, but missed.

The noise of another battle brought most of the Troop Bats overhead. Many of them cheered Tiathan on wanting him to kill Morgg. Tiathan intended to wound not to kill him if it were possible.

"Your rage betrays you." Tiathan warned him. "Your anger is useless because A I am not your enemy nor is Jesuar."

"Lost, lost, all lost!" Morgg wept as he swung his great

arms at Tiathan. Morgg beat his fists upon the ground in frustration.

"No, listen to me, Morgg." Tiathan dared not get too close.

"Kill him and be done with it!" Bazarath scream at Tiathan.

"No!" Tiathan's angry voice echoed through the caverns. "He is worth ten of you!"

"Really?" Bazarath gestured with his wing as ten Troop Bats swarmed around Morgg. The distraction kept Morgg busy while Bazarath came down to speak with Tiathan.

"Stop them!" Tiathan saw how terrified he was of them.

"Now, does our guest want to leave?" Bazarath showed his sharply honed teeth.

"On my own and without you at my back, yes, but I will not leave Morgg to you." Tiathan tried to think of a plan to save both of them, but his anxiousness dulled his thoughts.

"He is of no importance to us though we owe him the lives of our brothers." Bazarath wanted blood and Tiathan knew it.

"Then I will give you a blessing instead of a curse." Tiathan watch as Bazarath winced. "May Jesuar come to this place and may you find peace in Him."

The Troop Bats laughed convulsively, but not Bazarath. He had always been cursed by travelers never blessed. He quieted down the warriors with a wave of his talons, then retreated to the safety of the cave walls. Those who were attacking Morgg stopped their fight and retreated, too.

"For that gesture, mighty Ioroarka, go in peace." Bazarath struggled with the words. "We will not harm you."

"No! You die!" Morgg lunged at Tiathan grabbing the dagger from his hands.

Surprised, Tiathan ran toward the back of the cave finding a huge crevice before him. There was no escape from the lumbering Morgg racing toward him. Bazarath had no intention of helping either one of them since neither could help him in his leadership. Turning quickly he looked downward as Morgg slammed into Tiathan sending them both over the ledge.

"Mercy!" Morgg cried out, but it was too late.

****

"Stilkyl!" A weak voice cried out from the rubble.

"Agraine!" Stilkyl ran to her side holding her head in her hands. Agraine's face was pale as dark red lines formed around her shoulders as the poison from the Bantongue fangs swept through her body.

"What is happening?" Agraine looked around finding most of the Trag warriors dead or wounded.

"I do not know." Stilkyl had not looked outside to see what was going on.

"I heard trumpets." Agraine drifted slowly away. "So thirsty."

A loud bump and scurrying of feet alerted Stilkyl to warriors coming back. She readied her bow and waited to see who was coming. The hairy leg of a Bantongue slowly grabbed hold of the edge of the roof. Stilkyl waited until its head peered over the side.

"Do not shoot us!" A familiar voice called down to her. "It is Zarr and myself to help you."

"Show yourself then." Stilkyl took no chances, but when the ugly face of Tenca looked down at her she relaxed.

"Are we too late?" Zarr followed Tenca to the floor.

"She is dying." Stilkyl sadly cradled Agraine's head.

"We can help." Zarr looked down at Agraine as he nodded to Tenca who agreed with him.

"Too late, too late." Agraine closed her eyes.

"What can you do?" Stilkyl refused to give up as she pled with Zarr and Tenca to help her. She never could understand how Zarr and Tenca became Agraine's friends. However, now she was grateful they were there now.

"Do you have a cup?" Zarr saw the look of disbelief on Stilkyl's face.

Tenca looked around as some of the Trags began to

stand wondering what was going on. A couple of them picked up swords and lances before Stilkyl saw them. She waved her hands that it was all right so they relaxed and began treating each other's wounds.

"Yes, here." Stilkyl found a cup near the fire that still burning.

"You may want to turn your head." Zarr warned her.

"It may make you sick, but it is the only way we may be able t help her." Tenca drooled into the cup and gave it to Stilkyl for Agraine. "Give it to her to drink."

"She may be saved yet." Zarr was hopeful.

"I can't do this!" Stilkyl tried hard not to become ill from the odor. She would rather throw it away than feed it to Agraine.

"She will die without it." Zarr stuck his face close to Stilkyl. "That is for sure. Listen to us!"

"Trust us!" Tenca was just as sincere.

"I'm glad I don't have to drink it." Stilkyl raised up Agraine's head as she put the liquid to her lips. When she finished, Stilkyl looked up at them and asked, "What now?"

"Let her rest." Zarr relaxed a little.

"It will take time." Tenca rested his bulky body next to Agraine.

"No one will come for us now." Zarr looked out the broken portals into the valley.

The camps below were in flames as explosions and clashing of swords pierced the air. Harkies flew far into the distance while below the forest was running red and green with blood.

"What is going on?" Stilkyl stared out as Valkyrick fought Gimgiddean while Arbushi stallions galloped away from the battlefield. She could see Bantongues scurrying a a black cloud over the treetops to the east. Over the next few hours the fighting died out and warriors retreated, but it was only the beginning.

"It has finally happened and we are in the middle of it." Zarr was melancholy.

"What?" Stilkyl did not understand why they were fighting each other.

"War." Tenca was equally dismayed as he looked at the prone figure of Agraine.

"Tend to your warriors for their fighting is over for now." Zarr lay on the other side of Agraine.

The trumpets became silent. The sound of camps being struck and the march of warriors greeted their ears for hours. Fires consumed the forest beyond the mountains. Fighting was still heard in various parts of the valley. There was no doubt the War of the Seven Fortresses had begun.